ROGUE & REVENANT

THE FOURTH EMPIRE
BOOK 2

KAT ROSS

ROGUE & REVENANT

First Edition

Maps by the author.
Cover by Atraluna.

ISBN-13: 978-1-957358-12-3 (Ebook)
ISBN-13: 978-1-957358-15-4 (Paperback)

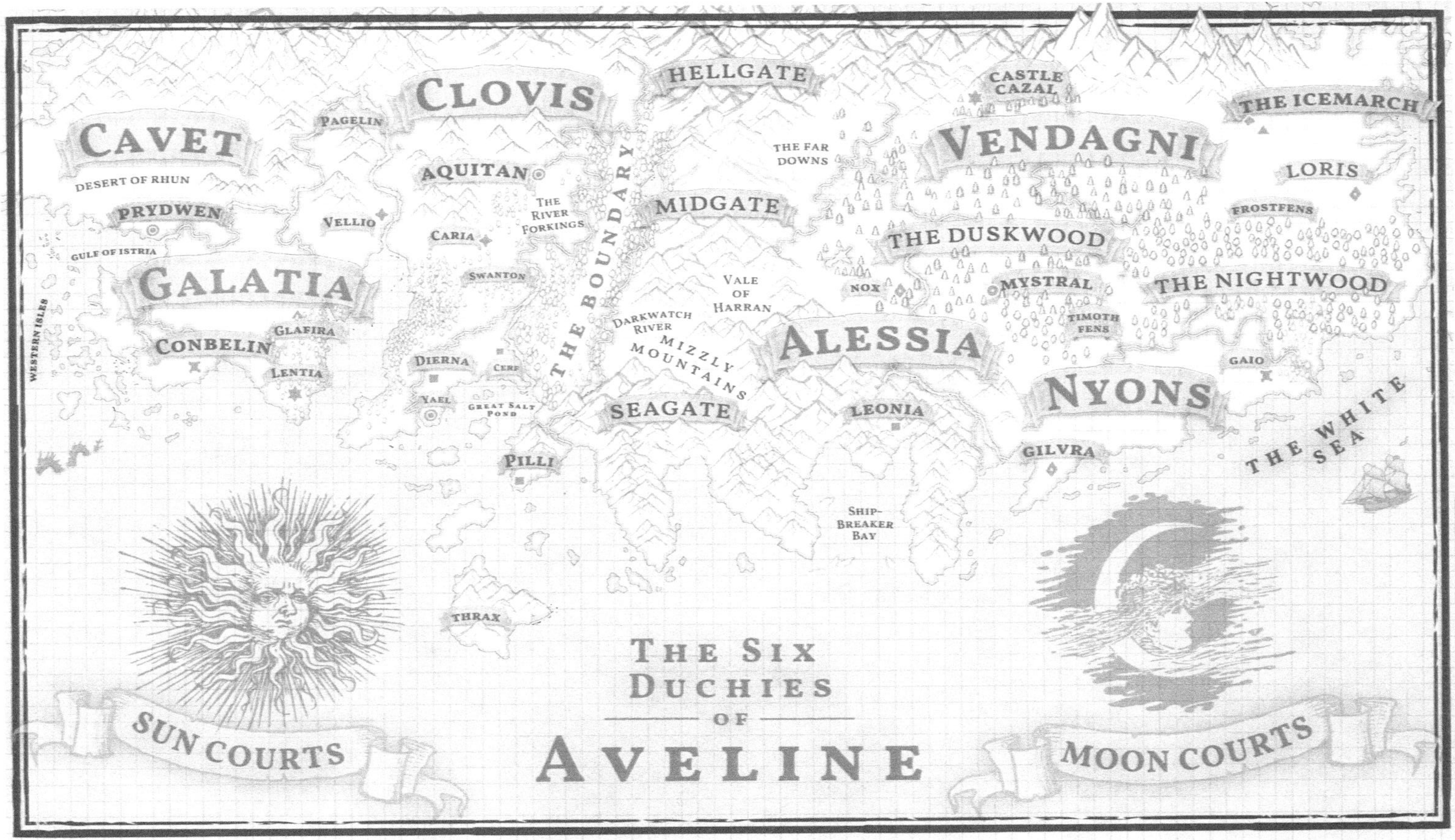

THE SIX DUCHIES OF AVELINE
CAVET
DESERT OF RHUN
PRYDWEN
GULF OF ISTRIA
WESTERN ISLES
GALATIA
GLAFIRA
CONBELIN
LENTIA
PAGELIN
VELLIO
CLOVIS
AQUITAN
CARIA
THE RIVER FORKINGS
SWANTON
DIERNA
CERF
YAEL
GREAT SALT POND
PILLI
THRAX
THE BOUNDARY
HELLGATE
MIDGATE
THE FAR DOWNS
VALE OF HARRAN
DARKWATCH RIVER
MIZZLY MOUNTAINS
SEAGATE
ALESSIA
LEONIA
SHIP-BREAKER BAY
NOX
CASTLE CAZAL
VENDAGNI
THE DUSKWOOD
MYSTRAL
TIMOTH FENS
NYONS
GILVRA
THE ICEMARCH
LORIS
FROSTFENS
THE NIGHTWOOD
GAIO
THE WHITE SEA
SUN COURTS
MOON COURTS

ONE

A*h, Swanton*, Cas thought dryly as he reined up on the outskirts of town. *My old nemesis.*

Thatch-roofed hovels dotted muddy lanes. Strings of washing swayed in a listless breeze. The half-naked children playing down by the riverbank weren't the ones he'd once known, yet they looked the same, with grimy faces and hollow cheeks. They stopped to gawk as he trotted past, but the rest of the village seemed deserted. Half the houses were abandoned, with leaves drifted against the doors and shutters hanging askew over dark windows.

He'd hoped to avoid the village, but the road from the northern ferry crossing dipped back down this way. Cas nudged unpleasant memories aside and set a brisk pace. With luck, he'd ride straight through without running into any familiar faces.

He planned to stop over at the Iron Bell, the same inn where Gui Harcourt had lifted a toast to the Ducissa Orlaith that day eight years ago when Cas was rescued from the margrave's jail. Then a hard ride and he'd be back in Aquitan. Kaethe only knew how bad things had gotten in his absence.

He began to whistle, an old ditty called *Anne of the Wildwood* that Ma used to hum when she weeded the garden. A minute later, the village green appeared. No unlucky miscreant in the stocks today. Cas's gaze flicked across the tumbledown barred enclosure that passed as the jail. For an instant, he saw a ghostly Teo, face pressed to the grille, whispering. Heard the crack of the reeve's cudgel as it slammed against the bars, nearly mauling his little brother's fingers—

"Hoi!"

Cas reined up. A red-faced man was hurrying toward him. *So much for stealth.*

"If you're aiming to flog me for the apples, it'll have to wait," he said with a chilly smile. "I'm on the Ducissa's business."

"What?" The reeve squinted up at him, befuddled, and Cas realized the man didn't recognize him.

Not surprising, perhaps. The last time they met, Cas was fifteen, skin and bones, clad in patched rags. But if he'd risen in station, his old enemy — one who, it must be said, had haunted his dreams for years — looked older and shabbier. Most of his hair was gone, along with half his teeth. Even the generous belly was reduced to a sagging paunch.

"Yer a Quietus, ain't ye?" he asked, glancing at the nine-pointed star inked on Cas's hand. "For the love of the Lady, help us!"

Cas was tempted to bark a caustic laugh and ride off. But he was oath-bound to aid any who asked – even his youthful tormentor – and he wouldn't break his vows. Best to get the job over with.

"Who's come back?" He realized he was thumbing the old scar across his palm and forced his hand to relax.

The reeve smoothed the gray strands clinging to his scalp. "We had a birth last night, sir. And, as often goes hand in hand, a death."

"The mother?"

"Aye. She rose before we could fetch the nuns and stole the wee babe from its cradle."

Cas's heart sank. "Then the child is dead."

The reeve shook his head. "Last I saw, the babe was still crying. He was all swaddled in blankets, you see."

"Where are they now?"

"The lichyard, sir."

Cas stared at him. "Then what the feck are you doing at home?"

The reeve flinched. "Ah, I just ran to fetch an iron poker and drive the revenant off myself. But then I looked out the window and there ye were, like a miracle!"

The man reeked of ale and onions. Cas suspected he'd been slow to locate the poker, but there was no time to berate his cowardice. He set his heels to the horse's flank and galloped off.

The lichyard was up the road near the convent. He found the family huddled at the gate. An exhausted-looking woman of middle years burst into tears when he appeared and was comforted by a lanky, raw-boned man who must be her husband. Cas vaguely remembered them both, but like the reeve, they saw only the blue tattoo on his hand and the braces holding the tools of his trade.

A much younger man with curly flaxen hair and a dazed look stepped forward. He pointed. "Up there," he said hoarsely.

Cas slid down from the horse, wordlessly handing over the reins. He unlatched the gate and stepped through. As he did, a thin cry came from over the hill. The youth, who was barely out of his teens, winced as though struck.

Cas climbed the hill, breathing in the cool, damp air, letting his emotions drain away. It never helped to bring your own fear into the mix.

Pale green willows dotted the lower edges of the field, their tangled roots furry with moss. It was the oldest section of the lichyard, the stones too weathered to read the names. He felt the girl's rage before he saw her, waves of simmering red. The sensation grew more powerful as he crested the rise.

The infant lay on the ground, near a cracked stone half-hidden by nettles. The swaddling blanket was in a tangle and it moved weakly. One pale, wrinkled foot stuck out. Its mother hunched over it, lank brown hair curtaining her face. Her head jerked up at his approach. Cas stopped, neck hairs rising at the ferocity of her gaze.

I've come to help you, he said in tongues.

She cocked her head. Her shift was stiff with dried blood. Fingers of shadow stretched back from the headstones, but she cast none.

You bore a fine child, Cas said. *He'll grow to be big and strong someday.*

Her lips peeled back in a silent snarl. Cas held her stare. He could feel her hatred like heat from an open forge. But there was something else braided through it ... pain, and loss beyond bearing.

He'll always be yours. But the Mother is waiting. The place beyond the Cold Sea is better than this one. There's green fields and all the food you can eat.

Cas hoped the words were true. Surely, it could not be worse.

He took another step. Atop the next hill, the convent of Kaethe looked over the valley. A plain whitewashed building with a bell tower and nine-pointed star above the wooden

4

doors. The low angle of the sun made the windows opaque, but he sensed watching eyes.

If it helps, I'll quiet the pain. Just give it to me now. Give it all to me.

How young she was. He'd taken the youth at the gate for her brother, but he realized now the boy must be the babe's father.

Her lips moved. The words were faint, as though whispered from a great distance, but the stillness of the lichyard carried them to his ears.

Coyus ru gano? *Who are you?*

Still holding her eyes, he unsheathed his iron knives and threw them down to the grass.

My name is Castelio.

The infant gave another weak mewl. She reached for its tiny foot, then snatched her hand back at the last instant. Cas's heart hammered against his ribs. He studied her. Tried to imagine how he would feel, if he were her.

You want to hold your boy. Just once more.

Her chin lifted. The sorrow and confusion in her eyes pierced his heart.

If you touch him, he will have to cross with you. And he has not yet lived. But I will hold him if you want to look on his face.

She hesitated, biting a fleshy lower lip. In a flash, he remembered her. Liza. Or Lissa. She would have been ten or eleven then. A boisterous lass with a crooked smile and scabby knees. Not one of the cruel girls, though it wouldn't have mattered. None of that mattered now.

Liza, or maybe Lissa, watched as Cas untied the bag of nails from his braces and set it down. One by one, he discarded the vials of Kaethe's Tears, until he stood defenseless. Whether she understood what the gesture meant, he didn't know. She skittered back like a shy animal as he walked over and rearranged the blanket, lifting the child to his chest. It stared up at him with puzzled gray eyes.

Cas rocked it gently. *Come*, he said. *Come see your boy.*

A bubble of cold pricked him as she crept closer. He tucked the blanket securely around the child, lending it his warmth. They stood together for a while. Perhaps a few minutes, perhaps much longer. The risen girl was so close, he could see the curl of each lash, the faint white scar on her chin. She gazed intently at her baby, memorizing every line of his face. Slowly, the anger and fear faded.

At last, the infant fell asleep. Cas carefully set him down and turned to her.

It's time.

Tears welled in her eyes, though they never spilled over. A tremor rippled her features. A final letting go. He'd seen this moment come countless times and braced himself, but it did little good when a red-hot knife ripped a bloody swathe through his abdomen.

Anger was always red. Sorrow pale blue. Yellow for regret. But agony . . . that was purest white. It erased everything like an exploding sun.

Cas doubled over, gasping. When he came to himself again, he was down on his knees, forehead pressed against a head-stone. The sweet scent of primroses filled the air. The young mother lay next to her child, eyes open and empty. He closed them and placed an iron coin on her tongue. Whispered a prayer for safe passage. Then he carried the baby down the hill. The old woman covered her mouth, smothering a sob. Cas gave the infant to its father, who took it awkwardly.

"Where's our girl?" the grandfather asked, his voice gruff.

"She passed well and willingly," Cas said, "to the embrace of the Mother."

The old woman hitched her skirts and ran up the hill. Her

husband followed, leaving Cas and the young man. They stood in silence for a minute.

"What's the babe's name?" Cas asked finally.

"I . . . we didn't have time to decide before Elizabet . . ." He swallowed. "If it was a boy, I wanted to call him Robert after the old Duc. But she wanted to name him for her Da."

"Then you might honor that wish."

"Aye." He gave a grim nod, cradling the sleeping infant against his chest, one hand cupping the tiny head. "I'd best take him someplace warm." Adding bitterly, "Before we lose him, too."

"The sisters will aid you. There's always a fire in the kitchens."

The young man looked away. "I don't . . ." He trailed off, lips tight.

Don't want to see Lissa like that, Cas guessed.

"We can take the long way round," he offered. "I'll go with you."

The young man gave a grateful nod. Together, they hiked around the base of the hill. By the time they reached the top, the nuns had come out from the convent and taken custody of the body. Cas accepted some water from one of the oldest sisters. From the sharp way she eyed him, he thought she knew exactly who he was. But the nun merely made the sign of Kaethe and escorted the family inside.

Then, lo and behold, the reeve appeared to take credit for sending him to their rescue.

"Come to the convent, sir," he said, beaming. "The sisters will give you a hot meal."

It was tempting, exhausted as he was, but Cas shook his head. "I must be getting back to Aquitan."

"Well, I'll go look in on the bereaved." He hooked his

thumbs in his stained breeches with a rueful air. "That lass was always trouble. Doesn't surprise me at all that she—"

The reeve took a quick step back as Cas loomed over him.

"I'm sure you aren't stupid enough to speak ill of the dead. Kaethe doesn't like it. And they hang around sometimes. You wouldn't want Lissa to pay you a visit while you're sleeping, now would you?"

The reeve shook his head so hard his jowls wobbled. "No indeed, sir." He knuckled his brow. "Have a safe journey!"

Cas watched him hurry up the hill, puffing for breath. Some things never changed. He turned and headed back down to gather his knives and vials. Many new headstones sprouted from the rocky soil of the lichyard, some with names he knew. Dorsey and Wandrill, Galdren and Blays. Entire families buried shoulder to shoulder, all dead in the same year.

Fever? A plague of risen? Or both?

Cas thought of all those empty houses and wondered how long it would be before Swanton faded away altogether, just another ghost town along the road. He found he had no anger or resentment left for this place. Only pity.

Everyone agreed the troubles with the dead were getting worse. He'd assumed it was the necromancers across the Mizzly Mountains, but having met Chaos and Caul Courtenay, Cas wasn't so sure. If they were bent on destroying the Redvaynes, why allow Enrigo to leave their duchy? He was Orlaith's only son and heir. In one stroke, the sisters could have ended Duc Robert's line forever. Yet they had spared the boy — and even allowed Lucius, whom they despised, to bring him home.

Nathan Ouvrard was another matter, but could one man be behind the rising tide of dead? And Nathan would have been a little boy when everything took a turn for the worse.

Cas was slipping the iron knives into their single sheath when his horse gave a whinny of unease, jerking at its tether.

He turned. Lucius stood at the gate, resplendent in his long cloak of blue woad and gold phoenix clasp. Twin flames danced in his pupils, yet he looked disturbingly human otherwise and seemed untroubled by the iron fence, which meant only one thing.

He'd fed, and recently.

"That was a risky maneuver, Quietus. She might have killed you." The mortifex smiled, revealing even white teeth. "Though I suppose it comes with the territory."

Two

Cas slid the knives into their sheath. Orlaith's mortifex was the last person he wanted to see right now. He no longer considered Lucius an enemy, but they weren't friends, either.

"What are you doing here?" he asked.

Lucius gazed up at the convent, his face impassive. "Her Grace sent me to find you. She was concerned for your safety."

The words warmed him, but he wasn't about to show it. "Well, you wasted your time. Nathan Ouvrard let us go."

"Both of you?"

"Aye."

Lucius made a show of looking around. "Where is the lovely khamoun now?"

Cas untied his horse's reins from the lichyard gate. "Delilah went home to Samarqand."

Lucius frowned. "How did she manage that? Her wind ship was destroyed."

"We ran into a group camped in the Vale of Harran. I took them for brigands, but they turned out to be traders from across the sea. Lo . . . " He caught himself. "I mean, the khamoun, she knew them."

"Traders?"

"Aye. Marooned here, so they said." Cas gave a careless shrug. "But they'd discovered a way to return. She went off with them. I could hardly stop her. They were armed."

"How fortuitous," Lucius said dryly. "Did you even try?"

"No, I didn't. She wasn't my prisoner anymore." Cas shoved the vials of Kaethe's Tears into his braces. "How is Enrigo faring?" he asked, hoping to change the subject.

"Recovering well. It was the first time since Duc Robert died that I have seen Orlaith weep. She was overcome to have him safely returned."

Lucius's emerald gaze was intent. The silence of the deserted lichyard felt oppressive.

"Well, of course she was," Cas replied in confusion. "She *is* his mother."

Lucius watched him a moment more, then turned and strode into the trees. He returned leading his own horse, a chestnut mare with white fetlocks.

"We'll ride back together," he said. "If you have no objection?"

Cas had several, but it might be useful to learn what had transpired while was gone.

"I mean to stop at the Iron Bell," he said.

Lucius inclined his head. "Of course. You must be tired."

"I suppose you watched the whole thing?" Cas asked, swinging into the saddle. In truth, it was all he could do to mount the horse.

"The end of it. That was a merciful thing you did."

Cas searched his face for mockery and saw none. "There was no need to be rough. She had it hard enough already."

"Still, you took a chance. What if the spirit had attacked you?"

Cas didn't care to dwell on it. He knew his actions had been reckless. Gui Harcourt would give him an earful if he ever found out.

"She didn't care about me," he said wearily, urging the horse forward.

Lucius said nothing more as they rode back through Swanton, and held his peace during the journey north. They took separate rooms at the Iron Bell, the innkeeper rushing to prepare his finest chamber for Lucius, whom he took for a noble.

Cas washed up and went downstairs, where he found Lucius lounging at a prime table nearest the fire, the iron menotte concealed beneath the sleeve of his doublet. The other patrons had no clue that a mortifex was among them, yet they instinctively gave him plenty of room. All the surrounding tables were empty, and the few men who remained avoided looking in Lucius's direction.

Smoke from the hearth mingled with sweat and roasting meat, a smell that never failed to curdle Cas's stomach. He had his usual vegetable pottage, washing it down with strong brown ale. It revived him somewhat. Lucius ordered only wine, which sat untouched.

"It seems certain that Nathan Ouvrard was behind Enrigo's abduction," Cas said, once the serving maid had cleared his bowl. No one else was near enough to overhear. "Does Her Grace plan to retaliate?"

Lucius laughed softly. "How? Nathan's castle is impregnable. No, she's preoccupied with another matter at the moment."

Cas feared it was the loss of the *Wind-Witch*. Orlaith had been bent on replicating the design. A fleet of wind ships would give her a strategic advantage over enemies like Nathan Ouvrard.

"Does she blame us?" Cas asked. "I know I should have spotted that lich before . . ." He trailed off. "Before we crashed."

The memory came unbidden. A shred of darkness drifting across the deck and latching onto Lo's wrist. Her tumble over the rail. The rope harness caught her, but then she dangled under the ship as it veered out of control. Cas and Lucius had hauled her up just before they hit the treetops.

"Yes, the lich," Lucius said slowly. He adopted a quizzical expression. "I wonder how Delilah managed to survive? I thought its touch was invariably fatal."

Cas had no intention of telling Lucius about the protective talisman. He shrugged. "I've no idea, though I'll admit it was peculiar."

Lucius grunted. "Well, it's nothing to do with the ship. Orlaith is most displeased at the news that the Duc of Cavet has been wooing the Damiata of Galatia."

Cas absorbed this for a moment. Galatia was the duchy that bordered Clovis to the west. "Isn't the Damiata a child?"

"Eleven. I assume Duc Marcel wants a betrothal contract for when she comes of age. Of course, Orlaith intends to wed her to Enrigo. I expect Her Grace will send me west to discover how far the courtship has gone."

"To Conbelin?" That was the Galatian capital.

"No." Lucius dipped a finger in his wine and idly traced a circle on the scarred table.

"To Prydwen?" Cas's scowl deepened.

Lucius noticed; of course he did. Cas silently cursed his lack of subtlety.

"Do you know something about it?" Lucius asked, his tone deceptively mild.

A knot popped in the fire, sending a tower of sparks up the chimney.

"No, how would I?" Cas swallowed the dregs of his ale. "Why does the Duc want to marry a little girl?" The thought was revolting, though he could guess the reason.

"She's merely a pawn in his ambitions for the west," Lucius replied. "Orlaith is determined to stop any alliance between Cavet and Galatia."

Cas knew Lucius considered him an untutored farmboy. He covered a yawn. "Makes sense, but it's none of my concern. I was just thinking I might ask for leave to visit my family."

And to seek out Delilah. He'd only caught a few words of her conversation with Nathan, but he'd heard enough to know she was headed for Prydwen.

"Ah." Lucius gazed into the leaping flames. "Well, you can ask the Ducissa yourself. She is eager to speak with you."

———

CAS BENT A KNEE, his gaze fixed on the thick carpet. His boots were still coated in mud from the road, but the summons had come immediately upon his arrival in Aquitan.

"You may rise, Quietus," Orlaith said.

He stood and met her blue eyes. She sat in a chair near the window, her posture rigid, pale hands gripping her skirts. As ever, she wore widow's black, with a silken hood concealing her golden hair.

"I'm sorry, Your Grace," he began. "I failed you—"

"You did not," she said firmly. "My son has been returned to me, and that is all that matters." Her gaze sharpened. "But I would hear the story of what happened at Castle Cazal."

Cas recounted their arrival at Nathan's keep. How Delilah

had gone inside to demand the return of her cat while he waited in a secret compartment of the coach. Cas had nearly been discovered by Nathan's mortifex, Vigo, but managed to get inside the castle through its only window. Then, an unfortunate misstep that led to sliding down a chute into Nathan's blood labyrinth.

Cas only left out the fact that he'd talked to Lo's cat. He had promised to keep Thistle's secret and the creature had saved his life, demon or no.

"So you don't know why Nathan summoned Delilah?" Orlaith asked, leaning forward. She looked pale and drawn.

"No, Your Grace. When I found her again, she refused to speak of it."

"Does she bear us ill will for this misadventure?"

"I do not believe so."

Orlaith gave a taut nod. "Well, it was honorable of you to accompany her. I regret the loss of the wind ship, but there's nothing to be done about that. And it was never my intention to hold the khamoun against her will."

Lucius had told him as much, but he still felt surprised at how quickly his mistress was moving on. Cas had wasted nearly two months in Tjanjin waiting for Delilah to show up so he could steal the *Wind-Witch*. Now Orlaith didn't seem to care that the ship was gone. She looked on edge and distracted — by the Damiata business, no doubt.

"So you did not speak to Nathan Ouvrard?" she pressed.

"No. He escorted us from the keep as soon as I found Delilah. Everything points to Nathan as the culprit behind Enrigo's abduction, but I have no proof."

Orlaith sighed. "That is the diabolical nature of sorcery. He's well aware his actions cannot be traced. I still believe the Courtenays also had a hand in it, but as you note, without proof . . . Well, we will be on guard henceforth." She smiled. "It is good to have you returned to us. You have been sorely missed."

Cas gathered his courage. "As to that, I would beg a favor, Your Grace."

"If it is my power, I will try to grant it."

"I would like to take a leave of absence."

The smile faded. She regarded him for a long moment, her face blank. He became acutely aware of the steady ticking of the ornate clock in one corner, the dry rustle of bombazine as her hands clenched her skirts.

"Has your service become burdensome, Castelio?" Orlaith asked at last.

There was a brittle, accusing quality to her voice he'd never heard before.

"No, my lady, not at all," he replied quickly. "It's just that more than a year has passed since I last saw my family. My brother and sister are still young. I hoped to look in on them and make sure they're well. It would only be a fortnight or so."

Orlaith seemed to relax, her expression regretful. "I sympathize, truly I do. But you're needed now more than ever. There's been an outbreak of risen in the south. Once that is suppressed, we can discuss the matter again."

Her tone left no room for argument. Cas covered his disappointment.

"I understand, my lady."

"That is all, Castelio. We can go over the details of your new commission tomorrow after you have rested."

He bowed and took his leave. He'd expected a refusal, but it still nettled. For the first time, he truly grasped what his oaths meant. All else came second. Family, friends . . . lovers.

You chose this life, he thought, heading to his rooms in the servants' quarter. *No one promised it would get better. And you saved a child today. That's something.*

Yet part of him wondered if the babe would survive to its next birthday given the squalid conditions of the village — which in turn led to darker thoughts. The reeve was a bastard, but he only enforced the margrave's will. And who did the margrave serve?

Orlaith, that's who. She acted like she cared deeply about her people, but she could change things if she wanted to. Stop her nobles from bleeding their vassals dry. A disloyal thought but true nonetheless.

I swore an oath, and now I must keep it. That's the end of the matter.

Once in his room, he washed in a bucket of tepid water, examining the new scars he had acquired on the bridge at Nox. One stitched across his ribs, with a deep pucker in the center where the centaur's arrow had punctured a lung. The other grazed his arm. Both made him think of Lo.

The silver chain on her talisman was broken, so he slid it off and pulled the lace from one of his camis. Cas threaded the disk — a moon on one side and a sun on the other — on the cord and hung it around his neck. He slumped down on his cot, staring into space. So Orlaith was sending Lucius to Prydwen. Neither of them could possibly know that Lo had gone there. Cas only found out because he chanced to overhear a few words at Nathan's castle. But what if Lucius found Lo somehow? What would he do?

Cas had spent more time with Lucius in the last week than he had over the past five years, yet the mortifex remained inscrutable. He needed some excuse to seek Lucius out. To gauge his true intentions.

Then he remembered what Lo had told him about the mortifex named Magnus the Merciless who had taken her parents prisoner. If it was the same one who had killed Ma, Cas had a powerful interest in following that lead as well. And if he was being packed off to deal with an infestation of spirits tomorrow, he'd better do it now.

He rose to his feet, filled with new energy. Lucius's rooms were buried in the deepest part of the manor where the sun never penetrated. Cas lit a candle and moved through the gloomy halls, wending his way downward. The manor was bigger than it looked from the outside, sitting atop a maze of low tunnels with flagstone floors.

He took a few false turns, first into the kitchen cellars, jammed with casks and barrels and smelling of apple cider, then into vaulted storage chambers where musty furniture sat beneath sheets to be quietly gnawed by woodworms.

Another room held rusting halberds and lances. The one beyond dated back to the days when the manor was a convent of Kaethe, with a nine-pointed star inlaid in the floor and a stone basin filled with mouse droppings. Lucius, Cas knew, would never tolerate such filth. He was far too *refined*.

Cas was starting to despair of ever stumbling across the mortifex's rooms when he heard voices ahead. He quickly pinched the candle flame. Even during the rest period, there were usually a few servants about. And he couldn't think of a good excuse for his presence.

Cas sank back into the shadows as a wavering light appeared ahead. He just had time to duck into another dark doorway and press against the wall. Two sets of footsteps approached, moving at a leisurely pace.

". . . must consult Robert. It is a delicate matter." Orlaith's voice.

"Of course, Your Grace. But you are satisfied he doesn't know?" That was Lucius.

"Robert?"

Surely they spoke of someone else. It couldn't be her

18

husband. Robert Redvayne had been killed long ago at the Battle of Hellgate.

"Castelio," Lucius clarified.

The footsteps paused a few paces away. Light poured through the doorway, illuminating streaks of white mildew coating the far wall, but the pair still stood in the corridor beyond.

"I do not think so," Orlaith replied slowly.

Cas didn't dare to draw a breath. He knew just how acute a mortifex's hearing was.

"I know you prefer to spare him," Lucius said.

"Of course I do," she snapped. "But I cannot risk discovery."

"No one suspects," he assured her. "How could they?"

Stars were starting to pulse at the corners of Cas's vision. His chest ached, made worse by the rapid drumbeat of his heart.

"We shall see what Robert says," Orlaith said. "His counsel is always wise."

At last, the footsteps continued.

Spare me what? Cas sucked a lungful of air through his teeth. Foreboding gripped him like an icy hand. He waited until the light faded to a pinprick at the end of the corridor. Then he tugged his boots off and crept forward in stocking feet, praying he wouldn't trip.

He kept as far back as he dared without losing them completely. In the blackness of the cellars, it wasn't hard to keep the lantern in sight, a bobbing spark ahead. The stealthy pursuit continued for several minutes. His eyes adjusted enough to avoid bumping the walls, though he bit back an oath when a rat skittered across his foot. The lantern paused, though the sound was faint and they were far ahead. Cas froze in the darkness. But Lucius must have decided it was simply vermin, for the light began to move forward again.

At last, it stopped at the end of a long corridor. A rattle of keys, then the pair entered another chamber. He counted to a hundred, then moved silently forward. Cas could see the lamp sitting on a table. Twenty more paces and he was near enough to catch the murmur of voices, oddly muffled.

He stopped, palms sweating. If they caught him, Lucius could easily murder him and no one would be the wiser. Part of him still couldn't believe Orlaith would sanction it, but another part knew that whatever they were up to, it was a grave secret.

I cannot risk discovery, she'd said.

There must be some explanation, he thought wildly. She might have meant anything. If I just turn back now—

But he couldn't. Not until he knew.

He stalked closer, blinking in the light. It was an old wine cellar. The walls were red brick, the ceiling a low arch draped with cobwebs. Bits of cork and broken glass littered the floor. The voices came from beyond a stout oaken door deeper in the cellar. They were too low to make out the words, yet he recognized the harsh cadence of tongues, the language of the dead.

Cas slipped through the entrance, placing each foot with care. A conversation was in progress, Lucius's voice interspersed with a rougher, throaty growl and occasional murmurs by Orlaith.

I must consult Robert. It is a delicate matter.

Cas wanted to believe the old Duc was simply a madwag, locked up down here for the last eleven years. But he could make out words now. Tongues for certain. And a metallic clink that sounded like chains.

"Ask him about Nathan Ouvrard," Orlaith said, her tone shrill. "His wraiths were supposed to return Enrigo at the border, not drag my son all the way to Nox. He betrayed our trust! And now Nathan refuses to speak to me. How should I proceed?"

Ene nofo net lilire samode hafil? Lucius inquired in a deferential tone. *Lani atun tohunin?*

How does it feel to know you will spend all eternity in this prison cell? And that I am the one who put you here?

Avano het tureca, rurunu! Duc Robert spat back.

Rot in hell, mortifex.

But I am already in hell, Lucius replied in tongues. *Your family saw to that. The least I can do is return the favor.*

Robert spewed a torrent of abuse.

"His Grace agrees that there is little to be done about Nathan," Lucius told Orlaith in plain speak. "Ouvrard cannot implicate you without implicating himself. Of greater importance now is the question of Galatia."

The pair stood just inside the doorway. Cas couldn't see them, but he *could* see the hulking shadow, pacing back and forth.

Now was the moment to creep away. To quit this manor and never return. Everything he had held as bedrock truth was crumbling around him. The woman he'd served since he was fifteen, the one he'd worshipped as a saint, was a figment of his imagination. Lucius might be using her, but she allowed herself to be used. To . . .

Cas raised an unsteady hand to his forehead. The magnitude of the betrayal was too much. He saw Enrigo in the sack, gasping for air. The fallen soldiers at Midgate. Redvayne soldiers.

He thought he'd reined in his boyish temper, but now it rose up in a hot flood. Through the thundering blood in his ears, he heard the rustle of skirts. Caught movement at the cell door.

He ducked behind the nearest wine rack, crouching down as Orlaith and Lucius emerged. He had a clear view of them. If she turned, she'd see him peering through the gaps.

Gone was the wan creature from before. Her cheeks were flushed, blue eyes bright with determination. Lucius held her elbow. His gaze swept the cellar — right across Cas's hiding place. Cas almost hoped Lucius would spot him. Provoke a confrontation. But the mortifex merely guided Orlaith back to the lantern, then returned to lock Robert's cell.

"It can all be salvaged," Orlaith said, hands clasped together at her waist. "The young Damiata is the key to the west. She *must* marry Enrigo. But we cannot afford any more mistakes." Her chin lifted. "We will speak more in my study. I have much to tell you."

Lucius nodded. He strode across the cellar, lifted the lantern, and stood aside for the Ducissa. Then he swept through the door, locking it behind him. Cas listened to their footsteps recede, leaving him alone in the dark. His breath quickened at a soft rattle from Robert's cell.

Not quite alone, actually.

Cas reached for his iron knives, then swore. For the first time since he'd spoken his vows, he'd left them behind. Ditto the vials of Kaethe's Tears and iron nails. The weapons were sitting on his cot, next to the bucket of washwater. A few weeks ago, he never would have approached a mortifex unarmed. But he'd grown accustomed to Lucius. A fatal mistake.

Cas's head snapped around in the dark as another rattle came from the cell, more forceful this time. Lucius and Orlaith might not have realized he was there, but Robert did.

Ghouls had a powerful sense of smell.

THREE

ours passed and the outer door refused to budge.

Cas pulled his boots on and tried to kick it down, but the door was solid oak and didn't budge. Repeated thrusts with his shoulder only left him bruised. He groped around until he found the table. It held a melted stub of candle but no means to light it.

Then an idea struck. He traced a nine-pointed star. Blue light flared, illuminating the cellar for an instant before darkness rushed in again. Yet that brief flash eased the first stirring of panic. The Lady was with him still.

From inside his cell, Duc Robert gave a guttural growl.

Don't like that, aye? Cas muttered in tongues.

The silence that followed was unsettling. He wondered what Robert looked like. There was a portrait of him in the North Wing, stout and bearded, posed with one shiny boot propped on a stool and a hand on his sword hilt, chin thrust forward in a challenge. But now? After eleven years?

The shadow he'd glimpsed against the cell wall didn't look

skeletal. No, it was large. Solid. They must have done something to preserve his body.

How often did Orlaith and Lucius come down here? She didn't speak tongues, relying on Lucius to translate, and he obviously told her whatever suited him. If Lucius went to Prydwen, would she venture into the cellars alone? Cas doubted it.

He shuffled to the wall, swatting away cobwebs, and ran his fingers along the bricks, searching for anything loose. Maybe, in time, he could find a way through. Smash up the table and use the legs to pry—

The slither of chains made him freeze.

Who's out there?

A dry whisper in tongues.

Cas sketched another star. Just to reassure himself that the cell door was secure.

Silence. Then a roar, muffled only partly by the barrier. *Who the fuck is out there?*

Cas kept quiet. He could barely find the spit to reply anyway.

More thumps. Then a rhythmic clanking, as of a chain being repeatedly stretched to its limit. Cas focused on the wall, prodding at each brick. Something landed on his neck and he slapped it away.

Let me out let me out LET ME OUT.

A small chunk of mortar crumbled away in his hand. He dug at it, but the main brick remained intact. Use the broken bit like a chisel. Yes, that'll serve.

Cas scratched at the wall, chipping away little slivers. Behind him, Robert was going mad. Shuffle, clank. Shuffle, clank.

It went on so long, he almost stopped hearing it. Half a

brick finally slid loose, enough to wiggle two fingers through. Stale air poured from the gap.

Shuffle, clank. Shuffle, clank.

He pressed an eye to the hole. Pitch black on the other side too. But wherever it led, the door might not be locked.

Robert spewed a stream of obscenities that made him wince.

Look, Cas told himself as the howls got louder. *They've held him prisoner for more than a decade. If there was any way to escape, he'd have found it by now.*

Shuffle, clank. Shuffle, clank. A mindless, repetitive rhythm, like a fly batting against a windowpane.

But then . . . He cocked his head. Aye, that was a new sound. A hard, definitive clatter, like a chain striking a stone floor. Then a thud, like a body hurling itself against the cell door. He had a sudden vision of some manacled appendage — hand, maybe foot — just . . . popping off.

Cas pried at the surrounding bricks, but they were firmly mortared. He kicked the wall, the dull smacks of his boot heel echoed by Robert's frenzied battering at his cell door. Then something gave a sharp crack. For a moment, he mistook it for the bricks giving. But no. That was *wood*.

Cas turned and sketched Kaethe's star. Blue light erupted. He glimpsed a fine dark line along the left side of the Duc's cell door. Another mighty blow and the fissure widened slightly.

The light faded.

Cas knew then that he wouldn't make it out. There would be no *quieting* of Duc Robert Redvayne. No peaceful passage to the beyond. He was well past that point. A ghoul now. Those could only be beheaded with an iron blade.

He staggered blindly to the table, smashing his hip into the edge. Rocked it over on its side and tried to snap one of the legs off. Something, anything, to defend himself.

Suddenly, the outer door flung wide. A light appeared, bright as the sun. Cas flinched back as a tall figure strode past. He heard tumblers click and the sounds of a brief scuffle. The Duc yelped like a chastised pup.

A great rattle of chains. A dismal, defeated groan. Then Robert's cell door slammed shut and Lucius stood there, cupping fire in his palm. He righted the table and used it to light one of the candle stubs, tilting his hand to pour the flames like liquid to the wick.

The mortifex regarded him calmly. "I'm sorry I didn't return sooner. Orlaith insisted that I—"

Cas lunged. He managed to land a single hard punch before Lucius spun him around and seized him from behind, pinning his arms to his sides. An icy chill sank into Cas's marrow.

"I'm here to save your hide," Lucius hissed in his ear. "I could have left you to rot, but I didn't. Think! If you want to stay here with the good Duc, I'm happy to lock you in again. Otherwise, calm yourself."

Cas vented a furious breath. He quit struggling. After a moment, Lucius released him and took a wary step back.

"You knew," Cas spat. "All this time. That it was *her*."

"Of course I knew." Lucius yanked up his coat sleeve, displaying the menotte. "And what exactly would you have me do? Refuse to cooperate? Expose her for the scheming fraud she is?"

Cas clenched his jaw and said nothing. Lucius turned away, wandering to one of the distant racks. He returned with a dusty bottle.

"I don't usually indulge," he said, prying the cork out. "But tonight is an exception."

He took a drink and held out the bottle. Cas shook his

head. "So Orlaith plotted with Nathan Ouvrard to stage her son's abduction. Why?"

"To cast blame on Chaos and Caul Courtenay," Lucius replied. "Orlaith is itching for any excuse to invade them and avenge her husband's death. It was their mortifex who killed Robert at Hellgate. But you and Delilah complicated her plans. You weren't supposed to go after Enrigo in the wind ship."

Lucius took another pull of wine, wincing at the taste. "The whole plot unraveled, as you'll recall. The Courtenays found us on the bridge at Nox, but instead of taking advantage of this windfall, they treated the boy with kindness and let him go home. Enrigo has no clue his mother was behind it all, poor bugger."

Lucius tipped the bottle at him. "But *you*, Quietus ... Orlaith was understandably worried about what you might have discovered at Nathan's castle. She sent me to intercept you, just in case."

Cas eyed him coldly. "Why didn't you just kill me before we arrived? You had a hundred chances."

Lucius gave a humorless laugh. "I'm not the one who wants you dead. And if you're smart, you'll keep what you know to yourself."

"I will not serve her. Never again!"

"If only I had the same choice." Lucius raised the bottle in an ironic toast. "Alas, I do not."

He offered the wine a second time. After a moment, Cas took it. His lips were so dry, they stuck to the rim. It was rough stuff, old and sour, but it dulled the urge to punch Lucius again. He wiped his mouth, then took another long draught.

"So you won't tell her I was down here," Cas said dubiously.

"Why should I? She would only order me to dispose of you, which I already told you I have no desire to do."

"I know your true name."

Lucius looked weary. "As do many others. I will not kill you for it. But if she orders me to . . . You might be bound by your *honor*" — this word was spoken with deep bitterness — "but I am bound in truth. If I disobey, Orlaith can hurl me into the depths of the Abyss, with no hope of return. Do you see the difference?"

The words held no trace of self-pity, but Cas realized how lonely his existence must be. An endless string of masters, and all those he cared about dead and gone.

"Aye," Cas admitted. "I suppose I owe you thanks. But what of the Duc? Did *you* bring him back?"

"At Orlaith's insistence. Why she mourned him, I cannot guess. Robert Redvayne was a monster. He murdered his first wife by shoving her down a flight of stairs. There are other crimes, too numerous to list." Lucius glanced around the dank cellar. "It is a fitting punishment to keep him here."

The cell had gone silent.

"And convenient," Cas said. "You exploit the arrangement to speak on Robert's behalf. I heard you talking in tongues. Taunting the Duc and making Orlaith dance on your strings. Makes me wonder who the real puppet is."

Lucius gave him a crooked smile. "When you are a slave, you fight back in any way you can."

Cas set the bottle on the table. "I cannot stay in Clovis."

"I understand. But you can't simply run off without a word. Orlaith will know you've discovered her secrets, and she will set hunters on your trail." He picked up the candle stub. In the warm light, Lucius's face looked almost human. "Accept the new commission in the south. Once you're past the city gates, you can go wherever you like. By the time she realizes you've vanished, it will be too late."

Cas nodded. "One more day, then."

"Less," Lucius said, his expression grim. "That's what I was trying to tell you. She kept me for hours, or else I would have come right away. I'd say you just have time to comb those dead spiders from your hair before she summons you again."

FOUR

The sour wine churned in his stomach as Cas knocked at the study door. He'd changed his clothes and scrubbed the grime of the cellars away, yet he still felt soiled.

"Enter," Orlaith's cultured voice commanded.

Cas came inside, grateful to bend a knee so he didn't have to look at her face.

"Did you rest well?" Orlaith asked, polite concern on her face.

"I did, Your Grace." Cas stood and forced a smile. "I'd hoped to see Enrigo before I left. Lucius said he is recovering from the ordeal."

Orlaith frowned and he kicked himself. *Why did I bring it up?*

"My son is a resilient young man," she said. "Like his father in so many ways."

The smile felt nailed to his face. "I'm sorry I never had the chance to meet Duc Robert."

"He would have liked you, Castelio, I'm sure of it. Now, I imagine you want to know what's going on."

He blinked. "I . . ."

Orlaith stared at him. "With the risen in Dierna. The town north of Yael?"

Cas recovered quickly. "Yes, of course."

She moved to her desk and picked up a written report. "Two dozen have come back in the last month. Four villagers are dead, touched by spirits. The place is infested. I've ordered a quarantine of the area, but someone must deal with them."

"I'll leave at once."

She studied him for an uncomfortably long moment. "I meant to ask you yesterday, Castelio. You met the Ducissas of Nyons. Chaos and Caul Courtenay. What was your impression of them?"

"Ah, they seemed wicked, Your Grace."

"Indeed they are. I understand they lent you a coach."

Was she trying to lead him into a trap?

"Not me, my lady. The khamoun."

As far as he knew, Orlaith still believed Lo to be a Persian princess.

"Yet they pretended to know nothing of the scheme to kidnap my son?" she persisted.

"I did not speak with them long. I . . . took an injury on the bridge at Nox. Nothing serious. A blow to the head. But I was unconscious for most of the time at Mystral."

"Yes, Lucius mentioned that." There was a chilly edge to her smile. "I am glad it did not hinder you in aiding the khamoun."

He nodded uncertainly. "I am fit for duty, Your Grace."

Orlaith moved closer. Once, he had thought her beautiful. Now she only seemed shallow and . . . brittle. As if she were made of fine-spun glass that might shatter at a touch.

"I hope I can count on your loyalty, Castelio. These are troubled times. We need men like you. Strong and true."

"It is my greatest honor to serve, my lady," he replied, praying she didn't see the lie in his eyes.

She walked back to her desk, laying the report atop a pile. "After you return, I will see you are granted leave to see your family."

He bent a knee, hoping it was a dismissal. When Orlaith didn't turn around, he backed from the study, gently closing the door behind him.

Alone in the corridor, Cas tilted his head back, blowing out a long breath through his mouth. Did she suspect something? It was impossible to tell. Every word, every gesture, was so laden with deceit. But if she did, it was Lucius she would set after him. And the mortifex had made it clear that he couldn't disobey a direct order.

Time to pack and get the feck out.

Cas hurried to his chamber. He was so lost in thought, he rounded a corner without looking and bumped straight into Esme. The basket of laundry in her arms spilled to the floor.

"Well, now look what you've done!" she scolded with a twinkle in her eye, hands propped on generous hips.

"I'm so sorry," he muttered, gathering up the linens and trying to fold them again.

"Head in the clouds," she laughed. "Where are you rushing off to, Cas? You only just got back."

"Dierna," he said. "The town's swamped in dead."

"But that's all the way south!"

He shrugged. "I don't get to choose, do I?"

"When are you leaving?"

"Now."

"Here, give me that." She snatched a tablecloth from his hands and whisked it into a perfect square. "And you're not going anywhere without a proper breakfast. Or a proper goodbye."

"Esme—"

"Don't start, Cas. You know you'll lose."

He opened his mouth, then shut it again. "Can you bring a plate to my room? I've got to pack."

Her brown eyes lit up. "Oooh, we'll have a picnic. Just let me drop these off. I'll be back in a titch."

Cas watched her stride away, strong arms balancing the basket on one shoulder.

I should have told her no. There's isn't time for a feckin' picnic.

But it was Esme. After Gui, his closest friend at the manor. Always cheerful and easy on the eyes, too. For some reason, this made him think of Lo with a pang of guilt — followed swiftly by chagrin.

Aye, you're just besieged by pretty women. Beating 'em off with a stick. Who wouldn't want an odd duck who spends all his time with dead people?

Back in his room, Cas tossed his travel bag on the cot. If he took everything he owned, it would be obvious he never intended to return. He began sorting it all into two piles: stay and go. His sister's letters definitely fell into the second category. Those he could never part with.

Of course, once he had them in hand, he couldn't resist reading them over again. Lippa always made things sound rosy, even when he suspected they weren't. He scanned the lines of perfect handwriting, searching for hidden clues.

Dearest brother . . .

The most recent had arrived only a few days before. Lip said they'd all found service at Duc Marcel's palace in Prydwen. She was working in the scriptorium, copying out letters and such. It reassured Cas to know they'd be easy to find. Surely not even Da could have mucked it up yet.

He regretted the unkind thought as soon as it came. Da had made mistakes aplenty — drinking, gambling — but it wasn't entirely his fault. He'd lost his wife, farm, and livelihood on the same day. Being a woodward was part of his nature. After that was taken from him, he was never the same.

None of them were after Swanton.

Cas stared at the letter, the lines blurring. Being a Quietus was part of *him*, too. The only thing he was good at. What would he do now? His jaw tightened, acid fury creeping back. Even if Duc Marcel kept Quietuses in his service, Cas would never trust another noble. *Never.*

But I won't end up like Da, either, he vowed.

The arrival of Esme dragged him from the well of dark thoughts. She was carrying a small wicker basket, which she set on the floor.

"No meat," she said. "Though how you survive eating like a rabbit I'll never know."

Cas twitched his nose. She gave him a slow, teasing scrutiny from head to toe.

"Well, you are a strapping lad," she said, propping her hands on generous hips. "I'll give you that."

"All the carrots," he said, plucking one from the basket and crunching it between his teeth. "I do have to shave the whiskers, though."

Esme laughed and started setting out the meal. Bread and butter, savory potato pastries, a few apples and pears. The pastries were still piping hot. Cas juggled one, half burning his fingers, while he stuffed the last of his clothes into the bag.

"I hear you had a grand adventure," Esme said, carving off a slice of pear and eating it with relish. "Did you really meet the Duc of Vendagni?" She gave a little shudder. "They say Nathan

Ouvrard is the most powerful necromancer in all the Moon Courts."

"I did. And his mortifex, Vigo, too."

Esme wiped juice from her chin. "Was he as frightful as Lucius?"

"He made Lucius seem like a dear little kitten," Cas said truthfully.

"Bel's balls, I don't envy you, then." She eyed him from beneath her lashes. "And the khamoun? She went home?"

"Aye."

A little smile curved Esme's lips. "I thought she was beautiful, don't you agree, Cas?"

"Aye."

She scowled and pointed the paring knife at him.

"But she doesn't hold a candle to the ladies of Clovis," he added hastily.

"Ah, but I'm not a lady."

"Which is why I like you."

Esme looked pleased at that. "I hope you won't be gone long. I thought we might go to the festival of Artemis together. Have a dance or two."

He turned away to hide his remorse. "I'd like that, Es. I'll do my best."

He heard her rummaging in the basket again and used the opportunity to dig out his smallclothes and force them into the now bulging rucksack. When he looked back, Esme pressed a cup into his hand.

"We must make a toast," she said.

He glanced into the cup, the fumes rising to his face. "Wine?"

"Ah, don't be such a stick-in-the-mud. What's a goodbye party without a toast?" Her brown eyes were bright as she raised her cup. "Come now, bottoms up."

Cas needed to keep his wits, but she'd clearly gone to some trouble.

"Just a sip," he relented.

"To old friends," she said, holding his eyes. "And new beginnings."

"To old friends and new beginnings," he echoed softly, bringing it to his lips.

It was a fine vintage. A hundred times smoother than the near vinegar he'd shared with Lucius. He savored a swallow, then took another. Gods, but it went down easy.

They sat in silence for a minute, watching dust motes drift in the shafts of low sun. *New beginnings.* It felt like a bitter irony. He'd wanted to go to Prydwen — but not like this. Yet Cas was glad she'd come. He'd miss her sorely.

Esme finished her cup and poured a bit more.

He eyed the dark green bottle. "Where'd you get it?" Servants drank ale. Wine was strictly for the nobility. He lowered his voice. "Did you steal it?"

She swatted his arm. "Course not. Cook'd find out and give me a switching." Her eyes sparkled. "The Ducissa herself gave it to me. A special vintage, she said, as a parting gift. She must be awfully pleased with you, Cas—"

His hand lashed out, knocking the bottle to the floor. The glass was too thick to shatter, but red liquid pooled across the flagstones. Esme lifted her skirts and leapt back. She stared at him in astonishment.

"What'd you do that for?"

"When did she give it you?" he demanded.

"What's wrong—"

"*When?*"

The look on his face made her go pale. "Just after you almost bowled me over. She called me to her study and asked me to bring it to you."

He snatched the cup from her hand and emptied the last of it into the chamber pot.

"Have ye lost yer mind?" Esme demanded, her Aquitan accent thickening with irritation.

He paced to the narrow window. Paced back and picked up the bottle, sniffing the mouth. He detected nothing out of the ordinary. He felt fine, and he'd drunk almost as much as she did. Esme watched him with crossed arms.

"Ye'd think Her Grace was trying to poison ye!"

He tried not to wince at the word. "I . . . heard someone fell ill from the Redvayne vintage," he said weakly. "A batch got contaminated."

Her brows drew down. "Who told ye that?"

"Just a rumor."

Esme shook her head ruefully. She was too merry to hold a grudge for long. "You shouldn't listen to every wagging tongue you meet, Cas." Her gaze landed on the puddle with regret. "It'll probably be years before I taste wine so sweet."

"I'm sorry." Cas rubbed the back of his neck, embarrassed. He reached for the linen lining the basket to mop it up and she grabbed his wrist.

"Not with that, you lummox. I'll never get the stain out."

"What then?"

She hadn't let go of his wrist. Esme stared at him. Her brown eyes seemed darker. Almost black.

"I've an idea," she said dreamily.

She stood up and untied her apron. Folded it into a neat square and set it on the cot. Then she started undoing the buttons of her dress. Cas couldn't quite make sense of it.

"What are you doing, Es?" he asked with an uneasy laugh.

She smiled impishly. Then, to his astonishment, she wiggled her shoulders and let her kirtle fall to the floor. She wore only a shift beneath, thin enough to see her breasts right through it.

"We'll just use this," she said, kneeling down and using her kirtle to soak up the stain.

His skin prickled. "Stop, Es," he said. "Please."

When she looked up at him, he realized why her eyes had gone so dark. The pupils were as big as ripe blackberries.

"I'm hot," she declared. A fine coating of perspiration dampened the curls at her brow. She started to pull the shift over her head. Cas yanked it back down. She resisted for a moment, but then her arms fell limply. He pulled her to his chest, a sick terror spreading through him.

"That went right to my head," she whispered.

"You need to sick it up, Esme," he said. "Right now!"

She shook her head blearily. "No, I'm fine."

"You're not!" He fetched the chamber pot and forced her to sit up. Big, strong Esme, who could lug two full pails of milk without a care, started to topple. He righted her and made her lean over the porcelain ewer.

Whatever was in the wine must be strong, but he still felt nothing. Nothing besides guilt. *The poison was meant for me.*

Cas tried to thrust his fingers into her mouth. She twisted away with a sudden burst of energy.

"Don't," she begged. "Just hold me."

Esme's heart fluttered against his chest, swift and erratic. Cas laced their fingers together. Hers were freezing, though her expression was peaceful.

"I always loved ye," she said, the words faint. "From the very first."

He cupped her freckled cheek with his free hand. Kissed her lips for the first and last time. Before he could reply, she was gone. He felt the passage of her spirit, like the brush of a sparrow's wing taking flight.

Tears blurred his eyes. He eased her down to the bed, an icy numbness creeping through his limbs. They'd been joking around just a minute before. How was it possible? "I'm sorry," he mumbled. "So sorry, Es—"

"*Fuck!*"

Lucius filled the doorway, features twisted in rage. It was the first time Cas had ever heard him swear. The flames of his irises were white-hot, practically glowing. He looked a creature out of nightmare.

"You should have just murdered me down in that cellar," Cas said, his voice a monotone. "Go ahead and get it over with. If I'd known what you had planned—"

The mortifex was upon him in an instant. He grabbed Cas's cami and pulled him close. "I had nothing to do with this," he snarled. "I came to stop it."

Cas stared at him, beyond contempt. "Then you came too late."

Lucius released him, rocking back on his heels. He regarded Esme's body for a long moment, lips tight. "I suppose you didn't drink the wine. But Orlaith will discover soon enough that you're still alive."

Cas found his pouch of iron coins. "Let her. I don't care anymore."

"Do you want to die here?" Lucius demanded. "Or live to get revenge?"

Cas placed a coin on Esme's tongue. Just in case she tried to come back. "Revenge? That's a feckin' joke. Orlaith's got you to guard her, doesn't she?"

Lucius audibly ground his teeth. "You have no clue how much I despise her!"

Cas sank down on the cot. "Aye," he said, gripping his head in his hands. "I do."

Esme's dress lay at his feet, stained a deep red. *But I did drink the wine. So why didn't it kill me, too?* A hand crept inside his cami, to the silver disk on a cord. Lo's talisman of protection.

An awful laugh bubbled up inside him. The one Orlaith wanted dead was immune to her poison. Something odorless. Tasteless. Nightshade family, most likely. But she had to know Esme would drink it, too. Knew and didn't care.

A spark kindled in the wasteland of his soul. *Revenge.* He might never get it, but at least it was something to live for.

"She'll have alerted the guards," Cas said. "I'll never make it past the gates now."

Lucius shook his head. "Not yet. I'm suppose to discover the bodies." He looked furious again. "You must believe me, she acted of her own accord. The instant she admitted what she'd done, I—"

Cas raised a hand. "I believe you. What next?"

Lucius strode to the door and cracked it, checking the hall beyond. "I will help you escape from Clovis," he said. "But you must do exactly as I say."

FIVE

"Is it done?" Orlaith demanded.

She sat at a mirrored dressing table, running a comb through her blonde hair. The Ducissa had taken to summoning Lucius directly to her bedchamber, but there was usually a maid present and she kept some semblance of propriety.

Of course, she wouldn't want anyone to overhear this particular conversation.

"Only by half," Lucius replied, hiding his disgust. "The serving girl is dead. But Castelio is gone."

She twisted around, blue eyes flashing. "*Gone?* I sent you to his room nearly an hour ago! What have you been doing all this time?"

"Alerting the guards at the gates, Your Grace. I hoped to catch him, but they said he had already passed through."

Her fingers knotted in the golden coils. "What did you tell them?"

"That he is wanted for murder."

Orlaith drew a deep breath through her nose. "Don't look at me like that, Lucius. Don't you dare!"

The menotte was a heavy weight around his wrist. It had been enchanted not to burn his flesh like most iron, but his control over his own emotions wasn't as firm as it used to be.

Careful, now. If she suspects anything, you're both done for.

"Like what, my lady?" he asked.

She threw the ivory comb down. "I had no choice. You claimed he didn't know, but I saw it plainly in his eyes! He hates me. This is *your* fault, Lucius. You should have gotten rid of him before he ever arrived at the manor. That girl would be alive now."

You're right, he thought bitterly. *Esme's blood is on my hands, too. I didn't know what you planned, but I've helped you carry out every other vile scheme.*

Lucius bowed his head. "I beg forgiveness, Your Grace. It was a grave miscalculation."

He felt the heat of his mistress's stare. "To say the least," she replied angrily.

A sweet, cloying odor wafted from bowls of rosewater and vases bursting with fresh lilies. She made the servants change them daily. It reminded him of the balms smeared on corpses to cover the stench of rot.

"If Castelio makes any wild accusations, no one will listen," he said. "Most likely he'll run to his family, although it would be prudent to comb the countryside as well. If he does flee to Prydwen, I will track him down there. But there's no time to lose."

She piled her gleaming locks atop her head and pinned them in place, regarding her reflection in the mirror. "Are you so eager to abandon me, too, Lucius?"

Something was different about her. For years, Orlaith had

been coolly formal with him. Self-contained and distant. But he detected a new neediness of late. A desire to be loved, as her actions grew ever darker. It reminded him . . . It reminded him of mad King Gaius in the last days of the War of Sundering. But that was a thousand years ago. Lucius had more immediate problems.

"I am eager to do your bidding," he replied evenly, "whatever that requires of me."

Her lips pursed. "Good. Then we will move on to weightier matters than a fugitive Quietus. What do you know of the Marcels?"

"Not a great deal," Lucius admitted. "They're one of the six great houses of Eddyn, who sailed here just before the Sundering. They disdain magic and have no mortifexes."

"Only partly true. The last Duc, Andrzej Marcel, kept a necromancer. A woman. But she disappeared more than twenty years ago, and he never took another."

"What about the current Duc?"

"I was friendly with Andrzej, but his son Vazsoly is young and ambitious. A threat to our interests in the west. I want him dead or deposed." Orlaith sniffed. "It shouldn't be too difficult. He's already unpopular. There have been riots — brutally put down."

"I've heard the rumors."

She dabbed two fingers in a pot and began to rub a pearly cream into her skin, sweeping it along her sharp cheekbones. "Once Vazsoly is gone, we can expect a bloody succession like the one that left that child on the throne."

"The Damiata of Galatia," Lucius said.

Aldonza Beatriu do Santillan had been the last one standing out of eight siblings when their parents were felled by an assassin. The girl was either lucky or uncommonly clever. For her sake, Lucius hoped it was the latter. The instant her twelfth birthday loomed on the horizon, the vultures began circling her duchy's carcass.

A sharp look. "Of course. Vazsoly's nobles can fight it out among themselves, while I betroth Enrigo to the girl. He's a far more suitable candidate. They're the same age. Vazsoly could almost be her father!"

Age had nothing to do with it, of course. Orlaith coveted Galatia's wealth. A union between Enrigo and the Damiata would double the territory under her control and leave Cavet ripe for the plucking. Once she solidified her hold over the west, Orlaith would again turn her gaze east, to the Moon Courts.

"How do you want me to proceed?" Lucius asked.

She moved to a side table and handed him a sheaf of papers. "There's already a faction that wants the Duc toppled. It seems simplest to align ourselves with them and offer support. Discreetly."

Lucius glanced at a gilt chair emblazoned with the phoenix of House Redvayne. "May I?"

She waved a hand and he sat down, scanning the documents. They were penned in Orlaith's own neat hand. A summary of Cavet's economy — fishing, limestone quarries, and gems mined from the rugged islands in the Gulf of Istria — followed by a brief recounting of the unrest, which began under the current Duc's father. It was led by—

"The Red Rogue?" Lucius said, meeting her gaze.

Orlaith looked amused. "That's what he calls himself. Wears a mask and preaches in the streets. He's also taken credit for several acts of sabotage."

"Like what?"

"Burning half the Duc's fleet in the harbor. Orchestrating work disruptions at the quarries. Now he's become some kind of folk hero to the peasants. Not even my sources know who he is, but he made himself such a nuisance, the old Duc finally relented and cut taxes."

"With the support of the Sons of Bel," Lucius said, flipping to the next page.

"That's right. The priests wield a great deal of authority in Cavet." A dry laugh. "Mostly because the Marcels owe them so much money."

"And then Vazsoly's father died."

She nodded, blue eyes glinting. "Less than a day before his son returned from a campaign to put down a rebellion in the Isles. Vazsoly was at sea when it happened."

"So he's blameless?"

"Not all believe so, but there is no proof. Another angle I suggest you look into, Lucius."

He inclined his head and curled the pages in one hand. "Let me guess. When the son took control, he reneged on his father's agreement with these rebels."

"The very same day," Orlaith confirmed. "It provoked an outcry, which he swiftly suppressed. I hear the mood in the city is tense."

Again, Lucius couldn't help but draw a parallel with his own brutal king and the great suffering Gaius had inflicted. General Claudius Quintus had cared about such things, but Lucius was no longer that man. *Dangerous to forget it.*

"What are we offering these rebels?" he asked, determined to preserve his objectivity.

All he wanted was to find Delilah — or better yet, her mother — and break the iron menotte that bound him to the Redvaynes' service. A goal that seemed ever more distant.

"If they're reliable, money and weapons," Orlaith replied. "But I want to know who this Red Rogue is first. His identity will give us leverage, should he try to betray us."

"That will be no simple task," Lucius warned.

"Which is why I'm sending *you*. Officially, you will be my envoy to Duc Marcel's court. Give him our condolences for his father and pledge friendship between our duchies, et cetera. He might let slip what his plans are." She turned back to the mirror and smoothed an errant curl. "But you will also meet secretly with these rebels. Play both sides." Orlaith studied him in the mirror. "You can do that, can't you, Lucius?"

He kept his face impassive, a mask of indifference. "As you command, my lady."

"In the meantime, Duc Scalici will escort my son to Galatia. Let Vazsoly court the Damiata from afar, while Enrigo spends the season at Conbelin and wins her tender heart."

"Isn't he rather young for wooing?" Lucius wondered. "The boy is only eleven."

Orlaith smiled indulgently. "He will not be seducing her, Lucius. Merely cultivating a friendship that will blossom into a deeper bond as they both mature. My son is charming and good-natured. If the girl has any sense, she will realize her good fortune and make an alliance. Leave all that to me, Lucius. *Your* task is to eliminate the competition should Enrigo fail to win her over quickly. As you noted, time is of the essence."

She turned on the vanity's padded bench. "Now, on to practical matters. You will need to take measures to protect yourself against the climate."

"I have free rein to feed?" Lucius asked bluntly.

"Of course. It is not only the sun that will be a bane, I'm afraid." A bitter tone crept in. "Prydwen does not have the same problems regarding the dead as we do. The founders were clever. The entire city is built upon a network of canals which flow from the sea."

He hadn't realized that. Lucius's gut twisted at the thought of all that running water. "I'll manage."

Orlaith eyed him in silence for a long moment. "I have

always worn the menotte with a light touch, wouldn't you agree?"

Lucius nodded — and drew a sharp breath as she clamped down on his elemental power. It winked out as if a razor had severed him from the Nexus.

"I prefer loyalty and respect given willingly," Orlaith continued, "to obedience inspired by fear and pain, but I will do what I must to prevail. The interests of House Redvayne come before all else. Do you understand?"

"Perfectly, Your Grace."

Invisible needles stabbed his skin beneath the iron band, but Lucius refused to give her the satisfaction of showing his discomfort. He wondered how far she would go. Her husband Robert had not been shy about inflicting a wide array of agonies.

"This is your chance to redeem your mistake with Castelio. Not to mention the disaster with Nathan Ouvrard and the loss of the wind ship." Orlaith's sapphire gaze bored into him. "I will be *most wroth* if you fail me."

Lucius bowed from the waist. "Consider it done, Your Grace."

Her grip loosened and power flooded back through the menotte. He had a nearly irresistible urge to hurl her across the bedchamber. To slam her against the wall hard enough to snap her slender neck. But if he tried, the talisman that bound them together would turn his own magic against him. The last time he had openly rebelled against Duc Robert, he'd writhed in agony for a month, covered in weeping burns.

"Take this." Orlaith thrust a small, cold object into his hand. "We will use it to communicate."

It was a shard of black mirror. Lucius slipped it into the lining of his cloak. He knew he should go before she changed her mind, yet he couldn't leave without asking.

"Where did you get it, my lady?"

"The mirror? Nathan taught me the trick of making them."

"I meant the poison."

His mistress's moods had grown so unpredictable, Lucius braced for swift punishment, but Orlaith merely nodded as if she'd been waiting for the question.

"I've learnt a few things on my own. Dwale aids me in achieving the trance state required to use the black mirror. Only two berries, of course. Four acts as an aphrodisiac. My husband sometimes . . ." She trailed off, heat rising to her cheeks. "Well, more than eight is fatal. But they say it is a pleasant way to die."

"That was merciful, Your Grace," he said, despising himself more than ever.

"I had hoped so." She sighed. "It seemed romantic for them to die together in the act of love. But the court gossips will weave their own tales. Perhaps Castelio dosed Esme and accidentally used too much."

She tilted her head, musing. "Or perhaps she took her own life because he spurned her advances. Myself, I favor the first version. His parents were woodwards." A tiny, satisfied smile. "Everyone knows about his skill with herbs."

SIX

Banners bearing a crimson phoenix on a field of gold rippled from the turrets to either side of the gates between the manor and the city. Cas didn't recognize the soldiers on duty. They watched him approach with slightly bored expressions, but that meant nothing. If a warrant for his arrest had already been sent, they'd wait to seize him until it was too late to run.

Archers in conical helmets stood atop the wall; *that* was a new development. The puckered scar on his chest itched at the sight of their bristling quivers. He slowed the horse to a walk, gaze purposeful. A man setting out on a long journey.

"Bonny afternoon," he called out cheerfully.

To his relief, the men stood aside with a nod and winched open the gates.

He trotted through, resisting the urge to look back. The itch moved from his chest to the spot between his shoulder blades, but no arrows were loosed. No cries of *"Traitor!"* pursued him down the road.

Knotted muscles relaxed as he entered the prosperous area

beyond the gates. Well-kept townhouses lined the boulevard, some with discreet brass plaques offering services for shipping, lawyers and notaries. Lucius had kept his word. *Feckin' hells, we actually did it—*

Cas's relief withered as he saw a tall, dark-skinned man, also mounted, coming at a slow walk up the street. Their eyes met. Gui Harcourt's bluff face broke into a grin.

"Ah, it's my favorite protégé," he cried, urging his mount forward.

Under any other circumstance, Cas would have been delighted to run into his old mentor. They'd barely seen each other these last few years, and then only briefly. But it was a delay he couldn't afford.

How much longer before the alarm goes out? Cas wondered, riding to meet him.

His worry turned to shock when he saw how old and tired Gui looked. The veteran Quietus was unshaven, his beard as white as his hair now. His cheeks were sunken and dark bags hung beneath his eyes. One knee was bound in a bloody bandage.

They moved the horses close enough to grip hands. Gui searched his face.

"I'd hoped to find you here," he said. "Wanted to catch up. Do this proper. But I see you're on you're way out again."

"To Dierna," Cas said, hating the lie. "There's been a mass outbreak of risen."

Gui gave a grim shake of his head. "It's as bad as I've seen it everywhere, lad. Worse." A sigh. "Well, I suppose I could have missed you altogether, so we can thank the Lady for crossing our paths."

They were still in view of the gates. Cas bit back impatience. He glanced at Gui's leg. "What happened?"

"Nest of ghouls." He waved a hand. "Never mind that. I

wanted to tell you myself . . . well, I decided it's time I stepped back. Don't have the reflexes anymore."

It seemed unfathomable that anything could stop Gui from carrying out his duty. "You're quitting?" Cas asked in surprise.

"Her Grace would never allow that. We serve for life." Giu gave him a wry look. "But I need a rest. Almost got myself killed too many times. But I did find some new recruits. I think Orlaith'll be pleased."

"Well, that's good news." Cas shot a casual look at the gate. The guards were watching them. "I'm sorry, Gui, but I'd best be off—"

"Hang on, lad. I have something for you." Gui reached back and untied his quarterstaff from the saddle. "Like I said, I hoped do this proper, but you're in a rush so . . ."

He hefted the staff, balancing it on his calloused palm. "This was given to me by the Quietus who trained me. Passed down through our number for Kaethe knows how long. Only to the best of us." A solemn nod. "And that's you, Castelio."

He stared at the staff. It was yellowed with age, covered in arcane symbols. Buried memories flooded back. Gui standing on the riverbank as the mortifex that killed Ma stalked forward with its bone-blade drawn. Magic meeting magic in a sizzling crack of sheet lightning.

Cas swallowed bile. "I can't take it, Gui."

White brows drew down. "If you think you're not worthy, I'm telling you different. It's mine to dispose of and I'm choosing you." He pressed the staff into Cas's hand, curling his fingers around the shaft. "You have talent and heart and courage. But that's not why I'm giving it to you. It's because you earned it. No matter what the world threw at you, you never gave up. And you always put others before yourself."

The words cut deep. Any minute now, a rider would gallop

up to the gates with news that the Quietus named Castelio zah Nerides was wanted for murder. The thought of Gui's face when he found out made Cas sick. But it was clear that Gui wouldn't accept a refusal, and there was no time to argue with him.

"I'm honored," Cas managed, tying the staff to his own saddle.

Gui patted his shoulder. "It has powers beyond just defending against the High Dead. I'll explain them when I see you next. Safe journey, lad." He touched his knee with a wince. "We'll share a mug of ale by the fire after you return."

Cas muttered a farewell and turned away before Gui could see his shame. He urged the horse to a brisk trot. *What the feck am I supposed to do with it? I'm no one now.*

A childish part of him wanted to throw the staff away, but he remembered too well what had happened the last time he'd rejected a gift from Gui. Maybe if he hadn't broken that vial of Lady's Tears, he could have used it against the mortifex and then Lippa would have grown up like all the other girls—

Cas severed the train of thought. He'd already been down that path a thousand times.

I'll find a way to give it back. Just like Lo's talisman. I don't deserve either one.

He thought of Esme dying in his place. How he wished it had been the other way around! The streets blurred past as he remembered the small kindnesses she'd shown him over the years. Badgering the cook for meatless dishes. Fussing over minor injuries. Making him laugh with her shameless flirting.

I always loved you, Cas.

Was it the poison twisting her mind, or did she mean it? He loved Esme, too, though more like a sister. But he would have lied, given the chance. Told her anything she wanted to hear. No, she deserved better than that. She deserved—

He realized with a start that he'd reached the huge statue of Kaethe at the center of Aquitan. Lucius had said to meet there. Cas reined up, looking around. Pilgrims streamed in and out of the temple doors. A fine mist hung in the air from the torrent of water that gushed from the statue's mouth far above.

Did he really trust the mortifex? Cas hesitated. If he rode for the city gates, he might just make it out ahead of the warrant. But he might not. Surely the guards behind him knew by now, and they'd be sending riders across the city. Lucius had only bought him a little time. *How does he plan to get us out of Aquitan?*

Cas drew up the hood of his cloak. No horses. Lucius had been clear about that.

He spotted a gang of street urchins on the other side of the shallow pool at Kaethe's feet. They were entreating passersby to purchase fake charms against the dead — bits of lead shaped like stars and dipped in lampblack, roughly the weight of cold iron and genuine-looking enough to pass casual scrutiny. Most were orphans from the villages around Aquitan.

Cas dismounted and assumed the goggle-eyed look of a newcomer. He led his horse in their direction.

"G'day, fine sir," one cried, swaggering over. "You look like you're in the market fer some protection—"

"It's a reaper!" his companion hissed, tapping the webbing of his hand between thumb and forefinger. The same place where Cas had a blue star of Kaethe tattoo.

The gesture was silently repeated about the square. The kids scattered, vanishing like smoke into the crowds, but not before Cas snagged the boy's collar. The kid tried to jerk away.

Cas leaned in. "I'm not here to arrest you, so knock it off."

The boy quit struggling, but he still looked terrified. Half-starved, too.

"You want a horse?" Cas asked.

The child blinked in confusion.

"You can sell her, barter her, or ride her round the square naked for all I care," Cas said. "But you must promise to be gentle with her, or I'll find you again and you'll be sorry. Understand?"

The boy gave a slow, suspicious nod. "What do I gotta do for it?"

"Nothing. It's a gift." He put the reins in the boy's hand. "But I want you to lead her away from this square. Someplace where there's grass and water."

The boy nodded again, still unsure of this sudden good fortune. "We sleep over by Six Stones Park."

"That'll do." Cas untied Gui's staff and his travel bag from the saddle. "You ever ridden before?"

"Aye." The boy swallowed. "My pa . . . he had a mule named Franklin."

Cas lifted the boy up and set him on the mare's back, adjusting the stirrups to fit his dirty bare feet. "Well, this horse is named Bramble. She's got a mellow temperament. But if I hear that you've beaten her—"

"Oh no, sir, I'd never do that. Pa taught us to be kind with animals."

"Then your father was a good man."

The child's face had a pinched look, the sort that comes from not enough food and too many cares. When he smiled, it gladdened Cas's heart. "Thankee, sir," he said, and trotted away, bouncing on the saddle like a sack of grain.

Cas watched him go, then drew his hood forward and started for the statue. He was supposed to meet Lucius at the base. The mist helped conceal him from prying eyes, but his staff and traveling bag marked him out. He was halfway around the pool when he heard the clatter of hooves. Cas peeked from the corner of his hood.

Four Redvayne soldiers rode past the temple steps, galloping hard for the city gate. The pilgrims parted to let them pass; some were forced to dive out of the way or get trampled. He heard a few disgruntled mutters, then spotted two more soldiers. These rode at a more measured pace, hard faces swiveling left and right.

Don't look so feckin' guilty. Cas quickly threw his hood back and joined a group of pilgrims who were gawking at the spectacle. A moment later, the two soldiers spurred their horses toward a cloaked rider, yanking his cowl back. It was an older man with a graying beard. Words were exchanged, too low to hear. Cas heaved a sigh of relief as the soldiers rode off. They were focusing the search on mounted men for now, but that wouldn't last long.

Cas walked around the base of the statue, his cloak sodden from the mist. Where in the nine hells was Lucius? It occurred to him that he could simply summon the mortifex with his true name, but Cas had a feeling Lucius wouldn't appreciate that. What did he say summoning felt like? A fishhook ripping into your soul—

"Sorry I'm late."

The dry voice came inches from his ear. Cas spun around. "How'd you manage to sneak up like that?"

"Practice." Lucius's gaze lit on Gui's staff. His eyes narrowed, but he made no comment. "Come on, before the next batch of soldiers shows up. They'll be tearing this place apart stone by stone in a minute."

Lucius led him around to the rear of the statue. It faced a blank wall of the temple, with only a strip of mud between. He stopped at a door set into the statue's base and produced a ring of keys. Hinges squealed as the door creaked open. Cas followed him into the dark interior.

A yellow flame bloomed in Lucius's hand, dancing above

his open palm. They stood on a narrow catwalk. A pool about forty paces wide lay below. It was quiet inside the statue, though Cas could still hear the distant roar of the cataract outside.

"I always thought it had some mechanism," he said, looking around in surprise. "To raise the water to the top."

His voice echoed hollowly against the walls. He peered upward, but the far reaches were lost in gloom.

"There is no mechanism," Lucius replied.

Was that a touch of awe in the mortifex's voice? Cas felt his neck hair prickle.

"So you mean to hide me here?" he asked. "For how long?"

Lucius smiled. "Oh, we're not staying."

Cas stared down into the pool, realization dawning. "It's a gate, isn't it?"

"Do you have a better idea?" Lucius arched a brow. "Even if you escaped the city, you wouldn't make it two leagues before they caught you."

Cas frowned. "Maybe if I'd kept my horse . . ."

"You'd be in irons right now," Lucius said reasonably. "But if we travel through the Dominion, it spares *me* the sunlight and *you* being stuffed into a sack and returned to Orlaith. We'll reach Prydwen in days rather than weeks. What's not to like?"

"Plenty. I thought you had enemies behind the Veil."

A dry chuckle. "I have enemies everywhere. And so do you."

Cas shook his head. He'd almost prefer to travel by wind ship. Or . . . what were those bird-lizards called? *Abbadax*.

"Don't worry," Lucius said, hefting his own pack. "I brought supplies for you. Food and blankets. You can boil water to drink."

"So there's another gate in Prydwen?"

"Of course."

"How many days of travel?"

"Three or four. I mean to set a brisk pace. Try your best to keep up."

"But you will let me stop to rest?" Cas pressed. "I haven't forgotten the way you left us behind in the Vale of Harran."

Lucius looked abashed. "You have my word."

Cas had no burning desire to return to the netherworld between life and death, but it was the only way out of Prydwen that didn't end at the gallows.

"How is it done?" he asked. "Do we jump in?"

Lucius shook his head. "This is a lesser gate. It requires a Talisman of Traveling."

He drew a spiral shell from his cloak. Cas studied it — or tried to. The light blurred, sliding around the twisted edges. Cas tore his eyes away, slightly nauseated.

"This comes from the shore of the Cold Sea," Lucius said, pocketing the talisman. Again, his gaze fixed on Gui's staff. "They are common in the land of my birth, but such things are hard to come by on this side of the world."

Cas gripped the staff, ignoring the question in Lucius's eyes. "You might have mentioned all this back at the manor," he said. "Given me a choice."

The fex's chuckle was a dry puff of air. "There are no real choices anymore, Quietus. Not for either of us."

"Don't call me that," Cas said, unable to keep the bitterness from his voice. "I am no longer a Quietus."

Lucius regarded him in silence for a moment. "Very well. Although I'm not sure it is a thing you can renounce so easily. The title, yes. That is just a word. It does not change the object it describes. I can claim I am not a mortifex until the sun moves again in the sky, but —"

"Enough," Cas growled. "I won't debate it! If we must travel together, just call me Cas."

Lucius nodded. "You have passed through a gate before. This will be much the same."

"It's not really water," Cas muttered, staring into the black depths. "I can breathe it just fine."

Lucius did not bother to reply. He was already descending the ladder set into the side of the catwalk. Not a ripple stirred as the mortifex vanished into the pool. With a last uneasy glance at the door, Cas shouldered his pack and followed.

SEVEN

Brother Symeon scattered millet across the broad stone sill, smiling at the eager flap of wings. Eight doves swooped down and began to peck at the grain. The sea breeze ruffled his thin white hair as he held out a palm. The smallest bird, who was missing two toes after getting tangled in fishing line, hopped to his hand. He stroked her gray feathers with one finger.

"Such a pretty girl," he said, as she cocked her head and regarded him with a bright eye. "My pretty little Pearl."

Brother Symeon couldn't help having his favorites, though he knew Bel loved all creatures equally.

The priest had a craggy, weathered face, roughened by sun and salt. His back was hunched from age, his shoulders stooped, but he carried himself with dignity and purpose. Brother Symeon had been Keeper of the temple's reliquary for nearly forty years. A solitary task, but by happy coincidence his quarters sat just beneath the dovecote. He found solace in caring for his avian charges, though he had a young novice to climb up the ladder and clean the little niches where they nested.

The doves cooed incessantly. Sometimes, their wingtips made little whistling sounds. Like the crashing of the surf below, it formed a tapestry of background noise that he had long ago stopped hearing.

He peered through the tower's high window. A storm was blowing in from the east. Far below, along the causeway linking the temple with the mainland, a line of pilgrims hastened back to shore. He gently set the dove down, kneading his achy joints. Even without seeing the black clouds, he could feel the damp they brought.

It seldom rained in Prydwen. Most days, his chamber was sun-baked, the oppressive heat relieved only by the cooler trade winds from the Gulf of Istria. Now he drew his robes tighter against a sudden chill. Yet it was not the storm that set his nerves on edge.

Brother Symeon sat down at his worktable and examined the messages for the tenth time. They were written in an abbreviated code known only to the Sons of Bel, each arriving on the leg of one of his birds. Once, he'd been able to read the messages with his naked eye, but that time was decades gone. He took a thick glass lens from a cloth case and held it above the scraps of parchment. Tiny letters snapped into focus.

You're an old fool, he thought wearily. *The contents will not change merely because you want them to.*

All spoke of a hooded stranger seeking an iron box, the last one dated from two weeks before. The report was quite brief and he wished it offered more details. Like the rest, the warning was vague. None of his informants had seen this individual themselves — only heard whispers. But each appearance of the hooded stranger had been accompanied by strange deaths in the surrounding countryside, the bodies unmarked by any wound.

Brother Symeon unrolled a map of the duchy of Cavet, setting each message upon the town or village from which it had been sent. He dipped a quill in the inkwell and drew a line from one to the next. It formed a rambling trail toward Prydwen, confirming his worst fears.

For nearly a thousand years, since the necromancer Jaskin Cazal had recovered from his madness long enough to entrust the iron box to the Sons of Bel, it had not left this tower. Brother Symeon had guarded it as one would a hibernating basilisk. Checking each day to ensure it still slept. Never, ever touching it.

Brother Symeon had hoped the talisman was forgotten; that only he and the arch-priest knew of its existence. But someone else had learned about it.

He stared at the pattern, feeling an odd sense of relief. He had done the right thing by hiding it away. When the danger passed, he would retrieve it. But he could not take the chance of it falling into the wrong hands. Just the idea drove a spike of cold dread through his chest.

He stared at the messages for another moment. Then he held each scrap to the candle flame and let them curl to ash. *I will carry the secret to my grave if I must. I will keep my vows.* A tremor shook his hand as he rewrapped the magnifying lens. *No matter what.*

His jaw firmed. Whoever it was wouldn't dare to enter the sanctuary of Bel Mara. The island fortress was guarded by dozens of Brothers. And the reliquary itself was more of an archive now. The most valuable objects had been moved long before to the shrine on the mainland to protect them from the corrosive salt air.

All but one.

What remained were ancient scrolls and personal correspondence between the arch-priest and the other temples, along with sensitive financial records, such as the loans extended to House Marcel. The old Duc had spent a fortune keeping up his extravagant palace and financing his conquest of the Isles.

Brother Symeon frowned in disapproval. War was one of Bel's domains, but here they focused on his aspect as a healer.

His knees popped as he rose and limped to the sill. The birds had devoured the millet and were waddling about hopefully, pecking at motes of dust. A glance at the causeway showed it to be empty.

"I'll fetch more," he said. "You must fill your wee bellies before the rains come."

His burly young novice Jerald had just brought up a fresh sack of grain, along with a bowl of clam stew. Brother Symeon used the shell knife to cut a slit in the sack and gather another handful of millet.

"Here you are, my dears . . ." The old priest trailed off, head cocked like one of his doves.

Measured footsteps echoed up the winding tower steps. It must be Jerald coming to clear his plate and cup. Yet . . . the boy was always in such a lather, darting up the risers two at a time. This tread sounded heavier. His eyesight might be fading, but his ears worked perfectly well. Brother Symeon gripped the small knife.

"Jerald?" he called, voice quavering.

A tall shadow fell upon the wall. Behind him, he heard the doves take flight as one, wings beating frantically. The grain trickled in a stream from his loose fingers, pattering against the stone floor.

Brother Symeon's last thought was that he was glad his pets could fly.

EIGHT

The ancient monastery of Bel Mara thrust up from the
bay like the summit of a massive seamount. From the
wave-battered curtain wall, clusters of red-roofed
buildings circled upwards to a rectangular temple capped by a
gold statue of the sun god.

Buttressed wings flanked the temple to east and west, with
soaring marble columns and tiers of stone balconies. Birds
swooped around a high, spindly tower on the north side, dark
specks against the clouds.

In short, the place was bloody *big*.

Lo stood at the entrance to the stone causeway linking the
peninsula called Jubert's Hook with the monastery. Waves
lapped at the edges as the elevated road surrendered to the
inrushing tide.

"You won't make it, girl," warned a plump woman in a
straw hat who was selling oranges on the pier. "Better to wait it
out."

The tide tables Lo kept in her captain's berth on the *Wind-
Witch* had proven worthless in Prydwen. When the three

moons aligned, the bay's funnel shape caused tides so low it became one big mudflat. And when the water came back in, it swamped everything — including the causeway road. The man who had rented her a slip called the phenomenon a *syzygy*.

"When will the the tide turn?" Lo asked.

The woman squinted up at the darkening sky and began loading her fruit in a barrow. "When Selene sets," she replied. "About six hours."

Lo eyed the rising water. It would be close, but she thought she could make it across. The object she had come to Prydwen for — an iron box belonging to the necromancer Nathan Ouvrard — was in the monastery's reliquary.

Get inside, get the box, get out. With luck, we'll be flying back to Castle Cazal within in a few hours.

She resisted the urge to tug up her sleeve and check the brand on her arm, a Hand Sinister with flames dancing above the fingertips. It was Nathan's sigil and the mark of the blood pact she had signed five days ago. The mark faded as the deadline of their bargain approached. Not that she needed a reminder; if she failed to bring Nathan his box within a week, she would die. *Again.*

How was not specified. Lo assumed it would be something horrific. But what troubled her more was that she might never learn where her parents were being held. Nathan *knew.* And he'd only trade the information for this iron box.

"Thank you for the advice," Lo said, "but I'll take my chances."

The woman shook her head. "Many have drowned, girl. The sea comes faster than you'd expect. I've seen it with my own eyes. Don't count on the brothers reaching you in time."

Lo gave in to a coughing fit, clutching her chest. "Then I'd better make haste," she managed.

Crossing the twilight mountains of the Boundary, she had

caught her first cold. At first, she didn't know what was wrong. Runny noses and sneezing were foreign symptoms. Then Thistle reminded her that she had given her protective talisman to Castelio.

"I'm *sick*?" she'd asked in disbelief.

"Drink tea," the cat advised.

It worked out in the end, because the reason pilgrims visited Bel Mara was to beg the god to heal their ailments. Now the woman gave her a pitying look. She hurried over and pressed an orange into Lo's hand. Her face was creased by the constant sun, her brown eyes kind.

"Bel watch over you, child," she said, wheeling her barrow away before the storm hit.

Lo stared after her for a moment. The peddler wore the popular shawl called a mantilla, or manty, a versatile garment that could be wound around the head and shoulders to block out the sun. Lo had bought one herself, so she'd blend in. But around the woman's neck, on a leather thong, was . . . well, a rather enormous wooden phallus.

"This is a strange city," she muttered.

"You should heed her advice," Thistle hissed from the wicker basket at her feet. "I don't care to go swimming."

At that moment, bells started tolling in the temple, no doubt warning pilgrims hoping to visit the monastery afoot that the way would soon be impassible.

Six hours until low tide? She'd already wasted nearly a week flying from Castle Cazal on the dark side of Aveline to the sun-drenched far west. Another four days or so to return . . . That left little time to find the box. And what was life without risk?

"We can make it," she said, pointing. "Look, there's someone!"

A lone figure strode across the causeway, heading land-ward. Too far off to make out any details, but they moved at a steady, unconcerned pace. Lo hoisted the basket. Besides the cat, it held her offerings for the sun god Bel, plundered from what was left of the ship's cargo. A few bolts of silk, some copper trinkets.

She tucked her chin against the rain and started along the causeway. The sea surged across the mudflats in a churning wall of gray water. All the boats in the harbor had already fled to deeper berths.

Lo was a quarter of the way there when a wave washed over the cheap sandals she'd bought at a local market. She paused to take them off rather than lose them to the tide. When she looked up, the figure was almost upon her.

It was a Son of Bel, clad in a pleated woolen skirt and tunic, dark hair plastered to his forehead. Chilly blue eyes regarded her through his golden mask. He gave a nod as he brushed past. A faint tingle ran down her left arm and she spun back, staring after him.

Everything was going numb from the rain and cold water. Surely, that's all it was. The man was obviously no wraith. She broke into a run, the soles of her feet prickling at the tiny mollusks clinging to the worn stones.

The road was completely submerged now. Water swirled around her ankles, then crept up her calves. She splashed forward in a straight line, plunging through the swells and trying her best not to veer off the causeway. From the darkness of the basket, Thistle gave an *I-told-you-so* growl.

Gods, but the current was strong. Well, too late to turn back now. The monastery was closer than the mainland. She used her arms for balance, sliding on the algae-covered rock, and kept going. The causeway began to slope upwards as it approached the abbey's circular curtain wall. A dark tunnel loomed ahead. Two priests stood in the opening. One shouted at her, but the wind whisked his words away.

Lo raised her hand in a friendly wave. They beckoned frantically. Seawater sloshed around her thighs by the time she clambered up a set of slippery stone steps to a gate where the brothers waited.

"Are you crazy?" one asked, leading her inside. He was young, brown-skinned like most Cavetti, with a head of tousled curls and single stripe shaved above his left ear. His dark eyes held a mixture of relief and irritation. "Didn't you hear the bells?"

"Easy, Kesh," said his companion, an older boy with a square head and big shoulders. "The girl might be deaf." *Or mad*, he mouthed silently.

Lo paused to catch her breath. She didn't have to fake the rattling cough that wracked her. "I can . . . hear," she gasped. "Just . . . didn't know. Tide came in so . . . fast."

The priests shared a worried look. "Are you fit to walk up to the sanctuary?" Kesh asked in a gentler tone.

Lo nodded, bending to put on her sodden sandals.

"Let me carry that for you," the heavyset priest offered.

She let him hoist the basket and followed the two young men into an enclosed courtyard. It was a stark contrast to the chaos outside, filled with peaceful cloisters, orange trees, and statues of Bel. As she'd suspected, he was a version of Apollo. They had many symbols in common — the laurel wreath, the bow, the lyre. Yet every nude statue also sported generous manly endowments.

Bel was the god of sex and money. So how did Nathan's family relic end up in this place? The young Duc had refused to reveal anything useful — not even exactly where in the monastery the box was kept. Despite the blood oath, Nathan didn't trust her. Lo touched the pocket of her skirts, ensuring the shard of black mirror was still there. She was supposed to contact him with it once she arrived at the monastery; only then would Nathan tell her the box's exact whereabouts.

Lo trudged up the steep road, pausing now and then to cough and catch her breath. Maybe she was on her last life. There was no way of knowing how many she'd used up.

That made her think of Castelio. Lo had thought of him often during the journey to Prydwen. They had been acquainted for only a week, but it was a busy one. She'd been killed by a lich, and he'd nearly died from an arrow through the lung. That bothered her more than her own demise, which she barely recalled. Castelio seemed unaware of how attractive he was, but it was his good humor she liked most, and the way she felt content in his company.

The road circled round and round, parts of it sheltered from the rain by narrow covered galleries. The lower reaches of the island were devoted to living quarters — the red-roofed buildings she had seen from the shore. A few priests passed by, eyeing her curiously: the reckless straggler who had barely made it to the walls.

The view of the bay spread out as she climbed higher. To the east sat a ramshackle port town of stilt houses and floating barges. To the west were high cliffs with gleaming white buildings that must be the seat of House Marcel. Twin lighthouses perched on distant spits of land at the harbor entrance, pulsing a warning to approaching ships.

At last, they reached the main temple, a grand space with columns as thick as five men soaring to support a domed roof far above. A haze of pungent incense hung in the air. Hundreds of candles burned in alcoves, casting a flickering light over a long line of people. Some had twisted limbs. Others were thin and pale. She heard the rustle of dry coughs, a few moans of pain.

At the center of the chamber stood another statue of Bel,

this one cast from mellow gold. A gaunt stone figure crouched at his feet as the god bent to lay hands on its head. Offerings were scattered at the base. A young man with a bulbous growth on his neck approached the statue, touching it with reverence. Lo felt a stab of sympathy.

"You may wait here," Brother Kesh said, setting her basket down.

Lo thanked them and took a place at the end of the line. She peeled the orange the kind woman on the pier had given her and shared it with the family in front of her.

The line moved slowly. The sickest people had to be carried to the statue by relatives, or, if they had none, the priests. Each pilgrim spent several minutes communing with the statue, lips moving in silent prayer.

The rigid division between rich and poor meant little here, Lo noticed. A middle-aged woman in a fine embroidered mantilla with dozens of silver bracelets rattling on her arms was followed by another in rough hemp and worn sandals mended with rope.

When each had finished, the priests would whisk them into a chamber beyond. It was all orderly and routine — but they were watched at all times.

When her turn came, Lo took her offerings from the basket: a bolt of fine red silk and a copper plate. She added them to the heap of coins and flowers, wax-sealed jars of honey and little cakes. Also a few pieces of very fine jewelry and raw gemstones.

No wonder the priests are so rich.

Lo knelt down and closed her eyes, laying a hand on Bel's foot.

I'm the last. It won't be easy to slip away. I wonder where they take us next? At least no one can leave until low tide. That's what . . . about five hours from now? She felt a sneeze coming and pinched her nose. *All those poor people. I wonder if it ever works? Touching a statue? Kaethe must be real enough, though, if my parents made a bargain with her.*

So close. She was so close to finding them, after eight long years. She would tell them everything. The whole shadow soul business. Assuming they didn't already know.

A disturbing thought.

Lo opened her eyes, hoping they'd forgotten her. The temple was silent. She rose to her feet and looked around. Which way now? The mirror was halfway from her pocket when Brother Kesh stepped out from behind a pillar.

"This way," he said briskly.

Lo coughed and shoved it back in her pocket. Brother Kesh brought her into the next chamber, where food and drink had been laid out on long tables. It was simple fare, bread and a fish soup, but the atmosphere was markedly more cheerful than the subdued line in the temple proper. If nothing else, these people had been given hope.

"Is there a privy?" Lo asked, clutching her stomach. "I feel queasy."

He nodded quickly and pointed to a door. Lo lifted her basket, trying to conceal how heavy it was with a fat cat inside, and hurried through, finding herself in a tiny chamber with a chute that dumped straight into the sea.

The instant she set the basket down, Thistle leapt out. He prowled to the chute, made a feline face of disgust, and moved to the far corner to wash his paws.

The door had no lock, so she stood with her back against it and dug out the black mirror. Lo gazed into the silver-framed oval. The mirror cast no reflection; it was like staring into a bottomless well. She blew on it and the surface rippled like disturbed ink.

"Nathan," she whispered.

A minute passed. Two.

"Nathan!" she hissed. "Whatever you're doing, I need you. Now! So put down your bones or corpse dust or whatever you're —"

The glass steadied and his face came into focus: shrewd dark eyes and raven hair swept back from a high, pale forehead. "Do you have it?" he asked without preamble.

"Not yet," Lo whispered. "I just arrived at Bel Mara."

Nathan peered at her. "You look awful, demoiselle. Perhaps you should have rested first."

She wished she could reach through the mirror and tweak his aquiline nose. "Just tell me about this reliquary. Where is it?"

"Beneath the dovecote at the top of the north tower."

Someone bumped the door. She leaned back, forcing it shut again. "Occupied!"

"Where exactly are you?" Nathan asked.

"Never mind that. How am I supposed to get inside? Is the tower locked?"

"I imagine so." He smirked. "But surely that will not prove a difficulty for you."

She scowled. "So you keep saying. But there are priests *everywhere* and—"

"How long are ye taking in there?" a voice called through the door. "There's others waiting!" Disgruntled murmurs followed this remark.

"Almost done!"

Lo leaned in so close her chin nearly touched the glass. Nathan recoiled slightly. "You'd better be right," she snarled, thrusting the mirror back into her skirts.

She turned to Thistle. "I need a distraction. Can you liven things up out there?"

71

He shot her a surly look. "Very well. But this is the last time I will suffer confinement—"

A fist banged on the door. Lo made frantic shooing motions. With a switch of his tail, Thistle hopped into the basket. Lo set the lid on and opened the door, wiping her forehead with a sleeve.

"Sorry," she muttered, elbowing a path through the small crowd gathered outside. An old man slunk in behind her, looking around with obvious trepidation.

She moved to a table, discreetly scanning the chamber. There were four priests keeping an eye on the pilgrims. Two doors, one to the privy, one back into the temple.

"Now," she said from the side of her mouth.

With a bloodcurdling yowl, Thistle exploded from the basket. He landed on the table, toppled a bowl of fish broth into its owner's lap, and leapt down the long trestle, wreaking as much damage as he could. Screams and curses erupted.

"Who brought that cat?" one of the priests shouted angrily. "No animals in the sanctuary!"

Lo stowed the basket under the table and looked around innocently. The priests lunged. One nearly caught Thistle's tail, but he dodged at the last instant and shot between the man's legs, causing him to stumble into the others.

Tin cups bounced and rolled across the floor. More soup bowls were upended. A few people laughed at the spectacle; others frowned in pious reproach. Lo inched her way to the doorway, unnoticed, as Thistle led the priests a merry chase over and under the tables. Several times, they seemed on the verge of catching him, but he always managed to scoot away.

With a last glance around, she darted into the temple. North tower. That would be at the far end. The multitude of candles flickered as she swept past, sprinting the length of the great pillared abbey. There were three archways at the end, but only one had winding stairs leading upward.

Lo pelted into the cramped space, sandals slapping the stone. Up and up she went, until she came to a wooden door. Locked, Nathan said, but when she gave it a push, it swung open.

One more twisting flight and she reached a round chamber of double-height. Lo stopped, chest heaving. Her spirits sank.

The walls were honeycombed with square niches. Each held a box. There must be hundreds. A rolling ladder sat on the far side. She made a slow turn, neck craning. Hundreds? More like thousands. It would take days to examine them all.

And yet . . . the boxes seemed to all be made of wood. She slid one from its niche. It contained an old, yellowing scroll. The end of the box facing outward had a series of numbers and letters. Some kind of archiving code.

Lo slid the box back into place. Of course, the iron box could be *inside* one of the wooden boxes. He said it was small.

Bloody Nathan.

She crossed the chamber. On the far side, several boxes had been pulled from their cubbyholes and hurled to the floor. The wood was splintered, as if they'd been stomped on in a rage. She could see the fragile scrolls still inside, partly torn.

That's peculiar.

Her skin tingled at a soft sound from above.

The staircase continued to a higher level. Lo crept up the corkscrew steps, moving with caution now. Yes, there were furtive sounds from above. She inched around the last turning, hand flying to her mouth to stifle a cry.

A desk sat near the window, with a well-worn, comfortable-looking chair. At the foot of the chair, an elderly priest lay in a pool of blood. The man was dead, that much was obvious. He eyes stared blankly at the ceiling.

Papers from the desk were scattered everywhere, some splattered with blood. The chamber must be the living quarters of the reliquary's guardian. A cot was pushed against one wall, the blankets torn away and thrown into a heap.

A woman stood amidst the wreckage. She had her back turned, hands propped on her hips. She was tall and dark, her hair woven into intricate braids. Her bare arms were slender but taut with wiry muscle. She wore heavy boots — of the sort that might easily have stomped one of the boxes in the archive below. A wicked curved sword hung at her hip.

Lo was inching away when she felt a rattle in her chest. A tickle in her nose. She slapped both hands over her face, trying to keep it in, but the woman had the hearing of a bat.

She spun around, her face a thunderhead. One hand fell to her blade. In a flash, she crossed the distance. Faster than a mortal had any right to. Lo swallowed as steel pressed against her throat.

"Keep quiet and you'll keep your head," the woman said softly.

She had a strange accent. Husky and musical.

Lo glared into her brown eyes, heedless of the blade. "What have you done?" she growled. "Who *are* you?"

The woman frowned. She opened her mouth to reply when they both heard feet pounding up the stairs. An instant later, two priests appeared at the landing below. One shouted urgently down the stairwell.

"Ah, Innunu," the woman muttered with a sigh. "You don't play fair, do you?"

To Lo's surprise, she tossed the blade away and sank down to her knees. Seconds later they were both surrounded.

"Brother Symeon is dead," one of the priests confirmed, crouching at the old archivist's side. "Murdered!"

"That much is clear," another muttered. "Seize them both."

"I heard a scream," Lo cried. "I had nothing to do with it! You must believe me. I just got here—"

Two glowering priests lifted her off her feet and hauled her by the arms back down the winding stairs. Ahead, she could just make out the killer's profile amid a crush of brawny Sons of Bel. The woman merely looked annoyed.

Lo was just thinking things couldn't get much worse when they reached the bottom and she was searched. A priest took the black mirror, regarding it with a grim expression. Then he dragged her to a tiny chamber, shoved her inside, and locked the door without a word.

Child's play to retrieve the box, Nathan had promised.

She almost laughed — except that it wasn't funny. That poor old man.

Lo gave an explosive sneeze and settled in to wait.

NINE

L o suspected her cell was not meant for prisoners. It held two bare cots and a dry washbasin containing a dead spider. Boys' names had been scratched into one wall, along with a series of large, detailed phalluses. Novice chambers, most likely.

She peered out the narrow window. It wasn't barred, but the drop would shatter bones. She could hear the killer whistling cheerfully in the cell next door.

A lunatic? They'd been searched at the same time. Lo had watched closely and knew the priests didn't take the box from her. And why would the killer hang around if she'd found it? Lo stuck her head out the window. It was raining, a steady, miserable drizzle.

"Hey!" she hissed.

The whistling stopped.

"You were searching for something, weren't you?" Lo called.

No response. Footsteps rang in the hall and she pulled her head back inside. Four priests escorted her through a tangle of corridors to another door. A curt announcement and she was hauled into a chamber with a single chair and table. A covered balcony ran along one wall, dripping curtains of rain.

The man who awaited her was garbed in a flowing white tunic with a laurel wreath on the breast and a braided yellow cord tied around one arm. He had a close-cropped gray beard and thin, patrician features. Judging by the deference the younger priests showed him, he was someone important.

"What is your name, child?" His voice was a mellow baritone.

Lo dropped to her knees, eyes welling with tears. "Ami. My name is Ami. I swear, I never saw that woman before. Oh, sweet Bel, I wish I'd never come here!" She wiped her nose with a sleeve and coughed miserably.

"You claim innocence in the heinous murder of the Reliquary's Keeper, Brother Symeon?"

"Aye, sir. Aye!"

"And where do you come from, Ami?"

"A village called Swanton, sir. It's in Clovis."

If she claimed to be from Prydwen, they could easily check the lie. But pilgrims journeyed from far and wide to Bel's temple. Cas had mentioned Swanton. He said he'd lived there for a time. Lo had an ear for accents and perfectly imitated his rapid, lilting speech.

"I have a sickness of the lungs," she said. "My Ma and Da saved enough for me to come and lay hands on the sacred statue. I swear on their names, I had nought to do with it. I heard a scream and ran to help, that's all."

The high priest gazed down at her. "You are from Swanton?"

"Aye."

He nodded. "I served as an initiate at Bel's temple in the

mountains where the Forkings River rises. We traveled a fair bit through Clovis. I know the village you speak of."

Lo clasped her hands. "Thank Bel! So you know—"

"It's odd, because your accent sounds more like the Boundary folk, not the good people of Swanton." His gaze hardened.

"Ah, that's because my Ma—"

"Enough lies!" the priest roared. He opened a small chest and brandished the black mirror. "What about this, Ami?"

"That's a family heirloom." She chewed her lip, flushing. Javid always said that when you're accused of a serious crime, it's wise to confess to a lesser one. "I was supposed to leave it as a gift for the god, but it's so pretty—"

"Do you take me for an imbecile? This a tool of necromancy. Who sent you here?"

Lo's eyes widened to saucers. "*Ne-cro-mancy*?" She knew she was caught, but stubbornness made her keep the bouncy, singsong accent. "Oh no, you're mistaken, sir. It belonged to my grandmother."

His jaw tightened. "Are you a follower of the Rogue?"

"Pardon, sir?"

"The Red Rogue!"

"I've no idea who you're speaking of," she replied honestly.

He returned the mirror to the chest. Then he folded his hands and leaned across the desk.

"I do not believe you killed Brother Symeon," he said. "You had no weapon nor blood on your clothes. But if you fail to offer a truthful explanation for what you were doing in the reliquary, standing over his body, I will be forced to order your transfer to Blackwater Jail. We are men of god here. We have no place to detain criminals."

Lo met his eyes. "I already told you all I know, sir."

He leaned back, studying her face for a long moment.

"Your lack of a reaction suggests that you are unfamiliar with Blackwater. It sits at the low point of the city. The cells flood with sewage when the tide comes in. I hear it is a pestilent place. Murder is a burning offense in Prydwen, but it's unlikely you'd survive long enough to reach the pyre."

She cast her gaze down, trembling. "It sounds terrible, sir. I can only beg your mercy, since I've nought knowledge of the crime."

The arch-priest sighed. "Let us see what your confederate has to say."

"She's not my confederate. I swear, I've never seen that woman before!"

He turned to the priests. "The moment the tide turns, alert the warden of Blackwater that he has two prisoners to pick up."

The priests dragged her out just as the killer was being dragged in. She winked at Lo and grinned. The door slammed shut.

"You saw that," Lo snapped, trying to jerk her arm free. "The woman's mad!"

"You should have confessed," one of the priests growled. "Now you'll be given to Duc Marcel. He's not half as gentle as we are."

They were a few paces down the corridor when a muffled thump came from behind. The priests stopped and turned. In that split-second of confusion, Lo slammed an elbow into the nearest one's jaw. His head snapped back, eyes rolling to the whites.

Forgive me, Bel.

Before he hit the floor, the other seized her from behind in a crushing bear hug. She struggled, heels drumming against his shins. Darkness threaded her vision. With a panicked burst of strength, Lo slammed her head back. It connected with a sickening crunch. The priest gave a guttural groan and let go. A kick between the legs left him writhing silently on the floor, blood pouring from his nose.

She leaned against the wall, catching her breath. Then a furry gray blur appeared, leaping over the fallen guards.

"Run!" Thistle growled. "Before more come along."

"Not . . . without Nathan's mirror," she wheezed. "I have to . . . tell him what . . . happened."

The cat bared his fangs. "Then I will do my best to draw them away."

He sped down the corridor, vanishing around a bend. Lo hurried back down the hall and pressed her ear to the arch-priest's door. More grunts and thuds came from within. She wrenched the door wide, steeling herself for a bloodbath.

The killer had gotten her sword back. Four Sons of Bel lay sprawled on the floor. Two were out cold, the other two groaning faintly, but none showed mortal wounds. Lo was relieved to see the arch-priest cowering under the long table.

She clutched her hands together and stepped between him and the killer. "Please don't hurt him, miss! You'll call down Bel's wrath if you do!"

The killer snorted and walked past her to bolt the door shut. Then she strode to the balcony, leaning out with one hand shading her eyes from the rain. The instant her back was turned, Lo slunk to the desk. The arch-priest flinched as she eased the chest open and slipped the shard of black mirror into her skirts.

What now? Lo eyed the fallen Sons of Bel, every one of them big and muscled. She had some fighting skills, but the killer was next level. Lo inched closer to the balcony. Lines of white-capped combers beat against the curtain wall, flinging gouts of spray into the air. The tide looked at its highest point now, a seething cauldron of treacherous cross-currents.

"Rough out there, eh?"

Lo turned. The killer had sheathed her blade. They eyed each other as bells started tolling across the island.

"If you want to get off this rock, girl," the killer said, "follow me."

At that instant, a commotion erupted in the corridor. Fists pounded on the door.

"Open up!" a stern voice commanded. "In the name of the god!"

TEN

The doorframe shuddered beneath heavy blows. The killer turned to the arch-priest, who huddled by his desk.

"Tell them you're alive," she said, "but that if they don't stop trying to break the door down, that will change."

The arch-priest relayed the message in a quavering voice. The pounding ceased, but every bell on the island was now tolling at once. Lo gripped the balcony rail and scanned the horizon. About a quarter league away, a dinghy bobbed on the waves. A cloaked figure bent over the oars, rowing with powerful strokes toward the monastery.

"You have an accomplice," she said.

"Partner," the killer corrected. She was stripping the four groggy priests of their red sashes and binding their hands. "Tie up the high muckety-muck, would you?" she called over her shoulder.

Lo met their hostage's flinty stare. "I swear, I've never seen that woman before. This is all just . . ." *Pointless.* He'd never believe she wasn't involved now. "Sorry, ah, your holiness," she muttered, as she tied up the arch-priest with his braided cord of office. "I really am."

Once he was securely bound, Lo followed the killer back to the balcony. They hooked their legs over the rail and dropped down to the next terrace. Four Sons of Bel were hiding beneath an overhang. Three went for the killer, and one — the biggest — for Lo. She ducked a meaty fist and hooked a foot behind his ankle. A quick shove and the priest tumbled over the edge of the terrace, straight into the water.

The killer fought like a cornered wolverine. By the time Lo turned back, one brother lay stunned on the blue floor tiles, and the others were floundering in the bay. The Sons of Bel atop the curtain wall rushed to their aid, throwing ropes down to fish the three priests out.

To Lo's surprise — and relief — the woman hadn't drawn her sword. It didn't add up. Why murder Brother Symeon, the one person who knew where the iron box was, yet spare the rest?

Lo was about to ask when she heard the door in the chamber above them crash open and the arch-priest's angry voice directing his rescuers to the balcony. "Down there!" someone shouted.

At least a dozen priests were gathered on the balcony above. Far below, green waves dashed against the curtain wall. And Lo could hear people coming down the corridor of the level they were on.

"Shit," the woman snapped, scanning for another escape route.

"What about that?" Lo pointed to one of the flying buttresses, which met the main structure of the temple a few paces down and to the right. The buttress was narrow, with a sheer drop to either side. The woman didn't look happy, but she gave a hard nod.

Lo went first, leaping across the gap. Adrenaline pumped as she skidded on the rain-slick stone, then caught herself. The woman followed, landing with the light grace of a dancer, and they ran along the sloping fortification, then dropped down again into a narrow alley. It left them at the ring road that circled upward to the temple.

For the moment, they seemed to have left their pursuers behind. All was quiet save for the hiss of rain and distant bells.

"What were you looking for in the reliquary?" Lo asked, holding the woman's fierce gaze.

"What were *you* looking for?"

They regarded each other in silence for a moment. Lo felt a sudden urge to trust her, to unburden herself of everything. It was madness. And she couldn't anyway. Nathan's bloody oath wouldn't let her.

"Go ahead," Lo said at last. "I'll fend for myself from here." She turned away, and the woman grabbed her arm.

"Don't be stupid. You'll never get off this rock alone. I'm offering you a way out."

"And I appreciate it." She pulled free. "But I have to find my cat."

The woman laughed. "You're kidding."

"Not at all. I won't leave without him."

The woman glanced out to sea, where the dinghy rowed by her confederate was slicing through the swells. "If you make it by the time he reaches the wall, you can jump in," she said. "But I'm not waiting around."

She strode off, leaving Lo to skulk through the wet foliage along the ring road. Shouts echoed through the temple complex from all directions.

"Thistle," she whispered, biting her lip. "Where the devil have you got off to—"

The cat came flying around a corner just ahead of a pack of

red-faced priests. Lo took off sprinting at his side, delving into a warren of twisting downhill paths between the houses. Sandals slapped against mud close behind as the priests gave pursuit. Red-roofed houses flashed past. Then the dwellings grew sparser and she glimpsed the bay. The boat was no longer in sight. She swore and cut through a grove of olive trees, the priests still on her heels.

They were calling for help. It was only a matter of moments before more arrived to cut her off. If she were taken to Blackwater Jail. . . Well, she might easily die within its walls before finding a way to escape.

"Stop!" came a cry from behind. "Or the archers will shoot!"

Lo refused to kill anyone to buy her own freedom, and certainly not a priest. But maybe she could slow them down a bit.

She sought the Nexus, the beating heart of the universe where her daēva magic waited. Her breath came faster as she whipped up a gust of wind. It tore loose a dozen red roof tiles and sent them flying like javelins. She glanced over her shoulder. The priests were forced to stop and duck the missiles.

Thistle's yellow eyes glowed as he cast her an accusing look. He did not need to say anything. They both knew the gambit was too little, too late. It had only bought them a few seconds. There was no way off the island — not until low tide exposed the mudflats, which was still hours away.

Yet somehow she felt certain that everything would work out. *Lo's luck.* She scooped up a bedraggled Thistle and kept running. They rounded a corner — and came face to face with the killer. The woman was leaning against a wall with her arms crossed, brown skin dappled with raindrops.

"I see you found your cat," she said.

Her eyes flicked over Lo's shoulder. Moving almost

languidly, the woman pushed off the wall. Her fist connected with a priest's jaw, sending him staggering back with unhinged knees.

"Go," she told Lo, waving at a carved archway. "I'll catch up in a minute."

The woman returned her attention to the priests, who had backed up and were eyeing her warily.

Lo dashed through the arch, Thistle's furry bulk clutched to her chest. It led into an enclosed courtyard with a statue of Bel and mounds of flowering herbs that gave off a sweet fragrance in the rain. Beyond sat a postern gate and small stone landing, where the dinghy bobbed in the choppy waters. The oarsman pulled hard with each stroke. It clearly took all his skill to keep the boat from dashing against the jagged rocks nearby.

The Sons of Bel patrolling the curtain wall had spotted him. Crossbow bolts buzzed around the boat like angry wasps. He laughed and shouted some taunt when a lateral swell dragged the boat sideways, away from the landing. Lo strode to the edge, gathering her breath.

"Do not even think of it," Thistle snarled.

Lo made sure the shard of black mirror was tucked deep into her pocket. Then she jumped feet-first into the water. Warm currents buffeted her. She surfaced a moment later to Thistle's loud yowling. His ears were laid back and his claws were tiny needles that pierced straight through her clothes.

The boat had drifted down past the rocks. Lo stroked hard with one arm, gripping the cat's scruff with the other. She managed to get hold of an oar and deposit a sodden Thistle in the bow.

The man on the bench hardly seemed aware of her. He was gazing intently back at Bel Mara. Lo searched for the killer, whom he obviously would not leave without. A minute later she appeared, jogging briskly along the landing. She was tensing to dive into the water when she winced and clutched her arm. She'd been hit by a crossbow bolt.

The oarsman cursed in a harsh accent and yanked at the oars. He looked startled to find Lo clinging to one.

"Please!" She held out a hand, spluttering as a wave slapped her in the face.

Without a word, he dragged her into the dinghy. By then, the killer had recovered enough to leap into the water and start paddling. The oarsmen angled for her as more bolts splashed around them. When they got close enough, Lo tossed a mooring rope she found coiled under the bow bench. The killer grabbed it and Lo reeled her in like the day's catch.

The man's relief was palpable as she flopped over the side and grinned weakly.

"We made it," she panted.

"Who is she?" he demanded, gaze flicking to Lo.

"No one," the killer replied, inspecting her bloody arm.

His tone softened. "How bad—"

"Just a graze. Now row, dammit!"

He cast Lo a narrow look. Then they were pulling away to a chorus of furious shouts from the priests. But the danger was hardly past. There was a hard bump and frightful scraping sound as the dinghy foundered on the reef. Lo clung to the bench, expecting the flimsy wooden hull to shatter at any moment. The waves nudged them toward the northern wall of the monastery — back into crossbow range. Once again, volleys hissed down around the trapped boat.

Lo batted them away with air as best she could, until a huge swell carried the boat past the rocky shallows into deeper water. Thistle crouched between her feet, his low growls muffled by the sloshing of swells over the gunwale. She stroked his sodden ears, whispering reassurances. But the tide was finally turning — and not in their favor. Despite the oarsman's strenuous efforts, the dingy was being pulled out toward the open sea. The priests seemed to realize this for they stopped firing, content to let Bel exact his own vengeance.

The killer's accomplice was lean and fit, with sandy hair and hazel eyes. He wore a manty around his shoulders and a sword buckled at the waist of loose trousers. His face looked young, around Lo's age, yet something about him seemed a great deal older and wearier.

The killer glared at him from the stern bench. She had managed to keep her own curved blade and seemed willing to use it. The dinghy drifted further from shore as the two criminals bickered with each other.

"Give me a turn," the woman insisted. "You're spent!"

"And you're hurt," he shot back, as a wave slammed them abeam and almost flipped the boat.

She glanced impatiently at the blood trickling down her arm. "I already told you, it's a scratch. Now give me the oars before we all go for a swim!"

He gazed at her with exasperation. "Liar. The wound pains you. I'll deal with it later, but we must—"

Lo tuned them out. Thistle looked disgusted by the entire affair. He met her eyes and blinked once, which meant *I'm done with this nonsense.* An instant later, the wind shifted direction. It gained force and began to push them toward shore, against the outrushing tide. The oarsman pulled hard again. They skimmed into the lee of the monastery and the battering waves subsided.

He aimed for a hodgepodge of stilt houses on the eastern side of the bay. With the wind at his back, the boat made swift progress. As Bel Mara dwindled in the distance, the clouds parted and blazing sun dried their soaked clothes. A short time later, they were gliding into a network of narrow waterways.

It was one of the oddest places Lo had ever seen, a mix of

grassy marshes and spits of dry land, through which a multi-tude of canals wound like silver serpents. There were boats of every description, as well as round stilt houses with thatched roofs that stood like wading birds in the reeds.

Red rags fluttered from rails and masts. About half the men wore red armbands, though Lo had no idea what they meant. Youngsters splashed in the shallows, their joyful shouts echoing in the shadowy recesses of the stilt houses.

Women sat with their bare feet dangling over the docks, mending fishing nets. The smell of woodsmoke and spices wafted through the air from countless braziers. It must be suppertime, for children ran about dispensing wooden bowls to their elders. The smaller ones gripped long, thin switches, which they used to discourage marauding gulls.

The oarsman pulled up beneath one of these stilt houses. Two bare-chested boys wearing their manties knotted at the waist like loincloths grabbed the mooring line. The woman hopped out first, offering a hand to the man. He seemed to have some old injury, for one leg moved stiffly. Lo and Thistle disembarked last. The boys hoisted the dinghy from the water and stowed it away on a wooden ledge.

The house perched at the edge of the canal, with catwalks of warped boards extending to either side. Lo considered making a run for it, but the man blocked escape on one side and the woman stood on the other, one boot propped on a piling. She gave Lo a toothy smile.

"Let's have a proper chat," she said.

Lo scooped Thistle into her arms. She opened her eyes wide. "I . . . whatever ye say."

"Not out here." The man jerked his chin at the house.

There was nothing sinister about the dwelling. A broad terrace on the bottom level held blue-glazed ceramic pots with lemon trees, and then a bunch of smaller pots with basil. A scruffy white dog dozed in a patch of sun.

Lo followed the pair up a rickety flight of stairs. The man limped the whole way, his face tight. On the second floor, a brazier held sizzling fish, tended by a doe-eyed girl of perhaps fourteen. A naked and rather dirty child crouched next to her, sorting through a bucket of oysters. An enticing blend of garlic and spices wafted from the brazier.

The woman tossed the girl a clinking purse. "Give it to your mother," she said. "Two weeks rent, as promised, plus extra for discretion."

The girl frowned. "What's that mean?"

"Keeping your mouths shut."

She nodded. "We never talk to no one anyhow."

"Filthy onions," the naked child put in.

"Who are the onions?" Lo asked. "The priests?"

The girl looked scandalized. "We'd never speak ill of the brothers."

"Onions are the Duc's soldiers," the woman said.

"Their uniforms are silver and gold," the girl explained.

"And they smell like the Duc's arsehole," the kid said.

The woman prodded Lo up the stairs to the top floor. It was little more than a loft, open on all sides to catch the breeze. Two hammocks hung from the rafters. Flies circled dirty plates on the floor. Two traveling packs sat against one wall, but it was otherwise empty.

"Why did ye bring me here?" Lo asked, clutching Thistle to her breast. "What do ye want?"

The woman shot her a flat look. "It's a bit late to play the innocent. I saw how you handled those priests. And you may as well drop the fake accent, too."

They stared at each other for a minute. Lo set Thistle on the floor. He began to prowl the perimeter, tail swishing.

"Fair enough," she said in a normal voice. "I was hired to find a relic. But you seem to have got there first. Why did you kill that poor old man?"

"His blood was already drying by the time I arrived." The woman turned to her companion, who lounged in a hammock, one boot on the floor. "Tell her."

He gazed at Lo impassively. "We only kill necromancers."

This statement set off quiet alarm bells. "If you didn't murder him, then who did?" Lo asked.

"The creature we're hunting," he replied. "Who slipped through our fingers yet again."

Creature? Lo thought of the Son of Bel she'd passed on the causeway. The tingling in her left arm, which she always felt around the dead. Not a priest after all.

"Is he a mortifex?" she asked.

The woman's eyes narrowed. "How do you know that?"

"I saw him as I crossed to the monastery."

"Describe him." She strolled closer, a hand resting on her sword hilt.

"Blue eyes. Dark hair. I can't really give you any more details. He was wearing a mask."

The words were soft. "Then how do you know he was Undead?"

Damn. "I felt a chill."

"Briefly passing someone on the road? In the pouring rain? Try again."

"Look, I just had a feeling." She lifted her chin. "All the women in my family have the gift of Sight—"

"Bullshit."

"Believe what you will. I can't really explain it."

"Not a word I like to hear. It's almost as bad as won't." The woman grabbed Lo's arm. "Why did you come to Bel Mara? What relic were you after?"

Lo tried to jerk away. Her sleeve rode up, exposing the Hand Sinister mark. The woman hissed between her teeth.

"She bears a necromancer's brand!"

Hatred twisted her face. She stepped back, blade sweeping free of its scabbard.

Lo spun out of reach and darted past. From the corner of her eye, she saw a gray blur shooting for the stairs. Shouts chased her as she sprinted for the edge of the loft, praying momentum would carry her past the wooden docks below. She leapt into open air, arms and legs flailing. Murky water rushed up to meet her. She just had time to draw a shallow breath before she plunged into the canal.

Lo touched a muddy bottom, kicked off, and swam as far as she could underwater. When she finally popped up with a gasp, she saw the man searching along the bank nearby. The little white dog was running up and down, barking madly. The man spotted her and shouted to the woman, who was launching the dinghy. Lo sucked in another breath and slid back beneath the surface, stroking hard.

Things bumped her in the gloom. The canal was full of floating garbage and dead fish and other nameless objects, many of them squishy. She ignored the vile taste in her mouth and found a rhythm: thirty strokes, then a quick surface for air.

At first, the man easily kept pace with her on the bank. Worse, the woman was closing in the dinghy, near enough for Lo to see her mouth set in a grim line. She was clearly strong, but she'd been grazed by a crossbow bolt and blood flowed freely down her arm. Had it been the man in the boat, Lo would have been caught.

Then she reached a crossing canal and took the way he couldn't follow on foot. Gradually, the dinghy fell farther and farther behind.

When her pursuers passed from sight, she spotted a slimy

rope ladder and scrambled up to a floating dock. The locals gave her unfriendly stares as she picked a path through a maze of catwalks and piers, some only wide enough for two people to pass. Lo kept her head down, hacking loudly whenever someone came near. She stank like a sewer and no one came too close.

The *Wind-Witch* was moored in the Docklands, an area south of the marsh with a deep-water harbor. It bristled with tall-masted ships that were easy to spot from a distance. Thistle waited on the deck. He'd clearly been grooming, for his fur looked immaculate.

"Don't worry," Lo said wearily. "I won't come near."

She drew a bucket from one of the water barrels and sluiced away the top layer of filth. Then she went below, stripped, and scrubbed down with a cake of soap, washing her hair twice. She wrapped herself in a blanket, shivering, and called Nathan with the mirror. This time, he appeared immediately.

"Do you have it?" he demanded.

"No, I don't." She sneezed. "The box is gone and a mortifex murdered the priest who oversees the reliquary. Know anything about that?"

Nathan looked even more pale than usual. "Are you sure?"

She sneezed thrice more, noisily blew her nose, and told him all that had happened. Nathan listened in silence. He seemed uncharacteristically subdued.

"Well?" she prompted. "You do know something. It's obvious."

He raked a hand through spiky black hair. "Demoiselle, you must believe me, I did not expect—"

"Save the apologies. Who is he?"

A deep sigh. "I fear it must be the same mortifex who killed my parents."

Lo blinked. "Oh . . . I'm so sorry, Nathan."

"He came for the box. It wasn't here, but he did not know that. He tortured my mother and father when they refused to tell him the box's location. I was six at the time. Vigo had gone to Mystral on an errand. He returned just in time to drive this mortifex off and save my life. But it is why I built the draw-bridge. Why I never leave Castle Cazal."

She sighed. "You have my sympathy, but you might have mentioned all this before."

"It was many years ago," Nathan said faintly. "He never came back. I hoped he had given up."

"Well, he hasn't. And these people looking for him really hate necromancers. Do you know who they are, too?"

"No, I swear it."

"Well, one good thing is that I'm not sure this mortifex found the box." She paused. "But it would really help if I knew what's inside."

Nathan's expression cooled. "I promised Jaskin I would keep it a secret. I gave my solemn oath."

Lo sneezed again. "What about your oath to me?"

"That's different. It is a family matter." He glanced at something out of view. She wondered if it was the creepy old sorcerer, lurking in his mirror. "But I am terribly sorry for this complication. Do not fear, I will set matters right."

"By cancelling our contract?" Lo asked hopefully.

"I'm afraid that's impossible."

She nodded. "Yes, of course. But I do wish you were here, Nathan."

His face softened. "Ah, demoiselle, that is touching—"

"So I could strangle you myself." She leaned into the mirror and held up her clenched fists. "Very slowly, like this . . ."

"*Fichu*, calm down. There is no need for threats," he said stiffly.

94

In fact, there was someone Lo did wish were with her right now — Castelio, the sleepy-eyed Quietus. They'd probably never see each other again. The thought made her sad, and then even angrier.

"Dead rats," she said.

Nathan frowned. "Pardon, demoiselle?"

"I counted seven floating in the canal. I hope I have at least one life left, because swimming in that water will probably kill me in the next day or so."

Nathan exhaled forcefully through his nose. "I understand your pique. Truly I do. But there is a simple solution."

She crossed her arms. "Oh, really? Let's hear it."

Nathan flashed her his most dazzling smile. "We will summon the dead priest and ask him where my box is."

ELEVEN

For three days, Cas and Lucius journeyed through a trackless forest of pale beeches and towering spruce. The sky was a gray slate, the woods stretching into blue twilight on all sides.

Kaethe's domain was just as unsettling as Cas remembered. There were no chirping insects or small creatures rustling in the undergrowth; only a deep, unnatural silence. Even their footfalls were hushed by a carpet of dry needles.

The gloomy landscape suited his mood. He'd promised to dance with Esme, but she'd never dance again. Merry, kind Esme was gone simply because he'd stumbled over the truth: that Orlaith had staged her own son's abduction and tried to blame the Courtenays for it. How often had he heard the Ducissa rail against necromancy . . . when all the while she was keeping her dead husband chained up in the feckin' *wine cellar*.

Before his world came crumbling down, Cas thought he'd left the suspicious, bitter boy he used to be behind in Swanton. A Quietus had to master his emotions. He'd heard tales from Gui about what happened when you allowed fear or anger to take over. Many had died after letting their guard down for a single instant.

So he'd spent the last five years locking the unruly parts of himself away. But that boy wasn't gone, only waiting in the dark. Now his old rage rekindled hotter than ever. He trusted no one — certainly not his travel companion. Lucius might have helped him flee Aquitan, but he served Orlaith, whom he didn't hesitate to betray when it suited. Cas had no illusions that Lucius wouldn't do the same to him if it was to the mortifex's advantage.

He gripped Gui's staff, using it to scramble up a steep hillside. For the hundredth time, he wondered if he should have told his mentor what he'd discovered in the cellar. But Gui Harcourt was Orlaith's man through and through, just like Cas used to be. He wouldn't have believed a word against her, not without proof.

The evidence against Cas, on the other hand, was damning. He had fled the manor, leaving Esme's body in his bedchamber. His familiarity with herbs and plants was common knowledge. Only Lucius knew that Orlaith had given Esme the poisoned bottle of wine.

The mortifex strode a few paces ahead. His midnight-blue cloak blended with the shadows, making the copper flame of his hair appear to float along disembodied. He'd obviously fed on blood before they left Aquitan, but that was days ago. Now the effects were wearing off. Lucius's skin was as white as freshly chiseled marble, his eyes reddened coals set deep in their sockets.

And he was acting strange. Every few minutes, his head turned, peering behind them at some distant point. His steps slowed, became almost clumsy. Then, with tight lips, he turned away and stalked onward with renewed determination.

What in the ninth hell is he up to?

Cas lengthened his stride until they walked abreast. So far, they'd met nothing besides occasional groups of the newly dead trudging along single-file — all in the same direction, as though pulled along by an unseen leash. As a living man, Cas was invisible to them. Each time, the mortifex would retreat into the trees to avoid drawing their attention.

The dead posed little threat. Beyond the Veil, most of them were weak. But black dogs called Shepherds also roamed the Dominion, harrying the dead to their final destination. And they didn't tolerate intruders.

"What's back there?" Cas asked, pitching his voice low. "Is it the hounds?"

Lucius looked startled. "No, just the Cold Sea." He sounded uncertain, oddly vulnerable. "Can't you smell it? The salt wind?"

An icicle touched Cas's nape. Every soul had to cross the Cold Sea or suffer damnation. Those who refused turned into ghouls and wraiths, existing only to be summoned by a necromancer, or to escape through a gate and prey on the living. Once the last ember of humanity faded, they became liches, drifting shades of darkness so tainted they could kill with a touch.

All the dead Cas had seen were headed in the opposite direction, toward the boats waiting on the shore of the Cold Sea. But for Lucius, the iron menotte anchored his soul. It stopped him from crossing, yet the current still tugged at him. A disturbing thought — and too close to Cas's own fear of coming back as a mindless revenant.

He shook the disquiet off and drew a deep breath. "I smell cedar and pine. But everything is . . . washed out. I don't smell the sea at all."

A flicker of intense longing crossed Lucius's face, there and gone in an instant. His expression hardened; his voice grew cold and distant again. "At least it is behind us," he said, resolutely staring straight ahead, "and falling farther with every step."

"How many more days to the gate?" Cas asked, glad to change the subject.

"We will reach it by midday tomorrow," Lucius replied. "But we cannot stop yet. There is a suitable place to camp in about ten leagues."

Cas adjusted his pack. Ten more leagues? His feet were blistered, his stomach grumbling. Well, he wouldn't complain. The sooner they reached the gate, the better. He felt a constant prickle between his shoulder-blades as though they were being watched. Yet whatever it was hadn't attacked. Perhaps fear of the mortifex outweighed its hunger.

They forged on. The land rose and fell, gradually changing from dense forest to rocky dales cloaked in burnt-looking heath. Streams meandered through the landscape, all narrow enough to step across. In the distance loomed the icy spires of a mountain range, its granite slopes luminous in the half-light.

Lucius did not look back again.

The hours crawled by, and Cas's thoughts turned inward. When he'd parted with Lo at the crossroads in Nox, he had secretly wished to be free of his vows so he could stay with her. Now that wish had come true, though not in a way he would ever have chosen. But wallowing in guilt wouldn't bring Esme back. If he could find Lo in Prydwen, he would offer his aid. That is, assuming he could convince her to trust him.

What bargain had she struck with Nathan Ouvrard? Nothing to her advantage, Cas felt sure. It was the woman's own business — he doubted she'd appreciate being told how to manage her affairs — but she struck him as someone who needed a friend.

That's not all you hope for though, is it?

Cas thought of her chaste peck on the cheek, and the look in her eyes that said different. He should have pulled her into his arms and given her a proper kiss to remember him by.

He lost himself for a while daydreaming about the sweet little notch in her upper lip. The bottomless blue of her eyes and long, silky mane of raven hair. Even her lightning scars fascinated him.

A strange woman, with an even stranger cat. And I can't stop thinking about her. Worrying about her, too.

At last, they reached a stand of firs nestled in the cleft of two hills. The ground was fairly level, with a bed of spongy moss that would serve to sleep on. Lucius threw down his pack, and Cas gratefully followed suit. A short distance beyond the trees sat a lake. Tendrils of mist drifted above the surface, exposing ragged patches of black water.

"Is that another gate?" Cas asked uneasily.

All three of the Greater Gates along the Boundary appeared to be lakes — until you took a closer look and noticed that nothing reflected on the surface.

"I don't believe so," Lucius replied. "But I wouldn't wash in it. Or drink it. We don't know what lives in there."

Wonderful.

Cas retraced his steps to the last running stream and filled his water skin. By the time he returned, Lucius had heaped up dry branches and was trying to light a fire. The first night they'd camped and he struck flint to tinder, Cas had been bewildered. A mortifex could unleash an inferno with a snap of his fingers. Then Lucius had explained, rather reluctantly, that his elemental power did not work beyond the Veil.

The kindling caught at once. Within minutes, a merry blaze crackled within a ring of stones. Smoke trickled up through the dense, spreading branches. If anyone were looking, the trees should conceal the location of their campfire.

Cas chewed a hunk of pungent white cheese, staring into the flames. Usually, Lucius would disappear into the woods while he ate a hurried meal and snatched a few hours of sleep. Lucius claimed he was scouting the trail ahead. Each time Cas woke, he expected the mortifex to have abandoned him, but Lucius always returned as he was breaking camp. They'd exchange a few terse words and begin the day's journey.

This time, Lucius unbuckled his bonewood sword and set the scabbard atop his own pack, within easy reach. Then he sat on a log, hands cupping his bent knees as he watched Cas eat.

"I'm sorry about the serving girl," Lucius said.

Cas glanced at him, then back to the fire. "Why should you be sorry? I'm the one who got her killed."

"Ah." Lucius tilted his head. "So you poisoned the wine?"

The anger jerked at its leash, but Cas kept his voice calm. "She died in my place. If not for me, she'd still be alive."

Lucius regarded him. His expression was hard to read. "That is all true, yet the fact remains that Orlaith murdered her, not you. It's lucky you didn't drink any."

"Aye." Time to change the subject before Lucius guessed he was lying about that. "So which side are *you* on?"

"My own."

Of course. "Then what is it you want? I doubt you're aiding me out of the goodness of your heart."

Lucius shrugged, but his gaze was keen. "Let's say I'm interested in knowing where Delilah might have gone." A wolfish smile. "And I'm not certain you've told me the whole truth."

Cas felt glad he'd kept his iron knives. Even without magic, Lucius was as deadly as a viper.

"The truth?" Cas arched a brow. "You know more than I do — such as the fact that Delilah wasn't royalty. Yet you went along with her game. Why?"

"Because I despise Orlaith. But you know that already." The embers of his eyes flared, then dimmed. "I find it hard to believe that Delilah would give up the quest to find her parents. Are you certain she went home with these traders?"

"I saw her leave," Cas replied. "She flew off on a winged beast called an abbadax."

Which *was* the truth, just not all of it.

"An abbadax?" Lucius's brows drew together.

"That's right. Do you believe me now? The man who rode with her was named Culach Kafsnjor."

Lucius gazed into the fire, distracted. "Kafsnjor . . . I remember that name. They were the masters of Val Moraine, one of the Valkirin high holdfasts of Nocturne." He seemed to be talking more to himself now. "Culach? No. But I remember one called Magnus. He died in the War of Sundering."

"Magnus the Merciless?" Cas prompted.

Lucius frowned. "How could you possibly know that?"

"Delilah mentioned the name. She said he was holding her parents prisoner."

Lucius looked amazed. "Who told her this?"

"The Ducissas of Nyons. Chaos and Caul Courtenay."

Lucius leaned forward, eager. "What else did they say?"

"Not much," Cas replied. "Only that Delilah's parents were hunting Magnus when they disappeared. But the Courtenays don't know where he is now. Do *you* know?"

Lucius slowly shook his head, gaze fixed on the fire. "It's been a thousand years since I last saw Magnus. I assumed he crossed the Cold Sea. I did not realize his soul had lingered."

A thousand years. Cas felt a twinge of pity and crushed it immediately. Lucius made his own bargain when he took the menotte. And his immortality had cost countless lives.

Cas wrapped the last morsel of cheese in waxed paper, his

appetite gone. "Tell me one thing. Is Magnus the same fex who killed my mother?"

Lucius's head snapped up. "I . . . I don't know."

"What do you mean, you don't know? I gave you the memories of what happened that night. You *fed* on them to heal yourself!"

"Yes, but I did not see the mortifex clearly," Lucius replied.

Images tumbled through Cas's mind. The vial of Kaethe's Tears slipping between Teo's fingers. Ma's white arms reaching for her children, and the way she cast no shadow. The terrified bleats of the sheep. Then the monster who came for Lippa.

"What if I don't believe you?" Cas demanded.

Lucius looked affronted. "Why would I lie?"

"I don't know. Any number of reasons. Because I remember exactly what he looked like. It's a face I'll never forget."

"That may be so," Lucius said, "but memories are slippery, especially bad ones. In the version I saw, everything about the creature was exaggerated. White teeth and burning eyes were all I could make out. The rest was a blur."

He did not quite meet Cas's eyes as he said this, and while Lucius was clearly aiming for sympathy, the words came out as evasive. It took every shred of discipline not to leap across the fire and bury an iron blade in the mortifex's heart. Two things stopped him. One, only Lucius knew the way out of the Dominion. Second, the bastard was already dead.

"Then we can't help each other," Cas said, the words hard and definitive.

Lucius was the first to look away. They sat without speaking for a while. Cas did an inventory of his charms, more to calm himself than out of any real need. Presently, the mortifex rose to his feet. Cas tensed, but he only added wood to the fire and sat down again.

"Did your sister survive the attack?" Lucius asked in a subdued voice.

Cas let out a sigh. "Aye, though it stunted her growth."

"Well, I am glad she's alive. You saved them both, Quietus—"

"Just Castelio."

"Right." Orange light gleamed on the iron cuff around his wrist. "I have never harmed a child and I do not condone it. So . . . she is well?"

"Felippa's got more wit in her little toe than three people of regular size," Cas said. "She's only thirteen and already a scribe for Duc Marcel."

"So you're going to the palace?"

Cas nodded.

"That makes things simple," Lucius said. "The gate leads out to the eastern side of the grounds."

He'd only seen the Duc's manor from a distance, perched on a high promontory above the Bay of Istria. "I've never been before. To Prydwen, yes. My family owned their own cottage until . . ." He trailed off. *Until Da gambled it away.*

"The palace is grand," Lucius said dryly. "Some say too grand. It is an exact replica of House Marcel's old seat in Eddyn."

Cas felt intrigued. Eddyn was the land across the sea where his forebears had come from centuries before. "You saw Eddyn before its destruction?"

"Yes. It was a beautiful place, all white marble and green parks." His lips quirked. "The Marcel motto is 'We yield to none.' They rebuilt the old palace in their new capital and replicated the grounds as well. But Eddyn had a very different climate. Mild and rainy, not hot and dry. Maintaining it all is a huge extravagance, considering that fresh water is at a premium in Prydwen." He stirred the embers with a switch of green wood. "It is another reason the people hate the Duc."

"Do you think the warrant for my arrest will be waiting?" Cas asked.

Lucius shook his head. "Not even the swiftest messenger could convey it in four days. And Orlaith has already set a hunter on your trail." His smile was chilling. "Me. But I'm afraid the scent has gone cold."

Cas held his gaze. "Thank you."

"Get some rest. I'll keep watch."

Lucius began feeding more dry branches to the fire. Cas rolled up in a blanket and whispered his customary prayer to Kaethe. He drifted off to the crackle and hiss of burning logs. It seemed like only a few minutes had passed when a cold hand shook his shoulder. Lucius crouched over him, expression taut. Cas sat up, instantly awake.

"What's—"

The words were cut off by a chorus of eerie, high-pitched howls.

TWELVE

Cas's pulse spiked as the howl came again. Its echoes had barely faded before it was answered by more blood-curdling cries and excited yips from across the valley.

"Shepherds," Lucius said. "Two packs at least."

He scattered the embers of the fire with a sweep of his boot. Cas quickly tied the blanket roll to his pack and heaved it over one shoulder. He grabbed Gui's staff, the hickory solid against his palm. If Lucius's magic didn't work here, the staff's power wouldn't either, but at least he could use it as a weapon in close quarters.

"They're three or four leagues behind, no more," Cas said as they fled the campsite. "How far to the gate?"

Lucius strode ahead, his face stony. "I cannot say for certain."

Cas glanced at the dark hills rising behind. The pack was still too far to see, but his imagination conjured them with ease. Black dogs the size of pack ponies, red tongues lolling between razored teeth. He could almost hear the rasping breath as they leapt through the forest in long bounds.

"I thought you knew where we're headed," he said.

"Gates distort the area around them," Lucius replied. "It is not always as one remembers. Landmarks can shift. Distances might shorten — or grow longer."

"You're telling me this *now*?"

"Let us hope it is the first and not the second," Lucius snapped as the harrowing cries came again.

They circled the western edge of the lake and struck out for the foothills of the mountains. Cas matched the mortifex's ground-eating strides, using Gui's staff to steady his footing on the uneven terrain. "What happens if the Shepherds catch us?"

Would they be taken to Kaethe? Dragged to the shore of the Cold Sea? Or—

"You, they would kill," Lucius said matter-of-factly, "but your death would be clean. A quick rending of the throat."

Cas scrambled up a steep incline. "What about you?"

"The hounds despise mortifexes even more than they do necromancers. They will tear me apart and fight over the scraps."

As if in agreement, the strident howls came again, echoing across the valley. One pack bayed off to the right and the second answered behind, their cries rising and falling in pitch. It reminded Cas of the wolves in the Boundary. As a boy, he would listen to them speaking to each other across the misty peaks. Wolves were smart. They worked together to bring down prey. Snug in his sleigh bed, with the quilt tucked around his ears, Cas had pitied the deer they stalked. Now he *was* the deer.

"Kaethe has abandoned us," he said, spirits sinking. "We must have angered her."

Lucius shot him a look. "All the more reason to leave her domain. Now, move!"

They hurried onward to the lower flanks of the mountains. Cas pushed himself but kept a measured pace, wary of tiring too soon. Branches lashed his face and snagged his coat. The hounds seemed tireless. No matter how fast they went, the sounds of pursuit grew ever closer. At last, Lucius stopped and threw his pack down on a wooded slope.

Cas bent over, trying to catch his breath. "How much farther?"

"A league or so." Even Lucius looked exhausted, his lips bloodless.

Cas spared a moment to gulp some water and discard his pack. He kept only a purse stuffed with silver. Five years' worth of wages. The rest he abandoned, even Lip's letters. With luck, he'd see her himself. If the hounds caught him, none of it mattered anyway.

Free of his burden, he broke into a sprint. They staggered up a rise and paused, shoulder to shoulder. Ragged breaths tore from Cas's throat as he looked back across the last valley. Nine dark silhouettes stood along the opposite ridge. The largest tipped its snout to the grey sky and bayed. The hair rose on his neck as the pack descended, a mass of fur and teeth flowing down the hillside. They were perhaps fifteen minutes behind.

"We're not going to make it," Cas said. "What about a tree? Can the Shepherds climb?"

"No, but once they have us trapped, more will come. They will wait until thirst or hunger drive you down. Or you grow so weak that you fall into their waiting jaws." The flames in his pupils danced with bleak mirth. "How fast can you run?"

They plunged down the steep slope. Loose earth crumbled beneath Cas's boots and he grabbed at tree roots to keep from sliding to the bottom. Once he did start to fall, but Lucius's hand shot out and steadied him. They half-slid through deep drifts of leaves, traversed another ridge, and descended into a mist-wreathed hollow. Cas heard the rush of water ahead.

Lucius gave a wild laugh and pointed through the trees. "It is the River Acheron. The gate lies on the far bank. We are nearly there!"

"Can you cross it?" Cas leaned on the staff, utterly spent. Wee trickling streams were one thing, but the High Dead could not abide larger bodies of running water.

"There is a stone bridge." Lucius's eyes sparked with fresh determination. "We can beat them yet!"

His faith gave Cas hope. They flew down the final stretch and stumbled out of the trees onto a muddy bank. The river was about as wide as the Forkings and swift-flowing. Angular boulders formed islands in the current, creating eddies and whirlpools. Across the foaming water, Cas spotted the gate. A doorway of dull pewter, its edges lit by a greenish glow. Beside him, Lucius slowed and muttered a heartfelt curse.

The gate was there but not the bridge. Traces of the old supports still stood on both shores, but the span itself was gone, crumbled into the depths. Cas realized that the square "boulders" must once have been stone blocks forming the arch.

Brush crackled as the hounds burst from the treeline a hundred paces away. The largest, a massive beast the size of a bull, growled deep in its throat. It sniffed the ground, then raised its head, hackles lifting. Cas saw his own death reflected in the creature's yellow gaze.

The pack coursed forward, black coats almost invisible in the twilight, like scudding moon shadows. He readied the staff, but Lucius shook his head.

"It is me they want the most. Ford the river. I will find you in Prydwen."

"But—"

"Just go! I will hold them." Lucius drew his bone-blade and turned to face the hounds.

Cas waded into the swift water up to his knees. On the far bank, the gate beckoned, the air around it shimmering like a heat mirage. He glanced back. The dogs were fifty paces away, paws tearing up clods of mud as they coursed across the flats.

Let Lucius make a stand. He's an expert swordsman. And if he falls...well, it would be a mercy if they forced him to cross the Cold Sea.

But the iron menotte bound his soul for eternity. He would be trapped here as they tore his body to pieces. And Lucius could still feel pain. Could still suffer. Cas had seen him after the Courtenays caught him, his face and hands raw with burns.

Nine hells, I'm a fool. Cas ran back and grasped Lucius's arm. "We cross together," he said. "I'll carry you if I must."

Lucius stared at the rushing river like a man contemplating a leap off a cliff, then staggered down the bank. He splashed into the shallows just as the lead hound sprang. Cas swung the staff. The butt connected with a muscled flank. The dog hit the water, lost its balance, and was carried downstream. Cas turned back to find Lucius on his knees, retching.

The other Shepherds spread out along the riverbank. Four crept forward, snapping and growling. A distraction, Cas knew. Like wolves, they were intelligent, drawing his attention while the rest flanked their prey.

"Get up!" he screamed, sweeping the staff in a wide arc, driving them back.

Lucius nodded, retched again, and gained his feet. Cas slung an arm around his waist. They waded into the surging whitewater. Within a few steps, it rose to their waists. Lucius sagged against him like a frail old man. Cas used the staff to probe the depths ahead — and to beat back their pursuers when snapping jaws came within arm's length.

Slippery stones lined the riverbed. With each precarious step, Cas expected to lose his footing. Lucius clung to him, shivering. His eyes were half-closed, their flames extinguished. Of course, the feckin' dogs proved to be able swimmers. Again and again, the hounds closed the gap. Cas lashed out, teeth bared, driving them back with Gui's staff.

The water was chest-deep when they reached the tumble-down bridge midstream. The stone blocks divided the current and made passage easier. Then Lucius's boot caught on some hidden snag — or his knees gave out. His weight dragged them both under.

Cas sank down, scraping along the murky bottom. The current dragged Lucius away. It nearly took the staff too, but some stubborn part of him refused to let go, even as he flipped upside-down. Then pain exploded in his shoulder. He was pinned against an underwater obstacle, probably a chunk of the bridge. Darkness began gnawing at the edges of his vision. Cas thrust out with the staff. With a hard shove, he pried himself free and broke the surface with a gasp.

The bull-hound was waiting. Cas swung the staff, but he had no leverage in the deep water. The blow glanced off its raised hackles. He struck again. The beast didn't even yelp. It was like beating an old stump. Lips peeled back from curving fangs. Then, a white flash as Lucius's sword swept past. Blood spilled and the hound vanished in the water.

Cas snatched at Lucius's doublet before they both sank down again. He braced his boots against the bottom and gave a mighty kick, propelling them into the shallows. The current had carried them downstream from the pack — and from the gate. Cas staggered up the bank, hauling Lucius's dead weight.

After slaying the bull-hound, his companion had promptly fainted.

Four of the Shepherds bounded from the water. They shook their coats, powerful muscles rippling, then broke into a lope. With a grunt, Cas hoisted Lucius over one shoulder. He started limping for the gate. Furious barks erupted. Cas could almost feel their hot carrion breath on his heels.

Ten paces to the portal. Five.

The air around the gate was distorted, as though it sat behind a sheet of thick, bubbled glass. Cas sensed something lunge. A shadow fell across them, like a swooping hawk. He pitched forward and they tumbled into a swirl of silvery light.

THIRTEEN

C as staggered through the gate, one hand steadying Lucius, the other white-knuckling Gui's staff. From one step to the next, hot sun seared his eyes. He squinted up at an azure sky and puffy yellow clouds. He was savoring the moment of triumph — they'd beaten Kaethe's hounds! — when the ground crumbled away beneath his boots.

Cas caught a flash of foaming waves far below. He threw his weight backwards, the soles of his feet tingling. Loose pebbles bounced as they landed in a graceless heap just shy of the cliff's edge. He lay there for a moment, knees wobbling. A salt breeze lifted the hair from his brow.

"Lucius," he croaked. "Do you hear me? We made it."

Ahead, the Bay of Istria stretched out like a sheet of beaten silver. In the middle was the island monastery of the Sons of Bel, tethered to the mainland by a slender stone causeway. Cas had seen Bel Mara many times before but never from this eagle's vantage point.

An ancient-looking cistern sat a few paces off, dead leaves

drifting across the surface. They must have come out of it; gates were always submerged in still water. Cas crawled over to splash some on his face. Despite the scorching heat, emerald lawns stretched out beyond a windbreak of trees. In the distance stood a palace with bright gold pennants whipping from the turrets.

"Lucius," he hissed, giving his companion a hard shake. "Wake up!"

The sun was raising welts on Lucius's hands and throat, yet it failed to rouse him. He might have been carved from a block of Galatian marble. Cas looked around for shelter. A small wood lay not far off. He hoisted Lucius under the arms and started dragging him across the rocky ground.

We'll find some shade. If he still won't wake . . . I'll think of something. He's fed on me before. What's one more time?

Sweat stung his eyes as he struggled with Lucius's dead-weight. For a revenant, the man was solid as a boulder. Somewhere nearby, Cas could hear the pounding of hammers and rasp of saws. He picked up the pace. *We'd better hide before—*

"Hoi!"

His head jerked up. Two soldiers in chainmail hurried towards him. Cas recognized the colors of House Marcel.

"Where'd you come from?" one demanded. He had a doughy, scarred, lopsided face that looked like it had been smashed up and poorly sewn back together more than once.

Cas raised his palms. "Well, now—"

"On your knees!"

He sank down, holding his palms up. The other soldier, a giant with no visible neck and deep-set, wintry blue eyes, walked forward and nudged Lucius with a scuffed black boot.

"Looks like a lordling from the mountain holds."

The men exchanged a speculative glance.

"And what might this young ruffian be doing out here, with him looking more corpse than noble?"

"You've got it wrong," Cas said quickly. "My master went for a walk and took ill. I was just seeking aid—"

"Aid, is it?" Dough Face's voice dripped skepticism. "Or did you fancy the cut of his cloak?"

No-Neck bent down and touched Lucius's wrist. "Body's already cold. We'll carry him back to the captain." He gave Cas a vicious smile. "Ready to meet Bel, boy? You'll burn for this."

"Wait!" Cas said, as Dough Face prodded him with a pike. "At least take an iron coin for my master so he doesn't come back."

No-Neck gave a rumbling laugh. "*You* have cold iron?"

"Aye." Cas slowly unhooked a pouch from his braces and tossed it over. "My master had a terror of rising again. He ordered me to carry this should any harm befall him. Please, let me do him a final service and put a coin on his tongue."

No-Neck opened the pouch. "There's enough iron here to drink and whore for a month!" he said with a grin.

"Iron?" Dough Face replied, scratching his head with an exaggerated look of puzzlement. "We never saw any iron, did we?" He gazed over the edge of the cliff. "The servant who murdered his lordling vanished without a trace. Perhaps he regretted the crime and jumped to his death, eh?"

Cas had met men like this before and knew it wasn't idle talk. They had no consciences to trouble.

He silently urged Lucius to wake. The mortifex lay with his head turned to the side and the iron cuff concealed beneath the edge of his cloak. With his refined features and expensive clothes, Lucius did look like a nobleman — and a very dead one. Cas cast a furtive glance at Gui's staff, which lay unnoticed next to the cistern.

"You see that?" Dough Face demanded.

Cas tensed, thinking they'd followed his gaze, but the two soldiers were staring at Lucius.

"See what?" No-Neck replied.

"His finger twitched."

No-Neck frowned. "Sure you're not imagining things?"

Dough Face looked a bit nervous. "Don't know. It was quick-like."

No-Neck regarded Lucius for a long moment. "I'm in no mood to deal with risen. We'll keep the purse but spare a coin for the corpse."

Dough Face nodded. "Toss it over, then." He plucked the coin from the air and hefted it in his palm. Then gave the coin a happy sniff. "Ah, it's pure, all right. I hate to waste it on the lordling but better to be safe."

He reached down, pried open Lucius's bloodless lips, and placed it on his tongue. "What in Bel's name...?" the soldier muttered as a curl of smoke wafted from Lucius's half-open mouth.

Two things happened next. First, Lucius's eyes flew open. Then a hand shot out and grabbed Dough Face by the throat.

No-Neck reacted faster than Cas expected. He lunged with the iron pike and drove it through Lucius's shoulder, pinning him to the ground. Lucius screamed and hurled Dough Face backwards like a rag doll. The soldiers crashed together as Cas dove for the cistern. He picked up Gui's staff and spun around just in time to parry a brutal downward blow from the pike.

Garbled noises were coming from Dough Face, but Cas didn't take his eyes off No-Neck, who stared at him with fear and loathing. The pike jabbed again, this time aiming for his legs. Cas pivoted away, hoping to drive the butt of his staff into No-Neck's throat. But again the soldier was too quick. A mailed hand jerked the staff away, then cracked him so hard he saw stars.

The world tilted. A boot drew back and Cas grabbed it with both hands, twisting. No-Neck crashed to the ground. Cas tasted blood as he leapt on the soldier, an iron knife in his hand he couldn't remember drawing. The blade slid into the juncture of his chainmail above the collarbone. A wet wheeze came out but nothing else.

Cas rolled away, head still buzzing. Lucius cradled Dough Face in his arms like a mother nursing a babe, except that his mouth was locked to the man's jugular and Cas heard sucking sounds. Dough Face's legs jerked weakly. One boot had come off and there was a hole in his stocking. Cas wondered if he had no one to darn it. The skin of his foot was pale compared to his face, which was tanned from the sun.

"We have to get rid of them."

He looked up, startled. Lucius offered Cas his knife, hilt-first. He must have cleaned it on the grass for there was no blood on the blade, although there was a great deal on his hands and face. Dough Face had stopped kicking. No-Neck was staring straight up at the sun with a look of surprise.

"What?" Cas managed.

Lucius jerked his chin at the cliff. "Before we're discovered. I imagine there are other patrols."

Cas pulled himself together and nodded. Together, they dragged the dead men to the edge and heaved them into the surf. Then Lucius crouched down at the cistern to wash up. Cas realized his own arms were speckled red and scrubbed until they were raw and stinging. It was the first time he'd ever used a knife on the living, but the only shame he felt was for not feeling something more about it. When the blood was gone, he retrieved the staff. For a moment, he hated Gui for giving it to him. The old Quietus was a gullible fool.

"Are you healed?" he asked.

Lucius pulled aside his cloak. There was a hole in his

doublet where the pike had gone through, but the skin beneath was unblemished. The burns on his hands and face had faded, too. Lucius looked as close to life as he ever got.

"I thought the river killed you," Cas quipped.

The ghost of a smile tugged at Lucius's thin lips. "We part ways here," he said. "Tell your family to leave. When the Duc is toppled, Father Chaos will reign."

Cas turned to the palace with its snapping pennants, each emblazoned with the Marcel cockatrice. "That's why Orlaith sent you, isn't it? To get rid of him?"

"Yes. And it is an order I'll enjoy carrying out." Lucius regarded him solemnly. "Thank you for your aid, Quietus — ah, Castelio. I will not forget it."

"And I won't forget yours. So let's call it even."

Lucius held out a hand. After a moment, Cas clasped it.

"I have an appointment in the city, but I will return to the palace later," Lucius said. "Find me if I can be of service."

Cas watched him melt into the shadows of the trees. Then he hurried for the palace, eager to see his family. Teo, Lippa — even poor old Da — they were the only ones he trusted now. They probably had no idea that the Duc's grip on power was so fragile. And living in the palace put them in the middle of everything.

He soon discovered that the hammering and sawing came from a long section of partly finished wall. Clearly, the Duc had decided that the sheer cliffs on every side were inadequate to keep out attackers, which spoke volumes about the political situation in the city. Cas kept his head down, walking briskly, and none of the masons on the scaffolding paid him much attention. Presently, the trees thinned and the full palace came into view. A hundred windows sparkled in the sun, turrets of ivory stone soaring high into the sky. As Lucius said, it was surrounded by lush gardens dotted with fountains spewing crystal-clear water.

Cas followed the smell of cooking around to the kitchens. Two girls emerged carrying baskets. Bright woven shawls were draped across their hair and shoulders.

"Good day," he said with a polite nod. "Do you know Felippa? She works in the scriptorium."

The taller one nodded with a smirk. "You mean the dwarf."

"She's not a dwarf. Just small."

The girl looked him up and down and didn't seem impressed. She pointed at some low wooden buildings a short distance away. "Her brother works in the stables. Go ask *him*."

The pair turned their backs and sauntered off, giggling. The girls in Swanton used to laugh at Lip, too, even though she was smarter than all of them put together. Cas started for the stables, doubly eager to be gone. He'd been here for less than an hour and already he despised the place. The fantasy of somehow finding Lo was rapidly fading. Family first. Teo and Lip *had* to listen to him. Prydwen wasn't safe—

Cas paused, instinctively drawing back as a large black coach drew up in front of the palace's main entrance. It was escorted by two dozen mounted guards and drawn by four magnificent white horses with feather plumes. Liveried footmen rushed up to open the doors. A tall blond man emerged first. He wore a silver cloak with ermine trim and offered his hand to a woman with strong, attractive features. The way the footmen fawned over them both, Cas assumed he was Duc Marcel, and she was either his wife or some high-ranking noble.

Cas was about to turn away when a second man stepped gracefully from the carriage. He had dark hair cut to the nape, a high, stiff collar, and gloves covering his hands. The only exposed skin was on his face, and this was white as chalk. The man was finely dressed in silks and velvets, but Cas hardly noticed. The palace melted away and he felt the rough planks of the Forkings ferry beneath his feet, blood soaking his bandaged hand, while the mortifex that killed Ma and tried to kill Gui stood on the bank, watching.

Cas wondered if the backhand from No-Neck had addled his wits. How could it be? Then a breeze caught the man's cloak just so, making it billow out above soft knee-high boots, and Cas saw the burning coals of his eyes and knew it was real. The thing of his nightmares was *here*. Duc Marcel said something and the monster laughed. Its voice raised the hair on his arms.

Gui's hickory staff warmed beneath his palm. The staff had faced this mortifex before. It, too, remembered.

His vision tunneled down to that white face. Eight years he had hoped to meet the creature again. It seemed like fate that Gui gave him the staff. Even Kaethe's hounds had forced them to make haste so he would be standing in this spot, at this moment.

Whether it was a chance encounter or the Lady's hand at work, Cas wouldn't waste it. He whispered a prayer and started for the coach.

FOURTEEN

C as was halfway to the group lingering on the palace's marble steps when he heard running footfalls behind him. He was turning to deliver a vicious right hook when he saw who it was.

"Stop," Teo hissed, grabbing his arm.

Cas tried to wrench free, but his brother's grip was annoyingly firm. Teo had grown in the last two years; they were almost eye to eye now.

"Let go," Cas snarled.

"He'll kill you. Don't be an idiot!"

The guards flanking the carriage were staring at them both. The mortifex's head cocked. He turned to see what had drawn the guards' attention. Cas clenched his jaw so hard it made his head pound, but he let Teo pull him inside the dim, hay-strewn stable. They watched from the doorway as the trio entered the palace, flanked by the Duc's soldiers.

The instant the doors closed, Cas took his brother by the shoulders. "My heart is glad to see you," he said with exasperation, "but I'd like to know why Lip failed to mention in her letters that the mortifex who attacked her is *here*?"

Teo flinched. "He only came a week ago."

"Has he seen any of you? *Does he remember?*"

"I curried his horse once. He looked right at me. I'd have known if he—"

"What about Lip? She's the one he'd know best."

Teo stared down at his sandals. "Lip's avoided him so far."

"Feckin' hells!" Cas threw his hands up. "Why don't you tell the Duc?"

His brother snorted. "Marcel wouldn't care, he burns people for fun. Not just lowborn. Nobles! What do you think he'd do to *me*? The fex serves him."

Cas wondered if Lucius had known about this all along. "Is it bound to the Duc with a menotte?"

Teo shook his head. "Don't think so. I mean, I haven't seen one. But it's not like I'm around either of them much."

"Why haven't you fled?"

"And go where, Cas?" Teo asked with maddening calm.

"Anywhere that isn't here!"

"You don't understand," Teo whispered. "There's too much at stake."

"Like your lives? Because if we stay, I can promise you—"

One of the horses whinnied and bumped the stall door. Teo grabbed a bucket of oats and gave it a handful, followed by a fond pat on the muzzle.

"Keep your voice down," he hissed when he came back. "The Duc's got ears everywhere."

The only other person in the stables was a boy about his brother's age, who sat on a bale of hay mending tack at the far end of the stalls. He gave them a curious glance and returned to his work.

"Lip's almost done with her shift." Teo shook a flop of

sandy hair from his eyes. "She can explain better than me."

Cas wondered when Lip had become the family's leader, though he wasn't entirely surprised. She was thirteen, younger than Teo by three years, but she had a firm head on her shoulders. Now that he was here, surely she'd listen to reason.

Teo brought him around to a side door of the palace and through a warren of narrow, dingy halls to a windowless chamber just big enough to accommodate straw pallets, a rickety three-legged table, and stools. It was a far cry from the bright two-story cottage Cas had bought for them years before — and that Da had lost to his gambling debts.

"Just wait here," Teo instructed, hurrying off.

Cas propped the staff in a corner and sank down on a stool. In her letters, Lippa had made their lives sound wonderful. She obviously didn't want him to worry. But this Duc Marcel sounded like a bastard of the highest order. Even the servants' quarters at Orlaith's manor were not half so cramped and miserable.

What was the mortifex doing in Prydwen? The High Dead hated sunlight, and it never set here. Marcel might have convinced himself that the creature was serving him, but Cas bet it was the other way around.

Footsteps in the hall tugged him to his feet.

"Cas!" Lip flung herself at him, long braid flying like the tail of a kite.

He sank to one knee and swept her into his arms. Her flaxen hair smelled like woodsmoke and beeswax. She hugged him with a fierce strength that belied her slight build. After a minute, she pulled back and searched his face.

"You look older," she said, freckled nose wrinkling.

"And every year you look more like Ma," he said.

She seemed pleased by this. Unlike Teo, who had shot up like a radish, Lip's size was about the same, but her face had lost its youthful plumpness and her blue eyes held a knowing depth. She wore a plain, dark dress with long sleeves and an apron with pockets of various sizes. It suited her.

"Where's Da?" Cas asked.

"At table," Teo replied, taking the other stool. His legs were so long and skinny, they hardly fit under the table. "He's the Duc's taster."

"Taster? For poison, you mean?" Cas asked in dismay.

"Aye. Da started as a serving man but . . ."

Cas could imagine the rest. "His drinking landed him in the shite."

Lip gave a resigned nod. "At first he was made taster as a punishment for pilfering ale. But the Duc found him amusing and decided to keep him." She scowled. "Sometimes Marcel throws scraps on the floor and makes him crawl after them like a dog."

Cas sighed. "How long ago did this happen?"

"Oh . . ." She picked at a splinter on the table. Her nails were bitten to the quick, the fingertips stained with ink. "A while, I suppose . . . How did you get here, Cas? You've been so busy. Did you finally get some time off?"

He knew she was changing the subject so he wouldn't get mad that she'd kept Da's humiliating — and perilous — situation from him. But he felt more exhausted than angry. It seemed a lifetime ago that Lucius had shaken him awake at the campsite.

"I'm not a Quietus anymore. I doubt I ever will be again." Cas gathered his thoughts and gave them a quick version of his falling out with Orlaith.

"That witch!" Lippa breathed. "Oh, Cas, I'm so sorry."

"So you're wanted for *murder*?" Teo whispered. He sounded both horrified and impressed.

"Aye." Cas reached into his coat and took out the purse of

silver. "But I saved up my wages. It's more than enough to get us out of Prydwen." He scanned the pitiful chamber. "Pack whatever you can't live without. We'll slip away as soon as Da shows up."

His brother and sister shared a look. Lippa cracked the door open and peered up and down the hall. Satisfied that no one was eavesdropping, she rejoined them at the table. "We can't, Cas."

"Why not?"

Lip's stare was unsettling. There was a distance in her gaze, a cool, businesslike measuring, he had never seen before. "If you still worked for Orlaith, I wouldn't tell you. But I suppose you can be trusted."

"Suppose?" Cas frowned. "Of course you can trust me. What's going on?"

"The nobles are rotten," she said, leaning forward. "All of them!"

"Aye," he agreed. "Which is why we need to go someplace far away."

Teo crossed his tanned arms. "We're not running."

"Not until the Duc's deposed." Lip's jaw set in that stubborn way she had.

Cas thought of Lucius's warning. *Father Chaos will rule.*

"Are you mad? By then it'll be too late." He studied them, the truth dawning. "So you're part of this . . . resistance?"

The revolutionary fervor in his little sister's eyes was answer enough.

"When the bear fights the wolf, it's the hare who loses," Cas told them.

"The Red Rogue isn't a *rabbit*," Teo protested. "He's a hero—"

They all jumped as the door banged open, but it was only Da. He'd aged a decade in the two years since Cas last saw him.

His skin was gray, his eyes dull. It took a long minute for him to register the fact that his eldest son was there.

"That you, lad?" his father asked, shuffling forward. He wore a long, shapeless tunic that hung like a sack on his skinny frame.

"It's me."

They embraced. Da reeked of stale wine and old sweat. A two-day beard roughened his jaw and he seemed to be missing more teeth than Cas remembered.

"Teo, go fetch supper, would you?" Da said, sinking down on one of the pallets. "How've you been, son?"

He didn't have the heart to tell the story again. "Fine, Da. I saved some coin. I was hoping we could start over somewhere new." Lippa shot him an annoyed look that Cas ignored. "Live together like the old days."

His father gave a forced smile. "Sounds nice. But what about your oaths?"

"I've been released from those," Cas said shortly. "Needed a change."

Da might be hung-over, but he wasn't a complete idiot. His gaze narrowed. "What happened, lad?"

Lippa arched a brow. "Yes, Cas, what happened?"

"Nothing," he muttered. "I missed you all so I'm here. Did you know about the fex?"

His father blinked. "Of course, but there's nothing we can do about it."

"What if I could?"

"No," Da said decisively. "We won't lose you, too." Sudden confusion clouded his eyes. "Is that why you came, son?"

"I . . ." Cas was spared another lie by the return of Teo, who carried four bowls of lumpy pottage.

"Sorry, best I could do," he said apologetically. "They cut rations a fortnight ago. The Duc's so far in debt to the priests, he hardly has two copper pyres to rub together. He'll probably raise taxes again."

"Of course, he blames the people," Lip put in heatedly, "when everyone knows he's the one—"

Cas raised a hand. He wasn't in the mood for politics. "Don't care, I'll eat anything."

He wolfed down the pottage with some watered ale. It reminded him of the worm-riddled fare in the margrave's jail. By the time he finished eating, Da had already passed out on one of the pallets and started to snore.

"Is that really Gui's staff?" Teo was staring at it with awe.

"Aye."

"Can I touch it?"

"Go on." Cas threw himself down on a musty pallet. "Just don't crack yourself in the head."

Teo grinned and took the staff, awkwardly spinning it with two hands.

"Stop," Lip protested. "I want to see the runes!"

"What for? You can't read 'em."

Her jaw came out. "Maybe I can, if I study them."

Teo laughed. "Doubtful."

Cas listened to them argue with half an ear. He was thinking about the mortifex. Even with Gui's staff, he had to admit the odds were poor. He was quick with his knives, but he'd never trained with a staff. No-Neck had taken it from him like stealing sweets from a child. Teo was right. If he'd gone after the fex, he would have gotten himself killed.

The High Dead didn't eat. Never slept. Chopping the thing's head off would only slow it down. If he knew its true name, he could banish it. But might as well wish for a mountain of treasure and a magic spear like Caddoc Godslayer.

Unless... Cas smiled in the darkness. Unless he fought fire with fire.

FIFTEEN

The boatman steered the gondola deeper into the Shambles, its prow slicing through the murky canal. Lucius leaned back in the shade of the canvas sunscreen. He could still taste blood on his tongue. Every sense was painfully heightened. The splash of oars and slap of waves against wooden pilings. Chattering voices and laundry flapping from railings. The pungent stink of fresh tar and woodsmoke.

He'd been given the meeting's location by one of Orlaith's contacts, a lawyer sympathetic to the rebels. The gondola was followed from the moment he left the woman's office. First by two boys in a canoe, then by two others leading a goat along the canal's footpath, and finally by a pair of young women toting wicker baskets of mackerel, which he could smell from forty paces.

All six did a fair job of ignoring him, but Lucius was too old and wily to overlook his shadows. He had expected to be watched. If anything, it meant the insurgents weren't sloppy.

"Over there," Lucius told the oarsman.

The man nodded and steered toward a stone landing.

"Shall I wait, my lord?"

The gondolier was clearly wondering what sort of business a finely dressed noble could have in the Shambles.

"That won't be necessary," Lucius replied, dropping two silver ferries into his palm.

The oarsmen gave a relieved nod and shoved off, steering back the way he'd come from. A group of young men lingered nearby, watching from the corners of their eyes. Each wore a red rag tied around their right bicep. Some gutted fish, while others scraped barnacles from an overturned canoe.

Lucius climbed the stone stairs and approached a barge moored along one of the piers that jutted into the marsh. Six burly men with bandanas covering their faces waited on deck. They led him down a cramped ladder to the hold. The space was empty of cargo except for a few crates. It stank of rotting wood and the sharp bite of mortal sweat.

More masked men stood along the walls, knives at their waists, along with a few women. The air was stiflingly hot. Only a few beams of dusty sunlight broke through the boarded-over portholes, but Lucius could see like a cat in the dark. Before going any further, he scanned the wooden floor for traps. There was no nine-pointed star drawn in blood. No iron except for the rebels' knives.

The Red Rogue waited in the center of the hold. He raised a hand in welcome. It was strong and tanned from the sun, the hand of a young man. "Thank you for coming," he said.

A scarf concealed the lower half of his face, winding loosely around his neck and forming a hood that shaded forehead and eyes. Like the others, he wore a coarse russet tunic over baggy trousers. There was nothing to identify him beyond his voice, which was self-assured and commanding. The voice of a practiced orator.

Lucius stopped a few paces away. "Thank you for

extending an invitation through our mutual friend. I'm sure you're a busy man, so I'll get straight to business. My mistress is willing to provide material support for your cause, but may I ask a few questions first?"

The Rogue nodded. "I expected you would."

"She backs a change of ruler in Cavet, but she wishes to know if you plan to seize power yourself."

"I have no interest in ruling anyone," the Rogue replied. "Only for my people to be treated fairly." Shrewd eyes studied him from the shadows of the hood. "I see you doubt me. What you fail to understand is that we have been slaves in all but name for generations. Every man and woman here is willing to die for freedom. If not their own, then their children's, or their children's children. That is why we will win. Because there is nothing more they can do to us. The only thing we fear is to continue living under the boot heel of Vazsoly Marcel."

He spoke with quiet conviction. The others nodded.

"My parents died in Blackwater Jail," the Rogue continued. "They went on a hunger strike. The Duc let them starve. Not the current one — the last one. Andrzej Marcel. He only agreed to lower the crushing taxes after we burned half his fleet in the harbor."

The hold was quiet save for the distant screams of gulls. Lucius felt them all watching him. There were things he might have said. *I know what it is to be a slave. I, too, would die for my freedom, but even that choice has been taken from me.* Instead, he said nothing. The Rogue seemed to take his silence for skepticism.

"Let us go back even further. Do you know how many rebellions have been brutally put down over the last eight hundred years? How many good, brave people have died at Blackwater from torture and pestilence? Do you know about the laws that were passed *taxing our dead?*"

Lucius shook his head.

"If we don't pay the soldiers in iron coin — coin few of us have — the bodies are denied proper burial. Instead, our brothers and sisters, our mothers and fathers, are taken to communal pits to be burned." Fury simmered in his voice. "The practice condemns them to eternal damnation."

Lucius knew this wasn't true, but he would never convince these people otherwise. Some Cavettis believed that since fire was the domain of Bel, his estranged wife — Kaethe — rejected any soul whose body had been touched by flames. The Duc had to know that. It was an especially cruel decision.

"So when you ask me if I want to seize power," the Rogue finished, "I think of the fine lords and ladies who have drained the lifeblood of this land, and I want no part of it."

The others muttered agreement.

"Here is what we do want. We want an end to the Marcels' tyranny. We want basic rights for all, not just those with land and power. We want *justice*."

It was standard soapbox fare, yet the passionate speech stirred something long dormant. Lucius crushed it immediately. Their fight had nothing to do with him. Even he had never been so stupidly idealistic. Tyrants could be killed, yes, but another always rose. In fact, the next one would undoubtedly be the man standing in front of him. And whoever won this conflict, they would take bloody revenge on the other side and call it justice, starting the cycle anew.

"Who's next in the line of succession?" Lucius asked, though he knew the answer.

"The Duc has two younger sisters," the Rogue said. "He exiled them to the convent of Kaethe up in the hills. The eldest, Dravka Marcel, is his heir."

"Why do you think she'll be better than her brother?"

"She can't be any worse."

A few people laughed. Most didn't.

"But we will insist on assurances. We want a new charter of rights. Dravka Marcel will sign it before the arch-priest of Bel or we will stop her from taking power."

"Fair enough," Lucius said, still doubting every word. "I heard rumors that Vazsoly murdered his father. Are they true?"

The Rogue sat down on a crate. "I'll give you the facts and you can decide for yourself. It was late one evening, just past eleven bells, when a cry came from inside the Duc's bedchamber. He always bolted the door from the inside when he slept. By the time the guards broke it open, he was dead. The room was empty, the windows securely fastened.

"No weapon was found, but his hair had turned white as flour, and my source at the palace said the Duc wore an expression of purest horror. He was not yet sixty, but he looked three decades older."

"And Vazsoly? I heard he was on a ship at the time."

"That is true," the Rogue admitted. "When he arrived a few hours later and viewed the body, he blamed poison. The cook and the Duc's personal manservant were both executed at Blackwater."

Lucius nodded slowly. "It could have been a spell. Do you have any evidence that Vazsoly knows necromancy?"

"None. But I promise you, the servants were innocent. It was well-known that Vazsoly had quarreled with his father. He opposed the easing of taxes that the old Duc had agreed to and made remarks at court indicating he thought his father was weak. Not surprisingly, Andrzej took exception to his son's willfulness. As punishment, he sent him on a five-year campaign in the Western Isles.

"The excuse was that the people worshipped pagan idols and needed to be brought into the fold of Bel, but everyone knew it was to get rid of his wayward son." Contempt entered the Rogue's voice. "Vazsoly took out his frustration on the villagers. Then he came back, and his father died hours before he made port. No one believes it is a coincidence."

"But without proof," Lucius finished, "nothing could be done. Well, I am satisfied that our interests coincide. My mistress has sent the first shipment of weapons. Delivery will be overseen by our mutual contact." That was the lawyer. "The shipment should arrive in another fortnight or so."

"I thank her for that. But there is a service you could perform in the meantime." A pause. "I believe you're uniquely suited for it."

This man does not speak like a fisherman, Lucius thought. *He might have been born in the Shambles, but someone gave him an education. A good one.*

"Go on," he said.

"There is one of your kind staying at the palace. A mortifex named Janus. I fear the Duc will use him against us."

Lucius frowned. "I don't understand. The Marcels never owned a menotte."

"Janus is unbound. He offered his service freely and the Duc accepted. But it makes Vazsoly that much harder to get to. If you wish to aid our cause, you could start by eliminating him."

Curiosity sparked. An unbound mortifex? Here, in Prydwen? "When did he arrive?" Lucius asked.

"A few weeks ago."

Janus. The name meant nothing, but it wouldn't be his true name. No mortifex would reveal that.

"I have not yet gone to the palace," Lucius said, "but I plan to once our meeting concludes. I'm sure I can find a way to deal with him."

"How would you do it?" There was frank curiosity in the Red Rogue's voice.

Lucius shrugged. "Cut him into pieces and throw them in the bay for the sharks."

The Rogue laughed. "You do not believe in half measures. Nor do I." They eyed each other appraisingly. "I think we will make successful allies—"

A series of whistles came from the deck, one long, two short. The mood instantly shifted. The Red Rogue made a subtle gesture and half the rebels scrambled up the ladder. The rest circled closer, hands dropping to their knives.

"What's happened?" Lucius asked.

"A patrol is coming."

"He led them here," someone snarled.

The Rogue's voice went cold. "Did you?"

"No," Lucius said in an equally frosty tone. "If I meant to betray you, I would have left first. *Then* I would have sent the soldiers to arrest you."

There was a tense silence. Lucius prepared to fight his way free of the hold. Then the Rogue made another hand sign. The rest of the rebels silently moved to the ladder and vanished.

"The patrols come through often," the Rogue said, "looking for any excuse to start trouble and then arrest us for defending ourselves. I choose to trust you until proven otherwise."

"Thank you," Lucius replied.

They climbed up to the deck. The soldiers were one street over. A dozen, their chainmail shining in the sun. An old woman in a white headscarf came out of her house, finger jabbing as she shouted at them. One pushed her aside with enough force to send her sprawling to the ground. She kept cursing at them as a group of scrawny, bare-chested boys hurried over. They gesticulated angrily at the soldiers and helped the old woman to her feet.

The patrol moved on, ignoring the stares of people who

were coming out of their stilt houses to watch. The other rebels were already paddling away in canoes toward the tall reeds of the marsh. One of the soldiers spotted them and gave a shout. The patrol started running down the pier toward the barge.

"Go," Lucius said. "I'll slow them down."

"Use fire and you'll expose yourself," the Rogue warned.

Lucius gave him a crooked smile. "I can be subtle."

He unleashed a whip-fine lash of earth power on a rotting support beneath the pier. With a loud crack, the center crumbled, sending half the soldiers into the canal. The rest beat a hasty retreat, straight towards a group of children gathered at the end of the pier. They began pelting the soldiers with stones. The missiles bounced harmlessly off their mail, but the act of defiance seemed to enrage them. They gave chase, heavy boots thudding against the wooden boards. The children scattered into a warren of floating docks beyond the canal.

"Meet again tomorrow?" the Rogue asked, hooking a leg over the barge's rail.

Lucius nodded. He turned back just as one of the children stumbled and fell. The smallest, no more than six or seven. The boy's face twisted as a soldier caught up to him. He raised his arms in a shield but didn't even try to plead for mercy. A boot drew back to kick the child's head.

Time slowed. The sounds around him dimmed until all Lucius heard was the soldier's steady pulse. How strong it was. He could almost taste the blood rushing through his veins. The weaving formed as swift as thought. Air and water, a touch of earth, all bound with fire. It made a cage around the soldier's heart.

Lucius clenched his fist.

Sixteen

L o slunk along the floating dock like one of the city's feral cats, a shawl tucked around her face and a dagger in her belt.

Six days left to deliver Nathan's box, and she had no idea where it was.

Being Nathan, he kept hounding her to steal the reliquarian's body, reanimate it, and interrogate his soul about the box's whereabouts.

"My first apprentice!" he'd declared, rubbing his hands together. "Do not worry, demoiselle, I will guide you through the process. We'll need grave dirt. Blood, as well, but any will do, I'm not choosy. And his bones, of course, preferably with the flesh boiled away. The spell is simple. We will practice the pronunciation together so you don't make any unfortunate mistakes."

Lo thought of his shambling dust servants and suppressed a shudder.

"You do realize that you're talking about a priest?" she had asked. "A holy man who dedicated his life to an order that aids the sick and infirm?"

Nathan stared at her with blank incomprehension. "What's your point?"

"Right. So the answer is still no."

He opened his mouth, but Lo never heard his response because she stuffed the black mirror into her sea chest and left the *Wind-Witch* with Thistle to pursue their own inquiries. These were hampered by the fact that every soldier in the city was looking for her. The Sons of Bel, too.

The sight of that poor old man lying in a pool of his own blood still haunted her. She had dreamt of it the night before — night being a relative term in a place where the sun never set — except that instead of the woman, it was Nathan standing over the body, tentacles of black dust coiling around him. She'd backed from the chamber, fleeing down the cramped spiral stairs, but they didn't lead to the great temple of Bel.

In the way of dreams, she found herself in a house of endless halls and doors, playing a game of hide and seek. She was a child again, and the person she sought was also a child because now and again she heard a peal of smothered laughter somewhere ahead. At first the hunt was lighthearted. But then the mood changed. Her quarry's giggles turned to faint whimpers of fear. Their timidity annoyed her.

"It's just a game!" she shouted. "Come out if you won't play it right!"

Silence.

She ran through the halls, braid flying, and caught a glimpse of movement ahead. Lo skidded around the corner and saw a door just closing halfway down. "Ha!" she cried, racing to the door and seizing the knob. Whoever was on the other side had hold of the knob, too, and they wrestled for a moment, but Lo was stronger. She gave a mighty yank, the door flew wide . . . and she saw herself, not with a pigtail but a chin-length bob, dusty tears streaking her face. A cruel urge took hold and she formed her fingers into claws as Scaredy-Lo shrank back with saucer eyes.

"I'm coming to get you—"

At which point, she had sat up in her bunk on the *Wind-Witch* with a start. Sunlight muscled through cracks in the makeshift blinds she'd hung over the portholes.

"That was a weird one," she'd muttered, swinging her legs over the bed.

She dressed and made tea. The dunking in the filthy canal hadn't helped her cold. A glance in the wardrobe mirror revealed puffy red eyes with dark smudges beneath. She blew her nose — gods, who knew such disgusting goop could come out of one's own head? — and had the fruitless conversation with Nathan. In the end, she decided to seek out the mercenary woman and her companion. At least *they* seemed competent. If she watched the stilt house and followed them, they might lead her to the mortifex.

And, with a little luck, Nathan's box.

Lo ventured deeper into the tangle of decaying barges and fishing canoes. The stilt houses all looked the same, but she did remember lemon trees in blue pots and the yappy white dog. Then a commotion ahead made her stop. She couldn't see what was happening, but angry shouts carried across the marsh.

"We should turn back," Thistle growled. "Circle around."

"Why?"

The cat stared at her. "Haven't you had your fill of trouble?"

Lo pointed at three red pennants fluttering from the mast of a small sailing vessel that was painted green with black trim. "But look! I recognize that. We're close."

He blinked twice, slowly, which meant dissent.

"Besides which," Lo added, "anything out of the ordinary might be worth investigating."

She crept down the floating docks and peeked between the stilts of a house. Six waterlogged soldiers were scrambling out of a canal. They wore only their quilted underjackets. Curses sliced the humid air.

More soldiers, these in full chainmail tunics, were pursuing a gang of children. Her breath caught as the littlest one tripped. The soldiers closed in, obscuring her view. Then one of them collapsed. He clawed at his chest, heels drumming, mouth gaping in a silent scream. Some kind of fit? To her relief, the boy scrambled to his feet and rabbited away. The other soldiers ignored him, kneeling around their fallen comrade.

Lo was scanning the docks for more patrols when she noticed the silhouette of a man on the stern of a barge. The pier it was moored to had broken in half, leaving a wide gap of splintered boards. He stood with the sun behind his shoulders, shadow obscuring his face, but the light caught his hair. It was a rich, dark copper, like the tail of a fox.

A hubbub of agitated voices drew her gaze back to the soldiers. The sick one had stopped moving. After a moment, his fellows lifted him up and carried him away, trailed by the ones who had fallen into the canal. The last were red-faced and obviously humiliated, shouting at the people who watched from the decks of their stilt houses to get inside or face arrest. The soldiers were such a sorry bunch, Lo doubted they'd follow through on the threat, but most of the crowd drifted away.

When she turned back, the red-haired figure was gone. She stared at the deserted hulk for a moment, brow furrowed. But no. It couldn't have been Lucius. He was five hundred leagues away in Aquitan, not in this sun-drenched western city.

"Shall we depart?" Thistle hissed. "Or do you prefer to wait until more soldiers come along and take you to Blackwater Jail?"

"The first," she answered with a grin. "I know the route from here."

They slipped away. Soon enough, she spotted the right house. Happily, the excitable white dog was nowhere in sight. With a little searching, she found a spot between a thick coil of rope and a mossy piling. It was tight, but she could just squeeze in with her knees pulled to her chest. Better yet, it gave a view of the docks leading to the stilt house. Thistle wandered off to find a sunny place to nap.

Lo settled in. Hours later, her throat was aching, her legs numb. No one had come or gone. She rose, flexing stiff knees — and something sharp pricked the small of her back.

"Don't move."

She knew that voice. It was the man. She almost reached for the Nexus, but the knifepoint didn't waver and now the woman was strolling up. She wore black leather from head to boots, her hair tightly braided to her scalp. The leather was nicked and scuffed, as though it had led a hard life.

"Well, look who turned up. It's the slippery little eel who swam away."

"I'm not a necromancer," Lo said tightly, as the man bound her hands behind her back.

"Never said you were." The woman smiled, her cheekbones sharp as sabers. "You're just a necromancer's plaything."

Lo grimaced. "I'm not that, either."

The woman tugged her sleeve up and examined Nathan's brand. "We haven't been here long, so I don't know who you belong to, but you're going to tell us."

The woman searched her, taking the knife from her belt.

They dragged her to the house and up the winding stairs to the loft. No one else seemed to be home.

"Sit," the woman ordered.

Lo sank down against the wall, blowing a lock of hair from her face. "Listen, you've got it wrong. I came back looking for you, didn't I?"

She turned to her companion. "Would you call that looking for us or spying on us?"

"Definitely spying," he replied.

"I got that tattoo on a dare, all right?" Lo said sullenly. "I was drunk at the time—"

"Try again."

Her shoulders slumped. "Fine. I was born into indentured servitude to a necromancer. My mother died when I was two—"

"Innunu save us, I think she' s allergic to the truth." The woman sank to her haunches so they were eye to eye. "Let's start with the relic you're hunting. Is it an iron box, by any chance?"

Lo opened her mouth and found she couldn't utter a sound. She cleared her throat and tried again. A guttural croak emerged, like a dying crow.

The woman frowned. "What's wrong with you?"

It had to be Nathan's blood oath. "I can't speak of it," Lo admitted. "I mean, I physically *can't.* I tried to tell you that before."

The pair shared a look. She'd seen it in the boat. As though they communicated a great deal without words. It felt familiar, though she couldn't say how.

"She's bound by a spell," the man said. He was dressed in the local garb of baggy trousers, tunic, and manty, but he looked nothing like the people from the Shambles. Too fair, for one thing. And he had a light, feline way of moving that made her think he'd be quick with a sword.

The woman rubbed her neck and stood. "Well, shit."

"But I swear to you," Lo said, "my reasons for . . . what I did . . . they're not what you think."

Her onyx eyes flashed. "That's what they all say. I ought to—"

"Don't, Tijah." The man laid a hand on her arm.

Tijah? Lo looked at them again, really *looked*. Then she saw it, almost hidden by the woman's long, tight sleeve. A glint of gold at her wrist. In a flash of sudden insight, she realized what she had sensed between them. They were bonded with talismanic cuffs. And the deep intimacy . . . it was just like her parents. Each would know where the other was, no matter how far away. They would share each other's emotions, their physical pains and pleasures.

More pieces clicked into place. The woman had taken a crossbow wound just the day before. Yet she gave no sign of pain when the man touched her. There were no bandages around her arm. Because she had been healed. *He* had healed her.

"Your name is Achaemenes," Lo said to him in a rush. "And you're a daēva."

They both turned to stare. Tijah's face went smooth and hard as carved wood. If anything, she looked even angrier. One hand dropped to her curved blade.

Lo frantically rifled through her memories. The stories Mama used to tell about the old days when she and Papa first met.

"My mother is Nazafareen," she said quickly. "And Darius is my father. You were novice Water Dogs together at Tel Khaluja. You fought demons." *What else? Think!* "Tijah means sword in your native tongue. You come from . . . from . . . "

The name eluded her, and then she remembered. "Al Miraj! *Please.* You were Mama's best friend."

Tijah's mouth was still set in a thin line. Achaemenes spoke first. Mama always said he was the more reasonable one. The cool water to Tijah's fire.

"What is your name?" he asked.

"Delilah. I was named for—"

"Your father's mother," Tijah finished. "I knew her." She regarded Lo with sadness in her eyes, her voice heavy. "That may be so, but you still bear the mark of a necromancer. There is nothing so evil in the world. They draw their power from human captives, draining them to the point of death—"

Lo shook her head. "No, I have met several. They speak with the dead and work magic with mortal remains, but none had slaves. Not living ones, at least." She thought of Nathan. "They can be arrogant. And irritatingly secretive. But I would not use the word evil."

Tijah seemed about to argue, but again Achaemenes intervened. "It could be different here," he said quietly. "She might speak the truth."

Tijah gave a curt nod. "But we're not turning her loose. Not until we know more."

She strode away, staring out at the canal, her back stiff. Lo knew she had lost her first daēva to the scheming of a necromancer in the Old Empire, a world on the other side of the Dominion's gates. They had been bonded from childhood and the death had gutted her.

Achaemenes sat down in front of Lo cross-legged. Now his left sleeve rode up enough for her to see the matching cuff around his wrist. It was engraved with a snarling gryffin. "The Drowned Woman sent us to find your parents," he said. "That is why we hunt this mortifex."

So it wasn't about the box at all. She had allies at last, if they would only trust her.

"Then we want the same thing," she said urgently. "Is he Magnus the Merciless?"

A brow lifted. "So you know that name. No, he goes by Janus. Even the Drowned Woman does not know his true name. But he is a minion of Magnus. We hope to capture him and force him to lead us to your parents."

"Eight years we've been hunting," Tijah said without turning around. "We scoured every inch of the Dominion. They are not there."

"I was told the same," Lo said. "By necromancers who knew them."

Tijah spun around. "They never mentioned that to me."

"So you have seen my parents?"

She nodded. "Not since they vanished, but our paths would cross occasionally. We both serve the Drowned Woman." Her face softened slightly. "Nazafareen told us about you. I have never seen her so happy. Darius, too." Her expression cooled. "But until I know the nature of this oath you have made, and to whom you have made it, you will remain a prisoner in this room. I will *not* lose Janus again!"

The tone brooked no room for argument. This time, Achaemenes only shrugged.

Lo's jaw clenched in frustration. Damn Nathan! They might know what was in the box, if she could only ask. Or at least why this mortifex wanted it.

Lo's bloody luck, she thought sourly. Why couldn't she have met them a week ago? Of course, she wouldn't even be here if she hadn't made that stupid, stupid pact . . .

A rumbling purr made her look down. Thistle had arrived, but it was not *her* he shamelessly rubbed against. It was Achaemenes, the little traitor.

Achaemenes blinked in surprise, then smiled and began to

stroke the cat behind the ears. Well, Thistle liked them. That counted for a great deal.

A thought struck her as she watched him rub his head against the daēva's knee. She knew the terms of her contract by heart. Not a single word of it forbade Thistle from talking about her oath. It was possible Nathan didn't even realize he had the power of speech. A loophole? Faint hope rose.

"Is he yours?" Achaemenes asked, scratching Thistle under the chin now.

"I wouldn't call him mine," she replied. "He is his own master. But we are friends." She caught Thistle's eye. "And we aid each other in times of need," she added pointedly.

The cat yawned and gave a luxurious stretch.

Lo leaned forward. "I'm in a tight spot," she whispered, as Achaemenes watched her quizzically. "I know you're not chatty with strangers, but an exception might be in order here."

She and Thistle were not bonded in the traditional way, but they understood each other. Lightning flared in the cat's green eyes. It was brief. No one saw it but Lo.

"Did the girl hit her head?" Tijah asked, hands on hips.

Thistle strolled away, prodigious belly swinging. He sniffed at the pile of dirty plates. Then he leapt into one of the hammocks, seemed to dislike the way it swayed, and leapt down again. After a cursory lick of his claws, he sat down to face them. Lo thought she detected a faint smile.

"The necromancer is named Nathan Ouvrard," Thistle said. "He claims to know where Magnus is hiding, and promised to trade that information if Delilah brought him an iron box held by the priests of Bel."

Achaemenes scooted back and gained his feet, looking around wildly. The blood had drained from his face. Tijah merely stood open-mouthed, too shocked to reach for her sword. Whether it was that a cat could talk, or Thistle's particular manner of speech — overlapping voices, some whispering, others shrieking and gibbering, all utterly inhuman, as if the wind itself was given voice — Lo couldn't say.

"Nathan is a scoundrel," Thistle finished, "but Delilah is not to blame. And she will die in six days if she fails to keep their bargain." With that, he blithely returned to washing his claws.

"Sweet Innunu," Tijah managed.

"See?" Lo said cheerfully. "I told you it wasn't my fault. Will you untie me now?"

"What . . . " Achaemenes swallowed. "What is he?"

"A cat," Lo said. "But his mother was a sea goddess. She's a cat, too. I can't say I fully understand the lineage, but he is descended from magical royalty." She gazed at Thistle fondly. "Thank you."

He gave no sign of hearing, having moved on to the other paw.

Tijah barked an unsettled laugh. "We have seen many strange things in our wanderings, but never a talking cat." Her brow furrowed. Well, I have my gods. You can have yours. And it seems I misjudged you."

She used Lo's dagger to cut the bonds, then returned it to her hilt-first. Lo tucked it back into her belt, rubbing her wrists. The rope hadn't been tight enough to break the skin, but they were still sore. She was feeling lightheaded, her skin too hot. The dratted flu.

"If this necromancer knows where Magnus is," Tijah said, black eyes gleaming, "then you must lead us to him. He might have refused to tell *you*, but I can promise he'll tell me."

Lo opened her mouth to clarify the dilemma. Not a sound emerged. Achaemenes came to her rescue.

"Didn't you hear the part about her dying if she breaks the bargain?" he asked Tijah.

She tilted her head. "I only caught about half of it," she admitted. "But can't we just . . ."

Achaemenes shook his head. "It's Nazafareen's daughter. What would you say if we did find her? That you let Delilah die?"

It was at this point that Lo might have clarified that death for *her* was not quite the same thing as it was for normal people. She didn't relish the prospect, but she didn't fear it, either. But they had just untied her and given her knife back. Perhaps they'd had enough surprises for one day.

More importantly, if this mortifex was looking for Nathan's box, she would do everything in her power to keep him from getting it. Bless Thistle, he seemed to be thinking along the same lines.

"The box," the cat said, his tail lashing now. "Do you know what is inside it?"

The pair still winced at his infernal voice, though it was nothing like the first time.

"No," Tijah replied. "I hoped you might."

Lo managed to shake her head.

"Whatever it is, Magnus wants it badly," Achaemenes said. "Janus is holed up in the Duc's palace. We tried to get inside. It's impossible." He shared one of those wordless looks with his bonded. "Not without killing a lot of people. Which we aren't supposed to do."

Tijah wore a disgruntled look but said nothing. Lo had a feeling she had been overridden on this point.

"If he's still there, that suggests he hasn't found it," Lo said thoughtfully. "We must make a plan . . ." She trailed off, nose twitching, and just managed to cover a violent sneeze. "Do you have any hot tea?"

"I'll make some," Achaemenes offered. "Do you need healing?"

She was about to gratefully accept, but what if he sensed something fey inside in her? A . . . darkness? Lo decided not to take the risk. She flapped a hand.

"It's just a cold. But I'll take the tea."

Achaemenes nodded seriously, his eyes green-gold in the sunlight. She had to admit that he was handsome. And Tijah was beautiful, when she wasn't glowering or waving her sword about. They made a striking pair. Lo wondered if . . . but no, Mama had always insisted they were merely close friends.

He slipped down the stairs. Lo and Tijah regarded each other. It was surreal to finally meet the legendary fighter from Al Miraj. Mama had always made her seem larger than life, fearless and lethal to her enemies, and the truth was not far off.

"You have your mother's nose," Tijah said with a lopsided smile. "And her habit of poking it into other people's business."

"Do you know . . ." Lo began. Her throat tightened and she had to start again. "Do you know for sure that my parents are still alive?"

To her surprise, Tijah came over and took her hands. Warmth seeped into Lo's chilled flesh.

"I am certain of it," she said.

"The necromancers, Chaos and Caul, they claimed my parents were under an enchantment. I . . . I saw them. In Nathan's mirror." This did not break the oath and the words flowed freely. "They were on a ship." She searched Tijah's dark eyes. "They seemed . . . well, they seemed all right. Mama was sharpening her sword and laughing."

Something unreadable crossed Tijah's face.

"What do you know?" Lo whispered. "Tell me."

"Oh, honey." Tijah squeezed Lo's fingers. "They're pirates." She gave a wondering laugh. "Magnus has them robbing the dead as they cross the Cold Sea."

SEVENTEEN

"Don't sulk, pet. It spoils your beauty."

Morgen turned to regard Vazsoly Marcel. He was stretched out on the massive bed, chin propped on the heel of one hand. Sweat beaded the hard planes of his chest.

"I asked you not to call me that," she said.

His lips twitched in amusement. "Shall I call you my lady, then?"

"Now you mock me."

"I would never," he murmured, distracted by his own reflection in a gilt-edged standing mirror strategically positioned opposite the bed.

The Duc of Cavet was an attractive man and knew it. His eyes were a clear sea-blue, his jaw firm, with a winsome dimple at the center of his chin. He wore his hair cut fashionably short; a single flaxen lock tumbled across one eyebrow. Now he sat up and reached for her. Morgen pretended not to notice, gliding away just before his fingers could catch her. She didn't need to see his face to know it tightened in irritation.

"You're angry with me," he said.

"Not at all, my lord." She wrapped a silk robe around her bare shoulders.

This was true. Morgen wasn't angry. She just hated him with every fiber of her being. One day, he would realize that. One day, he would kneel at her feet, broken and stripped of his titles, begging her to spare his life. And she would. Because death was far too easy a fate for Vazsoly Marcel.

He adopted a patient, condescending tone, as if she were a spoiled child. "Beloved, these are *our* plans, yes? We have discussed them a dozen times. I will restore the glory of Aveline, with Prydwen as the capital of a new empire. To do that, I must wed the Damiata and use her wealth to pay off those miserly priests. A political alliance only."

Bare feet padded on the rug behind her. Muscular arms circled her waist, his breath hot on her neck. "But my heart is yours, pet. Beatriz is an untutored child. She could never satisfy me as you do. Once she has borne me a son, I will send her away to the convent. She can live out her days milking goats with Dravka and Jaelle, and we will rule together."

Morgen endured his caresses in silence. Knowing Vazsoly, he would demand his marital rights from Beatriz the moment she had her first blood. He would not consider it rape, just expediency. He needed legitimate heirs to secure his name and the future of the duchy.

Of course, there would be no heirs. By the time Morgen was done, the House of Marcel would be razed root and branch, the ground it stood upon scorched and salted.

As for his two younger sisters, she would deal with them when the time came. Sometimes, she snuck up to the convent in the hills where Vazsoly had confined the two girls and spied on them at their chores — tending goats or hoeing in the fields, skirts tied up to their knees and straw bonnets covering the Marcel white-blond hair.

The first time she'd glimpsed Jaelle and Dravka Marcel, Morgen had expected to hate them, but she felt nothing. After some consideration, she decided it must be because they were not male heirs. Vazsoly, on the other hand, was a mirror image of his father. A self-absorbed brute who thought he could do anything to anyone and get away with it.

How wrong they both were.

When Morgen's mother lay dying of the wasting sickness that began with a radish-sized lump beneath her left armpit, she'd confessed the truth of her past. Why she didn't speak with the accented patois of the Isles, as their neighbors did. Why she and Morgen kept to themselves. Why they had no cousins or aunts or uncles, or any relations at all.

It was because her mother was originally from Prydwen. From the Duc's own court.

He believes me dead, her mother whispered. *And if he learns that you lived, he would come after you, too. When you are strong enough, you must destroy them all.*

Morgen had gazed into her feverish eyes and sworn it.

Her mother had already passed on all she knew of necromancy. Guided Morgen in developing her own special talents. Six years passed. She grew stronger, learned all she could of the Marcels, and honed her plans of revenge. When she turned twenty-four, Morgen decided she was ready to seek out her enemies — but then, Kaethe be blessed, Vazsoly came to her. He sailed his warfleet to the Isles, burning villages and slaughtering any who opposed him.

She found out where he was camped and managed to talk her way through six layers of guards, until she stood outside his tent. He had left her waiting for two hours, mosquitoes whining in her ears, eyes stinging from the smoke of five hundred campfires. At last, he had summoned her. Two of his hulking personal guards escorted Morgen into the tent. A mailed hand pushed her down to her knees.

Vazsoly was not yet the Duc of Cavet, but the way he sat in the folding camp chair, with one gleaming boot hooked over the arm and a gold breastplate that matched his gold hair, made him look every inch an arrogant prince.

Morgen had chosen her own attire carefully. A long piece of cloth dyed crimson with madder, draped in the traditional sheathe of the Western Isles, and yellowed bone bracelets on her arms. His eyes roamed the length of her body, his smile lazy.

"So you wish to be my necromancer."

"Yes, milord." Morgen kept her chin up and looked him straight in the eye. Interest kindled in his gaze. She understood now that he did not admire her spirit; he wished to break it.

"I might have an opening." His men laughed at that. Vazsoly flicked a finger. "Leave us."

The soldiers exchanged amused looks and withdrew, letting the tent flap fall shut behind them. She was prepared to seduce him, but it turned out that he did have a task for her. One she was happy to fulfill.

Vazsoly had beckoned her over. A dry, calloused hand closed around her wrist, pulling her close. Then he'd whispered in her ear. *I want you to kill my father, witch...*

"What's wrong with you today?"

The Duc's voice — here and now — dragged her back. It had an ugly edge that meant his temper was fraying. Morgen realized that he was cupping her breast, and that she was standing with her arms limp at her sides, as responsive as a dressmaker's mannikin.

"I'm sorry." She turned and eyed him through her lashes. "I suppose I am a little jealous of the Damiata."

He squeezed her bottom, too hard, then strode to the arched window. The sumptuous bedchamber was appointed with glittering tapestries of gold and silver thread, the Marcel colors. Candlelight from the round chandelier burnished his skin. Even that was honey-colored, as if he had been dipped in gold.

You are like a prettily embalmed corpse that does not know it is riddled with maggots, she thought.

Vazsoly gazed across the bay at the priests' stronghold of Bel Mara. "We owe them a bloody fortune," he muttered. "Do you have any idea what it costs to keep this place?"

It was a constant complaint. By Kaethe, he was tiresome.

"A great deal, I imagine," she replied, unable to summon any interest.

"I need money, pet. How long has it been since I sent that letter?"

He referred to an offer of betrothal that Morgen had penned for him. *Put a womanly touch on it,* Vazsoly had commanded. *Tell the fractious little brat what she wants to hear.*

"Two months, milord."

A heavy sigh. "What the fuck is taking her so long?"

What indeed? Vazsoly believed Morgen was jealous, that she wanted to marry him herself, when in truth she couldn't wait for him to wed the Damiata Beatriz. The higher he flew, the farther he would fall. Let him have all his heart desired. Only then would she cut his legs out from beneath him.

"Perhaps she thinks you should woo her in person," Morgen said. "Young girls are impressionable. Likely she has been raised on tales of romance and chivalry. A letter will not do."

He grunted and gripped the edges of the stone sill. At twenty-seven, Vazsoly's body was still firm and fit. Not like his father, whose red-veined nose and fat middle revealed a life of excess. His jowls had wobbled in terror when Morgen appeared in his bedchamber. This very same one, as a matter of fact.

"You could be right," Vazsoly said slowly, "but it is not a good time for me to pay her a visit. The recent unrest complicates matters." He was silent for a minute. When he spoke, his voice was soft but intense. Almost eager. She knew that tone. It raised the hair on her arms.

"Perhaps the people need to be taught a lesson. I'll set my dogs loose in that rat's nest they call the Shambles."

Morgen knew Vazsoly was already deeply unpopular. One spark might ignite a full-blown rebellion. The worst possible outcome would be if someone else killed him and deprived her of the pleasure. She'd endured his revolting company for too many months.

"The Sons of Bel won't like it," she warned, walking over and laying a hand on his arm. "They have much support among the poor. And you are not yet strong enough to challenge their authority directly—"

The sudden backhand blow knocked her to the floor. She cupped her stinging cheek but made not a sound.

"Not strong enough? I'll show you—" Vazsoly drew a deep breath, mastering himself. As always, the explosion of rage was followed by vague remorse.

"I'm sorry," he said gruffly, bending down to help her up. "Forgive me, pet?"

How tempting to kill him on the spot. To rip out his soul and hurl it screaming into the ninth abyss. But, unlike Vazsoly, she never lost her temper. If the Marcel motto was *We yield to none*, Morgen Nadezhda's was *Ice for blood and salt for heart*.

She made her expression soften. A woman besotted, willing to overlook any sin. "Your duties weigh heavily, milord. And your sleep has been troubled of late." She allowed him to help her up. "I know you didn't mean it."

Vazsoly looked relieved. Like most bullies, he was secretly insecure.

"It is this Red Rogue," he muttered. "Some fucking illiterate fisherman, yet he incites riots with a single speech. I still don't see why you can't get rid of him the the same way you dealt with my father."

Her cheek burned like a brand. Morgen tasted blood. She dabbed it with a sleeve. "That was different. I don't know who the Red Rogue *is*."

"Then work your witchery and find him!" Vazsoly roared.

She bowed her head. "I will try."

For a moment, she thought he would slap her again. The Duc's face darkened to a thunderhead. He *is* afraid, she realized with a jolt of unaccustomed glee. Of a fisherman!

"I will not count on *you* to dispose of my enemies," Vazsoly hissed between his teeth. "You've already had months, and I've suffered this insult for long enough. It undermines my position with the Damiata and makes me look as though I cannot even manage my own duchy! Small wonder she has not responded favorably to my suit."

He rubbed his square jaw, pacing the carpet. "The Rogue is a coward, hiding behind a masque, but he can be drawn out. Then we will behead the snake. As for the Sons of Bel, you will pay a visit to the arch-priest and tell him I need more time. Explain matters in a way that dried-up fart understands." Blue eyes speared her. "If they will not trust us, Morgen, then they must fear us."

"I will go tomorrow."

A knock came at the door. "Your Grace?"

"A moment, Rossignol." Vazsoly snapped his fingers and Morgen ran to fetch his breeches and doublet. Once he was decent, she belted her own robe and admitted the captain of his guard.

Galoy Rossignol was a career soldier and stalwart campaigner who had served the old Duc. He was in his mid-fifties with a neatly trimmed gray beard and watchful brown eyes. They widened a little at the sight of her face. Not from surprise — it was hardly the first time the Duc had struck her — but pity.

Morgen decided that Rossignol would die slowly, shrieking for his mother.

"Lady Nadezdha," he said with a courteous nod.

"Captain." She walked to the window, not bothering to correct him. Her only title among the courtiers was "the Duc's barbarian whore," but Rossignol was old-fashioned. He looked the other way when his soldiers raped and murdered, but Kaethe forbid he breached etiquette within the walls of the palace.

"What is it?" Vazsoly demanded, pulling on his boots.

"A small matter, but I know you wish to be informed of anything out of the ordinary. Two soldiers on patrol failed to report back after their rounds, Your Grace," Rossignol replied. "We have mounted a search."

"Deserters?"

"I think that is . . . unlikely. All the men know the penalty for leaving their posts without permission."

Death on the pyres. Morgen had seen the sentence carried out before.

"Then what?" Vazsoly stared at him, brows lowering. "You cannot be suggesting that assassins breached the perimeter? I've emptied the treasury strengthening the fucking defenses. You told me the new wall would keep them out!"

Rossignol licked his lips. "Surely not, Your Grace. As you say, it is impossible. More likely it will turn out they were drinking on duty and passed out somewhere."

This response seemed to make Vazsoly even more livid. "I will not have drunken louts in my service. In case you've lost count, there have been seven assassination attempts, Rossignol. Seven! When you find them, unless they tripped and fell off the fucking cliff, you'll make an example. Toss them into the lowest, filthiest cell at Blackwater and lose the fucking key."

"I understand, Your Grace," Rossignol said, his expression stoic. He was used to the Duc's outbursts.

Vazsoly rose and Morgen laid a light cloak across his shoulders. He frowned at Rossignol. "Why are you still here?"

"There is one final matter, Your Grace."

"What is it?"

"Orlaith Redvayne, the Ducissa of Clovis, sent an emissary. He brings Her Grace's condolences for your father and wishes you a long and prosperous reign."

"Who is it? One of her nobles?"

"Lucius Bittencourt, Your Grace."

"Orlaith's mortifex?" Vazsoly thought for a moment. "Give him rooms in the palace, neither the worst nor the best. Tell him I am indisposed and will summon him at my convenience."

"Yes, Your Grace."

"Find Janus," the Duc said. "Send him to the council room." His voice softened a fraction. "And fetch the Lady Nadezhda's maid. She had an accident."

Rossignol was staring at her. After a moment, Morgen realized her nose was bleeding again.

"Now," Vazsoly snapped.

Rossignol bowed and backed from the room. Vazsoly turned to Morgen. "Orlaith is painfully transparent," he remarked. "She has sent her mortifex to spy on me."

"Then send him away."

Morgen had no fear of the High Dead, but she didn't need anyone meddling in her own plans.

"If I insult him outright, Orlaith will know I've seen through her ruse. Worse, he might go to Galatia and press the Redvaynes' marriage suit to Beatriz. As you said, she's young and impressionable. No, best to keep Lucius at arm's length and let him stew." Vazsoly planted a perfunctory kiss on the uninjured side of her face. "Why don't you take a nap, pet? Janus and I will devise a plan to deal with this Red Rogue."

Morgen curtsied, but he was already striding to the door without a backward glance. She watched him leave, then sat on the edge of the bed, thinking. Presently, a young chambermaid entered. She glanced at her mistress and wordlessly fetched a bowl of warm water and a cloth.

Morgen let the girl dab the blood away. Chessamir knew better than to show any trace of sympathy. The last time she had done so, Morgen put her on scullery duty for a week, scrubbing burnt stew from the bottom of the great iron pots in the kitchen.

"Do you require anything else, milady?" Chessamir asked, not meeting her eye.

"No, you may go."

"Very good, milady." The maid left quietly, removing the bowl and the pink-stained cloth.

Morgen regarded her reflection in the mirror. A vicious bruise marked her cheek, and her upper lip was cracked and puffy, but it would heal. Vazsoly had done worse before. She opened a pouch and withdrew a finger bone and small pot. The bone had belonged to her mother. The pot contained a paste made from ashes, oil and antimony. With a steady hand, Morgen began to repair the elaborate pattern of runes and whorls on her forehead.

"You will die on your wedding day before all the noble guests and your sweet young bride," she whispered with a smile. The traces of red staining her teeth made it look ghastly, which pleased her. "But I will make sure that before you do, you know exactly who has done it to you, and why. *Brother.*"

EIGHTEEN

"Vazsoly Marcel is toying with us, Lucius."

He gazed at Orlaith's reflection in the black mirror. "So it would seem."

"The insolence," she muttered. "To not even grant you an audience!"

"Well, he didn't exactly refuse. Something along the lines of summoning me at his pleasure." Lucius glanced around the sunless chamber he'd been given deep below the palace. "He didn't send me packing."

"It is still a grave affront," Orlaith fumed, seeming to forget that she had sent him there to make sure the Duc was deposed. "His father would never have treated an emissary from Clovis in such a rude fashion."

"And now his father is conveniently dead," Lucius pointed out. "What about Castelio? Did your soldiers hunt him down yet?"

"No," Orlaith snapped. "But they're watching all the roads. He cannot get far." She leaned closer. "You made contact with these rebels?"

"Yes. They told me the Duc has an unbound mortifex in his service."

The shock on her face was priceless. "Unbound? Is Vazsoly mad?"

"By all accounts, no," Lucius said dryly. "Merely power-hungry. I imagine they've made a bargain."

"A bargain!" She gave a brittle laugh. "He is an even greater fool than I thought if he believes he can control that creature without a menotte."

Lucius ignored the implied insult. "The mortifex's name is Janus. Not one I've heard of. But I've summoned a maid on the pretext of wanting hot water for a bath. I'll see what else she knows—"

"You will get rid of this Unbound mortifex," Orlaith interrupted. "I don't care how you manage it. Just do it."

"That's what I promised the Red Rogue, my lady."

Her face hardened. Anger rolled through their bond. "Your oath is to *me*, Lucius. Do not forget that."

As if he could. "I merely meant that in this matter, your interests coincide."

"Speaking of the Red Rogue, I take it you met him?"

"I did."

"Any ideas about his real identity?"

"He was careful, but a few things stood out."

Lucius thought of the Rogue's voice. It had a natural confidence and charisma. A man used to having his orders obeyed without question. That suggested a military past, yet he lacked the arrogance of an officer. Lucius felt certain he believed every word he said about dying for his ideals. And the accent . . . A slight burr marked him as a native of the Shambles, yet educated. Not a noble but someone who had managed to rise in station.

"Well?" Orlaith snapped.

"He was very fat," Lucius lied with a straight face. "I heard a wheeze that spoke of ill health. And he smelled strongly of fish."

"A common ruffian, then," she said, lips pursing in distaste.

"He assured me that he had no desire to take power himself, only to see Vazsoly ousted."

She snorted. "And you believe him? No matter. The Cavetti nobles would never stand for some fishmonger ruling their city. If the Duc's sisters do not seize the throne, one of the margraves will fill the void."

Lucius marveled at her naïveté, but Orlaith had never witnessed a full-blown popular revolt. Once the tinder caught, there would be no controlling the blaze. The thought made him oddly happy.

"I'm sure you're right," Lucius said.

"But I still want to know the Red Rogue's identity." Her brow creased. "I dislike dealing with phantoms. You will discover the name."

"As you say, my lady. We meet again tomorrow. I will try to follow him afterwards."

A brisk nod. "And find out where Vazsoly stands with the Damiata Beatriz."

A rap came at the door. "That must be the maidservant," Lucius said. "They're always full of gossip. I'll see what she knows."

He bowed. Orlaith's image grew cloudy, the mirror's surface settling to a dull black again. Lucius tucked it away beneath his feather mattress and opened the door.

A tall man with cropped dark hair stood in the corridor. He had a strong, aquiline nose with a faint white scar across the bridge. A rich blue cloak hemmed in silver hung across broad shoulders. His face was youthful, his eyes ageless. Twin flames flickered in their depths.

A jolt of bone-deep shock made Lucius grip the doorframe. Words fled.

"Claudius Quintus," the visitor said slowly. "I never expected to lay eyes on you again."

The name struck him like a blow. It wasn't possible.

Is he here to drag me down to the Ninth Hell? If so, I deserve it.

Then the man pressed his right fist to his heart. The old salute of *celere* to *legatus*. Cavalry to general.

"Will you not invite me inside?" he asked with tentative warmth.

A strangled laugh escaped. "Justinian!"

Lucius pulled him into a hard embrace. He smelled the same, of leather and horses.

Memories crashed down in a tidal wave. Searing heat and smoke. The pain of his own burns, but far worse, the agony of knowing he had failed. That they would all die. Justinian's face hovering above as he drew his last rattling breath. The warmth of his fingers slipping away as life fled.

When Lucius stepped back, his cheeks were wet. It took him a moment to realize why. *I am weeping*, he thought in astonishment.

Justinian's eyes were damp too, the tears steaming against his skin. They regarded each other for a moment.

"How?" Lucius managed at last. "I assumed . . ." He trailed off, unable to speak the words.

"That I had died and crossed over? Gone to my just reward?" Justinian replied in a sardonic tone. "I thought the same of you."

They were still standing in the doorway. Lucius stepped back to allow his old companion inside.

"So they call you Lucius now," Justinian said with a mirthless smile.

"And they call you Janus." He glanced at Justinian's bare wrists, then held up his own, displaying the iron cuff. "At least you didn't make the same mistake I did."

As soon as the words were out, he saw the double meaning and felt the weight of his own guilt press down again.

"Perhaps not," Justinian agreed, "but I am bound nonetheless."

"To the Duc?"

Now he did laugh with genuine amusement. "That preening idiot? No. But there is another device that controls us."

"I don't understand."

"Nor did I expect you to. Few know of it." Justinian glanced at the cold hearth and flames erupted, driving back the dank chill of the underground chamber. "I have much to tell you, legatus."

"I am that man no longer," Lucius said, more harshly than he intended.

Justinian studied him in the frank way he had. "You were always the best of us, Claudius Quintus. A leader of unimpeachable courage and honor—"

"Stop, I beg you."

"If I had to do it all again, I would still follow you against Gaius's Praetorians," Justinian continued quietly. "Even knowing our bitter defeat was inevitable. There was no other choice."

His resigned tone was worse than anger or accusations. Lucius sank into a chair by the fire. "How long did you outlive me?" he asked in a whisper.

"Minutes. I died in one of the defensive trenches."

The legion had been called to a Danai settlement. It was still the early days of the daēva war, what become known later as the War of Sundering. They had expected to take hostages.

They failed to grasp the depths of their king's madness and hatred — not until they were ordered to burn two hundred women and children huddled in their homes.

General Quintus had refused. Incited his men to mutiny against the crown. For six long nights, the dwindling legion had held against wave after wave of Gaius's reinforcements. Long enough to buy time for the Danai to flee deeper into the forest.

It had ended with the surviving remnant encircled. A parley on the barren, charred ground around the village. A last chance to surrender.

Claudius Quintus had spat at Gaius's feet.

How young he had been. Just turned thirty and certain of his own judgment. Much like the Red Rogue.

"Some of us see you as a martyr," Justinian said. "I am one."

"A martyr? I accomplished nothing," Lucius retorted. "Except for the deaths of a thousand brave men!"

"You saved the lives of innocents," Justinian replied with a touch of impatience. "And Gaius was stopped eventually. But I am not here to debate the morality of battles a thousand years' past. I need your help."

Lucius looked up, shaking off his dark memories. "Then you will have it."

Justinian tossed his cloak to the other wing chair, putting his back to the fire. He wore a black doublet and breeches in the style of the Duc's court. It was strange not to see him in the padded tunic and ring mail of the cavalry, a crested helmet atop his head. Now his gaze settled on the iron band around Lucius's wrist.

"I will not ask what led you to enter Orlaith's service," he said. "But the talisman you wear is a petite menotte. A *small manacle*, in the tongue of the necromancer Jaskin Cazal." The name was uttered with quiet loathing. "It binds a single daēva. But he secretly forged another. The Grand Menotte."

Lucius blinked in surprise. "What does it do?"

"It holds the souls of one hundred daēvas. Mine included."

The implications landed like a gout of frigid water. "*What?*" Lucius shot to his feet. "How . . .?"

"I cannot tell you the *how*," Justinian said. "It has to do with our true names, of course. He discovered them and engraved them on this talisman. I imagine one hundred is all he could fit, else there would be more of us bound to it."

Lucius's thoughts scattered like pebbles on ice. The raw power bestowed on whoever wielded such a thing . . . He forced himself to focus.

"Jaskin Cazal is dead. So who has it?"

"No one at the moment, else I would feel them."

Even now, Lucius sensed Orlaith in a corner of his mind. As always, she was anxious and brooding.

"Yes," he murmured. "But I still don't understand. Did Jaskin ever wield this talisman?"

"Only once. It drove him mad." Justinian rubbed his hands as if he felt a draft, though the room had grown hot. "But you must hear my tale from the beginning." A dry chuckle. "Or perhaps, I should call it the end. After I died, I was met by Shepherds in the Dominion. Kaethe's hounds."

"I know them."

"I did not turn back for the gate and try to elude them, as some did."

Like me, Lucius thought.

Justinian avoided his gaze, focusing his attention on the hearth. "My soul was at peace, willing to make the passage to whatever lay beyond. The Shepherds led us to a black ship with black sails. We were halfway across the Cold Sea when the wind died. We drifted. I felt . . . a force. Pulling me back. Before I knew what was happening, I was climbing through a nine-pointed star at Castle Cazal."

A knot popped in the fire. Lucius waited, dread curdling the stolen blood in his veins.

"There were many daēvas already there, from all the clans, as confused and terrified as I was. Most had just suffered brutal deaths in the war. I think Jaskin did not truly understand what he had done. All those souls, clamoring for release. It . . . broke his mind. He used us for a time, but in the end, he did not want the power he had taken. So he rid himself of the Grand Menotte and took his own life."

"But you were not freed."

"From his service, yes, but not from the talisman. With no master, we found our way through Hellgate back into the Dominion." A deep bitterness entered Justinian's voice. "We tried to cross the Cold Sea again and found we could not. It was a miserable existence. Hunted by the Shepherds. Always fleeing, never able to flee far enough. But then one of us found a solution. There are isles in the Cold Sea beyond the reach of the hounds. Beyond even Kaethe's roving eye. It is there that we have made our home for the last thousand years."

Lucius gripped his head. "This is my fault—"

"No! Most of those he bound are not even from our legion." Justinian's eyes narrowed. "Unless you gave him our names?"

"No, I swear it."

"Then he learned them another way. Cazal traveled often in the Dominion, bending spirits to his will. It would be no difficult task for a necromancer. Not with so many newly dead streaming through the gates each day. But I am not finished with my tale, legatus."

Justinian smiled, the flames in his eyes dancing. "We found a Breaker. She is in our custody at this moment. If I bring the

Grand Menotte back with me, she can be made to destroy it forever." He glanced at the iron ring on Lucius's wrist. "And yours, as well."

"*You* have Nazafareen?"

Justinian's brows shot up. "You know her?"

Lucius gave a wondering laugh. "I've been searching for her for years. She is well?"

"She is alive. Then you will help me?"

"Of course! But where is the Grand Menotte?"

Justinian sank into a chair. Lucius joined him. "It has taken me an age of hunting, but I believe Jaskin Cazal gave it to the Sons of Bel for safekeeping. Why he trusted them, I cannot say. But his faith was well-placed, for not one of the priests has tried to use it over all the long centuries. However, if it fell into Duc Marcel's hands . . ."

"Or those of my own mistress," Lucius added. "They would be—"

"Unstoppable," Justinian finished. "Hardly short of a god on this earth."

"And if the talisman drives its wearer mad, we would be dealing with . . ."

"Another Gaius, yes."

Lucius was silent for a long moment. "It is why I agreed to the bargain with the Redvaynes," he admitted at last. "I wanted to come back and kill him myself."

"But they made you a slave instead." Justinian's mouth twisted. "That is the way of mortals. They are self-serving and treacherous."

"Not all of them," Lucius said, thinking of Castelio, who had carried him across the river. Of Delilah, who was half-human and had rescued him from the Courtenays' iron cage. They had both aided him with nothing to gain by it. He felt a stab of guilt, knowing she pined for her lost parents. But he didn't even know where Delilah had gone.

"If the Sons of Bel have this menotte, surely you can simply take it from them?" Lucius said.

"I already tried. I'm certain it was in the reliquary on that island fortress of theirs. But the cursed priest who ran the place must have been expecting me. He slit his own veins with an oyster knife before I could discover its whereabouts."

"You mounted a thorough search?"

"The Grand Menotte is kept within a box of cold iron to contain its power and prevent casual contact. Had it been inside the reliquary, I would have sensed it." He sighed. "And Kaethe has sent two of her mercenaries after me. A bonded human-daēva pair from the Old Empire. They are . . . formidable. The woman was hot on my trail. I had to flee the monastery." He punched his thigh in frustration. "But I do not think it was there. The priest must have given it to someone."

"Then it might still be here in Prydwen," Lucius said slowly.

"I pray it is so. But my movements are limited. The pair is watching. I was forced to shelter here in the palace."

"What did you tell the Duc?"

Justinian gave a feral grin. "That I would help him find this Red Rogue if he gives me an estate and title and slaves to abuse as I please. Terms a man like him would believe."

Lucius laughed. "Lord Justinian."

"Fah. As if I covet the trappings of mortal luxury." Justinian sobered. "All I want is for my soul to be free. I want to cross the Cold Sea, Claudius! It is my right!"

His sudden fury spilled over to the smoldering hearth. The flames leapt, scattering embers across the carpet. Lucius stomped them out before the blaze spread. The smell of burnt wool hung in the air.

"When that day comes," he said, "I will cross with you. But . . . would I be welcome among these fugitives?"

Justinian reached for his hand, gripping it tight. For a moment, Lucius lay on the battlefield, staring up at the soot-streaked sky, his most trusted cavalry commander kneeling in the mud at his side.

"If we bring back the Grand Menotte, we will be hailed as heroes," Justinian said.

Lucius had never seriously contemplated the possibility of redemption; only an end to his own suffering. But a return to the fold . . . a final way to serve his people. To make things right. It was his heart's secret wish, one he had never dared to examine until now.

"Time is running out," Justinian said. "Whoever has the Grand Menotte, it is no longer in safe hands. I could find myself bonded to a new master at any moment."

"But where to begin?"

"The priest who killed himself was named Brother Symeon. He might have given it to another priest, but if he were being careful, he would choose someone outside the order of Bel. I'm investigating all his contacts. Friends, relatives. If I find anyone promising, I will give you the name. Track them down and make them talk."

Lucius nodded. "What about this bonded pair?"

"As I said, they are dangerous." Justinian's tone turned dry. "Luckily for us, the Duc is so hated, his own people are endlessly trying to kill him. He fortified the palace with a new wall and extra patrols. So far, it's kept Kaethe's hunters out."

"And the Red Rogue?" Lucius leaned forward. "Do you know who he is?"

"Not a clue, but he is a thorn in the Duc's foot." A shrug. "I will do what I must to keep Marcel happy until we succeed in our mission."

"Of course," Lucius murmured.

He was about to say that he'd met the man just that afternoon, but something stopped him. A sense of honor he'd thought was dead and buried. The rebellion had nothing to do with the Grand Menotte. And despite his resolve to remain neutral, Lucius found he was sympathetic to their cause.

"I should go before the Duc suspects I've paid you a visit," Justinian said, rising. "But gods, it has been good to see you."

They embraced with a vow to meet in secret again. When he was gone, Lucius stood awhile, staring into the flames. The initial rush of euphoria was fading as the reality of his position sank in. He had told both Orlaith and the rebels that he would dispose of "Janus."

Little did he suspect it was the man he had known from childhood. The man who had fought at his side and willingly followed him to the grave. There was no possibility he would keep that promise now.

Which left him . . . where exactly?

Lucius rubbed his temples, lips curling in a pained smile. Strange, wasn't it? He had found a friend, yet never had he felt so alone.

NINETEEN

Cas hurried through the lower reaches of the palace, a bucket of steaming water in one hand. He wore the livery of a servant, thanks to Lip, though it had taken some persuading.

"You can't beat a mortifex," she'd said, crossing her arms. "Janus will kill you."

"I have a friend here," Cas said. "He might help us."

"What friend?"

"Orlaith's mortifex," he admitted.

Lip stared as if he'd sprouted a second head. "Why would a mortifex help you against one of his own kind?"

"Because he's not like the others. He helped me before, Lip."

"I don't want to be called that anymore. It's a little kid's name. I go by Felippa now."

"I'm sorry. *Felippa*." Cas grasped his train of thought. "The point is, I think he feels bad about what happened to you. When I tell him that Janus is the one who did it—"

"But what can he do? Janus is already dead."

The quiet despair in her voice broke Cas's heart.

"I know that, but there are ways to get rid of him. Maybe not forever, but for a while at least."

Cas had lain awake the previous night, Da's snores in his ear, thinking about the cistern that was really a portal to the Dominion. Together, he and Lucius could chop Janus's head off and throw him through the gate. Let the hounds find him.

Cas had laid out his plan, which he thought was fairly reasonable. Still, Lippa resisted for longer than he expected. She had a new self-assurance that was unnerving for a thirteen-year-old. He realized that in his absence, it was not Teo who had taken his place but Lip. She was more woman than girl now, gently managing their father, reminding Teo to plaster down his cowlick and clean his teeth. It made Cas both proud and sad. For her lost childhood, and for how much she reminded him of Ma.

He finally wore her down enough to find a spare servant's tunic so he could move about the palace. Shortly after, she learned that Lucius had ordered hot bathwater to be brought to his chamber. Now if Cas could only find it. The Duc's palace was even bigger than Orlaith's manor, and half of it sat underground.

"Sixth door on the right, second level down, south wing," he muttered, lugging the bucket along yet another long gallery with no windows. "Easy enough, if I knew where I was."

In truth, he wasn't certain Lucius would help. Not for free, at any rate.

I'll give him whatever he wants. Blood, nightmares, anything.

All the anger Cas had carried around since Esme was poisoned — and if he were being honest, since that night at the farm eight years ago — it had a focus now. With Gui's staff and Lucius at his side, Cas could finally pay the debt he owed to Janus. If it was his final service as a Quietus, so be it.

Cas spotted a page at a crossing corridor ahead. "Hoi!"

The boy turned.

"Which way to the south wing?"

"Back the way you came. Left at the buttery."

The page eyed him oddly. Cas muttered thanks and hurried off before the boy asked any questions. He found his way to the buttery, a large storeroom filled with oaken casks of all sizes, and was just turning leftward at the junction when Janus emerged from a room down the corridor.

The sixth on the right. Lucius's chamber. *That sanglant son of a—*

Cas ducked his head, but it was too late to hide. He moved over to give the mortifex plenty of room. Kept his gaze fixed on the stone floor and the Quietus tattoo hidden up his sleeve. The echo of boots came closer. Stopped. A waft of chill air raised gooseflesh on his arms.

"You."

He'd left his knives back in the room. His Kaethe's Tears, too.

"Milord?" he said hoarsely.

"Where are you going with that bucket? Look at me, boy."

Cas raised his head and met the mortifex's flaming gaze. A white scar crossed its face. He remembered swinging the iron hoe. The fex's hiss of agony as it struck home.

"I was told to fetch hot bathwater for the Ducissa Orlaith's envoy," Cas said.

Janus stared at him. A faint line creased his brow, then smoothed out. "Leave it outside his door. You'll escort me to my chambers."

"Aye, milord."

He deposited the bucket outside Lucius's room. His hands were shaking so badly, water slopped on the floor.

Does he not recognize me? Or is it a ruse to lure me away and murder me someplace quieter?

The reeve hadn't known him, and he'd been fifteen when he left Swanton. He was only twelve when Janus came to the farm. Cas looked up to see the mortifex waiting with a look of impatience.

"Coming, milord."

Cas jogged to catch up, keeping a pace behind.

"You're not from Prydwen. They don't say *aye* here."

"Aquitan, milord. I moved here as a boy."

Janus grunted and seemed to lose interest. But Cas's mind was spinning like a potter's flywheel. What was he doing with Lucius? Did they know each other? Had Lucius lied when he said he didn't recognize the mortifex from Cas's memory?

All his old mistrust came flooding back.

He took careful note of their surroundings, memorizing landmarks so he could find Janus's rooms again — assuming he was alive to leave them. Each torch they passed flared brighter in the mortifex's presence. Like calling to like, Gui once explained. Cas had never noticed it with Lucius, but maybe Janus was especially strong.

You know he is. He threw you across a fecking barn with a flick of his finger.

Finally, they entered a large solar with a massive cold fireplace dominating one wall. Arched doorways led to rooms beyond. Janus unclasped his cloak and tossed it over the back of a chair.

"Fetch my sword," he said. "And my riding boots need cleaning."

"Aye, milord."

Janus gave a brusque nod and disappeared through one of the archways.

Cas looked around. The bone-blade was propped in its scabbard against the wall next to the fireplace. A pair of muddy boots sat beside it; not the same ones as before. But the sword . . . yes, he remembered it well. Cas eyed it for a long moment. Had a brief fantasy of sliding it from its sheath, creeping into the next chamber, and . . .

Dying in a fiery whirlwind, no doubt.

He grabbed the boots and walked over to the table, keeping a close eye on the archway. Like the rest of the room, the table was covered in a fine layer of dust. The only semi-clean part had two piles of books. Cas gave them a cursory glance. All the titles were related to the history of Aveline and the Sons of Bel.

A slender volume bound in red leather caught his attention for two reasons. The oddly phrased title and the subject. It was called *The Lives and Deaths of Jaskin Cazal*.

Unease knotted his gut as he picked up the book. An edge of paper was sticking out between two of the leaves. He glanced again at the dark archway, then drew it out. It was folded into squares and speckled with brown droplets that looked like dried blood. He opened it and found a map of Cavet, with a ragged line that passed through a series of villages and led to the monastery of Bel Mara.

Where a priest had just been brutally murdered. Teo told him at breakfast. Everyone in the palace was talking about it—

Cas heard approaching footsteps. He quickly slid the map back into the book and grabbed the boots, making sure to keep the tattoo on his left hand hidden. Janus appeared in the doorway. He had changed from his doublet into a padded surcoat and quilted trousers.

"Pardon, my lord," Cas said apologetically, "but I couldn't find a brush and rag."

Janus jerked his chin. "Bucket in the corner."

Cas cleaned his boots, then buckled on his sword and fitted him with chainmail, greaves, and gauntlets. He had watched the Ducissa's soldiers in Aquitan do it a hundred times. His hands moved on their own, fastening buckles and lacings, his thoughts elsewhere, but Janus seemed pleased with the result.

"I need a manservant," he said. "You will serve for now."

Cas forced a smile. "Aye, milord."

"What's your name?"

"Castelio."

Janus clapped him on the shoulder. "Come, you can ready my horse."

A short time later, Cas stood outside the stables, watching Janus ride off with four dozen of the Duc's soldiers. The mortifex seemed tense, his gaze constantly flicking to the wall around the grounds. Cas had no idea where they going. A servant wouldn't ask. But his own revenge would have to wait.

Jaskin Cazal.

It could be a coincidence that Lo was sent here by Nathan Ouvrard, Jaskin's last living heir, but he doubted it. Something was afoot. Something bad. That blood-speckled map . . .

"I have to find her," he muttered.

"Find who?" Teo asked, coming up from behind. "And why were you helping that piece of flaming shite mount his horse?"

Cas turned. "I'm Janus's manservant now."

They looked at each other for a long moment. Then Teo started to laugh, and Cas couldn't help himself. All the nerve-jangling tension he'd held inside erupted in dark mirth. Their guffaws startled a white cat sunning itself on some loose bits of straw. It leapt up, shot them an irritated look, and strolled away with its tail in the air.

Cas's laughter faded. An idea was forming in his mind.

Lo could be anywhere in the teeming city of Prydwen. He might search for twenty years and never find her. But maybe . .
.

Maybe he could find someone else.

TWENTY

L ike the Shambles, the wealthy district of Rosnamore was criss-crossed with serpentine canals, yet the two places could not have been more different. These waterways had stone footbridges and smelled of seawater rather than sewage. Elegant stone mansions lined the streets above — proper paved streets filled with curtained palanquins borne by muscular bearers.

In a feature unique to Prydwen, the mansions all had several floors set below ground level where it was cooler. The entrances could be accessed from the streets above, or from broad stone landings in the canals themselves. Lucius sat in a poled boat, a white sailcloth fluttering above, and watched the well-dressed mortals sitting on their shaded terraces. Servants catered to their every whim, uncorking bottles of wine, setting out platters of fruit and cheese and smoked fish. A genteel hubbub of laughter and conversation filled the air. Other pleasure craft glided along (no fishing boats or flimsy canoes here), under the watchful eyes of hired guards stationed at the bridges.

Rosnamore sat across the bay from the Shambles on the same spit of land that held the Ducal Palace, perhaps two leagues in a straight line from the stilt hovels where their servants lived. They imagined themselves to be safe from the unwashed rabble.

Good luck to you, Lucius thought, *the day they rise up*.

He hadn't fed since draining the two soldiers and the chill was beginning in his core. Not a full-blown reversion to death. Not yet. But the sunlight hurt his eyes, pricked his skin. The gently undulating water of the canal made him queasy.

Well, those were the least of his problems.

He should be thinking about how to find this Grand Menotte. About what he would tell Orlaith when she asked if he had disposed of the Duc's mortifex. About how he would handle the Red Rogue when they met again.

He should be thinking about how he would feed next. *Who* he would feed upon.

Lucius wanted to do none of those things. What he wanted at this moment was to feel alive. To hold onto the man he had been for just a little while longer. After Justinian left, his thoughts had spun for hours, digging deep ruts that led nowhere. The same old guilt and recriminations. How wearying it all was.

What he wanted was a distraction.

Lucius saw the grand structure rising up in the distance. It sat at the juncture of four canals, an ornately carved square temple capped by a nude statue of Bel. Not nearly as big as the island monastery, but this temple did not cater to the sick and dying. This one catered to the rich and horny.

It wasn't his money, of course, but the thought of spending some of Orlaith's gold on a holy prostitute was too delicious to pass up. Lucius happened to know that she disliked the priests, devoting herself to Kaethe, which made it even more appealing.

The poleman steered over to the crowded landing and expertly wedged the boat between two others, both well-appointed private vessels awaiting the return of their owners. Lucius paid the fare and disembarked, moving quickly through the throngs to the shade of the temple's wide entrance. No one looked at him oddly. He still had a human appearance, at least.

Several good-looking priests stood on the steps, next to bronze kettles brimming with coins. They probably put the pretty ones outside, Lucius thought cynically, to lure in customers, the way a fishmonger displays the morning's catch on ice and keeps yesterday's riper goods in the back. He tossed six gold coronets into the kettle, earning a dazzling smile and blessing from a young priest, who nodded him through the doors.

The antechamber had the usual soaring pillars, each as wide as four men standing abreast, with braziers sending clouds of incense into the air. Lines of people wound among them like ants on the trail of honey. No one approached to explain what happened next. It had an air of cheerful chaos, with knots of men and women socializing, others praying before well-endowed statues, and the occasional brief dispute as someone tried to cut a line. Priests mingled with the devotees, some young, some older. The actual rooms where the transactions concluded were somewhere else, likely at the end of the lines.

Lucius chose one at random, wondering how long it would take. He knew a little about their doctrine. Copulation inside the temple was considered a union with the god himself. A brief joining of souls and purging of sins. Of course, it also happened to make the Sons of Bel very rich.

The line shuffled forward. He caught snippets of conversation around him, all of it banal. The outrageously high cost of silk these days, and when would it rain again, the heat was unbearable. Did you hear about Lord X's new mistress? He wrote her an awful love sonnet and his wife found it! Have you tried the iced cakes at the new bakery on Gannet Street? Well, don't, darling, they won't help your waistline.

Lucius thought of the scrawny children from the day before and found his enthusiasm waning. What was he doing here? None of the priests he'd seen sparked any interest. A shiver rippled through him from a place deep inside. He fought down a sudden impulse to tear someone's throat out. The tall gentleman in front of him, perhaps, with his oiled, perfumed beard and smarmy half-smile. Or the pair of ladies tittering behind their hands and whispering together at they stared at something behind him.

Lucius turned to leave and found his mouth going dry.

A priest had just come through the doors. Bronzed skin and hair as black as True Night, cut to the nape with a single stripe shaved above his left ear. Broad shoulders and muscled calves. Every eye turned as he walked through the crowd, which parted like water before him. He didn't seem to notice. His brows were furrowed in thought, his gaze distant.

"Who's that?" Lucius heard himself ask in a hoarse voice.

Oiled Beard laughed and gave him a languorous once-over. "You won't have that one, my friend."

"Why not?"

"Brother Brennos isn't available. Not for us, at any rate. Some claim he is Bel come down in mortal flesh. Don't you see how closely he resembles the god? The spitting image."

Lucius hadn't, but the statues were cold and white, with sightless eyes. As far as one could imagine from this living, breathing, gloriously perfect man.

One of the women heaved a wistful sigh. "They say he's endowed with *all* the god's bountiful qualities."

Lucius watched the priest approach with mingled longing and resentment. Well, now his plan was thoroughly ruined. If he couldn't have *that* one, what was the point? Six gold coronets, straight down the gutter. He stepped out of line, tearing his eyes away, and was turning for the doors when a hand gripped his wrist.

Oiled Beard, no doubt, urging him to stay and have a threesome. Lucius was about to jerk away when he looked up and met a pair of onyx eyes. The priest said nothing, but the heat in his gaze was clear. How long they stood there, Lucius couldn't say. He was too dumbfounded. At last, Brother Brennos released his wrist and walked away. Lucius gaped after him. After a moment, the priest stopped and looked back. One brow lifted slightly in invitation. *Are you coming or not?*

"You lucky bastard," Oiled Beard muttered in a low, angry voice. "I never . . ."

Lucius didn't hear the rest. It was drowned out by the thunder of his heartbeat. And who knew how much longer that would last?

Envious murmurs chased them to the doors at the end, and then he was following the priest up flights of stairs, the surroundings a blur. The chamber they entered was small and clearly the place where he lived, not an anonymous love nest. It smelled of him, for one thing, and his spare clothes — the dark, pleated skirts and white tunics with red sashes — were lying about, some dirty in a wicker hamper, others folded and waiting to be put away. There were pink seashells on the windowsill, alongside carved tokens to the god. A single cot was pushed against the wall.

Brennos sat down on it, forearms resting on his knees, and regarded Lucius with a frank gaze. The silence stretched out. Lucius began to feel unspeakably awkward. Like a cheap, graceless intruder. He had no idea what he'd done to be singled out. He wasn't terrible to look at, but surely there were more handsome men below if that was the criterion. Or, and this made him bite his lip against a bark of slightly hysterical laughter, Brennos really was Bel reborn and could see how much his soul needed purging of sin.

"You don't have to please me," he said at last. "Just tell me what you—"

The priest reached him in three strides. He shook his head and touched Lucius's mouth. Then he withdrew his hand, though the imprint of his touch remained.

All right. No talking.

Lucius saw kindness in his eyes, and curiosity, and the warmth of genuine desire. As Brennos undressed, revealing flawless skin and muscle dusted with wiry black hair, Lucius wondered if he even remembered how to do this anymore.

Then their bodies pressed together. Their lips met. He curled his fingers into the silky hair at the priest's nape. The last remnant of ice at his core vanished in a sudden contraction of heat.

And Lucius decided that he did indeed.

TWENTY-ONE

L o woke up with a pounding head and stuffy nose. She'd been too tired to return to the *Wind-Witch*, so Achaemenes had borrowed another hammock from the family who owned the stilt house.

"Girl, you look like warmed-over camel dung," Tijah remarked. She was sitting on the floor, oiling a long iron chain.

Lo squinted, the bright sun stabbing her eyeballs. "Where's Thistle?"

Tijah shrugged. "Roaming. Want something to eat?"

"Privy first."

It was a sort of hut next to the house. To her dismay, it emptied straight into the canal. *No wonder I caught the plague,* she thought as she hoisted up her trousers. *That could cost me one more life right there.*

By the time she crawled back up the stairs, Tijah had brought bowls of rice with clams and shrimp. Lo had no appetite, but she made an effort to get some down. It might have been delicious or terrible; she couldn't taste a thing.

"When did you come to Prydwen?" she asked.

"About a month ago. Janus went through a gate and the Drowned Lady sensed the ripples of his passage. She called us in." Tijah shook her head. "The way they treat people here . . . And I thought *my* world was tough."

"What about Nocturne? That's where I come from." Lo thought of her foster parents, Javid and Katsu. How worried they must be. "Have you been there?"

"No, though I heard about it from your mother." Tijah ate a bite of rice. "There are many mirror worlds, with portals between them. Some things are the same, others are different."

"Like the necromancers," Lo said.

Her gaze went flat. "Like them."

"What about Kaethe?" Lo eyed a wooden figurine with the head of a falcon that Tijah kept next to her hammock. "Is that her?"

Tijah shook her head. "That is Innunu, one of the old gods of Al Miraj. Achaemenes claims they are likely the same deity, but Innunu is the goddess of death in battle. Of sacrifice for a higher cause. She is not the Drowned Woman." A shadow crossed Tijah's face. "*Her*, I have met myself."

Lo leaned forward, intrigued. "What does Kaethe look like?"

"Pale. Creepy as all hells, until you get to know her."

"And then?"

"She's terrifying." Tijah laughed. "Kaethe claims she doesn't interfere in worldly affairs, but she breaks the rule when it suits her purposes — like sending us after this mortifex. There's a bunch of them who won't cross the Cold Sea. They're hiding out somewhere."

Lo poked at her food. "Are my parents actually pirates, or did I dream that part?"

"Not a dream." Tijah shelled a shrimp and popped it into

her mouth. "Apparently, they're pretty good at it. Kaethe's been getting a lot of complaints."

Lo's thoughts felt muddy. "But . . . what do the dead have to steal?"

"Believe it or not, some of them do wear jewelry and such. If they were buried with it." Tijah peeled another shrimp. "Don't ask me this shit. I know it's weird. I think Magnus is just mad about something. Or maybe he'd doing it for the fun of it."

"Then we should search the Cold Sea, right?"

Tijah gave her a level look. "You think we haven't tried? It's vast. Full of islands. Pirates' paradise. Achaemenes and I spent the last year sailing around that salty bitch and came up empty." She turned toward the stairs a few seconds before Lo heard footsteps. "Let's see what he found out."

Her partner slipped inside and pushed his hood back; his face looked grim. "Everyone's talking about the murder at the monastery. There's a bounty on all our heads but no mention of any missing relic."

Tijah sighed. "Okay, so we have two problems to solve. How to lure Janus out of the palace. And figuring out who has the box, if it isn't him. Any ideas?"

No one spoke. Then Lo tentatively raised a hand.

"Nathan wanted me to reanimate the dead priest and ask him about—" Her tongue did something strange and the word came out sounding like *zingabob*. She cleared her throat. "You know."

"That's fucking horrible," Tijah said. A slight pause. "Do you think it would work?"

"Well . . ."

A distant scream drifted through the windows, followed by splintering wood. Frenzied barking erupted below. Tijah and

187

Achaemenes hurried to the side overlooking the canal. Lo dragged herself to stand and followed.

Soldiers were swarming through the Shambles. Not a dozen this time. They were everywhere. Pulling people from their homes, smashing up the flimsy canoes with axes.

"Are they looking for us?" Lo asked with a pang of guilt.

"Maybe," Tijah muttered. "But I've seen this happen a lot. Not quite as bad though."

"The ones getting the worst of it have red pennants," Achaemenes said, his voice tight. "It's a sign of sympathy for those who oppose the Duc."

Lo leaned over the sill for a better look. She recognized the family who owned the stilt house. The girl held the squirming white dog in her arms. Their mother was trying to shoo them all back inside.

"Shit," Tijah hissed. "It's him!"

Lo looked up just as her left arm started to tingle. A mailed figure galloped along the docks on a midnight black horse. He raised his hand and a fireball engulfed one of the stilt houses.

Janus.

Tijah and Achaemenes wordlessly spun into action. Tijah belted her sword on and coiled the iron chain, hanging it over one shoulder. Achaemenes grabbed his own iron blade. In an instant, they were pelting down the stairs.

Six houses were ablaze now. People were running and screaming, many leaping into the canals. Others held their ground. Men and women both, all wearing red bandanas over their faces, who fought with the Duc's soldiers.

A wave of dizziness took Lo, and she braced a hand on the sill.

I could stop him. I could open a gate and send him through. Save countless lives.

And never learn where my parents are.

She bit her lip hard enough to taste blood. Something took her, a reckless urge to hurt him, and she flicked the horse's rump with a bee-sting of air. It reared up. Janus kept his seat, but his head snapped in her direction. Their eyes locked. Then he flung a fireball at the stilt house.

It roared toward her with a whoosh. Lo dove to the floor. She felt a tremor run through the boards. A wrenching shift to the side. Her skin prickled all over, but there was no fire in the loft. Not yet. It must have arced downward at the last moment. The house shifted again, the timbers groaning. Black smoke filled the room. She crawled down the stairs, coughing. The second floor was ablaze.

"Hello?" she cried.

Thank the gods, no one answered. They must have gotten out. She flung an arm up and started down the last flight, when a low whimper stopped her in her tracks. Through an acrid gray haze, Lo saw the white dog. It was backed into a corner, under a table. The tail thumped pathetically when it saw her.

Flames were licking up the walls. One had already fallen in, and the roof must be seconds from collapsing. She ducked her head and ran forward, groping blindly through the smoke.

"Come on, boy," she coaxed, her throat raw. "Come on out. . ."

The heat was withering. Then her fingers brushed a rough coat. Lo grabbed him to her breast and raced blindly down the last flight of stairs seconds before the whole structure tumbled down. The girl ran up, tears streaking her sooty face.

"I told you, Mama," she called out behind her. "He *didn't* run off!"

Despite the chaos all around, the family was still huddled a short distance away. Lo's chest tightened as she handed over the dog. They wouldn't leave him — or, judging by the mother's exasperated expression, the girl wouldn't. She nodded thanks and ran to her family, who quickly climbed into a waiting boat and paddled for the marsh.

The main fighting seemed to have moved away, probably because the houses and docks were on fire. The shattered remains of crockery, barrels, and boats lay everywhere. And bodies, too. Most wore red. Hot ash drifted on the wind.

Then Lo heard the faint clash of blades. She picked her way through the smoldering wreckage. Her head felt odd, as though it floated above her body.

A minute later, she saw Tijah and Achaemenes. They'd managed to unhorse the mortifex and were driving him back toward one of the canals. He wielded a flaming sword with one hand, the other streaking fire at them, but Tijah's curved blade absorbed it like water sinking into sand.

When Lo was young, Mama had tried to describe what it was like to see a bonded pair fight together. The perfect synchronicity of their attack. Two swords, one mind. Watching Tijah and Achaemenes, Lo finally grasped just how deadly a human-daēva pair could be. In one fluid movement, Tijah uncoiled the iron chain from her shoulder, holding the links loosely in her hand. Janus's lips pulled back into a snarl. Achaemenes ducked a lunge and circled behind him as Tijah's arm came back to loose the chain.

They've got you now, Lo thought with grim satisfaction.

Then Tijah stumbled, a black-fletched arrow jutting through the meat of her thigh. She sank to one knee. Janus raised his flaming blade. Achaemenes moved so fast he blurred, his sword parrying the killing blow.

Lo spotted the archer in the window of the only stilt house that hadn't burned. She gathered her wits. *Focused.* A gust drove smoke into the archer's eyes. Janus seized his chance to start backing away.

"Take him!" Tijah screamed, thrusting the chain at Achaemenes.

The Duc's soldiers were coming now, half of them mounted. Achaemenes threw a baleful look at Janus, then scooped Tijah into his arms. She was cursing him roundly, but he paid her no mind. He sprinted down the sandy path along the edge of the canal. The soldiers gave chase.

Janus, the coward, grabbed the bridle of a horse, yanked its rider from the saddle, and galloped off in the opposite direction.

Lo tried to find the Nexus again, to help her friends somehow, but she could no longer sense the place of stillness. Only an achy chill that inhabited her bones. She sank down on a piling. She ought to walk back to the *Wind-Witch*. Sort out what to do before she got arrested. But it all seemed too much effort.

After a time, boats appeared. They carried women in white with shaved heads. The women moved like pale ghosts among the dead. Some of the bodies were starting to twitch, but the women did something to make them stop. Two approached her with long sticks shod with iron at the tip. One was tall and weathered, the other plump and pretty. The tall one pressed the end of the stick to Lo's bare arm.

"What are you doing?" Lo asked. It felt like a strange dream.

The woman's face relaxed. She turned to the others. "Living!" she called.

"Who are you?"

"Nuns of Kaethe. You should go home, child." She looked around at the charred husks. "Or wherever they'll take you in."

The women dragged the bodies to the boats and paddled away.

How long she sat there, Lo wasn't sure. It could have been

minutes or hours. Then someone was coming towards her through the drifting smoke. At first, she thought it was the onions — funny word, that, for such ruthless men — because he wore a tunic of silver and gold. A moment later, she noticed the fat gray cat waddling along at his side. Thistle wouldn't associate with an onion.

Now he was running. Strong arms caught her as she started to slide off the piling. A face swam into focus, dark brows drawn together with a worried look.

Lo smiled. "Hello, Sleepy Eyes," she said.

TWENTY-TWO

Castelio carried Delilah to the *Wind-Witch*. She felt too light, as if she hadn't been eating. He was deeply relieved to find her, but she was burning with fever. Delirious. He kept thinking of Ma. Of Esme.

"Quit crying," she murmured in his arms. "Just quit! You're ruining the game . . ."

Whether she spoke to herself or someone else, he couldn't say. But he was terrified.

Thistle led him to the ship, which was moored not far off in the Docklands. Cas hadn't realized that the *Wind-Witch* could also sail on water, though it made sense. He'd first encountered the vessel floating in the emperor's pond in Tjanjin.

Of course she wouldn't just fly into Prydwen, he thought. *The docks is the first place I should have looked.*

At least the demonic creature Thistle — true name Chelithoth — had answered his summons. Not immediately, but the cat must have decided that his mistress needed help. On the way to the Shambles, the cat had related all that happened since they arrived, including the details of her pact with Nathan Ouvrard. Cas understood now why she hadn't told him the truth. It was worse than he imagined. Far worse.

Lo would die in less than a week if she didn't find this box. He was furious at Nathan Ouvrard for putting her in this position, but there was nothing he could do about that, so Cas pushed it out of his mind for now.

Two men were guarding the pier, but they recognized Lo and let Cas through.

"She need a healer?" one asked. "My aunt knows herbs."

"I do, too," Cas assured him. "We'll be fine, but thank you."

Of course, he had something better. Her talisman. It had brought him back from the brink of death. Surely it would cure her fever. He'd already returned it, hanging the silver disk around her neck. He hoped that would be enough.

Cas managed to get her down the ladder and lay her on the bunk. She'd rigged up makeshift blinds to keep out the sun. It was dim in the cabin, but not so dark he couldn't see her flushed cheeks and dry, cracked lips. He dipped a cloth in one of the water barrels and draped it across her forehead. Then he brewed some tea and put an arm around her shoulders, lifting her up. She managed a few sips and lapsed into delirium again. Thistle sat on her desk, watching them.

"When will the disk start working?" Cas asked.

"It should have already."

"What do you mean? Is there something more I must do?"

The cat didn't reply.

"If so, tell me!" he pleaded. "Whatever it is, I don't care. How do I make it work?"

"You have done all you could." Thistle's voice was subdued, a scratchy whisper. The cat leapt down and walked away.

Cas took her hand. It was frozen. He piled as many blankets as he could find on top of the bunk. Made her take some more sips of hot tea. She was shaking, convulsive shivers that rippled through her thin frame. More ominously, the delirious muttering stopped. She lay still except for the occasional bone-deep shudder.

"Feck!" He pulled his servant's tunic off and climbed under the covers, drawing her close. Parts of her felt hot, others freezing. She burrowed her face into the crook of his neck, flinging one arm across his bare chest. Slowly, her body relaxed.

Cas stroked her hair. Kissed the top of her head. "You'll be just fine tomorrow," he whispered. "After we find this box and give it back to Nathan, I'll throw him into the fecking chasm, Vigo be damned."

The weak grunt of agreement made him smile.

His thoughts whirled for a while, thinking about the box and the mercenaries that Thistle said Lo had fallen in with. The bloody map he'd found in Janus's room. Lucius's treachery. It all tied up somehow — and the picture wasn't a pretty one.

At last, Lo's breathing grew deep and even. He touched her brow. It was clammy with sweat. The fever had broken.

I should get up, he thought. *Put my clothes on and sleep in one of the empty cabins. She might be less than delighted to find a half-naked man in her bed when her head clears.*

But Lo felt nice in his arms. Like she belonged there. Cas's lips twitched in amusement. Sleepy Eyes, she'd called him.

"I have no oaths to keep me from you," he said softly. "Not anymore."

She murmured something, then rolled over and wedged a knee between his thighs, nestling closer. Cas stared into the semi-darkness of the cabin, trying to still his racing heart.

Think about mortifexes. Or those hounds of Kaethe nipping at your heels.

Still, it was a long while before he finally drifted off.

HE WOKE to find Lo gone. Cas found his cami and was lacing it up when she came back. Her hair hung wet over one shoulder and she wore a fresh jacket and trousers. Purplish bruises still lurked under her eyes, but they were clear. Like the shallows of a summer sea.

They stared at each other for a moment. Then she thrust a cup at him, rather violently. "Tea?"

Her hand was none too steady and the hot liquid splattered his wrist as he took it.

"Oh! I burned you, didn't I?" she said with a stricken expression.

He wiped his smarting hand on his trousers. "Not a bit." Cas cleared his throat. "Feeling better, I see."

She nodded, wary. Something was off. The woman he remembered always kept a level head, even in trying situations. He'd never seen her so unsettled.

"Look," he said, setting the tea down on the floor to lace up his own cami. "I only climbed in there because you were shaking like a wind-blown aspen. I—"

Lo waved a hand dismissively. "That's not it." She blew on her own mug, eyes darting around the room. "I . . . You talked to Thistle."

"That's right." He frowned. "You don't think I'm angry at you? Because I'm not. You did what you thought you had to. All of this is Nathan's fault."

"Yes," she said. "Well." Lo sank down on the edge of the bed. "He didn't tell you everything."

"There's more?"

"Quite a bit more," she said with a smile that held no trace of humor.

He nodded slowly. How much worse could this get? "Tell me if you want to. But only if you want to. I'll help you regardless."

She gazed at him. It was hard to read her expression. "I won't hold you to that, Cas. But you deserve to hear everything." She seemed to gather herself. "I think the best place to start might be on the bridge at Nox. It's true that my talisman saved you from the arrow wound. But that was only half our problems. The dead rose from the lichyard. They came to the bridge. I scattered some of your iron nails and it held them off for a little while."

Her voice grew steadier as she spoke. As if it were a relief to unburden herself.

"The dead?" he said. "I don't remember that."

"You were too far gone. After I lowered Enrigo into the river, the dead broke through. A great horde of them. Lucius had vanished. It was just you and me left."

He stared at her. "What happened, Lo?"

"They were coming. And they were saying something in tongues. Over and over. *Sarg erish'kigal.*"

"Shadow soul," Cas translated softly. "Do you know what it meant?"

"Not what. *Who.*" She held his eyes. "I was so scared. So angry. You were dying in front of me and they were coming for us and . . . something welled up inside me, like a . . . a black wind, and I made a gate and I threw them all inside."

He blinked in shock. "You made a *gate?*"

Lo nodded. "I'd been feeling strange ever since I first saw Lucius." She absently rubbed her left arm. "I sense the dead when they're near. Like a cold tingle. I didn't know what it meant, then. But I felt it strongly at Midgate." Guilt seeped into her voice. "Nathan said he had nothing to do with the spirits who broke through and killed all those soldiers. That I attracted them—"

Anger bubbled up. "Feck Nathan Ouvrard! He's a liar."

Lo eyed him sadly. "He's not. I am a Shadow Soul, Cas." She lifted the talisman from around her neck, cradling it in her palm. "The only thing holding my power in check was this. It's why I was able to banish the dead at Nox. I'd given the disk to you."

Cas tried to make sense of it. "So . . . you're like a Quietus. Only a lot stronger."

"A bit," she said. "Nathan claims it is a gift from Kaethe. He said the Drowned Lady's number is nine, and that's why she's given me nine lives."

"Shite, really?" The tea had gone lukewarm but he drained it in a gulp, wishing he had something stronger.

"The lich did kill me," Lo said ruefully. "Probably those lightning strikes too." She held up her forearms. Above the feathery, branching scars, Cas glimpsed the fading brand of her pact with Nathan. A Hand Sinister with flames dancing above the fingertips. "I've surely frittered some lives away crashing my ship, too," she added.

"I've never heard of such a thing," Cas said in wonder. "It must be rare."

"Jaskin Cazal was a Shadow Soul. So I'm not the only one ever."

Jaskin again. He seemed to be at the heart of this whole tangled mess. Cas remembered the odd title of the book he'd found in the mortifex's chamber. *The Lives and Deaths of Jaskin Cazal.* Now it made more sense.

"How do *you* feel about it?" Cas asked.

Lo wiggled her bare toes, studying them with a distracted frown. "Well, I'm not as scared of dying as I used to be. That's one thing. I must have a life or two left. I mean, I hope I do." She looked up at him and grinned. "Because this box is in the feckin' wind."

She imitated his accent with startling accuracy, but Cas didn't smile back. "How can you not know, Lo?"

"I've had some bad crashes."

"How many?"

"Lost count."

He rubbed his forehead. "Let's not test it, then."

Lo pulled her sleeves down, her tone brisk. "I'm not quite done."

Cas started to laugh. It just happened, and once it started, there was no going back.

"What's so funny?" Lo demanded, but she was laughing a little, too.

"I just can't see how you'll manage to top the last one."

"Oh, I think I can." Her good humor faded. "I'm half daēva. My father, Darius, is from the Danai clan. My mother is a mortal."

Cas shook his head, laughing even harder now. "You're not."

Her gaze focused. He felt a sudden force gather around him, gently squeezing. Lo's brows drew down in concentration. Then she let out a sigh. The force popped with a little rush of air.

"I can't budge you. You're too heavy, and I've never been strong in air. But you felt that, didn't you?"

He nodded, dumbfounded.

"So I am both one of those scary wolves you mentioned," she said, "and a Shadow Soul with death powers I barely understand. If that's not enough to put you off, I'm not sure what is."

Her tone was light, but he sensed a sudden vulnerability.

Cas realized that *this* is what she had feared telling him the most.

"Wolves?" he echoed.

"You told me that Lucius was a wolf on a leash," she reminded him flatly. "And then you asked me in the coach if all the demons in my land were dead. You said Lucius was scary enough, and you couldn't even imagine a live one."

Cas cleared his throat. "I'll admit I was raised on tales about the old days. But all that was what? A thousand years ago? You could have just told me. I wouldn't have run."

"No?"

"Feck no." He slid closer. "Look, hardly anything I've believed for the last . . . oh, eight years or so turned out to be true. I expect your people are like mine. Good ones, bad ones."

"Jaskin went mad." She chewed a nail. "What if I go mad?"

"Then we'll deal with that when the time comes. But you won't go mad, Lo. Or any worse than you are already."

She swatted his arm.

"Ow." He could smell her hair, a fresh, minty scent. "I'm sorry I gave offense. So your mother is mortal?"

Lo nodded.

"I didn't even know we could have children with daēvas."

Her cheeks pinked slightly. "Yep."

"And you have powers like Lucius?"

"Not nearly as strong," she confessed, "or you would never have managed to take the *Wind-Witch*."

His gaze narrowed. "But you did try to knock me down with magic, didn't you? I knew it!"

Lo chuckled. "Your face. It was priceless."

"Hmmm. And those supposed traders we ran into . . ."

"Daēvas," she said. "They feared that your Ducissa Orlaith would try to enslave them."

"I serve her no longer, Lo. I know what she did."

Cas saw sympathy in her face. And regret. "Nathan admitted the plot to me," Lo said. "I was going to tell you, *of course* I was. But Nathan said you wouldn't have believed me, and that if you said anything to Orlaith about it, she'd try to kill you. I'm so sorry, Cas."

"You were right," he said. "I wouldn't have believed you. And when I found out, she did try to murder me."

"What?" Lo leaned closer, eyes wide.

"Except that I was wearing your talisman. So I survived." He looked away. "The friend who brought the poisoned wine didn't fare so well."

"Oh no. No. Oh, Cas."

"Her name was Esme. One of the chambermaids." He thought of the light brush of her soul as it took flight. The things she'd said. "I'd rather not talk about it."

"No, of course. She was your . . . were you close?"

"Like a sister."

"I see." Lo tentatively reached for his hand. Cas wound his fingers with hers. A jolt of warmth ran through him. Part of him wanted to pull away, but it was just his own guilt, and that never brought anyone back that he'd heard of.

"So you left," Lo said.

"I fled," he clarified. "Ahead of an arrest warrant. Esme died in my chamber, you see. Everyone thinks I killed her."

Lo's jaw went hard. "Orlaith won't get away with it."

"She already has," he replied wearily. "Lucius helped me escape. I thought he'd changed. But the mortifex who killed my Ma is at the Duc's palace. His name is—"

"Janus," Lo finished tightly. "He serves Magnus. The one who has my parents."

"Sanglant bastard," Cas muttered. "He's brought us both grief." He was silent for a moment. "I became a Quietus so I could try to fix my worst mistake. Banishing the dead . . . it felt like sweeping away the past, over and over again. But we can't ever undo them, can we? The things we've done."

Lo nodded, though he could see she didn't quite understand. Only Teo knew about the vial of Kaethe's Tears he'd broken. The vial he might have used to stop the mortifex before it drained his little sister. Teo had never mentioned it once. He didn't have to.

"Cas," she said gently. "I think you became a Quietus because it's who you are. You're strong *and* kind. A rare combination. Now, I haven't a clue why Kaethe gave me this power, but there must be a reason. It's the same for you."

"Maybe we should ask her ourselves," he said, half-joking.

"That's a good idea," Lo said seriously. "I think we should. After we do something about Janus."

"As to that," Cas ventured, "believe it or not, he made me his manservant. I've been to his chamber at the palace."

"Did you see the box?" she asked eagerly.

"No, but it could be there. I've only been inside once."

Distant bells began to toll. Cas counted and uttered a soft oath. "It's six bells," he said regretfully, standing up. He walked to the porthole and peered through a gap in the blanket. "I had Teo cover for me, said I had the flux, but I can't be gone too long. Janus will come looking. And I'm not leaving Lippa alone with that monster roaming the palace."

"I'll go with you," Lo said at once.

"Aren't you wanted for the priest's murder?"

"Oh, that. I mean, yes. But I'll wear a manty."

He eyed her askance. "Are you still feverish? Because it's a shite idea."

Lo looked confused. "Why is it a shite idea?"

"Because they have your description, and there aren't that many young women with eyes your shade of blue around here.

Besides which, it's near impossible to get past the Duc's guards. And what would you do, anyway?"

"Go search Janus's chamber. If he turns up, I'll threaten to toss him into a gate."

Cas nodded slowly. "Right. And while you're threatening him, he'll burn us both alive. You see the problem?"

Her brows quirked. "But—"

"Shite idea," Cas said again. "Though I do appreciate the offer. Let me search Janus's rooms. Just give me one more day before you go off half-cocked, all right?"

"I have four left, Cas. It takes three to fly to Castle Cazal."

Her tone was not despairing. No, it was sunny and carefree. Shadow Soul had a grim ring to it, but Lo seemed blithely indifferent to her fate. Cas tried not to worry.

"We'll find this box," he said. "We will bring it to Nathan Ouvrard and he will fulfill his end of the bargain. And then we'll find your parents."

She stood up and came over. A smile played on her lips. "We will?"

"Aye," he said firmly.

Lo still held the talisman in her hand. She stepped up so they were eye to eye and hung it around his neck.

"I don't need this anymore," she said, so close he felt the warm tickle of her breath. "You should keep it."

Then they were kissing, and he completely forgot that anything was wrong with her because she felt so good, and he'd been dying to kiss her for so long. Cas cupped her face, running his thumbs along the sharp blades of her cheekbones. She tipped her head back, gripping his shoulders. The kiss deepened. She tasted like honeyed black tea, sweet and bitter at the same time. They fell sideways on the bed and she pulled his shirt free of his breeches, running warm hands up his chest. It took all his strength to catch her wrists and pull back, breathing hard.

"I can't."

She arched a brow and reached for him again. "Oh, I think you can."

"Bel save me, I want you more than anything," he said, his voice thick. "But if I'm not back soon, I daren't go back at all, and then we're screwed if Janus has the box."

His head was so muddled, he wasn't even sure the words came out in the right order.

She sighed. "I see that."

Cas pulled her close and kissed her again. It was delicious torment. "Besides which, I don't want a fifteen minutes under the clothes sort of tryst with you."

Now Lo laughed. "I'd take what I could get." She patted his rump. "But yes, later."

He kissed her palm. They would have time. Years. A lifetime, maybe. He would make sure of it.

"Stay out of trouble," he warned, pulling his boots on. "I'll be back soon."

Lo grinned. "Aye, Sleepy Eyes."

TWENTY-THREE

L ucius walked along the floating dock, a sick sensation in his gut. The stink of charred wood hung in the air, so strong even the sea wind couldn't whisk it away. Here and there, dried blood stained the wooden boards. The devastation was even worse than he'd feared. Water barrels smashed, boats turned to kindling, houses to piles of blackened timbers.

A dozen priests had turned up, handing out bowls of rice and dispensing some of the temple's hoard of coin to surging throngs of people, but it was a drop in the bucket. To his irritation, Lucius found himself scanning their faces. Looking for the priest from yesterday.

The one you took your pleasure with while these people were being burned out of their homes? an acid voice reminded him.

The wail of an infant came from the rubble of a house where a young woman stood staring with hollow eyes, the babe clutched to her breast. It was nuzzling for milk and she absent-mindedly put it to her nipple. A naked child of three or four squatted at the edge of the canal, trying to hook something from the water with a stick. It wasn't hard to picture her overbalancing in another few seconds and tumbling in. Lucius scooped her up and gave her a little push.

"Stay by your mother," he said.

She shot him a resentful pout and ran off. The mother didn't seem to notice. She was looking around with an expression of defeat.

Justinian had done this.

Lucius hadn't confronted him about it yet. The story put about by the palace was that the insurgents had started a riot, forcing the Duc to send soldiers to protect the good people of the Shambles. A brazen lie, probably for the benefit of the Sons of Bel, since everyone knew what had really happened. There were no soldiers in sight now. They'd done their job and retreated back to the barracks.

"Hoi!"

Lucius turned. A dinghy pulled up to the landing ahead, with six men wearing red bandanas. Their eyes were not friendly. He climbed down and got in. They rowed in silence to a place deep in the tall grasses of the marsh, where a cluster of stilt houses sat intact. The boat glided up to one, accessible only by rope ladder. Two men held it steady as Lucius ascended.

The Red Rogue was inside, masqued as before, alone this time. He said nothing. Just waited.

"I know you blame me for this," Lucius said. "But I . . ."

He'd concocted a story about why he hadn't killed Justinian, a failed attempt, but now he abruptly changed his mind. Let him have the truth.

"It turns out I know this mortifex," Lucius said heavily. "From the time before . . . " *Just say the bloody word.* "From before I died. He was a good man, then." Lucius drew a breath.

"He was killed because of *my* actions, do you understand? And he does not even hold it against me. So I couldn't do it."

The Rogue was sitting against the far wall, knees bent. He made a gesture of invitation, and Lucius sat across from him.

"I saw you save the boy," he said. "You have honor. I do not blame you. It was the Duc who gave the order."

"Which is why I have another proposal. I'll kill Vazsoly myself."

The idea had come to Lucius in the blissful aftermath of his dalliance with the priest. The solution to all their problems. Everyone wanted Vazsoly dead, so why not just finish him as he'd done to the soldier who tried to kick that child?

"I thought your mistress wanted to keep her hands clean," the Rogue said with a note of surprise.

"Oh, she does," Lucius agreed.

She *always* does, he thought to himself. Orlaith's defining trait. Even the poisoned wine meant for Castelio was delivered by its unwitting victim.

"Which is why I won't tell her beforehand. If she doesn't know, she cannot forbid me." Lucius frowned. "The problem is access. The Duc still refuses to see me. I haven't caught a glimpse of the man since I've arrived."

Dark eyes studied him. "You are really willing to do this?"

"With pleasure," Lucius said honestly.

"Then you're in luck. I have been invited to a parley at Bel Mara." A mirthless laugh. "To settle our differences."

Lucius leaned forward. "When?"

"Tonight."

"He must intend to betray you. It's fairly obvious."

The Rogue inclined his head in assent. "I had no intention of going. But now . . ."

"You trust me?" Lucius asked dubiously. "After I failed you once already?"

The Rogue sighed. "I should not have asked you to kill Janus. I fear the request angered Bel."

Lucius knew these people were deeply religious. Devotion to the sun god was an integral part of their world. It was the same in every culture he had seen. The poorer and more downtrodden you were, the more you needed to believe in some power of higher justice. But the only deity he *knew* existed was Kaethe, and she didn't care what happened to the living.

In Lucius's experience, justice was a commodity you had to take yourself, usually at the point of a sword.

"Why would it anger Bel?" he asked. "You were right. Ju —" He almost spoke the true name before catching himself. "Janus burned your people out."

"It must be because his soul grew corrupted in Kaethe's domain. Don't misunderstand. I do not revile the Lady of the Still Waters." Lucius sensed a smile behind the masque. "She serves her purpose. Not all of us can, or should, be immortal like your race."

"Daēvas are not immortal," Lucius corrected. "But our life spans are akin to an oak tree, while mortals are mayflies. No offense intended."

"None taken. But the fire daēvas are the favored children of Bel. He created you in his image."

Lucius nodded politely. He had never heard this particular mythology. It must be local to Prydwen.

"What do your own people say?" the Rogue asked, genuine interest in his voice. "About where the Vatras come from?"

The question surprised him. Lucius was accustomed to being treated like a monster. A *mortifex*. He thought of himself in those same terms now. But this man knew his clan's name. How? It was all ancient history. The Rogue was educated, Lucius thought again. By whom?

"We have no gods," he replied. "We were makers of talismans who lived peaceably with our neighbors until a king named Gaius took the crown. He was a fair ruler at first. Then . . . he changed for the worse. I still don't know why."

Lucius gathered his thoughts. "As to your question, some believed our ancestors came through a gate from another world. There is no way to prove it one way or another. I never gave the matter much thought, to be honest." He smiled. "Soldiers tend to be literal-minded. Tactics, strategy. The logistics of feeding legions and their horses. That's what I did best."

"I know the stories of your mad king," the Rogue said. "There are still a few old scrolls that tell the tale. So you knew him."

"I served under him," Lucius admitted. "For a time."

"We cannot choose our rulers," the Rogue said. "Only whether we follow their orders without question."

His gaze was piercing, as though he knew more than he ought to. But that wasn't possible. The name of Claudius Quintus was long forgotten. Even Lucius was tired of remembering it.

"Then we are agreed," he said. "Vazsoly will die tonight. I will keep my identity a secret. Blend with your escort, if that's acceptable?"

The Red Rogue inclined his head. "You can't harm any Sons of Bel. I must have your word."

"Only Vazsoly," Lucius promised. "And his soldiers, if necessary."

The Rogue regarded him quietly for a moment. "It's strange," he said. "You seem like any other man. Not at all like the stories I have heard."

"That's because I fed last night."

"You killed?"

"I have before," Lucius admitted. "But no. I fed another way. One I think you'll appreciate."

A quizzical look from the depths of the hood.

"Fire and air can be woven to create dreams," he explained. "I had a modest talent for it when I was alive, and the gift remains." He shrugged. "The trick doesn't work so well on other daēvas, but mortals are more susceptible. I constructed a nightmare and unleashed it on everyone who slept in the palace. Their fear gave me sustenance."

"Truly?" The Red Rogue leaned forward now, his voice hoarse. "What was it?"

"Vazsoly, stark naked, standing over his father with a sword and hacking him to pieces." Lucius smiled. "It was chilly in the old Duc's chamber. I'm afraid Vazsoly's manly parts were rather shrunken. An unfortunate side effect."

There was a shocked silence. Then the Rogue burst into laughter. It was rich and deep and Lucius liked it very much.

"I trust the Duc shared in this dream?" he managed.

"Most definitely. I wonder how he's faring with his council this morning? Not to mention every soldier, steward, cook, undercook, manservant, stableboy, groom, scullery maid—"

"Enough," the Rogue waved a gloved hand, still chuckling.

"So you can expect him to be in an ill humor tonight," Lucius said.

The Rogue's high spirits faded. "I do not believe the man has any other mood." He rose to his feet. "Meet us at the same landing. Eighteen bells, sharp. We will go direct to the monastery from there."

Suddenly, Lucius wanted to see his face. Wanted to talk more. It had been a long time since he'd felt so at ease in someone's presence.

"I've been wondering about something," he said. "You told me that the old Duc, Vazsoly's father, only capitulated to your demands after you burned his ships in the harbor. How did you manage it?"

The Rogue paused. "We discovered the formula for a substance called Bel's Fire. It keeps burning even when doused with seawater. We are trying to adapt it into a weapon that can be used on land as effectively, but Bel's Fire is . . . explosive. A dozen men have died working with it."

"I would like to see this Bel's Fire," Lucius said slowly. "I might be able to advise you on it. But you are right to be cautious. There were zealots among my clan who claimed that flames transform and purify. That fire is the most sublime of all the elements." He smiled. "It can be a thing of beauty. But in the end, fire simply destroys. It's a greedy creature — always hungry, never satisfied."

"I hope we never have to use it against men again," the Rogue replied grimly. "I did not relish their screams."

"Where are you going now?" Lucius blurted.

Another low laugh. "That, I cannot tell you. There is a matter of some urgency I must see to. But I do trust you, Lucius. And if your plan succeeds, you have my thanks."

He gripped Lucius's forearm, then brushed past and climbed swiftly down the ladder to the waiting boat. Another rowed over and Lucius climbed in. The two boats glided together back to the Shambles. Lucius was deposited on the landing. His dinghy turned back for the marsh, while the other carrying the Red Rogue continued on.

He stared after it for a minute, letting the boat gain some distance, then slipped into the crowds and followed. There were other vessels on the water — the soldiers had not burned all of them — and enough people about that he could conceal himself when one of the Rogue's men looked back. Which they did frequently.

He kept his eyes fixed on the red bandanas, skirting along behind the houses. *Just a glimpse*, he told himself. *Then I'll go back to the palace and find Justinian and ask him what in all hells he was thinking.*

The boat eventually landed at a stone jetty and the Rogue leapt out. It was the border of the Shambles, where the houses became somewhat more respectable and grew into the hodge-podge of covered markets around Jubert's Hook.

The Rogue strolled along between rows of open-sided tents crammed with vendors selling all manner of goods. The first bazaar was occupied by wiry nomads from the Desert of Rhun. Both men and women wore scarlet robes with bright indigo head coverings. People crowded the stalls, haggling in at least four different languages. The air was thick with a smoky haze and a pungent, heady scent halfway between dried animal dung and singed skunk.

Orlaith's report on the region's economy, which was excru-ciatingly detailed, had noted that the nomads specialized in fragrant, creamy soaps made from the milk of the shaggy beasts they called xaks, along with a vibrant red dye derived from the blood iron in the rocks of their barren homeland. Both things turned out to be true, though the report failed to mention the strong hashish the vendors smoked in long water pipes.

Next came the market of the sea folk from the Western Isles, whose tables were crammed with bowls and drums carved from flingen wood, a tree unique to the isles. The wood also made exquisite flutes and woodwind instruments, the finest in the world some claimed, and snatches of gay music filled the air. The Rogue paused at one of these tables, clapping as a group of musicians gave a demonstration, then moved on.

Next came polished armor chased in silver from Galatia, exotic fruits from the hothouses of Loris, and potions to ward off illness brewed by the reclusive druids who dwelled in the mountains north of Hellgate. The bazaar seemed the one place in Prydwen where rich and poor mingled, though the wealthy trailed entourages of servants and hired guards.

Lucius made sure to keep his distance as he followed his quarry's meandering path through the bazaar. At last, the Rogue stopped in front of a table overseen by an old woman selling trinkets of Kaethe. Woven knots of reeds and silver bells and little rosettes you could pin to your clothing. Prydwen was firmly Bel's city and business was slow.

The Rogue glanced around. Lucius went still as he unwound his manty . . . and a tumble of long chestnut hair spilled out. The young woman, tall and exceptionally broad of shoulder, turned towards him. She had the audacity to wink. "Buy me a charm, fine sir?" she called merrily.

Lucius shook his head in amused disgust. When they'd made the switch was impossible to say. He could have sworn he'd never let the man out of his sight.

I've been outfoxed, he thought, plucking a green grape from a produce vendor's basket and popping it in his mouth. *So much for my unblemished reputation.*

"You'll have to buy those," a kid sitting on an overturned crate told him. "They ain't for free."

Lucius took a coin from his purse and tossed it over. When he looked back, the girl was gone.

TWENTY-FOUR

Felippa hunched over her slanted table in the scriptorium, copying contracts related to the Duc's new defenses. Shipments of brick, mortar, stone, and timber. Payments to the masons and builders. Even plans for various parts of the wall. She suspected her overseers gave them to her for copying because no one thought a wee lass would put it all together, but she happened to have a good head for numbers, too.

For the last several months, she had secretly written summaries of any documents that seemed important. A soldier was stationed inside the room, watching all the scribes, but he was easily distracted. On the days when she planned to smuggle out her reports, one of the comelier serving girls would happen by and flirt with him while Felippa stuffed the papers into her skirts.

She liked the scriptorium because it was big and airy, with a high vaulted ceiling and good light coming through the tall windows. She liked the scratch of quills and the dry smell of the parchment and the sharp tang of fresh ink. She would lose herself in fierce concentration, forming each letter with precision and ensuring that the ink flowed smoothly through the nib. Hours seemed to pass in the blink of an eye.

Then she sensed an odd quiet. The scratching of the other scribes had stopped. Felippa looked up and saw a Son of Bel standing in the doorway. He said something to the guard, then stared at her. She dropped her eyes back to the parchment. She knew who he was, though they had never spoken. His name was Brother Brennos. He was very handsome, and the kitchen maids were always swooning over him. But they said he was a fanatical supporter of the Duc, so Felippa hated him on principle.

Now he was walking over to her table. She felt a thrill of fear.

"Come with me," he said in a curt tone.

She didn't dare look at his face. "Yes, Brother," she said meekly. A glance at the parchment showed she'd ruined it with a splotch of ink.

I'll have to redo it all again, she thought, trying to pretend to herself that she wasn't in deep water. But there was no reason she could imagine he'd want her unless he knew what she'd been up to.

Felippa followed him between the tables, feeling the other scribes watching them. There was a small chapel around the corner, lit by a hundred flickering votive candles. Brother Brennos was so tall, she fit inside his shadow with room to spare. No one else was there. Her palms felt sweaty and she surreptitiously rubbed them on her skirts.

"Kneel before the god," he commanded.

That came easy since her knees were wobbly. She sank down in front of the statue of Bel. He was holding a lute in one hand, a bow in the other. The priest knelt at her side. He traced a circle in the air and bowed his head.

"When does the cockatrice crow?" he asked softly.

A tingle of bright terror walked down her spine. It was the code phrase she'd been given. The way she'd know if someone was a sympathizer. They changed it every week, but that was the new one.

Felippa stared at the hyacinth blossoms mounded at the god's feet. The sweet smell of them made her nauseous. "I'm sorry, I don't understand," she mumbled.

"When does the cockatrice crow?" Brother Brennos asked again with dreadful patience.

Her mouth had gone dry as sand. Wings of panic fluttered in her ribcage. *He knows. He knows. They'll send me to the pyres. Tie me up and pour oil over my head and . . .*

Then a pragmatic voice spoke up. The one that had seen her through those dark days after Cas left and Da was gambling all their money away, even though he kept promising not to.

It said, *If he already knows, then you're damned anyway. Just tell him, or he'll never stop asking.*

"At the red dawn," she whispered, fists so tight the nails dug into her palms.

"And when will it fly?"

Felippa gathered her courage and turned to face him. "At the rising of the red tide."

Brother Brennos smiled. It was like a shaft of pure sunlight pierced the gloom of the chapel. "You are named Felippa, yes?" he whispered. "Recruited by the chambermaid Chessamir?"

She nodded, somewhat relieved. She had seen Chessamir at breakfast, alive and well and flirting with the baker's boy.

"We are in debt to you, Felippa. Your information about the Duc's fortifications has proven invaluable."

"I . . . Thank you. I mean, I'm glad." She felt confused. *Had he come here just to thank her?*

"I have a task for you, if you're willing," he whispered,

glancing at the door. "But it's dangerous, so if you refuse, I'll understand."

"What is it?"

"There's something in Galoy Rossignol's bedchamber I need you to steal."

"You mean . . . the captain of the Duc's guard?" The last words came out squeaky. She cleared her throat. "Are you mad?"

He took this in stride. "I wouldn't ask if it weren't important, Felippa. I can't do it myself. Rossignol would know immediately that I was the one who took it. But the object is small. An iron box."

She vented a long breath. "What's inside?" she whispered.

"He claimed not to know. He said he broke two good knives trying to pry it open." Brother Brennos leaned closer. He smelled nice. A clean, masculine smell that reminded her of Cas. "But Rossignol confessed that it was given to him by the priest who was murdered two days ago at the monastery."

Felippa's brows lifted. "I heard about that. It's terrible." A hand rose to her mouth as she made the connection. "Did *Rossignol* kill him?"

"No, but Brother Symeon was his uncle by marriage. He entrusted the box to him for safekeeping. Now Rossignol is in a panic. He confessed all to me after we . . ." Brother Brennos trailed off. "Perhaps you are too young to hear of such things. Let us just say that he rashly confided in me during a moment of weakness."

Everyone in the palace knew he was Rossignol's lover. Felippa felt her cheeks flush, but she gave him a level look. "I am not as young as I seem, Brother."

He had the grace to look embarrassed. "I'm sorry. It must be tiresome to have people talk down to you all the time. But let our enemies underestimate you, Felippa. And remember that *they* are the fools."

The heat in his voice warmed her in . . . unfamiliar places. Felippa gazed into his dark eyes for a moment, mesmerized. The lashes were thick and curling, the brows above straight and fine. It was easy to imagine Rossignol spilling his secrets to this priest. Not only because of his perfect face, which did resemble the stern, chiseled features of Bel, but because of the way he looked at her. Like he really *saw* her. No one else did except for Cas and Teo. Da, if he wasn't in his cups.

Sometimes she felt like the court jester, an aged man with a hunched back who kept the Duc and his nobles entertained. An oddity who was beneath notice when she wasn't being laughed at. But Brother Brennos was taking her seriously. Treating her like an equal. His manner was open and confiding, yet slightly aloof, as if he existed half in the realm of the gods . . .

Pull yourself together, the voice said briskly. *You can moon over him later, after you steal this box.*

And Felippa realized that with a few words, he had somehow talked her into it. That she would do anything to make him keep trusting her. To please him.

And for the revolution, of course.

"Where is it?" she asked.

"Hidden in a locked chest at the foot of his bed." Brother Brennos produced two keys, one large, one small. "The first is to Rossignol's door. The second is for the chest."

Felippa tucked them in her pocket. "I think I can get to his chamber without too much trouble," she said slowly. "But I will have to carry it out again. Is it heavy?"

"It is made of iron, but the box itself is small. I saw it myself." He formed a square with his hands. Even those were deep-tanned and gracefully formed. "About this big."

Felippa nodded briskly. "I made a sort of sling that fits under my skirts. I use it to bring the bigger scrolls out. The box should fit inside."

"Tell the guards that you're delivering a message to me. They'll be new ones by then. They won't know I've already gone. I'll be sure to back your story later, if it comes up." He smiled reassuringly. "Don't worry, I know how to manage Rossignol. Leave the window to his chamber open. He'll think the thief came in that way. But he's not even supposed to have this relic, so how can he claim it was stolen? If he does, it will connect him to his uncle's murder, which he wants to avoid at all costs."

"And after? Where should I hide it?"

"Keep the box in your room for now. I'll find a way to get it from you later."

It all seemed a little flimsy. She wasn't quite so dazzled by his charm that she couldn't see that. When you were a small person, and a girl to boot, you had to speak up for yourself because no one else would.

"Are you certain it's worth the risk?" she asked. "We could *burn* for this. And you don't even know what *it* is."

"A fair question," he conceded. "The priest who was killed, Brother Symeon, said only that it was an object of great power. That he feared someone dangerous was coming after it. Rossignol didn't want to take it, but he agreed in the end. A decision he now regrets. But this might be something we can use, Felippa. And if *we* don't, I fear he might give it to the Duc."

She bit her lip, fresh misgivings rushing in. Just the night before, she'd had a vivid dream about Vazsoly Marcel. He was covered in blood and stabbing his sword down, again and again. "I heard you were one of the Duc's greatest supporters," Felippa confessed in a rush.

Brother Brennos studied her for a moment. "Have you ever played a role out of necessity?"

"Every time I curtsy to the Duc!" she whispered fervently. "I hate him!"

"As I hate Rossignol. But I will do anything required of me to see them all defeated." His voice went flat and she caught a flash of carefully controlled anger. "Will you do it?"

She thought of the pyres in the yard at Blackwater Jail, where the Duc burned people he didn't like. She'd only seen it once, when they first arrived in Prydwen, but she had never forgotten. The high-pitched screams still echoed in her nightmares.

"Yes," she said.

His face relaxed. "I will tell the Red Rogue of your courage when I see him."

Felippa had no idea who the Red Rogue was. Teo said no one did, not even his inner circle. It was why the Duc hadn't caught him yet. She longed to get out of the palace and hear one of his fiery speeches, but it was impossible. Da always insisted that the Shambles was too dangerous. And the rallies were never planned in advance. The Duc might get wind of them and set a trap.

But she'd heard stories. The Red Rogue would appear, and word would go round, and people would come from all over in their boats to hear him talk. She'd wanted to write his words down so folk could read them who weren't able to go, but Teo had pointed out that most couldn't read anyway.

Felippa thought there was still value in it. How would they know about any of the things that had happened so long ago if someone hadn't written it down?

"I have to finish my shift first," she said. "Then I'll do it. I'm done at five bells. Is that enough time for you to get out of the palace?"

"It's perfect." He rose and offered her his hand. It was large and warm, swallowing hers completely. "You are a brave and loyal woman, Felippa," he said, tracing a tiny circle on her forehead with one finger. "Bel blesses you."

Brother Brennos nodded to her and strode away. He had nice legs, too, lean and strong. She sighed. Some people were born with everything just right.

She returned to the scriptorium, ignoring the curious glances of the other scribes. This time, the hours dragged, but at last she heard five bells tolling through the open window.

She'd already slipped a blank piece of her parchment up her sleeve. She tidied her table, sharpening her quills and refilling the wells of ink. The overseer came out and collected their work for the day. Then she set off for the wing of the palace where Galoy Rossignol kept his chamber. It was near the Duc's quarters, though not past the final cordon of guards. Now *that* would have been impossible, even for her.

When she reached the outer garrison, she held up the rolled parchment, which she had tied with a black ribbon. "I carry a message for Brother Brennos."

They all knew of his association with their captain. The guards waved her past with bored expressions. To most eyes, she looked like a child of six. Felippa had given up hope that she would ever catch up to the other girls her age. They were starting to notice boys and act silly around them. She'd heard two of them whispering about something called *Hecate's blood,* who had already had it and who didn't. What did a moon have to do with blood? Lip hardly remembered her mother, but it would have been nice to have someone to ask about these things.

She rounded a corner, too fast, and bumped straight into a person coming from the other direction. A tall woman, who gave a muffled gasp of surprise. Thick hair hung in an elaborate braid over one shoulder. She wore a black dress with ample cleavage spilling out. A dark bruise marked one cheek. In the shadowy hall, it nearly blended with the odd swirls and runes drawn on her face.

Felippa backed away. It was the Duc's consort from the Western Isles, Morgen Nadezhda. Some said she was a witch, but Felippa thought it was probably just because they didn't like her.

"Oh," she said, dropping into a deep curtsy. "I'm so sorry, milady. Forgive my clumsiness."

Unlike the soldiers, Morgen *did* seem curious. Instead of chastising her and moving on, she studied Felippa in silence for a long moment. "I've seen you before," she said at last. Her voice had the harsh, throaty accent of the Isles.

"I'm one of the scribes, milady."

Her shrewd gaze noted the scroll in Felippa's hand. "I'm not a lady. I'm the Duc's heathen whore. Isn't that what they call me?"

There was no bitterness in her voice. It was merely a statement of fact.

"I never . . . do not say such a thing, milady." Felippa swallowed. "Everyone says you are very beautiful."

"You are polite, child. What is your name?"

"Felippa."

"Ah. Do you know what your name means?"

She wordlessly shook her head.

Morgen smiled. "Lover of horses. A pretty name for a pretty girl."

It was a kind thing to say, but there was no warmth in her voice. Or in her smile. *There's something odd about her*, Felippa thought uneasily. Something missing.

Morgen reached out and smoothed her hair back. Her touch was cool. "Well, Felippa, it was a pleasure to meet you, but I must join the Duc. We are making a grand procession through the city. His subjects love him so, do they not?"

"Very much, my lady."

Morgen gave a dry laugh and passed by, her silk gown rustling against the floor.

At least she didn't ask what I was doing here, Felippa thought, unsettled by the encounter.

She quickly found the captain's chamber, looked both ways to ensure no one was coming, and gave a brisk rap, just in case. When no one replied, she unlocked the door, slipped inside, and leaned back against the wood.

It was a single large room with a bed and sitting area. The sheets were disarranged and she stared at them for a moment, wondering what sorts of activities went on there. She wasn't stupid. She knew a few things. But Rossignol was old enough to be his father. Poor Brother Brennos. His sacrifice made hers seem minor in comparison.

"Chest," she muttered, fishing out the smaller key. The lock opened easily. She groped beneath a stack of musty doublets and felt metal. Felippa lifted the box out. It was heavy for such a small object. No lock or any markings. Not even scratches from the knives Rossignol broke trying to open it.

Felippa wondered what was inside. An object of great power, Brennos had said. It did seem sinister, dull in color and freezing to the touch, like a cube of black ice. Even the bright sunlight dimmed when it struck the box.

She lifted her skirts and adjusted it in the sling so that it pressed against the backs of her thighs. The chill made her flinch. Walking would be awkward. She'd just have to hope the guards didn't notice.

She went to the mullioned window and unhooked the center latch. The hinges gave a rusty protest as she pushed the panes open. A hot breeze blew inside. Her heart leapt as voices floated up from the courtyard below, but they quickly faded. She tried to open the panes a little wider, but the hinges wouldn't budge any further. She was attempting to force it when she heard faint footsteps in the corridor. They stopped in front of the door.

Her scalp tingled. She looked around wildly for a hiding place. Under the bed? Inside the chest? But what if he checked on the box? And if it was missing, he'd make a thorough search.

All this flashed through her mind in seconds. Then her frantic gaze settled on the cold hearth. It looked too clean, like he never used it. Felippa waddled across the chamber, the box swinging, and stuffed herself up the chimney. It was narrow, but she could just fit. The door swung open as she hoisted her legs and braced her feet against the stone.

Rossignol came inside and closed the door. She heard the sounds of rummaging. The chest lid slammed down and the steps moved toward the bed. The legs creaked as it shifted position. A soft thump, followed by a crash.

Suddenly, she was glad she hadn't hidden underneath it.

Felippa squeezed her eyes shut as the steps moved about the room, rapidly now. More loud banging. A muttered curse. Then they moved toward the fireplace. That's when she felt the unearthly chill. It seeped into her flesh like liquid death. Her heart started to thump so fast her whole chest ached to contain it.

Not Rossignol. *The mortifex, Janus.*

Cas had taught her everything he knew about fexes. He said it might help keep her safe one day. Iron burns them, he'd said. They can sense it, even from a distance. That's why charms work to keep them away.

But this one wasn't scared of iron. This one must be looking for the box.

Now he was close enough to see the scuffed toe of his boot.

She breathed through her mouth, shallow, silent breaths that made little spurts of fog in the dark chimney. The leg braced against the wall was starting to cramp. The sling was heavy between her legs, pulling her down.

She didn't remember the attack eight years ago. Didn't remember anything about that night, only falling asleep in Cas's arms at supper. She was grateful to be alive at all. But she knew that if Janus found her now, he'd kill her for certain.

Please, Kaethe. Not like this. Not like this.

He stood there for a minute or two that seemed like hours. Then he turned and strode to the door. It opened and shut again.

Felippa waited a while to be sure. When he didn't come back, she released her madly shaking legs and crawled out of the hearth. She was trembling all over, her palms black with soot. She stood up and her kneecap bumped something hard. She winced. It was the iron poker.

She pictured him standing there, *feeling the box*, so close. Maybe he didn't think anyone could fit up the chimney. Or maybe the poker had saved her. Confused him.

She wiped her hands on her skirts. Luckily, she always wore dark colors to cover the inevitable ink stains and the soot didn't show. But the room was a mess. He'd tossed the feather mattress on the floor and snapped one of the legs off the bed so that it sagged down. Torn Rossignol's clothes from the wardrobe and left them scattered about. Maybe that was even better. It looked like someone broke in. No one would think a little girl did all that.

Felippa pressed her ear to the door. All quiet. She slipped out and hurried back the way she'd come, savage triumph lightening her steps.

TWENTY-FIVE

"I still don't see why we couldn't watch the procession from the shade of your terrace," complained a woman whose auburn hair glittered with jeweled pins. "I haven't been down in the *streets* since . . . oh, *ages*."

Her thickly-powdered companion leaned in, forcing the boy holding a paper parasol to shuffle forward. "Are you truly so dense?" she hissed. "Only archers are permitted on the balconies. Have you forgotten what happened last time? That knife-wielding maniac who came within six paces of the Duc?"

A dry chuckle. "Darling, I barely remember what I had for breakfast."

Lo stood close enough to the two women to smell their jasmine-scented perfume and the sour sweat it was supposed to mask. She wasn't entirely sure how she had ended up jammed shoulder-to-shoulder with rich people waiting to see Duc Marcel pass by. It was blazing hot, with barely a hint of breeze from the bay. Flinty-eyed soldiers occupied every rooftop and balcony, and more manned barricades at the intersections. The crowd was obviously hand-picked. Nobles and their trusted servants only.

Lo had trailed the two chattering women through a gap in the barricades. She wore a wide straw hat and blue cotton dress, plain but of good cut. The soldiers had given her no more than a cursory glance. They were looking for supporters of the Red Rogue, not the girl calling herself Ami who had escaped Bel Mara after tying up the arch-priest with his own braided cord of office.

Ami would have to be crazy to show up here.

A tail hooked around her calf and she crouched to meet Thistle's luminous yellow eyes.

"You were always incautious," he growled softly, "but now I wonder at your sanity. Why are we doing this?"

"I just want to see what this vile Duc looks like," Lo whispered. She pretended to shake a pebble from her sandal, glancing around. No one was looking down. "It's not like I planned to come."

After Cas left the *Wind-Witch*, she had gone back to the Shambles hoping to find Tijah and Achaemenes. The family and their little white dog were at the burned stilt house, picking through the ruins, but hadn't seen the bonded pair since the attack.

Lo tried not to worry. The last she'd glimpsed of them, Achaemenes was sprinting away with Tijah in his arms and a pack of soldiers on his tail. Lo reminded herself that they were seasoned hunters for Kaethe who had faced down far worse things. They must be holed up somewhere while Achaemenes healed Tijah of the arrow wound in her thigh.

Lo didn't feel like waiting on the ship until Cas returned, so she'd gone walking, hoping it might clear her head. If he failed to find the iron box at the palace, they needed another plan. Unfortunately, her thoughts kept wandering to his soft lips and strong hands, and she made little progress on averting her own imminent death.

After an hour or two of meandering, she'd found herself in a district of limestone mansions with elegant columns and wrought-iron balconies overlooking picturesque canals. The area was abuzz, knots of people calling and waving to each other and jostling for prime positions against the sawhorses lining the streets. She had learned that the Duc was making an impromptu processional.

"Did you have the dream? I mean, the naked one?"

The voice of the bejeweled woman floated down. She wore silk slippers with tiny lavender pearls sewn along the seams. Her friend's lumpy feet were crammed into silver-painted sandals with criss-crossing straps. The boy shading them with the parasol had no shoes at all.

"Of course you *would* fixate on that part. I assume you refer to the dream of Vazsoly butchering his father? No, but I heard about it." The voice lowered further. "His Grace has forbidden anyone to mention it, so hold your tongue, Karima." A soft laugh. "At least until we share a drink in the garden later. Bel, it's hot! How long must we wait?"

Thistle shot Lo a disgruntled look and flopped down in a patch of sun. Lo rose up on her toes, craning her neck. She stood near the front of the crowd and could see parts of the street beyond. The cobbles were strewn with flowers, now limp and wilting. People fidgeted and fanned themselves with hats. Their expressions ranged from annoyed to glassy and glazed, as if they were on the verge of fainting.

The nobles of Prydwen, Lo reflected, were not a hardy bunch. They seemed unused to being out of doors and standing on their own feet rather than being whisked along in a covered palanquin or gondola. A few called out to the soldiers, demanding to know when the procession would begin and why it was delayed.

"We could be sipping iced wine in the shade," Karima griped. "How would Vazsoly know the difference?"

"Keep your voice down. Lord Baruda lost his left hand for missing the Duc's inaugural ball, and I happen to know Baruda was bedridden with an attack of gout. His Grace is sensitive to anything that smacks of disloyalty."

"I'm not disloyal. Merely bored and overheated . . . *And now there's sun in my eyes!*" Karima whacked the boy on the crown of his head with a folded fan. He had dozed off; now he blinked and quickly adjusted the parasol.

Lo caught his gaze and made a face. The boy pinched his lips together to smother laughter.

Then a fanfare sounded. A tremor rippled through the crowd, whether of genuine excitement or relief that the ordeal would soon be over, Lo couldn't tell. She heard the distant thunder of an army on the move. First came the cavalry on powerful destriers, the warhorses sporting headpieces with white plumes and stepping in perfect unison. They were followed by ranks of foot soldiers in chainmail and the silver-gold surcoats of House Marcel. The soldiers held lances and shields bearing a cockatrice, a serpentine creature with the head of a rooster.

The crowd clapped politely with fixed smiles for the next several minutes as the advance guard passed. Then a wild bout of cheering erupted down the line and the Duc's coach came into view. It was pulled by six black stallions, their manes and tails braided with gold thread that glinted in the sun. The carriage itself was lacquered with gold and lined with white velvet. Two bannermen walked ahead, carrying pennants with the same cockatrice device.

The coach moved at a crawl, a ceremonial guard of two

dozen armored knights flanking the sides. Archers on rooftops and balconies scanned the surging crowd, arrows notched to bowstrings, ready to loose at any threat.

The Duc waved, acknowledging the adulation with a faint smile. He was younger than Lo had imagined, no more than thirty or so, and handsome in a white-toothed, chiseled way. He wore a silver breastplate extravagantly etched with gold. A light, silken cloak flowed down his back, but his head was bare, revealing cropped, wavy blond hair.

Lo could see right away that Vazsoly Marcel was not soft like his nobles. He wore heavy armor and stood in the full sun but showed no sign of fatigue. His skin was deeply tanned; not a man who spent his time sipping iced wine on shaded terraces.

She watched the coach draw closer, the straw hat shading her own face. So this was the infamous Duc of Cavet. A petty tyrant enamored of his own charms, yet still insecure enough to demand this display of fealty.

The woman at his side . . . now *she* looked more interesting. She wore a plunging, tight-bodiced gown, her dark hair braided and hanging nearly to the waist. Bracelets of wood — or possibly bone — ran up her brown arms. She had markings on her face, either painted or tattooed. She did not smile or acknowledge the crowd, which ignored her in turn. Her gaze was fixed straight ahead, her chin lifted at a defiant angle.

Lo tugged the parasol boy's manty. "Who's that? The Ducissa?"

The boy glanced at his employer, but she was too busy gossiping to notice.

"No miss, that's His Grace's consort. Brought her home from the Western Isles as spoils of war. Everyone says he'll marry the Damiata of Galatia."

Spoils of war? The woman turned her head, revealing a dark bruise on one cheek. Lo hadn't thought it was possible to hate

Vazsoly Marcel more than she already did, but it turned out she was wrong. So he had kidnapped some woman from her homeland, dragged her to Prydwen, raped her no doubt, and now he was forcing her to stand at his side like a human trophy. Lo stared at his smug face, wishing an assassin would leap from the crowd and plant a dagger in one of his blue eyes.

A commotion at the barricades raised her hopes, but it turned out to be two prettily dressed little girls running out to present the Duc with a laurel crown.

"As if he's Bel himself," the Lady Karima murmured. "An audacious move."

The Duc feigned surprise, though it was clearly planned in advance. He leapt down from the coach, hoisting each child up for a kiss, then sank humbly to one knee as they placed the wreath on his pale curls. The crowd was lapping it up, but Lo sensed the braided woman's gaze settle on her.

"What is the consort's name?" she whispered to the boy.

"Morgen," he whispered back. "Morgen Nadezhda."

Morgen tilted her head, brows drawing slightly together. She was staring at Lo with a puzzled expression. Lo felt it, too. A vague familiarity, as if they had met before.

Or . . . Morgen had heard the description of Ami and put it together with the woman in the blue dress who stood twenty paces away.

The crowd was jammed against the barricades. Lo had sharp elbows, but using them to force her way out would draw unwanted attention. Morgen was still staring at her, and the coach hadn't moved. The Duc was making a speech.

Lo crouched down and whispered to Thistle. He lashed his tail, looking happier. The wind freshened. Ominous black clouds raced down from the north. The Duc squinted up at the darkening sky and climbed back into the coach, shouting at the driver. A powerful gust tore the straw hat from Lo's head.

The Duc began to wrestle with the coach's canopy, which appeared to be stuck in the folded position. His curses were audible even over the muttering of the spectators. After a moment, Morgen Nadezhda turned to help him.

"Hurry, boy!" Lady Karima snapped, loose strands of auburn hair whipping in the sudden gale. "Clear a path for us before the storm hits. It will ruin my silk slippers!"

The paper parasol was already torn. The boy threw it aside and began hollering for the other nobles to make way. Lightning streaked down from an angry sky, followed by an ear-splitting boom of thunder. Someone gave a shrill scream. People started to push and shove as the heavens opened and torrents of rain pelted down.

Thistle leapt into Lo's arms and they joined the stampede. The last she saw of Duc Marcel, he was gesticulating and hurling threats at his bannermen, who were tugging frantically at the furled canopy. His laurel crown was askew, his blond curls plastered to his forehead. Morgen Nadezhda stood with her face tipped up to the rain. Lo thought she was smiling.

The barricades had been thoroughly trampled by the panicked crowd. Soldiers shouted for calm, but they were swamped in a tide of screeching nobles. As Lo crawled beneath a sawhorse, she saw one of the soldiers bowled over by an immensely fat man with a pointy beard and silver walking stick that he was using to smack anyone who got in his way. Lost shoes, soaked shawls, and broken parasols littered the drenched streets.

It was perfect chaos.

Lo ducked her head and ran, laughing, all the way back to the *Wind-Witch*.

Lucius found Justinian sitting beneath a pavilion in the palace gardens, incinerating the roses on a bush one by one. Heavy rain drummed against the copper roof, but it wasn't enough to save the roses; elemental fire burned too hot for that. They were going up in little wisps of flame that sizzled and spat. Half the delicate pink blooms were already withered to ash, the leaves and stems around them untouched.

Justinian looked up as he approached, mouth slanted in a grim line. "So you got my note. We must talk, old friend."

Lucius stepped into the shelter of the pavilion and shook the rain from his cloak. "I agree," he said coldly.

Justinian frowned. "Is something wrong?"

There were two stone benches. Lucius sat down on the one facing him. "I saw the Shambles. What you did to those people. They had so little to begin with. Now they have nothing."

Justinian looked away, sullen. "I had no choice. The Duc ordered it."

"You could have refused," Lucius replied, his tone scathing. "Or is Vazsoly Marcel your master now?"

Embers flared in Justinian's eyes. "No, but I still need his protection. I was almost captured by that bonded pair yesterday. They came out of nowhere." He grimaced and the rosebush burst into crackling flames. "If they drag me back to Kaethe, I'm fucked!"

"Leash your temper," Lucius said. "And it's still no excuse. The man I knew wouldn't murder innocent woman and children."

"They're mortals," Justinian replied absently, watching the bush blacken and die. "Had they been daēvas, I would never have done it." He shook his head in disbelief. "How can you defend their race? They've enslaved you for the last thousand years."

"I enslaved myself," Lucius corrected. "It was *my* choice to enter the bargain, if admittedly a stupid one. I understand your bitterness, but these are not the people who forged the Grand Menotte. They are not all like Jaskin Cazal."

Justinian stared at him. There was an emptiness in his gaze. A black pit behind the flames of his pupils, like the eyes of wraiths. How could Lucius not have seen it before? Justinian's long exile in the Dominion had indeed changed him.

Water trickled in a steady *drip-drip* from the roof corners. The air smelled of damp earth and sweet smoke. In the distance, a trumpet fanfare announced the arrival of the Duc. Lucius didn't notice any of these things. He was too busy facing an unpleasant but obvious truth.

He might hate his bondage to the Redvaynes, but it had kept his soul intact over all the long years of his service. The iron cuff tethered him to a world of light and warmth and emotion. To living, breathing people. Oh, Lucius had schemed and raged and wallowed in his own misery. Yet he knew now that Claudius Quintus was never truly gone. Coming to Prydwen had drawn him out of hiding.

Not the city itself — but those he had met here. The Red Rogue and the comely priest, Brother Brennos. Each, in his own way, reminded Lucius of the man he used to be. Whom he could be again if he chose to.

But Justinian's soul was tied to a talisman that belonged to no one. Jaskin Cazal was the only mortal to wear it and he'd been dead for hundreds of years. It was a basic law of Kaethe's realm that those who lingered too long without crossing the Cold Sea lost themselves forever. Without the Grand Menotte, Justinian would be a lich by now, his soul decayed to a dark essence that knew only hatred and destruction. The talisman had preserved his form, even his personality, to some degree, but inside he was something else. Something *less* than a man — and far more dangerous.

Justinian leaned forward. His voice held soft menace. "If you want me to stop, Claudius, find the iron box. Then we can both be gone from this place."

"Give me a lead, and I will."

Justinian's mouth twisted. "I did have a promising one. Galoy Rossignol, the captain of the Duc's guards, is the nephew of the priest who guarded the box at Bel Mara. I searched Rossignol's rooms, but it wasn't there."

"He might have hidden it elsewhere," Lucius said, adding silently, *Please let him have it so this creature leaves before killing anyone else. And so I can cross the Cold Sea before I become like him.*

"Oh, I haven't ruled it out," Justinian agreed. "As soon as Rossignol returns, I plan to torture the truth from him."

"Where is he?"

"Some processional." A hollow laugh. "The Duc staged it at the last moment so his enemies wouldn't have time to organize an assault. Then they'll be going to the parley at Bel Mara. I'll do it after. I'll need time with Rossignol if he doesn't break quickly. Burn him by inches, starting with his feet. You'd be amazed how long someone can live when it's done right. The wounds cauterize, you see. It prevents the blood loss that would otherwise lead to death."

Justinian might have been discussing his choice of saddle for all the emotion in his voice. Beyond his broad shoulder, Lucius saw a young girl leading a man by the hand down one of the paths. The man was stumbling. At first, Lucius thought he was sick; then he realized the man was simply drunk. As the pair drew closer, he felt a tingle of recognition.

The man was an older, careworn version of Castelio. And the girl . . . Lucius hadn't quite told the truth when he said he couldn't remember the details of Castelio's worst memory.

Parts were blurry, but the little sister, Lippa, looked much the same. Fair hair, freckles, a stubborn chin.

As for the mortifex who had drained her life force and would have killed her if Castelio hadn't smacked him with an iron hoe . . .

Lucius's eyes flicked to the thing sitting across from him. He hadn't seen it at first because the memory distorted the mortifex's features, made them more terrifying. But yes, it could be Justinian.

Before the Shambles, Lucius wouldn't have believed it. He had killed mortals himself but not children. Never children. Yet Justinian had already shown himself capable of anything.

They sat in the shadow of the pavilion. Castelio's father and sister had not noticed them yet. Justinian started to turn, following his gaze, and Lucius knew that if Justinian saw them, he would burn them without hesitation, just as he had done to the rosebush.

"What about this parley?" Lucius said quickly. "Is it genuine, or does the Duc plan a betrayal?"

Justinian turned back with a look of irritation. "How the fuck would I know? The Duc doesn't confide in me. And what does it matter? Let them all kill each other. Just help me find the box!"

From the corner of his eye, Lucius saw Lippa and Castelio's father round a bend in the path and disappear from view. He relaxed slightly. "What do you want me to do?"

"When this parley is over, we'll bring Rossignol to your chamber." Justinian's smile reminded Lucius of a barracuda, toothy and dead-eyed, lurking in the icy depths. "The Grand Menotte is close, Claudius. I can feel it."

TWENTY-SIX

Heavy gray clouds swirled above the small sailing vessel as it approached Bel Mara. Lucius fixed his gaze on the monastery's hulking silhouette. The choppy, white-capped water made him want to curl up at the bottom of the boat.

He'd often wondered why rivers and oceans were such a bane to the dead. His theory was that it had something to do with the Cold Sea. If souls refused to cross as they were meant to, any other body of water would be a torment.

"Can we be certain the Duc isn't bringing his mortifex?" The Red Rogue's voice was muffled by the scarf covering his face.

"Fairly sure," Lucius replied, swallowing a bout of queasiness. "Janus didn't seem to care about this parley. He has no idea we've been meeting. He thinks I came to Prydwen to seal an alliance between Orlaith and the Duc."

"But if he is there?" the Rogue persisted. "You said you owe him a debt."

"Janus is not the same man I knew." Lucius sighed. "I prefer not to fight him openly, but I will if I must. That I swear."

The Rogue adjusted their course, aiming for a stone landing. "I trust your word."

"Why?" Lucius asked bluntly.

"Are you saying I shouldn't?" Now he sounded amused.

"No, but you don't strike me as a man who operates solely on instinct. Most of those end up in shallow graves by the age of twenty-five."

The Rogue laughed. "I have my reasons. Ah, we are nearly there."

Rain squalls swept the monastery's outer wall, where a line of priests stood with their cowls pulled forward against the storm. Lucius drew his own hood up and tied a red scarf around his face.

"What if the Duc agrees to your demands?" he asked.

The Rogue snorted. "An unlikely outcome."

"I mean, should we let him live?"

"Do you think he'd keep his promises?"

"No."

"Nor do I. But we wait for him to betray *us* first. I want the arch-priest to witness it with his own eyes. He has given the Duc far too much credit."

Lights shone from the windows of the temple. Lucius had no doubt Marcel intended to spring a trap, but how exactly? What dirty trick did he have up his sleeve?

"The Duc owes the Brotherhood money, doesn't he?" Lucius asked.

The Red Rogue nodded. "The Marcels took out loans to finance their wars — and their palace. The Sons of Bel should never have agreed to the debts, but now they are in too deep." He gazed at the monastery. "But I think they are finally losing their taste for Vazsoly. He is too extreme, even for the arch-priest. The younger sisters would be more malleable."

They lowered the sails and glided up to the landing, where the arch-priest waited. He wore white robes with a golden sun on the breast. His expression was solemn but not unfriendly.

"The Duc and his men are waiting," he said. "A token force only."

"How many?" the Rogue asked. His voice sounded deeper. Rougher.

"Seven, like your own party," the arch-priest replied. "They consented to a search and I can attest that they are all unarmed. Now you must show the same courtesy."

Lucius submitted to a groping by a pair of priests, his attention focused on a fresh insight. The Red Rogue was trying to disguise his voice. There could be only one reason — the arch-priest might recognize him. If the Red Rogue were a priest himself, it would explain both his education and knowledge of military strategy.

Lucius smiled beneath the red scarf. It all fit, including the fact that young men from the Shambles often joined the priesthood to escape crushing poverty. Once, the Sons of Bel had been a well-armed, disciplined fighting force. If they had not mellowed and chosen to devote their energy to enriching Bel's coffers, at least half the duchies of Aveline would probably be under their control.

A mule-drawn cart waited to carry the delegation to the main temple, and Lucius found himself on the far side between two rebels he didn't know. Names were never used, at least not in front of him. Neither spoke as the cart wended its way up the ring road. With each turn, the bay spread out wider, presenting views of the Shambles on one side and the gleaming white marble of the ducal palace on the other.

At last, the cart stopped before the temple's great bronze

doors. Inside was a long chamber with thick pillars and a statue of Bel healing the sick. Duc Marcel waited at the far end. He wore a black doublet and cloak that made his fair hair gleam. Lucius sharpened his hearing, filtering out the distant sounds of the sea and the rain, the shuffling of feet and clearing of throats. Despite the Duc's outwardly cool demeanor, his heart was beating swiftly. Whether he was nervous or eager to confront the phantom who had plagued him, Lucius couldn't say.

Marcel was flanked by six guards, including a man with the red-and-silver knot of a captain on his shoulder. Galoy Rossignol — the one Justinian planned to torture. Rossignol was in his middle years, bearded and heavyset. Deep lines bracketed his mouth, tugging the corners down. He gave off a cynical weariness Lucius was familiar with. Rossignol knew better, but he'd committed too many sins to turn back now. Both the Duc and his captain had dark pouches under their eyes as if they hadn't slept well.

About two dozen Sons of Bel stood along the walls. A parley table had been placed in the center of the open space, under the blank gaze of the statue. The arch-priest motioned for the two sides to take their places. The Red Rogue sat down at one end, Lucius standing behind him. The Duc and Captain Rossignol assumed the same positions at the other end of the table. The chamber fell silent. All eyes focused on the arch-priest.

"I am saddened by the loss of life on both sides of this conflict," he began. "It has caused great suffering and displeased the god." The arch-priest shot a quick frown at Marcel, which the Duc pretended not to notice. "But I am certain we can achieve a fair compromise. Bel and his servants will bear witness to any agreement struck this day. Your Grace?"

The Duc rose. "First, I thank you for coming. Given the ill will between us, I was uncertain if my invitation would be heeded. But it is for the greater good of Cavet that we must find a way forward. As the lawful sovereign of this duchy, I have the right to speak first, but I cede the honor to the delegation from the Shambles." He made a gesture of invitation. "Present your terms."

The Red Rogue stood up. "They are the same as they have always been. First, an end to the death tax and proper burials for all. Second, aqueducts to carry clean water. Don't claim it's impossible or blame the supposed drought. If the palace didn't siphon off freshwater from the Auberjon River to keep your gardens and lawns green, there would be plenty for all."

The Duc nodded thoughtfully and signaled for him to continue.

"Third, we want the prisoners who have been held in Blackwater for more than five years without charge to be released at once," the Rogue said.

Those would be the political prisoners, Lucius realized, guilty of no crime other than speaking against the Duc.

"For the rest, we demand impartial hearings to review the evidence against them." The Rogue's voice hardened. "But there is another category that comprises hundreds of people. It is those who have vanished, either from their cells in Blackwater or after being dragged from their homes by your soldiers."

The Duc folded his hands on the table and regarded him without expression.

"If they are dead," the Rogue said, "we want to know what happened to them. I doubt the bodies can be returned to their families since you have a habit of burning corpses, but at least their fates will be known."

"Is that all?" the Duc asked.

"That is all." The Red Rogue sat down.

The Duc rose to his feet, bracing his palms on the table. "We shall take your demands singly. Regarding disposal of the dead, the nuns of Kaethe can hardly give charity to all who ask. You complain that your people are burned, but what am I to do with them? Wait for them to rise again and kill others?

"As for the criminals in Blackwater Jail, they shall remain until they have paid their debt. By law and tradition, I have the right to dispose of miscreants as I see fit, and this will not change." He gave an incredulous laugh. "You even blame me for the disappeared." His blue eyes glittered with amusement. "Little mystery there, I expect. You will find most of them at the bottom of the bay. Drunks and canals are a perilous combination."

His soldiers laughed.

"As for the Auberjon River, I can hardly have my lawns turning brown. You moan over the lack of freshwater, but if you didn't live and rut like pigs in your own squalor, I suspect you wouldn't die so often from ill humors. So here is my counter offer: I will give a cake of soap to each household." He turned to his men with a shrug. "Assuming they even know how to use it?"

The arch-priest licked his lips, eyes darting between them. "Duc Marcel, you assured me of your good faith!"

"Faith?" the Red Rogue echoed with contempt. "Clearly, he has none. The parley is over."

"Yes," the Duc agreed, "it is. Arrest this man. He is a traitor to the realm."

His soldiers stepped forward. So did the Rogue's men. Tension crackled in the air.

Time to end this farce, Lucius thought. He wove a net of earth, air, and fire around the Duc's heart, then yanked the threads tight. Marcel jerked, clawing at his chest. His men rushed to surround him.

"What is happening?" the arch-priest demanded.

"He's having a paroxysm!" Rossignol cried. "Give him air."

The Duc wheezed and choked. Rossignol loosened the clasp of his cloak and shouted for water. Lucius clenched his fist, savoring the moment. The bastard was strong, fighting with all his will, but another thirty seconds and he'd be—

An arrow punched through Lucius's shoulder, knocking him back. More hummed through the air. The Red Rogue heaved the parley table to one side and crouched behind the makeshift barrier, shouting at the rest of their party. Arrows thwacked into the oak, raining down like a storm of deadly wasps. Three rebels dropped dead before they'd taken a step. Lucius looked for the archers and realized it was the Sons of Bel.

He dropped down next to the Rogue. "They've betrayed you," he hissed.

His dark eyes were dazed and disbelieving. "You're hit."

"Forget that," Lucius snapped. "Give me leave to fight back. Now!"

The Rogue gave a slight shake of his head. Lucius was about to argue when a gout of flame shot past. He peeked around the side of the table. One of the priests was staring back at him. Red embers glowed in the shadowed eye-holes of his mask. *Justinian.*

Justinian ducked behind a pillar just as Lucius hurled a fireball. From the corner of his eye, he saw a woman helping the Duc to safety. *Not a chance.* Lucius raised a hand to finish him when he sensed a strange power radiating towards him. His knees buckled. Pain exploded at the back of his skull.

Fire flowed along the walls and ceiling. Then a force sent

the oaken table tumbling the length of the chamber like a child kicking a toy. Lucius lay with one cheek pressed against the stone, his back riddled with arrows. He couldn't move, couldn't even blink, but his eyes were open and he saw soldiers drag the Red Rogue to the Duc.

Marcel tore the scarf from his face. Lucius would have laughed if they weren't so completely fucked. The Rogue's coal-black hair was in disarray, his face blazing with fury. Rossignol flinched as if he'd been struck.

Lucius couldn't see the Sons of Bel gathered along the walls, but he heard their gasps and murmurs.

"You know this man," the Duc said. His voice was hoarse, and he was leaning on the woman's arm. She had strange symbols painted on her skin. Lucius realized she must be Morgen, his consort from the Western Isles.

Rossignol's mouth opened, but nothing came out. His jowls had turned the shade of a ripe plum.

"Well, who is he?" the Duc demanded.

"Tell him, Galoy," their prisoner said with a twisted smile.

"Shut up." The Duc turned to the other soldiers. "Do you recognize this man?"

They exchanged looks. Several nodded.

"It's the captain's bedmate, Your Grace."

"Bedmate?" the Duc repeated. "Is this a jest? If so, it is in poor taste!"

"No, Your Grace. He's a Son of Bel. Or at least he dressed like one when he visited Captain Rossignol in his chambers." The soldier managed to keep a straight face, but he seemed to be enjoying himself. "On a regular basis, my lord."

The Duc rounded on Rossignol, stark disbelief on his face. "The Red Rogue is one of your *prostitutes*?"

"Ah . . ." Rossignol blinked rapidly.

"Somebody fucking speak!" the Duc bellowed.

"His name is Brennos Fearghal," the arch-priest stammered. "Yes, he is a brother. But he has served with devotion since he was a little boy. We all hold him in high regard. I promise you, I had no idea . . ."

Rossignol's paralysis finally broke. He stalked over and backhanded Brennos so hard the crack echoed through the temple. Brennos licked his bloody lip and spat at Rossignol's feet.

"I loathed every minute of your company," he said with a dry laugh. "But Bel, you loved to talk! Did it never occur to you that I took an excessive interest in the Duc's movements?" Brennos shook his head in wonder. "If he hadn't gotten lucky, he'd already be a dead man."

Rossignol's chest heaved. He looked on the verge of having a paroxysm himself. "You lying whore!" he spat. "It was you who took the holy relic from my chamber!"

"Relic?" the Duc echoed. "What relic?"

The arch-priest jolted as if he'd been goosed. He stared at Rossignol in astonishment. "Brother Symeon gave the box to *you*?"

"For safekeeping." Rossignol stabbed a finger at Brennos. "Until he stole it from my chambers!" Wounded humiliation twisted the captain's face. He'd fancied himself in love, Lucius realized. "I never should have confided in you—"

"Gave him *what*?" the Duc roared.

"An iron box," Rossignol gabbled. "Symeon was my uncle. He asked me to hold it for him. Only for a week or so, he said. I don't know what's inside, it wouldn't open." He turned from purple to a sickly green under the Duc's withering glare. "I intended to tell you, Your Grace. I was just waiting for the right . . ."

"So you told your lover, and he took it from you," Justinian said, walking forward. The mask of Bel was pushed up on his forehead. He was smiling, a frozen rictus that was terrible to behold.

Rossignol gave a vigorous nod. "Yes. Yes! He must have it."

"I don't," Brennos said. "Rossignol is lying."

"But why would he lie?" Justinian asked softly. "Why bring it up, if you didn't steal it from him?" A ball of flame danced above his palm. He began to roll it from hand to hand.

"Go ahead." Brennos spat blood again. "I don't have it, nor do I know where it is. Burn me. Kill me. I don't care."

But I do, Lucius thought. Part of him had wondered all along if the Red Rogue and Brother Brennos might be the same man. Why else would the priest have refused to speak? And Justinian . . . *I should have stopped him in the garden. Now it's too late.*

Brennos tried to lean back as Justinian reached for him, but the Duc's soldiers held him fast.

"Where is it?" Justinian asked.

"I don't know."

Brennos bit down on a scream as Justinian trailed a finger along his jaw. Lucius smelled burning flesh. The Duc was watching with an avid expression.

"Melt his eyes," he urged. "Blind him."

Lucius tried to stop them, but his limbs wouldn't respond. No one paid him any attention. They thought he was one of the dead rebels. Justinian knew better, but he didn't seem to care anymore.

"Where is it?" The question had the exact same inflection. He would keep asking, Lucius knew, until there was nothing left to burn.

"I don't know!"

Brennos screamed again, and then an arrow took Justinian through the throat. He coughed up dark blood.

"Touch him again and Marcel dies," someone shouted. "You all die."

The two soldiers holding up their slumped, bloody prisoner suddenly looked nervous. The Sons of Bel stood beyond Lucius's line of sight, but he guessed their bows were now trained on the Duc and his men.

"Stand down!" the arch-priest snapped.

"We didn't know he was one of our own," came the angry response. "Have you no loyalty?"

"Brother Brennos is favored by the god!" another added. "Bel will never permit—"

The rest was drowned out in a blast of heat so intense it turned the world white. When Lucius's vision cleared, he saw Justinian yank the arrow from his throat and throw it down.

"Where have you hidden the box? Tell me!"

No voices were raised in protest this time. They were all dead.

Brennos blearily raised his head. "Go back to hell," he whispered.

Justinian reached for his battered face. White-hot flames wreathed the mortifex's hand, crackling and hissing. Lucius did not want to see what came next, but he couldn't close his eyes against it. They were already damned. Surely hell could not be worse—

"Enough," Morgen snapped.

Justinian's grinning rictus vanished in a whirlwind of black dust. Pulsing tentacles filled his mouth, made his throat and eyes bulge, bound his arms to his sides. Lucius realized that she was a necromancer — a very powerful one. He let out a silent cheer.

"What are you doing, pet?" the Duc demanded. "We were making progress."

"He's telling the truth," she replied with a touch of impatience. "He doesn't have the box. But I think I know who does."

"Who?" Rossignol demanded.

"Hold your faithless tongue before I cut it out," the Duc snarled. He gripped Morgen's face, forcing her to look him in the eye. "Have you betrayed me, too? Did you know about this?"

"No, my lord," she said quickly. "But I saw someone else near Rossignol's rooms. Let me handle this. I will bring it to you, I swear. When have I ever been wrong?"

The Duc's anger faded. He released her, though the imprints of his fingers remained. "That is true enough." He turned. "You, Rossignol, are going to Blackwater with your lover. The two of you will burn together."

Rossignol blanched as his own soldiers surrounded him. Morgen approached the arch-priest. His eyes flicked between her and Justinian, who lay insensible on the floor.

"Speak or she will kill you as she killed my father," the Duc said. "What is this relic?"

The arch-priest's mouth sagged in defeat. He looked like a broken old man. "It is called the Grand Menotte. It was given to the Sons of Bel by Jaskin Cazal. But Your Grace, please listen to me. The talisman cannot be used. It is far too dangerous—"

"What does it do?" the Duc interrupted.

"It binds one hundred mortifexes." The arch-priest swallowed hard. He raised an imploring hand. "But the talisman drove Jaskin to madness. Please, my lord, when you find it, you must return it to us . . ." He rambled on, but Marcel had clearly stopped listening. He stared through the windows with a far-off, dreamy look.

"Your Grace?" the arch-priest finally prompted.

The Duc looked at him. "Yes, of course." He turned to one of his men. "Your knife."

The man drew a dagger from his boot and handed it over. So the arch-priest had lied when he said the Duc and his men were searched for weapons. Well, the poor bastard was regretting it now.

"Hold him," Marcel ordered.

The arch-priest looked alarmed. "But . . . but you promised to spare me if I helped you take the Red Rogue alive," he stammered. "We had a bargain!"

The Duc gripped the arch-priest's gray hair and yanked his head back.

"No!" Brennos shouted. "You cannot do this. Not in the god's own house—"

Marcel slit his throat with one practiced slash. A fine red spray speckled the Duc's face, but the blood did not show against the black doublet. Lucius wondered if he had worn it for that very reason.

"We'll call my debts to the brotherhood paid in full," the Duc said cheerfully, stepping back.

A contingent of fully armored soldiers spilled inside the temple from the far end. They must have arrived by boat.

"We secured the monastery, Your Grace," one said, lifting his helm and bending a knee.

"And the other priests who live here?"

"All dead, Your Grace."

"Good. What is your name?"

"Roger LaHay, a knight of the Fifth Rank."

"I'm promoting you. You are the new captain of my guard," Marcel said. "Have these prisoners taken to Blackwater and ready an escort back to the palace. See that the bodies are thrown into the sea."

The man saluted.

"Janus will try to cause trouble when he wakes," Morgen told the Duc in a low voice. "But I took the precaution of bringing cold iron. We must bind him."

The Duc gave the order. Brennos, half-conscious, was dragged off with a subdued, trembling Rossignol. As the soldiers wrapped Janus in thick lengths of iron chain, he revived enough to meet Lucius's eye. The fury and desolation there lifted Lucius's spirits. Morgen Nadezhda had trounced them both. *How,* Lucius still had no idea. He had never met a necromancer so strong. Never even suspected they could wield such power. So what was she doing with that strutting sadist Vazsoly Marcel?

"Come along, pet," the Duc called, striding with his men to the door. "I want this box taken into custody immediately."

"A moment, my lord," Morgen said. "I must first ask Bel to forgive the blood spilled inside his temple."

The Duc halted. "When did you ever care about Bel? You islanders are godless heathens."

"I would not spit in the face of any deity." She gazed up at the huge statue. "It is foolish to overstep without making proper atonement, Your Grace. Would you risk Bel's wrath?"

Vazsoly waved a hand impatiently. "Very well. But don't take too long."

Their footsteps receded. Morgen knelt in front of the statue and bowed her head. Silence fell. Lucius listened to the rain and distant cries of gulls. Every single priest at Bel Mara was dead. What atonement could she possibly seek?

"The Duc does not realize you are here, Lucius Bittencourt," Morgen said at last, "and I will not tell him. If you want to save your meddlesome priest, you'd better hurry." She turned her head and stared straight at him. "But heed this warning. Vazsoly Marcel is *mine*. Kill whomever you want except for him. If you betray me, I will deal with you more harshly than you can imagine."

She stood and left the temple. The terrible weakness gripping his limbs gradually eased. Oh, he hurt badly, but he could manage the pain. Lucius bit his lip and pulled the arrows out, one by one. Then he limped for the door as fast as he could.

TWENTY-SEVEN

Cas scoured every inch of Janus's chambers, even tapping the walls and floor for secret compartments. The iron box wasn't there.

He slapped dust from his hands, surveying the two adjoining rooms one last time. *Is there anyplace I missed?* But no, he'd gone through the monster's meager belongings twice, taking great care to leave them exactly as they'd been before.

If he didn't find the relic in the next few hours, they'd never make it back to Nathan in time. Maybe Lo had heard something. Found a new lead. Cas clung to this slender hope as he left the mortifex's chamber. *If not, there has to be a way to void the pact. I'll gladly throw Nathan Ouvrard into his own crevasse if that does the trick—*

Rapidly approaching footsteps made him duck into a side passage. The group passed in a flash, but he was pretty sure he saw Janus, bound from neck to ankles in thick iron chains, being dragged along by four soldiers. Cas stared after them. *But why would...?*

Lippa. Had Janus recognized her? Had he...?

Cas took off at a sprint for the servants' quarters, torchlit corridors blurring past. He couldn't bear to finish the thought, but the words came anyway. *Child murder.* That might be enough to get Janus thrown in irons.

He burst into their room to find Da with his nose buried in a mug of ale and Lippa trying to coax him to eat a bite of pottage. Cas pulled her into his arms, dizzy with relief. She hugged him back for a minute, then squirmed loose.

"What's wrong with you?" she asked with a quizzical look.

He caught his breath. "The Duc's punishing Janus for something. I saw him in iron restraints. And I thought . . . I feared . . ."

"That he'd hurt me," she finished briskly. "Well, I'm glad to hear that, but I don't know why. Where have you been, Cas? I was getting worried."

He glanced at his father. As usual, Da looked disheveled and glassy-eyed, showing little interest in their conversation.

"I found my friend, Delilah." Cas shut the door and sat on a pallet. "The one I told you about."

Lip gave him a perfunctory smile. She seemed preoccupied. "That's nice, Cas."

He rubbed his face, desperate to confide in someone. Lip had grown in the last two years. She might have sensible advice. "Yes, well. We have a big problem."

"What is it?"

"Delilah came to Prydwen to find something. We thought Janus might have it, but I just searched his rooms. No luck."

Lip pushed her spoon around the bowl of pottage, not quite looking at him. "What is it?"

"An iron box."

"Oh."

The lack of curiosity from his nosy sister set off alarm bells. "Have you seen it, Lip?"

"I told you, it's Felippa now." She spooned some mush into her mouth and chewed it like a cow, slow and deliberate and staring off into space.

"Felippa." He watched her closely, excitement building. "You *have* seen it."

"What? I haven't."

"*Please.*"

There was a lengthy silence as she gazed down into her bowl.

"I promised I wouldn't tell anyone," she whispered.

Cas came closer, though he didn't crowd her. If she thought she was being bullied, she'd just dig her heels in. "My friend will die if we don't find it. No exaggeration. A necromancer put a . . . a curse on her."

Lip finally met his eyes. "Do you know what's inside?"

He shook his head.

"Nor do I," she admitted. "But I think it's evil. A priest was murdered for it."

"Janus killed him," Cas said. "That's why I thought he might have it. But the box originally belonged to a necromancer named Jaskin Cazal. His heir wants it back, and he's using Delilah to get it."

Lip set the bowl aside and went to the basket where she kept her writing tools. She dug down and took out an object wrapped in an ink-stained cloth.

Cas let out a strangled laugh. "You actually have it *here*?"

She flushed. "I know it's a terrible hiding place. I was trying to think of a better one when Da came back."

She handed Cas the box. He knew right away that it was the real thing. An icy chill seeped through the wrappings, numbing his fingers. It was heavy, even for iron. He peeled back a corner of the cloth, then quickly covered it again.

"Where on earth did you find it, Li...I mean, Felippa?"

"You'll never believe it! Captain Rossignol's chamber, inside a chest. His uncle was the priest who got killed at Bel Mara." She suddenly looked miserable. "But I'm supposed to give it to Brother Brennos."

"Who's Brother Brennos?"

"A priest who comes to the palace sometimes. I thought he was loyal to the Duc, but it turns out he's on our side. He gave me the key to get into Rossignol's room and told me where to find it." She rubbed her arms. "Janus came while I was there. I'm certain he was looking for it, too—"

"Wait, *Janus* came?"

Lip nodded. "I thought for sure he'd catch me. I hid up the chimney. He stood there for the longest time, Cas. I thought he'd sense the iron box, like you warned me they can."

"Feckin' hells. But he didn't?"

"No. I think the poker by the fireplace confused him."

Cas regarded his little sister, his throat tight. She'd risked everything to get the box. Not for herself but for the cause she believed in. He couldn't take it from her by force. Well . . . he would if he absolutely had to, but he'd rather she gave it to him willingly.

"Listen to me, Felippa. You must let me take it to Delilah. She needs it more than Brother Brennos."

"But what do I tell him when he asks for it?" She looked distressed. "We're giving it to the Red Rogue. To help the cause."

"I understand, but like you said, this box is evil. It wouldn't do the rebels any good. If anything, it would be a danger to them."

Lip silently picked at the strings of her apron.

"The box must be given back to the necromancers who made it," Cas said firmly. "Delilah can do that. And if she

255

doesn't, the curse will kill her. So I think she needs it more, don't you?"

Cas could see her working through all the angles. At last, she gave a slow nod. "I'll tell Brennos I couldn't find it."

He swept her into another hug. "Thank you," he whispered into her hair. "You've saved us."

"Is she . . . is Delilah your beau, Cas?"

He grinned. "She started as a friend, but yes, she's my beau. I can't wait for you to meet her someday—"

The door crashed open so hard it rebounded off the wall. Guards swarmed inside, along with the tall, dark-haired woman he'd seen the day he arrived. Her gaze fell on the wrapped bundle. Before Cas could move, she darted forward and picked it up. For a wild moment, he imagined grabbing the staff from its place in the corner and knocking them all out, then running with the box. Perhaps Gui could have managed it. But Cas knew he didn't stand a chance, and he couldn't leave Lip and Da to take the fall, anyway.

"Who are you?" he asked, pushing Lip behind him.

"Shut your mouth, thief," one of the guards growled, "or I'll—"

The woman raised a hand and he fell silent. "I am Morgen Nadezhda." She looked Cas up and down. "Who are you?"

"Felippa's brother. Please, she's only thirteen—"

"I took it." Da lurched upright, steadying himself against the wall. "Stole it from that idiot Rossignol." The name came out slurred. "They don't know anything 'bout it."

The guards grabbed his arms. Cas tried to intervene and earned a clout to the ear that left his head buzzing.

"He didn't do it!" Lip burst out. "It was me—"

"Don't lie, child," Morgen interrupted sharply. "We all know it couldn't have been you." Her cold eyes fixed on Da. "I know you. You are the Duc's taster."

The guards regarded Da with scorn. "He's an old sot. Just look at him. More likely it was the young fellow. Shall we arrest them all, milady?"

Cas found Lip's hand and gave it a reassuring squeeze, though his heart was thumping. Ten minutes later and he might have been gone with the box. The thing truly was cursed.

"No," Morgen replied after a long moment. "Just the one who confessed. But the girl and her brother are not to leave this chamber. Guard the door."

They dragged Da from the room, Morgen walking after them. The moment the door closed, Lip burst out sobbing. She was crying so hard, Cas could barely make out the words.

"I'm sorry, I'm sorry!" she wailed, as he held her tight. "It's all my fault. Now they'll burn Da. They'll take him to Blackwater and they'll burn him!"

Duc Vazsoly Marcel hammered at the iron box with the hilt of his sword, cursing and sweating. Morgen watched in amused silence. Typically, he thought every problem could be solved by brute force.

"I shouldn't have killed the arch-priest," he panted. "The idiot might have known how to open it. Assuming his tale is even true."

"There is a way to test the claim." Morgen fetched a candle, holding it just above the lid. In the guttering light, a glowing sigil appeared — a left hand with teardrop flames above the fingertips.

"That is the device of Vendagni," Vazsoly said. His blue eyes widened. "So it is authentic?"

"Yes, but the arch-priest did not tell you everything, my

lord." She lowered her voice to a confidential whisper. "Jaskin Cazal couldn't risk the talisman falling into the hands of uncouth peasants. During its making, he included a spell to ensure that only a man of pure breeding and noble blood could wear the Grand Menotte. That is why the priests never wielded its power themselves."

Every word was a lie, but Vazsoly wouldn't trust her with the box otherwise.

"Of course," he murmured. "But how do you know this?"

"It is my business to know such things, my lord. Rumors of the Grand Menotte have circulated for centuries. I assumed it was just a child's tale, like Kopala's treasure."

"Can you open it?"

"In time, I am certain I can."

He smiled. "I can't wait to see Beatriu's face when I show up at the Alcazar with a hundred mortifexes. She'll wish she had responded favorably to my marriage suit then." His gaze went distant. "We will take Galatia, then Clovis. Hang Orlaith and her brat from the walls. And after that, we will conquer the Moon Courts. I will make you a dark princess, pet." Vazsoly exhaled slowly. "How did you know where to find it?"

Morgen guessed that Felippa had the box from the moment Rossignol said it was stolen from his chamber. When she ran into the girl in the hall, Felippa had been as furtive and skittish as the wild rabbits in the heath behind Morgen's childhood cottage.

Morgen had not spared her out of pity. No, she felt a kinship. They were both outcasts. If the girl's father wanted to trade his life for hers, Morgen had decided to let him.

"I saw your taster leaving Rossignol's room," she said.

The Duc scowled at the mention of his disgraced captain. "I will enjoy watching him burn. He's made me a laughingstock."

You were already a laughingstock, Morgen thought. She had shared the dream of Vazsoly murdering his father and suspected Lucius Bittencourt was behind it. Janus might have the power, but he lacked the imagination.

"So you still plan to attend the executions?" Morgen asked, knowing the question would goad him. "I thought you might remain here."

Vazsoly eyed the box, chewing his lip. "No," he said at last. "I want to see the Red Rogue dead myself. There can be no doubt, or else the rabble will simply revive the legend and some other masked fool will claim to be the Red Rogue." His jaw set. "Why can't I bring Janus with me for protection?"

Kaethe, he was stupid. "Because he wants this Grand Menotte, too," she explained patiently. "He would kill you for it, my lord. But after you put it on, he will be bound to you forever."

"Just get this box open by the time I return. Then I'll pay a visit to the Shambles with my new army and finish the job. Perhaps I'll make Bel Mara my new garrison. We can replace the statue of Bel with one of myself." He laughed. "Or a nude of you! What do you think, pet?"

Morgen smiled. "Whatever pleases you, my lord."

He kissed her. Then he gripped her arm hard, eyes glittering. "Do not think of betraying me."

She held his menacing blue eyes. "I have always been loyal to you. I already told you, I could not wield this power even if I wanted to."

Another lie, but he wouldn't leave her alone with it otherwise.

"Good." He released her and stepped back. "I'll return soon. My men will guard the door until then. No one is to enter or leave."

Morgen watched him leave. She had seen firsthand how he

treated those he conquered. Vazsoly had burned and slaughtered his way across the Western Isles. He was sorely mistaken if he imagined he would ever wield the talisman. No, she was meant to take it herself. With the Grand Menotte, she could make Vazsoly suffer beyond his worst nightmares. She could stop other evil men.

Morgen sat before her mirror with the pot of ash, drawing jagged symbols of power on her cheeks and forehead. Tongues, the language of dead. Very few could read the written form, but her mother had been one. When Morgen was done, she rested a palm on the box, allowing the chill to seep into her bones. She sensed no seam or joint, but it had to be there.

Open for me — before my scheming brother returns.

Twenty-Eight

Lucius limped across the causeway, hood drawn against the pitiless sun. Blood oozed from a dozen arrow wounds. His heart had stopped beating, which slowed the loss considerably, but he still felt weak. The tide was coming in, lapping at the edges of the road, and this made him even sicker.

If he went directly to the prison, he might save Brennos, but he would lose the Grand Menotte. He no longer cared about giving it to Magnus. The only thing that mattered was stopping Vazsoly Marcel from opening the box. If he did, a new empire would rise within a matter of months, perhaps weeks. And when he went mad, Aveline would burn.

If that weren't bad enough, Orlaith might summon him back to Aquitan at any moment. And if she discovered the lies he'd been feeding her . . . His own punishment would make the pyres pale in comparison.

Yet Lucius found that he longer feared her wrath the way he used to.

I've been the Redvaynes' monster for far too long. They made me believe there was nothing else left. But they were wrong.

His heart urged him to rescue a single man, but it was obvious what Brennos would choose. Everything he had fought for would be lost if Vazsoly wore that talisman.

THE HEAVILY ARMED guards at the palace let Lucius get within a hundred paces before ordering him to halt. He raised his hands in a gesture of surrender.

"I come with a message from the Red Rogue!"

"Archers take aim!"

The men atop the wall readied their bows.

"The Rogue's already in custody, you fool," someone shouted. "You can join him or die where you stand. Now kneel and throw down your weapons!"

Lucius had a good laugh over that. "I can't!" he shouted back.

The captain made a slashing motion. "Fire!"

Arrows rained down. Lucius batted them aside with shields of air. The archers drew a fresh volley and let loose with the same results. Their captain issued a series of feverish orders, but Lucius was no longer listening. The sun filled him with boiling heat, filled him to bursting.

He held up his hands. "These are my weapons! And if you want fire, you shall have it!"

Balls of flame streaked from his palms in a roaring arc. They consumed the archers in a heartbeat. The soldiers below barely had time to draw their swords before Lucius unleashed a wall of boiling orange fire as wide as the gates. It raced across the open ground, faster than a galloping horse, and engulfed them. There were a few ragged screams, but the sentries were consumed so swiftly and completely, all that remained was smoking armor.

Shouts erupted from various distant points as he raced across the charred earth and forced his way through the sally gate. It had all happened in a matter of seconds. The handful of guards on the other side were woefully unprepared to deal with him. Lucius set the nearest one alight, took the man's red-hot blade, and carved a path through the others. Then he ran with all the haste a daēva could muster to a rear entrance of the sprawling palace.

He cut down the pair of sentries there and looked back. The guardhouses along the wall were in quite a stir, but his passage had been of such blurring speed that mortal eyes could not follow. They were focused on the carnage at the gates.

Lucius slipped through the door, sagging against the frame. Dangerous, how good it felt to channel so much fire. To obliterate his enemies. Of course, Orlaith had sensed the outburst through their bond. It worried and puzzled her, but she hadn't severed his power. Not yet. She was too cautious for that. When she learned what he had done, though . . .

Lucius yanked the scarf down. The entrance led into the servants' quarters. He strode along a low, dim hall, hoping his red cloak covered the worst of the blood. A door opened ahead and one of the young maids stepped out, holding a mop and bucket. Lucius caught her wrist before she could run.

"Where are the rooms of the Nerides family?"

She pointed down the corridor with a shaking hand. "That way."

"And?"

"T-turn left at the crossing, then right."

Lucius released her. She darted away, leaving the mop and

bucket behind. He followed the directions and found two soldiers standing in front of a door. Lucius was on them like a leaping tiger, snapping a neck and impaling the second with his own blade. He kicked the bodies aside and opened the door.

Castelio was sitting on a pallet with his sister. He jumped up. The girl scooted back, terror on her face.

"Lucius!" His gaze narrowed. "What the hells happened to you?"

"There's no time," Lucius snapped. "I need your aid."

"And I need yours. My father was arrested and taken to Blackwater. We have to stop—"

"I'll take care of that," Lucius said impatiently. "But you must do something for me here. There's a talisman, a dangerous one. It's fallen into the Duc's possession and he can't have it."

Castelio nodded slowly. "What is it?"

"A menotte." He raised his wrist. "Like this one, but it controls a hundred mortifexes. It's inside an iron box. If we're lucky, the Duc will have taken it to his chamber. He has a necromancer . . . Are you listening?"

Castelio blinked. "Did you say . . . a hundred?"

"It's why Janus is here. He's been looking for it. And we're going to give it to him, understand?" Lucius glanced at the sister. She'd turned a sickly shade of green. "Then he'll go away and never come back."

Castelio studied him for a long moment. "Your friend, you mean? I saw him leaving your rooms."

Lucius bit back a surge of irritation. "I knew him a long time ago, but he is my friend no longer. If you need proof, I will give you his true name. Then you can banish him. But only after he gets the box."

Castelio's brows furrowed as he considered the offer. "If I do this, you'll promise to free my father?"

"I swear that I will do my utmost. There are others who will be burned, too, and one in particular that I happen to care about. But I must go to Blackwater now, or they will all die." He sighed. "I cannot banish another mortifex myself. That power is forbidden to me. But you are a Quietus. You know how it is done." When Castelio hesitated, he added, "Janus might be a devil, but he is the only one I trust with this menotte. He cannot use it and wants only to see it destroyed. You would be rid of him forever."

"What's his true name?"

"Do you agree to my terms?"

Castelio gave a reluctant nod. "Aye. And I know where to find him."

A weight slid from Lucius's shoulders. "His name is Justinian. For what it's worth, I did not know that he was the one who came to your farm. Not until today. I never lied to you, Castelio."

"How do you know I won't steal it myself?"

"You're not that stupid." He arched a brow. "Unless I have sorely misjudged you?"

"I have no desire to wear this thing."

"But the Duc would." His sister's voice was soft but steady. "He would command an army that couldn't be killed because it is already dead. An army that wields magic."

Lucius met her eye. She looked so very young, but she clearly had both wit and backbone. "That sums it up." He turned to Castelio. "As I said, the Duc has a necromancer. The strongest I've ever met. No doubt she is working on getting the box open right now."

"Then you do your job, and I'll do mine. I assume the guards outside . . . ?"

"Will not trouble you unless they rise again." Lucius

opened the door and paused. "I'm putting my faith in you, Quietus."

Castelio gave him a level look. "And mine in you. Go. I have a plan."

Lucius nodded and swept out the door.

TWENTY-NINE

"I'm coming with you," Lip said.

Cas gripped her small hand. It felt surprisingly strong. "You're brave, I know that, but if I have to worry about keeping you safe, we might fail."

"But it's my fault that the Duc got the box—"

"It's not your fault." He rummaged through his travel bag for the iron knives and vials of Kaethe's Tears. "That priest shouldn't have asked you to steal it."

"Why didn't you tell the mortifex what happened? You pretended like you'd never heard of the box."

"Because it's none of Lucius's business. But we know the sanglant bastard's true name now, Lip!" He cast her an apologetic look. "I mean, Felippa."

"If he told the truth," she said with a note of skepticism.

"If he did, aye. I hope he did." Cas shoved the weapons into the waist of his breeches. "It fits though. A mortifex's true name must contain the letters of its false name. Lucius is Claudius. Nathan Ouvrard's mortifex Vigo is Vergilious."

"And Janus is Justinian," Lo finished. She held out Gui's staff. "Don't you want this?"

Cas eyed it regretfully. "I can't. He'll recognize it. Do you have a scrap of paper? Something official-looking?"

Lip's corner was the neatest part of the room. She kept an old crate filled with quills and ink pots and other items related to her work in the scriptorium. He watched her roll up a blank leaf of parchment and tie it with a ribbon.

"Will this do?" she asked.

"It's perfect." Cas glanced out the door. The guards were still dead, but someone could come along at any moment. "Cover your ears."

"Why?"

"Please, just do it."

Lip sighed and covered her ears. Cas turned his back. "Shelithoth," he whispered. "Show yourself. I must tell you something important."

"What are you doing?"

Cas spun around. "Ears."

She sighed and covered them again. Cas bent down to check under the bed. "Shelithoth! I summon you, if you'll come. I found the box—"

Lip gave a startled cry as the fat gray cat materialized at her feet. She lurched back a step, eyes wide.

"You found it?" Thistle growled.

"Tell your mistress to come here right away. I hope to have it by the time she arrives."

The cat blinked. "This is good news."

"And I know what's inside. A menotte to bind a hundred mortifexes. Er, that's all. I must go before the box is lost again. Do you require . . . banishing?"

Thistle gave him a look of utter disdain.

"Cas!"

He turned. Teo stood in the doorway, jaw gaping. "There's dead soldiers out here!"

When Cas looked back, Thistle was gone. He yanked his brother into the room.

"Da's been arrested," Teo hissed. "I just heard it from the head groom. The palace is under attack and—"

"He's been taken to Blackwater, but help is on the way," Cas interrupted. "I need you both to find a good place to hide until this blows over. The stables might work." He gripped Teo's shoulder. "Don't worry, Da will be fine." He prayed it was true. "I have to go, but I'll find you both later."

Teo shook his head. "What? Where are you going—"

"Lip will explain. Just hide!"

He pushed them out the door and hurried down a nearby flight of stairs into the sunless depths of the palace. He knew the way by heart now, his feet taking each turn through the maze of underground passages as his thoughts raced five steps ahead. No wonder Nathan Ouvrard wanted the box so badly. Cas had speculated about what might be inside, but not even his worst nightmares had come close to the truth.

As he neared Justinian's rooms, he almost walked straight into a group of guards. Luckily, they were talking and he managed to duck into the buttery before they saw him. From what he gathered as they passed by, they'd been summoned to the wall. Less luckily, one remained at his post in front of the mortifex's door. But it was still better than Cas had hoped for. He straightened his tunic and approached.

"That's far enough," the guard snapped. "What do you want?"

Cas held up the rolled parchment. "I have a message from your lieutenant."

The man frowned. "We just received new orders. What's this one?"

Cas shrugged. "I'm sorry, sir, I can't read."

The soldier threw him a look of contempt and snapped his fingers. "Bring it here."

He trudged over and handed him the rolled parchment. The guard set his halberd against the door. The instant he began untying the ribbon, Cas grabbed his head with both hands and slammed it hard into the corner of the stone lintel. He crumpled in a clanking slither of mail. There was a smear of blood on the wall, but Cas didn't stop to see if he lived. He dragged the body around the corner. Then he opened the door and stepped inside.

Justinian paced the confines of a nine-pointed star formed from some dark, ashy substance. Human remains? Something with enough power to hold him, at any rate. The mortifex's head snapped up. Relief and surprise flooded his face.

"You! Get over here and let me out."

Cas stared into the coals of his eyes. *I could banish him right now and be done with it. Send him straight back to whatever hell he crawled out of.*

The temptation was strong. He might never have Justinian at his mercy again. Knowing his true name wasn't enough. He'd have to trick the mortifex into another star.

But he couldn't reach the Duc's chamber alone. There was no chance the inner sanctum would be left unguarded. And even if by some miracle he did make it, he'd still have to get past Marcel's necromancer.

I called Lo's plan shite. Mine is even worse.

"Come on, lad," Justinian wheedled. "It'll take but a moment."

"What'll you give me?" he asked in a sly tone.

"I've got a chest of gold hidden away," Justinian said quickly. "It's yours if you aid me. Enough to live without a care for the rest of your life. Seize your chance, boy! It won't come again."

Cas pretended to mull it over. "Did the Duc put you in there?"

"It was that bitch whore of his," Justinian snarled. "The Duc knows nothing about it. I'm his trusted advisor. Now, break that line and you'll make your fortune."

Cas ignored the voice of reason that told him he was about to die. He used the toe of his boot to scrub a gap in the ash. The mortifex stepped out and clapped him hard on the shoulder.

"Where's my reward?" Cas asked, gut tensing.

"You'll get it. But I need you to carry something out of the palace for me first. Run and you'll end up a greasy smear, understand?" This warning was issued with no change in inflection. "Do as you're told and you can keep everything in this chamber. I have no use for any of it."

He bobbed his head and swallowed hard. *Perfect.* He'd expected to trail the fex at a distance, but Justinian was actually bringing him along, the great idiot. It made sense that he wouldn't want to touch the box himself. Cas wondered what his plan was. If he knew about the cistern gate within the palace walls, he would have Cas carry it there, and then kill him.

"Now," Justinian said, "where is the Duc?"

"He went to Blackwater Jail." Cas glanced at the door and lowered his voice. "But if it's revenge you want, I heard a guard say that the Lady Morgen retired to his chamber and left orders not to be disturbed."

Justinian's eyes glowed with anticipation. Cas would have pitied her if she hadn't sent his father to be burned.

"She has something that belongs to me," the mortifex said. "We're going to get it. And like I said, if you try to run off—"

"I w-won't, milord," he stammered. "I swear it."

Justinian paused only to buckle on his bone-white blade and they left his chamber together, heading for the upper levels. The mortifex ignored the servants, who wisely fled in the opposite direction the instant they saw him. But when they reached the first sentries of the inner palace, he decimated the guards without a word, using his magic to lift them up like straw dolls and smash them headfirst into the walls.

Cas remembered being thrown across the barn like that. He'd known full well what he was unleashing when he let Justinian out, but his stomach still did a queasy roll as he stepped around their broken bodies.

They met three more checkpoints. Justinian used both fire and air to clear the path, not even bothering to draw his sword. As the corpses piled up, Cas began to question his own plan. And the knives were slipping down. He should have secured them better. He was about to adjust them when a frigid hand clamped around his arm.

"You still with me, boy?" Justinian asked softly.

Cas nodded, nailing his gaze to the floor. *Don't sense the iron. Just don't.*

Gui said the knives were too small to alert a mortifex unless it came very, very close. As Justinian was right now.

"Good. We're nearly there, so keep your mouth shut."

He turned away and Cas jammed a hand down his breeches, quickly rescuing the errant blades. They climbed a broad flight of steps to a wide, ornate hall with coffered ceilings and a marble floor inlaid with the cockatrice of House Marcel. The largest group of guards yet stood before a pair of carved double doors. Their heads turned as Justinian stepped into view. One opened his mouth to shout, but no sound came out, and then they were all sinking to their knees, eyes bulging.

The mortifex strode into their midst and proceeded to snap

their necks with economical precision, just the way the butcher in Swanton would wring the necks of chickens. It was all conducted in perfect silence. He must have used air to cushion their falls, for the men drifted down so slowly that not even their armor made a sound.

This grisly task complete, Justinian stared at the doors, gaze narrowing. A tendril of darkness was worming beneath them, slithering across the marble. The mortifex's face went taut. Then he thrust his arms forward and blew the doors off the hinges. Cas caught a brief glimpse of Morgen before one of the doors swept her away. Justinian stepped into the chamber. The heavy slab of wood lay on top of her, pinning her from the waist down. Blood ran from her nose. Her eyes were huge with shock. With a sweep of his arm, he sent the door flying like a leaf in a stiff wind. Then he lifted her bodily and hurled her through the windows on the far side. Glass shattered.

The necromancer was gone.

Let the bear and the wolf fight it out, Cas thought, his pulse hammering. *That was the idea. Except they were supposed to tear each other to shreds before the rabbit seized his chance.*

"Get in here, boy!" Justinian bellowed.

Cas picked his way through the rubble. The Duc's chamber was gaudily appointed in silver and gold, with mirrors everywhere that caught various angles of the mortifex's reflection. The canopied bed alone was bigger than his family's room. The iron box had tumbled to the foot of the steps leading up to the monstrous bed. Justinian stood over it.

"Wh-what is that, milord?" Cas asked, inching closer.

"The thing you will carry for me." His voice was distant, his expression curiously blank. He crouched down and made a small flame, holding it above the lid of the box. The line of his shoulders sagged. He turned to Cas with wide, staring eyes. "This is the one—"

Cas emptied a vial of Kaethe's Tears directly in his face. The mortifex screeched, throwing an arm up. Cas swept his knives free and drove one to the hilt into Justinian's chest. It scraped against bone, but he kept them wickedly sharp.

The fex unleashed a wild gout of flame. It whooshed past, setting the velvet drapes alight. Cas thumbed the stopper from the last vial and doused him with the contents. The skin on Justinian's face bubbled and steamed. One eye actually *popped*, running in viscous white fluid down his cheek.

Cas dropped the vial. He adjusted his grip on the second knife, aiming for the other eye, when a coil of air cinched tight around his throat, yanking him off the ground. Justinian roared with pain and fury. He tried to pull the knife from his chest, then screamed again as the iron hilt seared his palm.

Cas's vision started blacking at the edges. He tried to draw air, but the invisible garotte around his neck kept tightening. Justinian staggered towards him through a haze of smoke. The single eye blazed like a forge.

Then something whacked the fex across the legs. He lurched sideways and dropped to one knee. Lip stood behind him, her mouth curved down in lines of grim determination. Gui's staff sliced the air. There was an audible crack as it connected with Justinian's skull. The bonds of air vanished and Cas dropped to the carpet. He rolled over on his back, gasping.

Lip ran over and patted his cheeks. "Cas!"

"Thought I . . . told you to . . . hide."

She sniffed. "You're lucky I didn't."

"Where's Teo?" he croaked.

"Fighting at the wall." Her face shone with excitement. "The revolution's happening, Cas!"

He'd been too focused on Justinian to notice before, but

now he heard the sounds of a pitched battle through the broken windows.

"Feck," he groaned, sitting up. "Does no one listen to me anymore?"

Justinian lay unmoving, his face a ruined horror. Cas crawled around until he found the second iron knife. He briefly considered trying to saw the fex's head off, but that might just wake him up. Instead, he drew the blade across his scarred palm. Then he set about drawing a nine-pointed star around the stunned mortifex.

"How did you find me?" he asked, surprised at how fast the rawness in his throat had faded.

"I followed you from the start," Lip admitted. "I thought you might need the staff after all." She shuddered. "But it wouldn't have been hard. Justinian left a trail of dead people."

Cas glanced up at her. "Bet it felt good to whack him."

Lip bounced on her toes, still clutching the staff. "Really good." She gave him a nervous smile.

He had finished three points when his hand stopped bleeding. He studied it in confusion, then drew the knife across his palm again and made a fist. Red droplets pattered down, soaking into the carpet. He went back to work. Justinian was tall, and lying flat, so it was a larger star than he would have liked.

"If he starts to stir," Cas said, "whack him."

Another point and he was more than halfway done. Then the bleeding stopped. Cas stared stupidly at the knife, then at his palm. The cut had sealed again.

He was feeling lightheaded. Dangerously fuzzy. But there was a reason, wasn't there? A reason he was healing so fast.

"Cas?" Lip ventured. "You don't look well."

"I'm fine." Sluggishly, he grasped the problem. "Come here, Lip."

He realized he'd called her by the wrong name, but this time she didn't bother to correct him.

"Want me to cut myself?" She glanced anxiously at the mortifex. "I don't mind."

"No. Just wear this for me." He lifted Lo's talisman from his own neck and hung it around Lippa's.

She fingered the silver disk. "That's pretty. Where'd you get it?"

"A friend."

Cas slashed his palm again. It stung sharply this time. He crawled around the prone mortifex, counting the points. Six, seven . . . The blood kept flowing, though his hand was shaking now.

Justinian's unburned skin was bluish-white, like the belly of a rotting fish. His good eye was closed. He'd fallen on the knife, but had his head been turned that way before? The angle looked . . . slightly different.

Cas formed the last point and was closing the gap when Justinian reared up. Quick as a blink, he pulled Cas to his chest in a hard embrace. The smell of charred meat filled his nose. Cas drove the second knife clean through the back of Justinian's left hand, but the fex no longer seemed to care. His other hand gripped Cas's face, forcing it up. Shriveled lips parted, revealing a pink cave lined with white teeth.

"I will drain you, boy," he rasped, "drain every drop of you—"

"Stop!" Lip screamed. "Just stop!"

His head turned with a wet crunch. The single eye widened in recognition. He laughed, a grating rumble, and beckoned with the hand impaled by Cas's knife.

"Come over here, little one. Pull this out."

Lip raised the staff. With a contemptuous flick of his wrist, the mortifex threw her backwards. She hit the bed and bounced off, tumbling out of view. Justinian had Cas in a crushing hold, both arms pinned to his sides. Cas leaned forward, caught the hilt between his teeth, and twisted the knife. Justinian made a terrible sound. With a furious burst of force, Cas wrenched free and tried to crawl away.

"Run, Lip!" he cried. "Run!"

Flames licked at the walls. Shadows skittered and danced. For a moment, he was back in the burning barn, screaming at Teo, the lantern swinging wildly, the sheep bleating in terror.

Cas was almost out of the star when a hand closed around his ankle. He looked back and saw an inferno raging in the mortifex's eyes. Any pretense of life, of sanity was gone. Behind the forge-fires, there was only a bottomless black void.

"How does it feel to burn, mortal? I will devour you an inch at a time. Flay you slowly, like a pig roasting on a spit."

Cas realized the hem of his tunic was alight. He beat at the flames, trying to kick free. Where was Lip? Where—

She barreled past and hit Justinian hard enough to carry them both back across the line of blood. Time stretched as he saw her reach out and seal the star with her own bloody hand.

No, no, no . . .

"I banish you, Justinian!" Felippa cried in a high, clear voice.

Sudden darkness fell. Cas lunged at the star, but a wall of white-hot flames burst from the edges, driving him back. The swirling forces beyond whipped them higher and higher. He heard his little sister scream before the sound abruptly cut off.

Cas had no idea what happened to a living person if they were *inside* a banishing. Such a thing had never happened.

He ripped off his burning tunic and threw it down. "Felippa!"

The flames withered, sinking back into the carpet. Daylight

gradually returned. He stared through the haze of smoke and drifting ash, hope leaving him in a knee-buckling rush.

The star was empty. They were both gone.

The drapes still smoldered, but the walls and ceiling were stone. Nothing else had caught, though the chamber was streaked with black scorch marks. Cas viciously squeezed the cut on his palm. The pain was bright and welcome. He knelt and dripped fresh blood into the star.

"I summon you, Justinian," he snapped, stepping back.

Brief darkness. Then a cackle of unhinged laughter.

"I should have killed you when I had the chance, boy. Back when you were a stripling. But no matter. By the time I'm done, you'll wish you'd never been born."

He looked a nightmare. Most of his dark hair had burned away and half his skull was seamed with raw, weeping tissue. He gave a skeletal grin that twisted his flesh in strange ways.

"Where is she?" Cas demanded.

Justinian eyed the iron box. "Give that to me and I'll tell you."

Cas nodded slowly. He picked up the box, wincing at the chill. After a moment, he pressed it against the reddened skin above his navel, where the flames had raised a blister. Cold sank in, numbing the burn and raising goosebumps across his chest.

"What are you doing? Give it to me!"

Cas winked at him. Then he sauntered for the doorway.

"Wait! Come back! She's alive!" Justinian sounded genuinely surprised. "I don't know how. The banishing should have torn her to pieces."

Cas stopped, throat closing around a hot lump. The hallway ahead of him blurred. If he hadn't given her the protective talisman . . . Feckin' hells, Lip! She hadn't even known what it did.

"I'll tell you exactly where she is," Justinian said. "Just toss that box in here, boy."

Cas shoved down a toxic stew of hatred, fear, and guilt, locking it all away. That, at least, he was good at. When he turned, his eyes were dry, his voice steady.

"I already know where she is. With Magnus the Merciless, aye?"

Even wrecked, Justinian's face registered shock. He went perfectly still. Cas held up his hand, showing him the tattoo.

"I happen to know a few things about your kind. One is that when you're banished, you return to whatever place you call home."

He hadn't been sure of this at all, but the mortifex's reaction confirmed it. Rage twisted Justinian's gash of a mouth. He laughed again, though it sounded forced.

"Did you become a Quietus because of me, boy? It won't save you. First, I'll kill your sister. Then, I'll come for you."

Cas studied him. "How do you plan to do that?"

Justinian's head cocked, the single eye rolling in its socket. Cas watched with cold glee as he figured it out. "That's right, you piece of shite. I won't be banishing you again. You can rot in there."

"It won't hold me long!" Justinian shrieked. "I'll come after you and when I do—"

Cas turned his back. At least Lip had one less problem to deal with. Justinian would escape eventually, and he would follow, but he'd have to go the long way — through a gate. And Cas planned to get his sister back well before the bastard arrived.

He tore a strip from his burnt tunic and bound his hand. Then he searched for the staff; it had been hurled with Felippa across the room and rolled beneath the Duc's massive bed. When he picked it up, the runes flickered with faint blue light, so brief he might have imagined it. Cas bit his lip in frustration. He had no idea how to control the power inside. Gui knew, but they'd probably never meet again. For one deranged moment, he was tempted to hurl it out the window.

Patience rarely gets you killed.

It was one of Gui's favorite pearls of wisdom and used to irritate Cas no end, since it was usually whispered hours into the dogwatch at some abandoned lichyard, when Cas was stiff and cold and dreaming of his bed. But the words came back to him now.

"It might not be yours anymore," he muttered, striding from the chamber with the staff in one hand and the box under his arm, "but it sure as hells isn't mine."

THIRTY

The moment Lucius saw Blackwater Jail, he knew he was in trouble. The long, squat building was surrounded by a thick iron fence. Pure iron, not an alloy. It made his skin crawl even from a distance.

He paused at the top of the hill, cursing his own stupidity. He should have anticipated iron defenses. Considering the number of prisoners who died within the prison's walls, they would need to contain the risen. He'd have to find a way past the fence.

A sea of bodies churned before the main gates, which were secured by heavy iron chains. Soldiers watched from circular stone towers set at intervals along the fence. Lucius hurried to the outer fringe of the crowd and grabbed a scrawny teenager by the arm.

"What's happening?" he demanded.

"The Duc's burning the Rogue and them others," the boy replied. "Says they're traitors."

Lucius's grip tightened. "Has he done it yet?"

The boy flinched. "Not yet!" he squealed, trying to twist free.

"Is the Duc here himself?"

The boy nodded. Lucius released him and tried to push through the crowd, but it was packed into an unyielding wall. The iron weakened his power, but with a concentrated effort, he managed to conjure a wedge of air. The people closest to him staggered back, cursing as they bumped into those behind them. Lucius took advantage of the gap, slipping through the opening before it closed again.

After several agonizing minutes, he drew near enough to see through the bars. A dozen prisoners were bound to pyres in the muddy yard. They all wore black hoods so it was impossible to tell who was who.

Well, I meant to save the lot of them anyway.

Duc Marcel stood on a raised podium surrounded by soldiers. Archers lined the roof behind him. The sun burnished his breastplate and cast sharp-edged shadows from the finials atop the iron fence.

"Silence!" the Duc bellowed. A tense hush settled over the crowd. "You are here to bear witness to divine justice. I offered these men fair terms at the parley, an end to their pointless rebellion, and what did I get in return? The Red Rogue and his followers betrayed me. They attacked and killed the Sons of Bel in their own temple—"

Lucius shoved his way forward. "That's a lie!" he shouted, voice carrying across the yard. "I was there! It was your men who attacked first! Your men who massacred the priests!"

The Duc's cold blue gaze fixed on him. "And who are you?"

"Lucius Bittencourt, emissary of the Ducissa Orlaith Redvayne of Clovis!"

Surprise made the Duc's face go blank for a moment. Then

he smirked. "We both know your mistress seeks to wed her own son to the Damiata of Galatia. Take your serpent's tongue and go home!"

"You know I speak the truth," Lucius shot back. "You murdered the arch-priest with your own hand!"

Angry murmurs rippled through the crowd. The Duc flushed. He said something to one of his guards, who signaled to those in the nearest watchtower.

"Let the accused speak for themselves!" someone called out.

The crowd took up the chant. "Let them speak! Let them speak!"

Marcel's angry gaze swept the gates. "They had their chance to speak at the parley," he said loudly. "Instead, they broke the peace. They are no longer *accused*. Judgment has been passed. They are condemned. There will be no clemency this day!"

The Duc made a sharp gesture. Soldiers moved along the pyres, upending clay urns over the prisoners' hoods. The stench of oil filled the air. Lucius spotted more knights forcing their way through the crowd, their gazes fixed on him.

He reached for the Nexus, trying to send tendrils of power through the bars, but the iron absorbed it like water seeping into sand. The soldiers finished soaking the prisoners in oil. The Duc raised a burning brand aloft, ignoring the shouts of the crowd beyond the prison fence.

"Let these traitors' souls be cleansed in holy flames!" he cried.

A dozen mailed soldiers had nearly reached Lucius now. They carried iron lances. His own power was a candle guttering in the wind.

Then a commotion erupted around a tall woman wearing a red manty. Lucius recognized her. She'd impersonated the Red Rogue at the bazaar the day Lucius had tried to follow him.

"Get back!" she yelled, brandishing something that glinted in the sun. "I have Bel's fire!"

Bel's fire. The volatile substance that had burned half the Marcel fleet in the harbor.

People screamed, pushing and shoving to get away. A clear space materialized around her within seconds. "Death to the cockatrice!" she cried, hurling the glass vial to the ground.

Emerald flames clawed skyward, followed by a shockwave that knocked Lucius sideways. Smoke billowed around him, thick and blinding. When his vision cleared, he saw the iron gates lying in a twisted heap. Sparks from the explosion had already caught some of the pyres. Eager flames raced across the yard, leaping from one oil-soaked pyre to the next.

Lucius staggered past the wreckage, knowing he'd never reach the prisoners in time to free them. There was only one chance left. Teeth clenched, he drew the heat into his own body. Fire shimmered along his skin as the blood boiled in his veins. One by one, the pyres winked out.

For a moment, Lucius thought the fire would get the better of him. It was far easier to conjure flames and hurl them outward than to quench them. The inferno writhed inside him like an animal caught in a trap. It needed fuel and only the force of his will kept it from devouring him to ash.

I must get rid of it . . . I must . . .

Through a red haze, he caught sight of the Duc. Their eyes locked. Lucius remembered Morgen's warning — "Vazsoly Marcel is *mine*" — but he no longer cared. The Duc turned to flee as a firestorm engulfed the podium.

Without pausing, Lucius ran to the nearest pyre and yanked the charred hood back. Captain Galoy Rossignol. *Good riddance*, he thought savagely. The next prisoner was burned beyond recognition. The third had escaped the flames by inches, the kindling at his feet still smoking. Under the hood was an older man with sweat-soaked brown hair fading to white at the temples.

"You are Castelio's father," Lucius said.

The man gave a dazed nod. "Who are you?"

"A friend. He sent me to . . ." Lucius was about to say "save you" but trailed off. The father was looking at him closely. Too closely.

Lucius stepped aside as others arrived to give aid. *Did you see the flames vanish? A miracle. Saved by Bel!* Their joyful exclamations washed over him. He ran to the next pyre, where a man struggled against his bonds. The prisoner got a hand free and pulled his own hood off. Lucius winced at the state of his face, but he felt a sudden euphoria, a lightness in his chest, as if the flames had left him hollow and buoyant as an empty cask.

"You came," Brennos rasped.

"I failed you again." Lucius knelt to sever the bonds at his feet. "You were right about Janus. And the Duc's necromancer—"

"Forget that! Where's Marcel?"

Lucius's gaze sliced past the chaos in the yard to what remained of the podium. Bodies lay among the charred timbers, but there was no sign of the Duc's distinctive silver and gold breastplate.

"Gone," he said angrily.

"I'll hunt him down. He will answer for what he did at Bel Mara." Brennos turned to the pitted gray hulk of Blackwater Jail. "But first we're going in there."

THE STENCH HIT Lucius the instant he stepped through the scarred wooden doors, an unholy brew of tidal mud, human waste, and misery. Beyond was a dingy antechamber with corridors branching off in three directions. The ceiling was so low, it nearly brushed his head. He saw no sign of guards; they must have already fled.

Brennos pointed to a cramped staircase. "Up there are the cells for those with titles or coin. The worst are below."

Lucius steeled himself as they descended. The darkness grew thicker, as did the reek. He conjured a flame and covered his nose with the scarf. "How can anyone survive this hell?"

"Most don't," Brennos replied. "I only know of it from the fortunate few who were eventually released, but this is my first time inside." He sounded shaken, and Lucius wondered if his parents had died in this place.

The cramped stair finally ended at what could only be described as a mud pit. The walls were furred with black mold and the ground squelched underfoot. On each side were doors with tiny grilles at the bottom. When their light appeared, thin, pale hands reached through, imploring.

"They say not even the rats will come down here," Brennos said, his voice thick with pity and revulsion. He set his shoulder to the first cell door, but it wouldn't budge.

"Sweet Bel, the hinges are rusted solid," he said, turning to Lucius. "I don't think it's been opened in years."

"Step back," Lucius said.

He gripped the iron handle, ignoring the lance of pain that shot up his arm, and tore the door from its frame. Inside, bodies stirred, eyes blinking against the sudden intrusion of light. Brennos went to their aid as Lucius moved from cell to cell, wrenching the doors open.

One by one, skeletal prisoners stumbled or crawled out of their filthy cells. By this time, more rescuers had arrived to help them up the stairs. For a while, it was a confusion of bobbing lights and shouting voices, broken sobs and jagged laughter. Lucius lost Brennos and was about to seek him out when he noticed a bundle of rags in a far corner beyond the reach of the torchlight and realized it was in fact a person. If not for his ability to see in darkness, he would have missed them entirely.

The figure didn't move when he came near. Lucius feared they were dead, but then he heard a faint heartbeat and found an old woman. Cloudy eyes opened when he touched her shoulder. She was little more than skin stretched over bone, but her toothless mouth formed a welcoming smile.

"You're a handsome boy," she said, patting his face, "just like my Tomas." The woman struggled to sit. "Don't worry, I'll help you. Never give up hope."

Lucius stared at her in wonder. "I won't," he said. "May I carry you, grandmother? The Duc has fallen. You are free."

She blinked at him. "Andrzej Marcel is dead?"

Of course she had not heard about the succession. "He is," Lucius confirmed, "at the hand of his own son, Vazsoly, who is now a fugitive."

She sucked her lips. "I would like to walk out on my own two legs."

Lucius eyed her doubtfully. Her limbs looked like twigs. "Very well. Let us try."

She surprised him by hobbling all the way to the stairs, at which point he insisted on scooping her up. Her body felt warm and fragile in his arms, like a baby bird.

"I never thought I would see Bel's face again," she remarked as they went up the stairs. "But he answered my prayers. Are you a believer, son?"

Lucius covered a smile. He had called her grandmother, but he was ten times older. "I am," he said, thinking of Brennos. Lucius paused in the grim little antechamber. "Are you ready?"

She nodded and they stepped out into the bright sunlight. "Oh!" the old woman cried, pressing her forehead against his chest. She made choking sounds, though whether they were laughter or tears, he could not tell.

A girl with long, graceful limbs and a mop of reddish hair climbed atop one of the pyres and waved a red banner on a pole.

"The cockatrice has flown!" she shouted.

The sea of people outside Blackwater Jail raised their fists, bellowing the next line with her. "The red tide is rising!"

THIRTY-ONE

P andemonium reigned at the Ducal Palace.

From her vantage atop the wall along the west-facing cliff, Lo saw pockets of fighting everywhere. Laborers and men with red armbands skirmished with soldiers wearing the silver and gold of House Marcel. Swords clashed against shovels, pikes against thick planks of wood.

Only about two-thirds of the new wall had been completed, leaving gaps that were being fiercely defended by a group of archers positioned on the palace roof. The archers rained down arrows on a crowd attempting to storm through the openings. Smoke stained the sky at various points over the city. She didn't know what had lit the spark, but Prydwen's simmering discontent was boiling over and it wouldn't be long before the Duc's men were overwhelmed.

Of course, that was assuming he didn't get his hands on the Grand Menotte. When Thistle told her what was inside the box, Lo wanted to strangle Nathan all over again. For the first time, she wished she had her mother's breaking talent so she could destroy the vile thing. There was no way she could give it to Nathan now. The best thing would be to find Tijah and Achaemenes. They might know a safe way to dispose of it.

The fighting looked hottest to the north where the main gates were. Lo found handholds and dropped lightly to the ground. The palace sat on the other side of a vast lawn. If she tried to cross, she'd be an easy target for the archers.

"Do you think Cas is still inside?" she asked, crouching behind a hedge.

Thistle had wormed through a tiny crevice, then slunk over in a gray flash.

"He said only that the talisman was in the palace, and he was going to find it." The cat's tail switched. "This is madness."

Lo scanned the grounds. Servants and retainers were fleeing in droves, but she didn't see Cas.

"We're nearly out of time, and this delightful town is going up in flames. He needs me."

"If you get yourself killed—"

"Then I'll come back, won't I?"

"You treat your gift like it is a golden goose that will never cease laying," Thistle replied severely.

"Surely I have a few lives left . . ." She trailed off as her left arm began to tingle.

Bodies lay everywhere. Some sprouted black-fletched arrows; others had gaping wounds. At least half were stirring. Shattered limbs twitched. Eyes opened in faces streaked with mud and blood. They made low, guttural sounds like a herd of frightened animals. The archers noticed them first. Alarmed shouts went up from the rooftops. They began to take aim at the dead, for all the good it did. The force of the arrows knocked them flat, but they just got up again.

"Do something," Thistle growled.

Lo watched the macabre scene unfold. Most of the risen

looked confused, though a handful were expressing interest in the soldiers guarding the palace doors.

"Not yet," she said. "They're drawing the archers' fire. We can slip through."

He stared at her with flat disbelief. "There's too many."

At least a hundred corpses were now shambling around the Duc's lawn. Screams filled the air as the nimbler ones overtook six soldiers in chainmail. Steel flashed, but it took only a single touch for the victim to collapse, clutching his chest. An unearthly frost crept across the grass, turning it brownish-white in patches. The crowd swarming through gaps in the wall started to fall back. Even the elite guards stationed at the palace were abandoning their posts, pursued by a horde of dead.

The rest were slowly turning in Lo's direction. She felt the weight of their eyes. The sharpness of their hunger. A whispering went up like wind through dry grasses. *Sarg eresh'kigal. Shadow Soul.*

The green of the grass bled away to slate gray. The sky slowly faded to a dull, monochromatic palette. She sensed the barrier between life and death growing thinner by the second.

Lo took off sprinting across the lawn. Thistle growled somewhere behind, and then he was leaping at her side, belly swinging like a pendulum. She took a zig-zagging path through trampled flowerbeds and over some more low hedges. Some of the risen moved with a stilted, staggering gait, but others were quick and agile. Lo slid between their grasping hands. Arrows whistled past, thunking into the ground at her feet.

She was halfway to the palace when a great herd of the dead rounded the corner of the east wing. In life, they had been bitter foes. Many were soldiers, ashen and hulking in their armor. Others wore rags around their arms and faces, gray in the half-light, though they must be bright red. A few sported the doublets of the nobility. They rushed toward her in a seething mass.

The tingling along her left arm became an iron band across her chest. Her pulse began to slow. Lo stumbled to a halt as they closed the gap. Bluffing death, Nathan called it, but it didn't feel like a bluff. *I'm dying.*

Thistle nipped her numb fingers. Lightning crackled in his eyes. "Now, Shadow Soul!" he snarled.

She stood at the threshold — warmth and light on one side, a yawning black chasm on the other. And the doorway . . . she *was* the doorway. Lo felt a wintry gust as the gate blew wide. A whirlpool of flickering light spun around her, rippling the dead grass as it widened outward in a spiral. It pulled the risen down in a fierce undertow, the bodies collapsing in rows as the gate reached them. Their cries rent the air, but she listened only for the faint thump of her own heartbeat. All was rushing darkness, the downward pressure of the gate and howling wind.

How long it went on for, she couldn't say. Thistle's sharp teeth brought her back.

"Ow," Lo muttered. She opened her eyes, blinking against the bright sun. Another nip to the flank and she sat up with a gasp.

"Move!" he hissed. "Before they shoot us with arrows!"

She clambered to her feet. It was eerily still. She saw a few archers left on the roof, but none of them fired as she crossed the lawn. The doors of the palace stood open. A dozen fallen soldiers lay on the steps leading up to the entrance.

In the grand pillared hall beyond, Lo passed a group of nobles huddling in a corner, their faces frozen in terror. A young woman with pale blonde hair leapt up and grabbed her sleeve.

"What is happening?" she demanded shrilly. "Where are

the guards?"

"Run," Lo advised, "while you still can."

She left them behind, following Thistle through the opulent halls, her footsteps muffled by plush carpets woven with threads of gold. He led her down a flight of stairs and through a maze of corridors to a humble room with three sleeping pallets. Cas wasn't there.

"Did he say where the box was?" she asked.

"No," Thistle growled.

Lo waited for a while, hoping he might return. When he didn't, they set off looking. Together, they roamed through austere libraries and flower-filled sitting chambers, cavernous banquet halls and gilded ballrooms. Twice, she glimpsed someone running down a distant corridor and called out, but both times they ignored her. She searched the deserted servants' quarters again, and the vast, steamy kitchens. Poked through storerooms and barracks. Her anxiety grew with each passing minute. Then, Thistle cocked his head.

"He calls."

Lo let out a soft whoop. "Where is he?"

"Come, I have him now."

He wasn't far at all. They turned down a gallery lined with ornate mirrors and she saw him. Shirtless, his back streaked with soot, one hand wrapped in a bloody bandage. He was leaning on a staff, peering in the opposite direction. The box sat at his feet, but she barely glanced at it. Lo started running, all thoughts obliterated except for the glorious fact that he was alive.

"Cas!"

He turned and she threw her arms around him, knocking him back a step. His hair smelled of smoke.

"Thank Kaethe," he murmured, hugging her fiercely.

She fingered a singed lock at his forehead. "What happened

to you?"

Her happiness faded as he briefly related his struggle with the mortifex, and the fate of his little sister, Felippa.

"Wherever your parents are, she's with them," Cas said grimly.

"It's my fault. I should never have asked you to look—"

"No," he said, squeezing her hand. "And your talisman saved her."

Thistle twined between his legs with a consolatory purr, and Cas bent down to scratch his ears.

"We'll get her back," Lo vowed. "Whatever it takes."

He gave a weary nod. "Is there time to bring the box to Nathan?"

"I think so. But we'll have to get the information without giving it to him." She glanced at the box. "No one can wear that talisman."

"Agreed."

"So this mortifex is still inside the star?"

"I feckin' hope so. Do you have any news about Blackwater Jail? My father was taken there."

"What? I'm so sorry, but no. There's fighting everywhere though."

Cas swore. "I need to go myself and make sure he's been freed. I sent Lucius, but—"

"Lucius is here?"

"That's who told me Justinian's true name."

"I knew I saw him!" Lo exclaimed. "He was standing on a barge in the Shambles when I . . . Never mind. We'll go to Blackwater on the way to the *Wind-Witch*." She paused with a frown. "If you need to stay in Prydwen, I understand. I'll bring your sister back."

Cas looked torn, and her heart broke for him. Then he shook his head. "No, I'm coming with you. I have to — for

Lip's sake. But we must hurry. Justinian won't be contained for long."

Lo picked up the box. It was much heavier than it looked. Her shadow power stirred uneasily at the contact. The talisman was soaked in death. In greed and corruption. She could feel the taint of it, a dark knot in the Nexus. No wonder Jaskin Cazal had sent it to the priests at Bel Mara. The sunlit temple in the bay was the only place its power could be safely contained.

"We'll go out the back," Cas said. "I know the way."

They had almost reached the end of the gallery when a woman stepped into view. It was the Duc's consort. Dark hair hung in a long braid over one shoulder. She looked different somehow; then Lo realized that the bruise on her face was gone.

"That box belongs to me," Morgen said calmly. "Give it back and I'll let you walk away."

"It doesn't belong to you," Lo said. "It belongs to the Duc of Vendagni."

Morgen walked towards them. "Then you know what is inside. What do you think he'll do with it? Do you trust him with a talisman of such power?"

The words echoed her own doubts too closely.

"No," Lo retorted, "but I certainly don't trust *you*."

"I would use it for good. To punish the wicked and protect the weak."

"Sure you would. And I'm the khamoun of Samarqand."

Her brows knit. "What is Samarqand?"

"That's far enough," Cas said, moving to stand between them. "Go, lady. We're not giving it to you."

"Then I will take it." The words were spoken with total assurance.

Lo lashed out with a bludgeon of air, shoving Morgen back

a step.

"You are a daēva," she said in surprise.

"That's right. So skedaddle. I'd rather not hurt you."

Morgen found this funny. She gave a bleak laugh, then pursed her lips and blew. Tentacles of smoky darkness snaked from her mouth. More of the ashy substance stung Lo's eyes. She flailed blindly, one arm smacking into Cas's staff. The box was yanked from her hands. He shouted something, and then a wind was roaring down the gallery. It swept the fog away in time for her to see Thistle rake his claws down Morgen's leg. Lo stumbled forward and grabbed the iron box.

"Give it back!" Morgen screamed.

Sharp fingers dug into Lo's hair and hurled her into the wall of mirrors. Pain tore through her, deep inside, like a tree being ripped out by the roots. In a panic, she reached for the shadow power. It hummed through her in a wild vortex. The mirrors all turned black. With a hard twist, Lo broke free of Morgen's clutches, but another force had her now, pulling her through the shattered glass.

Blood rushed to her head. Everything tilted and blurred, as if she had stood up too quickly. Her mind went blank — where she was, *who* she was — but that only lasted for a moment. The world righted itself and her vision cleared.

My name is Delilah. And I am . . . where the hells am I?

She stood in a long passage lined with doors. Right away, she recognized it as the place of her dream. Morgen lay on the ground, coughing weakly. Lo still held the box. It felt real enough, solid and heavy as an anchor. She tried to tear open a gate back to the palace, but she couldn't seem to focus. The necromancer was stirring. She reached out and Lo kicked her away.

"Wait, come back!" Morgen cried as Lo took off running.

She rattled doorknobs as she flew past, but they were all

locked. She rounded another corner and sprinted down an identical passage. Footsteps pursued behind.

"Please! Don't leave me!"

The desperation in Morgen's voice irritated her. This was all the necromancer's fault. Yet . . . Lo had a peculiar feeling she had been to this place before, and not just in a dream. But when? How?

She shifted her grip on the box. It was hellishly cold. At least she didn't sense any spirits nearby. There was nothing but endless hallways, each the same as the last. Finally, she tried a knob that turned. Lo threw herself inside and slammed the door.

A young man in a purple robe covered with astronomical signs stirred a bubbling pot of stew on a woodstove. He had a dark beard and a gentle, scholarly face. A pile of shelled pistachios sat on a cutting board. Fragrant spices wafted through the air.

"Oh my," he said, brows lifting. "You aren't supposed to be here."

"Does this lock?" Lo braced her back against the door, breathing hard.

"I'm afraid not. How did you get here?"

She scanned the kitchen. It looked ordinary, with rows of shelves that held blue-glazed crockery and a sturdy worktable in the center. There were no windows, but she did spot a door on the other side. Lo hurried across the kitchen and flung it open. A small pantry lay beyond, with glass jars and sacks of rice and flour.

"Is there another way out?" she asked the man.

He tugged at his beard unhappily. "Well . . ."

The door to the passage banged open and Morgen stumbled into the kitchen. She was crying, her eyes red and puffy. "Give me that box," she sobbed. "I need it!"

"Go copulate with a goat," Lo retorted, making a rude gesture.

Morgen's lower lip quivered. "You're a horrible person."

"Me? Why don't you tell this wizard how you tried to kill me, eh?"

"Astrologer, actually," the man muttered.

Morgen stared at her feet. "I'm sorry," she said in a small voice. "I shouldn't have."

"And I'm supposed to believe that? You're just trying to trick me!" Lo shook her head in disgust. "I'm not that stupid, lady."

"Now settle down," the man said. "What are you fighting over? I'm sure we can resolve this peaceably over a nice bowl of—"

Morgen darted forward with a crazed look in her eye. Lo grabbed an open sack of flour from the pantry and flung it one-handed at the necromancer. The sack exploded, coating her in white dust. She gasped and started crying harder. Lo burst out laughing.

"Stop at once!" the man scolded sternly. He wrung his hands. "This is Kaethe's House. You must leave before she comes."

"K-Kaethe's house?" Morgen stammered.

"You are not supposed to be here," he repeated, casting an anxious glance at the door.

Lo blew out a breath. So she'd accidentally made a gate to the Drowned Woman's dwelling? Expect the worst and you'll never be disappointed.

"Look, I didn't mean to come here," she said. "Just tell me the way out and I'll leave."

"It's too late now," he said in a resigned tone.

The kitchen door stood ajar, the passage beyond cloaked in darkness. Lo heard footsteps. They had a slapping quality, as of bare feet in shallows. A rivulet of water trickled beneath the door. It crept across the kitchen floor, winding through the cracks and low places.

Lo shifted out of the way, dread congealing in her gut. Or perhaps it was the stench of burned stew. With an oath, the man lifted the steaming pot from the stove and hung it on a hook. She noticed that he used his bare hands to do this.

More rivulets joined the first until a tide of icy water crept across the flagstones. The young man had gone still, eyes locked on the dark doorway. "She won't be pleased to find you here," he whispered. "Not a bit."

Morgen scurried over to Lo's side but didn't try to take the box. As much as Lo disliked her, she didn't mind the company. Neither of them could drag their eyes from the encroaching flood and the slice of dark passage beyond. A moment later, the footsteps arrived. They paused outside for a moment. Then the door blew wide.

Kaethe, the Drowned Lady, stood on the threshold. She was pale as moonlight, her tall frame filling the doorway. Water streamed from the corners of her thin lips, gushed from flared nostrils. Her eyes were dark wells.

"Give me that box!" she thundered. An arm reached out, blue veins wriggling like worms beneath the skin. Lo's feet started sliding along the wet flagstones as an invisible force pulled her toward the doorway. Morgen grabbed her waist. The necromancer was sniveling in fear, but she dug her heels in and tried to hold Lo back.

"Feck off," Lo growled at them both. "It's mine!"

Morgen chanted under her breath. Weird, jangling words. Tongues? Whatever it was, it set Lo's teeth on edge.

Kaethe laughed and water spurted from her mouth. "I must thank you for —"

She never finished the sentence because the world spun

again and Lo was falling through a half-light of swaying reeds and murky shapes. There was no up or down, no left or right. Strange vistas spun before her eyes. An octagonal black tower. A dark vale with a circular lake at the center. She smelled salt and death. A figure drifted near and she lashed out, shoving it away.

Then something hard slammed against her back. Her eyes opened and Cas's face swam into focus. Lo sat up, bruised and bewildered. The iron box lay next to her. Somehow, she'd held onto it. Morgen sprawled a short distance away. Her face was ghoulish with flour dust; that part had been real, at least.

"What happened?" Lo asked hoarsely. "What did you see?"

"You both disappeared for a moment." Cas looked shaken. "Then you came flying out of *that*."

He pointed to one of the mirrors. The glass had shattered, exposing the wood backing. Lo got up and ran her hands along the stone wall to either side. It felt solid.

"I was gone for much longer than a moment," she muttered.

He shook his head. "By my reckoning, it was only a few seconds." He turned to Morgen, his expression grim. "I think she's . . . Her neck looks broken."

Lo hurried over. The woman's head was twisted at an awkward angle. Her lips moved, but no sound came out, not even a whisper of air.

Once, as a child in Susa, Lo had come across a baby sparrow in their garden. It had fallen from its nest and had blood on its beak. She had carried it to her father, begging him to heal it. He tried, but the poor thing was too tiny. The shock had killed it. She'd cried for two days. The look in Morgen's eyes now, glazed with pain and fear, made her think of the poor wee fledgling.

"We have to do something!" Lo stared up at Cas, stricken. "She's suffocating."

He crouched down. "She did try to kill you."

"And she said she was sorry." Shame filled her. "I treated her badly. I think . . . I think she may have saved us both."

"How?" he demanded.

"I'm not sure. She was speaking in tongues, I think."

Cas looked wary. "I saw Justinian throw her out a window and she came back from it. We should get out of here."

Lo knew he was right. But Morgen had suffered terribly at the Duc's hands. Now she lay dying in a foreign land, far from anyone who cared about her.

And it's my fault. I shoved her just as we were coming out.

"I can't leave her to die alone." Lo gave him a mutinous look. "It isn't right."

"Right or wrong," he replied heatedly, "I don't trust her!"

"You don't trust anybody," Lo snapped and immediately regretted it.

Hurt flashed across his face. "I trust *you*. But your judgment isn't what it was. You can't see that, but it's true."

He glanced over at Morgen. Her chest hitched in shallow spasms, trying to draw air through the ruined passageway. The fingers of one hand trembled. Lo reached for it, but Cas stopped her.

"Are you crazy? Don't touch her!"

The light was fading from Morgen's eyes. Lo tried to remember the woman who had stood smiling up at the rain on the day of Duc Marcel's processional.

"Do you have an iron coin?" she asked.

Cas shook his head. "I could speak the catechism though." He cleared his throat and sketched a nine-pointed star above the body. "May Kaethe guide you through the thickets of night. May your feet not lose the path, and at the last hour, when Her cold hand beckons, may you have the courage to cross the stormless sea. May Kaethe seal gate and tomb against you. May you not rise again."

He said it so quickly, the words ran together. "Can we go now?"

"Yes." Lo swallowed. "I met her, Cas. I met Kaethe."

He looked startled. "What?"

"She had water coming out of her mouth, and all around her."

He gave a low whistle. "White as bone? Skin you could see right through?"

Lo nodded.

"I saw her, too," he said. "When I almost died on the bridge."

"She wanted the box," Lo admitted. "I told her to feck off."

"You didn't." His brows lifted.

"I did." She laughed, though there was little humor in it. "You're right, Cas. I think there is something wrong with me."

Thistle padded over and butted his head against Lo's knee. She was reaching out to pet him when he hissed, fur rising. Morgen sat up with a gasp. Her pupils were huge. Instinct made Lo rear back — an action she would curse herself for later. Morgen snatched the iron box and sprang away. A single image filled each of the mirrors along the gallery. A windswept, rocky place with a thatch-roofed cottage. Gray waves heaved in the background.

Morgen smiled through red teeth. "*Sarg eresh'kigal*. We are the same, Shadow Soul. But like I said, I am the stronger one."

She stepped into one of the mirrors. It all happened in the space of seconds. Lo ran at the glass. She bounced off, cursing and rubbing her nose. The bloody thing was solid again. All she saw was her own scowling reflection.

Morgen was gone.

THIRTY-TWO

Their flight from the palace was a blur of shouts and cheers and breaking furniture.

Angry crowds milled outside and, with no soldiers in sight, they poured through the main doors to run gleefully through the halls and give the place a thorough plundering. Anything with the despised cockatrice was hurled through the windows and tossed onto a bonfire in the middle of the lawn.

Cas and Lo were taken for part of the mob, an impression he encouraged by raising his fist and crying, "Death to House Marcel!" whenever they ran into a group of looters. By the time they reached the gates, a fluttering red pennant had replaced the Duc's sigil atop the highest tower.

"What now?" Cas asked flatly, leaning on his staff.

Lo had been silent since losing the box. "We go to Nathan as planned. He knows where Magnus is hiding and he's going to tell us."

"What about the pact?"

She shrugged. "It will cost me a life. But I hope he resists,

303

because I will enjoy beating it out of him." She vented an irritated breath. "And to think I pitied that woman."

Cas refrained from pointing out that her pity had cost them the box. That Morgen might be opening it as they spoke and summoning an undead army.

They set off through the wealthy district of Rosnamore bordering the palace. Its residents had fled, and folk were streaming in and out of the houses, carrying off any valuables that remained. Young men hung over the balconies, drinking wine and singing. A group of women had set up shop in a bakery, handing out cakes and pies to a merry crowd.

Yet just beyond, bodies floated in the canal, and the next street held a makeshift infirmary in one of the grand mansions, where the wounded were being carried in a ceaseless line.

Barricades blocked the major thoroughfares around Blackwater Jail, and it was at one of these that Cas found his father and brother. He embraced them both, teary with relief, and introduced them to Lo. She gave a shy smile, but seemed as pleased as he was to see them unharmed.

"Where's Felippa?" Da asked. He wore a dented breastplate and helmet that were both too big.

Cas didn't have the heart to tell them the truth. "She went to my friend's ship," he said. "Let me keep her safe for a while. Until all this settles down."

Da sighed and nodded. "Aye, Prydwen's no place for her. There's fighting still. But where will you go?"

"I know people in Aquitan who will put us up. But I'll return with her, I promise." He paused. "What happened at the jail?"

"It was the most peculiar thing." Da squinted, but he looked — and smelled — sober. "The pyres caught, and I thought I was done for. Then the flames just winked out."

"And came racing back at the Duc and his men!" Teo put in excitedly. "Everyone says it was Bel's hand at work."

"A red-haired fellow untied me," Da said. "Friend of yours?"

"Aye." So Lucius had kept his word. With luck, he'd gotten rid of the Duc, too. "Is Marcel dead?"

"We hope so," Da said. "All was chaos, though I can't see how he could have survived it."

"Who's in charge now? The Red Rogue?"

Da and Teo shared a look. "Don't know," Da admitted. "But we have orders to hold this barricade for now." He awkwardly gripped a sword. Cas prayed he wouldn't be forced to use it. He hugged them again and promised to return in another cycle of Selene.

The Docklands were relatively quiet. As they neared the *Wind-Witch*, two figures slipped from the shadows of another vessel. The woman wore battered leathers. Her sandy-haired companion was dressed in a simple tunic and trousers. Both carried weapons and, unlike his Da, looked like they knew how to use them.

Cas gripped the staff. He wondered if he'd be better off giving it to Lo, since at least she knew how to use it, but a glance at her face told him the newcomers were friends.

"Tijah!" she cried. "And Achaemenes! I'd hoped to find you. Your timing could not be better."

"Did you find the box?" Tijah asked, her sharp gaze assessing Cas and, to his amusement, dismissing him entirely.

"And lost it again," Lo replied cheerfully. "But we are going back to the necromancer who sent me here looking for it, and I plan to smack him around until he tells me where Magnus is. Does that plan appeal to you?"

A slow grin spread across her face. "It does."

"This is Castelio, a Quietus formerly of Clovis."

He nodded at them both.

"Greetings," the one called Achaemenes said in a pleasant voice. Tijah grunted.

"Cas took the . . . object in question . . . from the mortifex you seek," Lo said, "and my own stupidity allowed it to slip away."

"Who has it now?" Tijah asked.

"A woman named Morgen. I think she has gone to the Western Isles." Lo strode across the gangplank leading to the ship, Thistle at her heels. "We will find her. But Nathan first."

"Without the box."

"That's right." She began untying ropes from their cleats. Cas joined her, following her muttered orders, as the others climbed aboard.

"But . . . you will die," Achaemenes said. He was frowning deeply. So was Tijah.

"That is true," Lo replied, not meeting their eyes, "but I might not be quite as dead as you'd expect."

Tijah stared at her. "What's this? And where's Janus?"

Cas was helping to hoist the mainsail. Movement in the distance caught his eye. Justinian was limping down the pier. Flames blazed in the ruin of his face.

Tijah gave a low whistle. "Damn, you really fucked him up."

She drew her curved sword and took two steps toward the gangplank before Achaemenes blocked her path.

"I'll slow him down."

"What?" She shook her head. "You're not going alone."

"One of us has to remain aboard to question this necromancer. You know I'm right, Tijah."

A stream of fire shot down the pier. It fell short of the *Wind-Witch*, but the nearer crafts caught in a great whump of flame.

"Then I'll kick his ass and you stay here," she said fiercely.

"I'm faster and stronger. There's no time to argue." Achaemenes gripped her forearm. "I'll find you!"

Before she could reply, he leapt across the gangplank and drew his sword. Tijah slammed her own back into the sheath, looking like she'd bit into something rotten. Achaemenes ran down the pier and was swallowed by black smoke.

"Hurry up!" she shouted angrily. "Get us out of here!"

Lo tied down the mainsail while Cas raised the jib. Thistle stood on the ship's prow, his fur stiff. Wind filled the canvas and the ship started to rise. Janus appeared through the smoke. He raised his hand to unleash another fireball. It would have incinerated them if Achaemenes hadn't stabbed him through the chest. Janus staggered back, the fireball going wide.

It exploded off to starboard, rocking the hull, and then they were soaring into the skies above Prydwen, the mortifex a tiny figure wreathed in flame far below. Achaemenes circled him, blade flashing in the sun.

Tijah stared down at the two of them with a grim expression. She gripped the rail. "You might have mentioned that this ship flies." A baleful look. "And what did you mean by *not as dead as I'd expect*?"

THIRTY-THREE

Hecate hung low on the horizon as the *Wind-Witch* crossed the border with Vendagni. The Mountains of Nightmare reared up below, their snow-clad peaks glittering in the moonlight. Cas was bundled up in one of Lo's heavy woolen cloaks. He turned from the rail as she clambered out of a hatch leading belowdecks.

"What does Nathan say?"

She smiled, cheerful as ever. It made him want to kick something.

"The ladies Chaos and Caul Courtenay answered his summons. They have been helping him search for a way to cancel the blood pact, or at least extend it."

"And?"

"He implied there might be an answer, though he would not tell me what it is."

"Is he still angry?"

The first time Lo contacted Nathan with the black mirror, his shouts and curses had been audible throughout the ship.

"He has calmed down since the last time we spoke. He even

said he would tell me where Magnus is, regardless of whether I gave him the box."

Cas glanced at Tijah and Achaemenes, who sat sharpening their blades at the stern. "Because of them?"

"Possibly, though I think he feels genuine remorse now. Especially about your sister."

Cas clenched his jaw, biting back a sharp retort. "I still say we should have taken him by surprise. Who knows what he really has in store?"

She slung an arm around his waist, her gaze fixed on Hecate. "You could be right. But I think Nathan isn't quite as bad as he'd have people believe. He didn't mean for any of this to happen. And he does seem to be trying to make amends. I saw the Ducissas in the background. They were poring through books." She glanced at him. "I do trust them. If there's a chance, I had to try."

Cas hugged her close. He found it hard to stay mad at her, especially since . . . He cut off the thought before it led him down dark paths again. He'd barely eaten or slept for three days, imagining what form her death might take.

"Does he know if the box has been opened?"

"He says it hasn't, so that's one piece of good news. Morgen must not know the right spell."

"Thank Kaethe for that." His gaze lifted to the small silvery moon, which was steadily sinking. "How much time do we have before Hecate sets?"

"An hour, I'd say."

They stood in silence as the Nightwood unfurled below, a vast evergreen forest unbroken by roads or human settlements — but not empty of life. As a boy, Cas had heard stories about the creatures who dwelt in the furthest reaches of the east, where Bel had not shown his face in a thousand years. The loup-garou scared him the most. They looked like beautiful women until the moons were full. Then they became ravening beasts who lured their prey into the shadows with whispered promises of—

"Look!" Lo gripped his arm.

A league ahead, the land dropped away to a misty chasm. Castle Cazal stood like a spike of black ice beneath the stars, a yellow gleam high in one of the towers the only sign of life. Lo took the wheel, steering for the obsidian span leading to the keep. Cas followed her orders, lowering the jib and then the mainsail.

The bridge was only a few paces wide. When the hull scraped down and the ship began to list to one side, he decided that crossing it in a coach was by far the preferable method. Tijah had her eyes squeezed shut and was fervently whispering to some deity called Innunu.

Cas couldn't see what Lo was doing, but the *Wind-Witch* held true to the glassy substance of the span, gaining the other side just as he felt sure they were about to tumble into the chasm. A sudden violent headwind, likely conjured by Thistle, and they lurched to a halt before the entrance.

"I will not enter the keep," the cat growled, laying his ears back.

"And I do not blame you," Lo said soothingly. "You may guard the ship. With luck, this will not take long." She dropped the rope ladder over the side and turned to the others. "Shall we?"

They climbed down. Tijah studied the snarling, bat-winged statues above the entrance with a smirk. "You know what they say. The bigger a necromancer's gargoyles, the smaller his—"

The door swung open, revealing Nathan's mortifex, Vigo. Jeweled pins gleamed in his long white hair. His gaze immediately fixed on Cas, who stared back coldly. From the corner of his eye, Cas saw Tijah's hand drop to the hilt of her sword.

"Is there a problem?" Lo asked. "I informed your master whom I was with. It is unfortunate that my companion was forced to banish you the last time we were here—"

Vigo cleared his throat. It sounded like rocks falling into a meat grinder. "His Grace will receive you in his atelier," the mortifex rumbled, stepping back.

Cas's scalp prickled as he walked past, and not just from the chill of his presence. The mortifex ignored him, leading them up a winding flight of stairs directly to Nathan's workshop. There was no door, rather a curtain of clacking bones on wires. Vigo parted them with sausage-like fingers, each sporting several rings.

"Your *guests* have arrived," he declared, coating the word in distaste.

Nathan Ouvrard leapt to his feet and strode over, eyeing Tijah warily. He bowed at the waist. "Welcome to Castle Cazal," he said, nodding at Cas. "Quietus. Demoiselle Dessarian."

The room was littered with grimoires, some in tottering heaps, others hurled face-down on the floor. Nathan's dark hair stood on end; deep shadows lurked beneath his eyes. It certainly *appeared* that he had been making an effort to undo the pact, though Cas still didn't trust him in the least. Nor, it seemed, did Tijah.

"Undo your filthy spell, necromancer," she snapped. "Now!"

Nathan arched a brow. "I cannot."

Cas resisted the urge to lunge at him. "But you said there might be a way to save her!"

"In the language of the bargain itself," a new voice said.

Lady Chaos approached from the recesses of the chamber,

leaning on her silver canes. Her twin, Lady Caul, walked at her side. Again, Cas was struck by the contrast between them. Caul was nearly as tall and sturdy as Vigo, with dozens of bone bracelets circling her muscular arms. The look she cast Nathan, of unbridled disgust, endeared Lady Caul to him immediately.

"We may have found a way out of your latest scrape, Nathan," she said tartly. "Though it should never have come to this."

He bristled. "We are nearly out of time. What have you found?"

Chaos held up a heavy volume bound in pale leather. "The *Archidoxis Notoria*, ninth edition, claims that intentions count for a great deal in the execution of blood pacts. You said the exact language was that Delilah would make her *best effort* to bring you the box, is that correct?"

Nathan tugged at his hair, brow furrowing. "Yes, those were the words." He beamed and dashed over to Lady Chaos, pressing her hand to his lips. "You are a genius!"

Her sister scowled, but Chaos did not snatch her hand away. She merely shook her head with an expression of exasperated fondness. Cas thought of the unsent love letters he'd found before he fell into Nathan's blood labyrinth.

"As long as you intended to honor the terms of our bargain, you are in the clear!" Nathan said happily, performing a little jig.

Lo nodded with a weak smile. "I'm so relieved."

She did not look at Cas, whose last hope was now withering.

"Who decides the meaning of the words?" he ventured. "I mean, how can the magic know what a person is thinking?"

"What does it matter? Surely this is enough," Nathan said. "You have all done your utmost to find the box and deliver it here, to my hands." He looked abashed. "And, er, you have made great sacrifices, above and beyond what was required. Truly, I had no idea that anyone else was even looking for it—"

"And what," Tijah demanded, "did you plan to do with the Grand Menotte?"

Nathan snorted. "Certainly not to put it on myself. Do you think I'm a complete idiot? Wielding such power would drive anyone mad. Look!" He flung a finger toward the wall of mirrors, where a slug-white face watched from the depths, the features too blurry to make out. "That is my unfortunate ancestor, Jaskin Cazal. Do you think I wish to end up like him?"

"You certainly seem reckless enough to try," Tijah retorted.

Lady Caul nodded in vigorous agreement, but Lady Chaos leapt to Nathan's defense.

"And who *should* safeguard it?" she asked. "This talisman is far too dangerous to allow mortals to keep it—"

"So a bloody necromancer should have it?" Tijah asked incredulously. "You're the worst of all!"

Then they were all shouting at once and Cas realized that Lo had disappeared. He hurried to the winding staircase and parted the bone curtains. Faint footsteps rang out below. Cas followed, taking the risers two at a time. He found her sitting on the top step under the gargoyles, hugging her knees to her chest, breath steaming in the frigid air. Cas sat down next to her. Lo leaned against his shoulder.

"You'll get your sister back," she said. "With the Courtenays here, he won't dare go back on his promise." A faint smile. "Tijah would skewer him if he tried."

"We'll both get her back," he replied stubbornly. "Your parents, too."

"Tijah said they're pirates now. Did I mention that?"

"Pirates?"

She settled against his shoulder again. "Magnus has them robbing the dead."

Cas pondered that for a moment. "Of what?"

"That's what I asked. What do dead people have to steal?" She laughed quietly, then pointed to a bright scattering of stars just above the horizon. The cloak fell back, revealing her lightning scars and the brand on her forearm. It was just a faint outline now. He could scarcely make it out. "In Susa, we call that the Nemean lion. It guarded the temple of Zeus. Do you see?"

Cas squinted. "Hmmm, not really." *Just keep her talking.* "Tell me the story."

Her finger traced an outline. "There's the head and the back. Anyway, the Nemean lion was fierce and cunning. No weapon could pierce its hide. Until the warrior Hercules came along. He had promised Apollo — the god you call Bel — to perform twelve impossible labors. Killing the Nemean lion was the first labor."

Cas studied her arm, which lay propped across her knee. A vise inside him ratcheted almost unbearably tight. The brand was gone, leaving pale, unblemished skin. Hecate must have set behind the keep's highest spire. "How did Hercules do it then?"

"He tried shooting it with arrows. Didn't work. He finally strangled the lion with his bare hands. Hercules was famously strong. Then he made a cloak of its skin to wear in battle."

Her voice sounded heavy, yet she was still alive. He felt her warm breath stirring the fine hairs on his wrist. Maybe the magic *doesn't* know. Maybe . . .

Cas said, "Feck Hercules. I feel sorry for the beast."

"The goddess Hera did, too," Lo agreed. "So she transformed the Nemean lion's spirit into a constellation so he would be forever remembered."

314

Cas tipped his head back. On the *Wind-Witch*, the ship's lanterns had made it seem like they drifted in an empty void. But here, on Nathan's front steps, with the moons hidden behind the keep and the skies clear, the expanse above was a maelstrom of stars. Bright ones and dimmer ones, flowing like rivers of light. He studied the sliver above the horizon she had pointed to, searching. Suddenly, the winking dots rearranged into the shape of a stalking beast. Its mane streamed in a celestial wind, forelegs bent to pounce. And there . . . a regal tail. Even a suggestion of sharp teeth.

"I see it, Lo," he cried in excitement. "I see the Nemean lion!"

She didn't answer. Cas turned her to face him, his smile fading. Her blue eyes were open and rimed with frost. It sparkled in her lashes under the pale starlight. Sudden anger burned the back of his throat. Her soul had snuck away like a cutpurse in the night. How could he not have felt it?

"Come back," he whispered roughly. "I'll wait."

He held her close, resting his chin on the top of her head. *It takes a little while. Just like before, when the lich took her. A few minutes, that's all.*

The stars wheeled their slow dance above, carrying the Nemean lion below the horizon. Thin clouds drifted down from the mountains and drew a wispy veil across the heavens. It was the first time Cas had ever wanted a corpse to stir. Wanted it desperately. But Lo did not come back. His feet were numb when he finally lurched back up the steps, carrying her in his arms.

"Nathan!" he bellowed, kicking the door open. "For feck's sake, help us!"

His shouts summoned the master of the keep, who blinked in surprise. "What has happened?"

"What do you think? Bring her back!"

Nathan hesitated. "You would not like what my power conjured," he said at last in a subdued tone, "if it was even possible. She is . . . special—"

"I know what she is," Cas ground out, "but it's taking too long. Something is wrong."

Nathan turned ashen. "I do not know why she died, but I am certain she will return. It cannot be . . ." He swallowed. "Surely, it could not have been the last."

Cas felt like he was drowning. The black walls blurred as Nathan led him to a stark, forbidding chamber with a pointy ceiling and even pointier furnishings. He blew a pinch of dust into the hearth and flames erupted.

"These will burn for hours. Vigo can bring food and drink . . . or perhaps you are not hungry."

"Just get out," Cas snarled.

Nathan backed away, closing the heavy door behind him. Cas laid her down on top of a hard bed with a stiff, embroidered coverlet. Her face was serene, her eyes staring at nothing. The flames gave off little warmth, but it was enough to melt the frost on her lashes. He sank down next to her, trying not to think of Esme, how she had lain just the same and never gotten up. When he touched Lo's cheek, it was cold and waxy. *If she rises and takes me*, he thought wildly. . . *I do not care. I won't leave her.*

Sheer exhaustion finally dragged him into slumber. He woke some time later to a furtive rasping. Cas's eyes flew open, one hand automatically reaching for an iron blade. His breath hitched as he studied her. Then he started to laugh. The sound made her stir. Lo blinked sleepily.

"What's so funny?" she murmured.

"You were snoring."

She gave a luxurious stretch. "Was I?"

"Yes, you were. Even louder than my Da when he's in his cups."

Her eyes cleared. She gazed at him seriously. "I died, didn't I?"

"You don't remember?"

She shook her head. "We were speaking of the Nemean lion and then . . . Was it bad?"

"Yes."

"Bloody?" She held up her arms, studying herself.

"Not bloody. But I thought you weren't coming back."

"Oh." She gave an unsteady exhale. "You must be . . . well, rather repulsed. I mean . . ." She winced, her mouth turning down at the corners.

"Despairing, more like," he said. "There are no ill effects?"

"None." She eyed him warily. "I am sorry you had to see that."

"Again? So am I. I do not care to repeat it."

She chewed her lip. "Does Nathan know?"

"He brought us here."

"Then he must realize I never intended to give him the box."

"I think he isn't sure what happened." Cas propped his head on one hand. "Lo?"

She met his eyes.

"May I kiss you?"

A flurry of emotions crossed her face. "You still want to?"

"Gods, yes," he replied with feeling. "I might die myself if you turn me down."

She shook her head sadly. "You aren't normal, Cas."

"More than you are," he managed before she pulled him close. The kiss deepened, lighting fires that tightened the muscles of his stomach. Clothing sailed through the air, catching on the sharp curlicues of the bedposts. Lo sneezed as motes of dust billowed up from the coverlet.

"Feckin' hells," Cas muttered, jerking his chin at the oil portrait sneering down at them from the opposite wall. It was some Cazal-Ouvrard ancestor with red lips and a mane of blond hair that he wore in cascading ringlets across his shoulders. The flickering firelight made his cold eyes very lifelike.

"This is the worst room," Lo said, shoulders shaking with silent laughter. She was naked and the most beautiful thing he had ever seen. "Plus it's freezing!"

He rolled her to her back, kissing the tender juncture of her throat. "Then we must do our best to warm it up," he whispered.

THIRTY-FOUR

L ucius followed the elderly priest up Bel Mara's ring road. As they climbed higher, the air grew thick with salt from the bay, mingling with a faint coppery tang. The stones had been scrubbed with lye, but the smell of blood clung like a stubborn shadow.

"I hid when the soldiers came," the priest said. He had a fringe of white hair and gentle eyes. "Praise Bel, they didn't find me. Most were not so lucky."

"How many died?" Lucius asked as they entered the temple. Sunlight poured through the high windows, gilding the statue of the monastery's namesake.

"One hundred and eighty-seven brothers and fourteen serving folk from the Shambles, including a six-year-old boy." The priest angrily shook his head. "The Marcel name will be cursed for ten generations!"

"So you witnessed the Duc's treachery?"

"With my own eyes. So did others who survived. Messengers are already carrying word of his heresy to shrines across Aveline. Soon, the whole brotherhood will know the truth."

The priest halted at a tower on the north side, its walls honey-combed with ancient scrolls. "You may go alone from here. Bel's light shine upon you, my lord."

"I'm not a lord," Lucius said, but the priest was already hobbling down the stairs.

He climbed one more winding flight to a round chamber with a simple cot and oaken table. Doves clustered on the broad windowsill, cooing and pecking at seed. Brennos sat at the table, quill in hand and a stack of letters at his elbow. He looked up with a smile. The burns were starting to heal, though they'd leave scars. Which, Lucius thought dourly, would only make him more appealing.

"Strategos," he said, pressing a fist to his heart.

"Is that what they're calling me?" Brennos asked in an amused tone, as if he didn't know.

"Yes, it seems the old rank has been revived." Lucius pretended to think, though he remembered it all clearly. The curse and blessing of being over a thousand years old. "I believe General Gregorian was the last one. About three centuries ago?"

"That's right." The smile didn't waver. "He was a blood-thirsty lunatic."

"Well, I'm sure you'll be an improvement," Lucius said.

The strategoi had led the Sons of Bel back in the days when it was a paramilitary order. Lucius had met Gregorian once. He hated the nuns of Kaethe with the passion of a true zealot and made it his crusade to wipe them out. After a particularly heinous massacre that earned him the epithet "The Butcher of Lentia," cooler heads prevailed. The priesthood shifted its focus to aiding the sick (with prostitution and money-lending as lucrative sidelines). Gregorian was exiled to a distant mountain shrine where he died of fever.

Now times were changing again. The arch-priest was dead,

and no successor had been named since the hierarchy at Bel Mara was all dead, too. But word was spreading that the Red Rogue and Brennos Fearghal were one and the same. Surviving Duc Marcel's treachery had elevated him to near sainthood among the faithful. He'd become more myth than mortal in the eyes of the young priests Lucius had met in the streets.

Brennos glanced around the chamber. "This was Brother Symeon's. He oversaw the reliquary for decades. A good and brave man. Janus murdered him for the Grand Menotte."

"So he told me," Lucius admitted. "Though he claimed the priest killed himself rather than confess where it was."

Brennos's stare was hot, and for an instant, Lucius remembered seeing those black eyes through a red mask. "Is Janus gone for good?"

Lucius chose his words carefully. "I found traces of a nine-pointed star in the Duc's bedchamber. Someone banished him."

"*Someone*?" Brennos repeated flatly.

Lucius had spent the last few days searching for Castelio, but finding anyone in Prydwen was near impossible. The city was in a state of upheaval. People were occupying the palace and the mansions in Rosnamore, barricades had sprung up everywhere, and only the canals kept the dead from overrunning the living.

"A man I trust," Lucius said. "He was a Quietus in Aquitan and had personal reasons to despise Janus. I gave him the mortifex's true name and he got rid of him, along with the Grand Menotte. It is better this way, believe me. The talisman would have brought you nothing but grief."

Brennos leaned back in the chair. "As long as I can be assured Marcel won't get his hands on it."

"I promise he won't. Do you have any word of his whereabouts?"

"There are a hundred rumors, few credible. The nobles who managed to flee are holed up in their walled country estates. He could be at any one of them." Brennos sifted through the papers and pushed a crude map toward Lucius. "I do know how he escaped, though. We found tunnels running beneath Blackwater that lead outside the city. No doubt the same ones Marcel used to 'disappear' prisoners from their cells."

"The war is not over," Lucius said softly.

"It has just begun," Brennos agreed. "And the uprising is splintered into a dozen factions, none of which will listen to me."

"They followed you because they believed you were one of them."

"Which I am. But I am also a Son of Bel." Brennos sighed. "At least what is left of the brotherhood remains unified."

Lucius watched the doves jostle each other for seed. "To what purpose?"

"Are *you* asking?" Brennos asked with narrowed eyes. "Or is it your mistress?"

Lucius felt a spark of anger. "Whatever you say will be held in complete confidence. I risked a great deal for your cause. Orlaith might possess my soul, but my mind and heart are my own."

"I'm sorry." Brennos sounded chastened. "I know you are an honorable man, but I have spent the last week dealing with ones who are . . . less so. The burning and looting, the violent reprisals. I expected it, but not to this degree."

"Then you were naïve," Lucius said bluntly. "War unmasks the beast in men."

"I suppose you're right." He gave a weary shake of his head. "I would not care if they drove Vazsoly naked through the streets, but women and children have been attacked as well.

The mobs will not heed me anymore. I fear for Marcel's sisters."

"Where are they?"

"Still up at the convent, as far as I can tell. I sent a group of brothers there to offer our protection, but the nuns drove them off. There is no love lost between us, as you know," he added wryly. "However, our purpose remains the same — to carry out Bel's will on earth. We lost our way and became overly fond of gold, but that is over now." His dark eyes shone with conviction. "What this land needs, Lucius, is a just and impartial force to protect the weak and stop men like Vazsoly Marcel from rising in the first place."

"I thought you didn't seek power," Lucius said dryly.

He scowled, his black hair untidy, and Lucius wanted badly to kiss him. "I don't aspire to rule. But nor will I leave the people to be governed by another series of tyrants, whether highborn or low. This is partly my doing and I will set it right."

"Well, I wish you luck. But I came to say goodbye."

Brennos looked surprised. "I thought you'd stay for a while longer. Your advice would be welcome."

"It is not my choice. Orlaith requires my immediate presence in Galatia."

"Where does she stand on the rebellion?"

Lucius shrugged. "She is displeased with the results of her meddling, of course. She'd convinced herself that Marcel's nobles would take control. The thought of people governing themselves is repugnant. It could light a fire in her own domain."

"I'm sure the other duchies share her sentiments," Brennos muttered. "The question is, what will she do about it?"

"At the moment, nothing. Orlaith is still determined to wed her son Enrigo to the Damiata Beatriu. She has no desire to wade any deeper into this mess. I assured her that the current situation is only temporary, and the nobles will return eventually."

"Well, that buys us some time. I mean to leave a small garrison here and march through the countryside gathering new recruits."

Lucius frowned. "You're abandoning Prydwen?"

"What would you have me do?" Brennos looked weary. "The Duc's men killed more than half of our order. The priests at the temple in the city were trained to be courtesans, not soldiers. I must build an army if the Sons of Bel have any chance of guiding events."

"Good thing you can afford it. Assuming the treasury is intact?"

"The rebels have not looted us yet," Bren replied with a snort. "Some of the brothers say it is because they fear Bel."

"Or the pickings at the palace are still rich enough to distract them."

"That is what I think," he conceded. "Another reason to leave while we still can. I need our coin. Armies don't come cheap."

Lucius glanced at the books piled on the table. "You are reading the works of the great strategoi, I see."

"Re-reading," Brennos replied with a smile. "It was Symeon who taught me my letters when I first came here as an orphan. He said I should have a proper education, and not only in the bedchamber."

To Lucius's vast irritation, a flush of arousal tightened his groin. "Tell me something. Why did you choose me that day?" He kept his tone light as if he didn't care either way, but suddenly he couldn't bear to leave without knowing the answer. "Wait, let me guess. I was a novelty. Or perhaps you planned to pump me for information like Rossignol?"

Brennos's smile died. It was as though black storm clouds

obscured the sun. "That would have been difficult since we never spoke."

"Why then?"

"I needed to know if I could trust you."

"And when one has sexual congress under Bel's own roof, his soul is laid bare?" Lucius said acidly. "You expect me to believe that nonsense?"

"I don't care if you do or not." Brennos stood up, his gaze intent. "But it is true. I saw inside your heart."

"To the man behind the mask?"

Brennos flushed. "I suppose I deserve that. I wanted to tell you . . . Look at me, Lucius."

He tried not to appear sulky. "What?"

"You are broken in places, poisoned with regret and cynicism, but your spirit remains pure. It shone with the brilliant radiance of the sun—"

"Stop," Lucius snapped, entirely unnerved.

"Why does that bother you?" Brennos looked puzzled.

"Because . . ." Lucius exhaled sharply. "Because it is easier to hate than to love."

"Ah." He rose and came around the table. Shiny pink scar tissue puckered his jaw where Justinian had tortured him. Lucius wished he still had the power of healing. "But it is not nearly as much fun."

Lucius laughed despite himself. "I suppose not."

"I chose you because I wanted to," Brennos said firmly. "It was expedient, yes. But I was attracted to you from the moment we met. And I rarely enjoyed the pleasure of bedding men I actually desired." A glint of amusement entered his dark eyes. "When I saw you standing there, looking attractively annoyed, I decided I'd earned a reward."

Lucius arched a brow to cover his confusion. He'd been

certain Brennos had simply used him in some way. And the man *had*. But not quite as badly as Lucius had feared.

"Thank you," he said quietly. "You gave me back a piece of myself I believed was lost forever."

"I am glad. Yet you are still chained to Orlaith's will," Brennos observed with a hint of bitterness.

"Chains can be broken, or they can be borne." Lucius's fingers brushed the iron cuff at his wrist. The gulf between them felt unbridgeable. "And I chose this shackle."

"Choice or not, freedom is the goal we both seek," Brennos replied.

He was close enough for Lucius to smell the clean salt of his skin and feel the warmth of his living, breathing body. Yet he felt something else, too. A thread tugging at his core, just short of pain. *Not yet*, he thought desperately.

"My true name is Claudius Quintus," Lucius said in a rush. "You can summon me with it. Draw a nine-pointed star in blood, light a candle, and speak my name. If you need me, I will come." *And rain hell on anyone who tries to harm you*, he added silently.

Brennos blinked in surprise. "That is an unexpected gift."

"Just keep it to yourself, please," Lucius whispered, and pulled him into a hard embrace. Their lips met and he savored an instant of happiness. Here was a man he would gladly die for again and again . . . Then Brennos drew back, alarmed. He said something but Lucius could not hear the words over the roaring in his head.

He could still taste the kiss when the first knives lanced through his body. He tried to hold on, but Brennos slipped through his grasp like smoke. Tendrils of agony branched out, as if he were being stretched upon a rack, but it did not last long. The restless murmur of the sea faded. The quality of the light changed as sunlight yielded to standing braziers.

Lucius raised his head to see a tiny girl perched upon a throne made of yellowing skulls. Her lips were bloodless and she wore a pearl-encrusted gown with a frilled collar that made her look like a porcelain doll. Dainty slippers dangled above the floor, swinging idly to and fro.

"Welcome, Lucius Bittencourt," she said in a high, sweet voice.

"Molti graciosa, Damiata," Lucius replied, sinking to one knee within the nine-pointed star. It had been laid out at the center of a gloomy chamber adorned with faded, threadbare tapestries. A gust of icy mountain air stirred the flames in a great hearth behind the throne. The skulls were dedicated to Kaethe, he knew. Galatia belonged to the Drowned Woman as surely as Cavet belonged to the sun god.

An excited whisper ran through the nuns gathered at the periphery, all clad in virginal white with their heads shaved to the scalp. Lucius had not anticipated being called directly to the Alcazar. What was Orlaith playing at now?

"The summoning, it is like a magic trick!" The Damiata's reddish ringlets bounced as she clapped her hands with delight. Her eyes were a cool gray. "I never expected to own a mortifex, but Her Grace has generously included you in Enrigo's dowry."

Lucius slowly turned his head to Orlaith, who stood next to Enrigo at the foot of the throne. Centuries of practice kept the shock from his face, though it surged through their bond. In turn, he felt her angry satisfaction. So this was to be his punishment.

"He served me well in the past," Orlaith allowed, breaking the awkward silence that settled over the room. "Although I must say, recent events leave much to be desired."

Her gaze was sapphire-hard. She was quietly seething, even if her countenance was as serene as his own. As always,

Orlaith wore widow's black, her fair hair caught beneath a net.

"Poor Duc," the Damiata mused. "I wonder what has become of him?" She leaned forward on the throne. "Do you know, Lucius?"

"I am afraid not, Your Grace," he replied. "Vazsoly Marcel disappeared."

"If he had not ruled with such a heavy hand," Orlaith remarked, "his fall might not have been quite so precipitous."

She jabbed an elbow into Enrigo's side, and he cleared his throat. "Let us hope that order is restored soon," Enrigo added.

The boy looked distinctly uncomfortable in a doublet modeled after the Galatian fashion, with a ruffed neck, narrow waist, and puffy sleeves. A silver rapier hung at his side. He cast Lucius a look of both apology and commiseration, but Lucius was happier than he had expected to be. Thrilled, in fact.

"I would be honored to serve the venerable house of Do Santillan," he said to Beatriu with a bow, one hand behind his back, the other pressed to his heart.

You couldn't possibly be a bigger hell-bitch than my current mistress.

The Damiata looked pleased at his familiarity with local etiquette. Her pale lips curled in a smile — one that gave Lucius pause. The warmth did not reach her eyes, which were guarded and assessing.

The story of her ascension to the throne was this: Two years before, the Duc of Galatia's third wife had poisoned him at the behest of her lover, a much younger viscount, and then thrown herself from the battlements when the crime was discovered. Aldonza Beatriu do Santillan, nine years old at the time, was hidden away by the nuns while her five older siblings killed each other off in a bloody year-long power struggle. When the dust settled, Beatriu was the last living heir. A sheltered innocent, people said, who had only survived by the grace of Kaethe.

Now Lucius wondered about the tale.

"I am certain we shall get along splendidly," the Damiata said. She flicked a finger and servants rushed forward to help her down from the grotesque throne. "Come, let us adjourn for lunch!"

THIRTY-FIVE

I n the scorched hills above Prydwen, Morgen sat in the crook of a milkthorn tree watching the convent of Kaethe. It was a drab, no-nonsense building, just like the women who lived there. The pits where the nuns burned the bodies of the poor lay downwind, but the smell of ash lingered in the air.

Her shadow power thrived in this place. Not only because the convent was dedicated to the Drowned Woman and had been for a thousand years, but because of the pits. The nuns had been hard at work these last few days, white cloths tied across their faces as they tumbled bodies from barrows onto the smoldering bone heaps. It made her wonder what would happen when she died for the ninth and last time. Her mother had known a great deal — but not that.

The iron box holding the Grand Menotte was safe inside an oilskin bag she'd retrieved from her cottage on Juniper Island. The box had no visible lock, and none of her mother's grimoires offered any useful advice about how to open it. After a day of fruitless attempts, Morgen had disguised herself in the scarlet robes of a Rhunish peddler and made a gate back to Prydwen. Chaos ruled the streets. She'd been afraid she might find Vazsoly's abused corpse being paraded around town, but the word was that he'd vanished.

His younger sisters, however, were still at the convent. The day before, she had glimpsed one of them peering through a window in the upper story. It was only an instant before a nun came and drew her away, but her head was uncovered and Morgen recognized the trademark Marcel white-blonde hair.

She could have killed the girls then, but she decided to wait a bit longer on the slight chance Vazsoly would come to spirit them away and save her the trouble of finding him. They were the last of his kin, after all.

Of course, he never turned up. He probably hadn't given his sisters a second thought. When her business here was done, Morgen would track him down, a moment she was already savoring. Perhaps she'd have the box open by then. She pictured the look on his face when Vazsoly saw her wearing the menotte. He would be furious at first, but that would change when he realized what she had planned for him.

Her lips thinned as she thought about almost losing the box to another Shadow Soul. Not only that, but the woman had cost her a life.

It was simple bad luck that I broke my neck coming out of the gate, Morgen thought with a touch of unease. *Nothing more.*

The other Shadow Soul obviously knew little about her own powers. She hadn't been able to follow Morgen back to her home on Juniper Island, yet she had made a portal to Kaethe's house behind the Veil.

Recalling that humiliating episode nearly cracked Morgen's icy reserve. How she despised the fearful, soft-hearted wretch she became behind the Veil! It was the only weakness of a Shadow Soul, that troublesome other half. Fortunately, she rarely had reason to venture into the Dominion, and the *other* Morgen, whom she thought of as Mara, stayed locked up where she belonged.

Distant voices broke her reverie. A grim-faced crowd was marching up the road to the convent. She scrambled down from the tree and slipped through the woods. By the time she reached the bottom of the hill, the mob had reached the convent's wall. A barrel-chested man with a wild, bushy black beard pounded on the wooden gates.

"Sisters of Kaethe!" he bellowed.

The mob milled around, shouting threats and imprecations up at the nuns.

"Come out, or we'll tear these down!"

Morgen clambered up the far edge of the crumbling wall and crouched behind the jagged remnants of a squat tower. She saw the abbess and four others emerge from the convent, hurrying down the path. The abbess was a stout woman with a perpetually displeased expression. She opened a small grilled window.

"What do you want?" she demanded.

"We heard the Duc's sheltering inside your walls."

"Are you mad? Why would he come here?"

"Sanctuary." The bearded man raised a fist. "But he'll not escape justice so easily!"

His companions gave a roar of approval.

"Duc Marcel is not here," the abbess hissed.

"So you say." The man slammed a meaty palm against the gates. "If you've nothing to hide then open up so we can see for ourselves."

"I won't have you ransacking my convent, terrorizing the nuns. You'll bring down Kaethe's fury—"

The man gave a bitter laugh. "For years you've done the Marcels' bidding. But that's over now." He raised his voice.

"There will be no more burning, except for your own convent!"

Jeers went up from the mob. Morgen had seen Vazsoly's soldiers sack villages. These people radiated the same eagerness to destroy. The abbess and her sisters conferred in soft voices.

"Wait here," she commanded.

She went back inside and returned a minute later with Vazsoly's sisters. Jaelle, a doe-eyed, delicate child of nine or ten, was being half dragged by two nuns. The older one, Dravka, who was about sixteen, shook off her escorts and strode up to the gate. The abbess opened the grille.

"I swear by my vows, Duc Marcel is not here," she said in a brittle voice. "But you are welcome to his heirs. They have been nothing but trouble. Do what you will with them, just leave us be!"

Morgen watched as the nuns lifted the bar from the door and shoved the girls through, then sealed it again. Jaelle was crying, but Dravka stared poison at the mob. She had the Marcel looks that Morgen so despised, with high cheekbones, a firm jaw, and flawless caramel skin, though her face was thinner and harder than Vazsoly's.

"My brother is a pig," she spat, "and so are all of you. If it satisfies your blood lust to tear us apart, go ahead. I would rather die than live out my days in this dung heap!"

The bearded man grabbed her arm, and Dravka Marcel brought her knee up between his legs. He doubled over and clutched his balls with a strangled wheeze. The crowd surged forward. A bony woman with wide-spaced eyes like a flounder shoved Jaelle to the ground. Dravka crouched over her sister, teeth bared.

"Where is the Duc?" the woman demanded.

"How should I know, you old bitch?" Dravka snapped. "He left us here to rot! I haven't seen him in almost a year."

The woman kicked Jaelle, who yelped and crawled behind her older sister's skirts. Morgen found to her surprise that the icy disdain she felt was no longer directed at the girls but at their tormenters. Dravka at least had spirit. And they *were* her half sisters, even if they took after their bastard father.

She vaulted lightly down from the wall, allowing her hood to fall back. Heads turned as she approached.

"Hoi, it's the Duc's fucking witch," someone said in wonderment.

Angry murmurs ran through the crowd. Morgen realized that they hated her even more than the girls. She drew a slow breath. The air tasted of death, past and future.

"Leave," she said. "These two are mine."

The bearded man was on hands and knees, retching, but the flounder-faced woman shared a look with the mob's other leader, a slightly built fellow with a wispy mustache. Dravka and Jaelle backed against the wall. Jaelle was weeping loudly. Dravka merely studied Morgen with suspicious blue eyes.

"Maybe *you* know where the Duc is," wispy mustache said.

"Would I be here if I did?" Morgen replied. "He fled the city with his tail between his legs." She glanced up at the convent, where the nuns were watching from the windows. "Go ahead and burn it down, but lay another hand on these girls and you'll regret it."

"Will we, you heathen whore?" the woman said with a derisive laugh.

A stone flew from the crowd, grazing Morgen's cheek. She touched her face, feeling the familiar liquid warmth. How many times had Vazsoly struck her hard enough to draw blood? Morgen found she'd lost count.

"Yes," she said, pointing. The man with the wispy mustache went rigid, mouth working soundlessly. It was just like when she killed the old Duc in his bedchamber. She was a flaming beacon and his soul was a helpless moth, drawn inexorably to wither in a blaze of glory. A shining silver ribbon came out the crown of his head and drifted towards her. The instant it left him, the man collapsed. Morgen opened her palm and pressed gently downwards like a trainer bringing a hound to heel. The soul sank into a tiny black whirlpool and disappeared.

About half the crowd broke and ran back down the road. The rest gave a wordless howl and attacked. More rocks hurtled through the air, striking chips from the wall behind. She lashed out at the front ranks, unmooring spirits and forcing them through the Veil, but the crowd was maddened now, bent on revenge. A man lunged at her with a pike and screamed as a rock split his forehead.

Suddenly, Dravka stood next to her, hurling the missiles back. Her lip was bloody, one eye swollen shut. Morgen wanted to kill them all, but if she was knocked unconscious they'd be on her like a pack of wolves, and she couldn't afford to throw away any more lives.

She gripped Dravka's hand and found Joelle's collar with the other. Then she tore open a portal and dragged them both through. The girls fell to the ground beneath the milkthorn tree on the hillside above the convent. Far enough to be hidden from sight, but close enough to hear the frustrated cries of their would-be murderers.

Dravka scooted back, trembling. "Who are you?"

"That," Morgen replied, "is a question that will take more time to answer than we have at the moment." She glanced down the slope. The mob had broken through the gates. Some were storming the convent, while others fanned out to search the woods. "If you come with me, I will take you to your brother."

Dravka's tone turned frosty. "I never wish to lay eyes on

him again."

Morgen shrugged. "Then you can sit here and wait for the mob to string you up. Perhaps they'll listen to reason."

The hunters were drawing closer. Dravka stood and hauled her younger sister to her feet. "Stop crying," she hissed. "They'll hear you."

Jaelle cast her a resentful look. Her face was red and puffy, but she looked unharmed.

"What if I told you that we can make Vazsoly pay for what he's done?" Morgen said. "To all of us?"

Dravka gave her a considering look. "How?"

"Do you doubt me?"

The girl licked her lips, eyes darting to the convent gates. A dozen bodies lay sprawled in the dust, none with any visible wounds. "No."

Morgen prodded the girls up the hill. Jaelle stumbled along with the blank expression of someone whose life keeps going from bad to worse and who has given up hoping for rescue. She was younger than Morgen first thought, no more than seven. Their mother had died in a fall from the sea cliffs near the palace when Jaelle was an infant. Officially, it was deemed an accident, but Vazsoly had confided one drunken night that he felt sure she had jumped.

"That is good," Morgen said, "because I know where your brother has gone."

"Where?" Dravka asked with a sneer.

She might have been pretty; it was hard to tell. Her face looked pinched and hungry. Dirt crusted her claw-like finger-nails. And her hair — silver-blond waves that were the Marcels' crowning glory — was matted and uneven, as if someone had seized random hanks of it and sawed the locks off with a dull blade. Punishment for some infraction? The abbess had claimed they were "nothing but trouble."

"The Alcazar," Morgen said. "It is the summer palace of the Damiata, in the northern province of Vellio."

They clambered up the steep slope, then half-slid down the other side.

"How far is that?" Dravka panted.

Morgen knew the old Duc held his female offspring in contempt, but were they so untutored that they had never seen a map?

"Far," Jaelle muttered. It was the first word she'd spoken. "Can't we buy horses?"

"I will not risk you two being recognized, not until we're across the border. You are novices who misbehaved, and I am taking you home." She cast them a warning look. "You are neither wealthy nor titled. Keep your mouths shut if we meet anyone and get used to walking."

"We're not weaklings," Dravka spat. "The nuns worked us like mules. I could walk all the way to the Frost Fens if I had to."

"Good," Morgen replied with equal tartness. "Though it will not be quite as long a journey as that."

They cut through a rocky vale and angled southward. The sun beat down. Morgen stopped at a stream to shed the scarlet robe and rinse her face. The cut on her cheek had stopped bleeding, at least. The girls crouched next to her, gulping handfuls of water and dousing their heads.

"I still don't understand," Dravka admitted, after they had washed the sweat away. "The nuns told us next to nothing. Only that the people had risen up and cast my brother from the palace. Why would Vaz go to the Alcazar?"

Morgen adjusted the strap of her pack. Her smile was as thin and deadly as a *stochatto*, the favored blade of Galatian swordmasters. "Why, to beg for aid from his little child bride, of course."

THIRTY-SIX

"Uncle?"

Nathan stared into the black mirror as if he could summon Jaskin Cazal by sheer force of will. "Come out, I beg you. We must discuss a matter of the utmost importance."

The young Duc was bloodshot and disheveled, his raven hair uncombed and his velvet half-cape creased with wrinkles. Lo thought he'd probably slept in it.

Across the chamber, Tijah and Cas sat on a table cluttered with the tools of necromancy — hooked knives that gleamed dully in the candlelight, chalices stained a chalky white with the residue of past concoctions, scrolls etched with symbols that seemed to squirm when glimpsed from the corner of an eye. The air was thick with a metallic tang, as if the stone itself had absorbed the essence of a thousand dark spells.

"Uncle Jaskin," Nathan repeated, his tone stern now. "I insist you speak to us."

The silence was broken only by the furtive whispers of other ancestral spirits stirring within their own silver frames.

"Threaten him," Tijah suggested.

"With what?" Nathan retorted. "He is already dead."

"Let me try." Lo walked up to the black mirror. "Heed me now, Jaskin Cazal. The mortifex known as Magnus the Merciless, whom *you* bound in service, is holding my parents captive, along with a living child. You will tell us where to find them, or I'll kick you downstairs to the ninth and foulest hell."

Nathan winced. Tijah gave a satisfied nod.

Lo leaned closer. "Like you, I am a Shadow Soul," she added, "if you doubt my ability to keep that promise."

In the charged moment that followed, she sensed something stirring in the mirror's lightless depths. The other spirits vanished like rabbits beneath a swooping hawk.

"You dare to command me, girl?" came a dry voice.

"You will not address me as *girl*," she replied firmly. "My name is Delilah Dessarian. I made a bargain for Magnus's whereabouts, and you will uphold the terms."

An unpleasant laugh echoed though the chamber. "Your pact was with Nathan, not with me. And you failed to uphold your promise to bring us the Grand Menotte. Why should I help you for nothing?"

Cas watched the exchange with hooded eyes, but the fingers gripping his staff were taut with tension. "What do you want, Cazal?"

"Let me out and I'll tell you," the spirit rasped with malevolent glee.

Tijah looked ready to wrench the mirror off the wall and beat Nathan over the head with it. "Not a chance," she growled.

"Show yourself," Lo said, "and we'll discuss terms."

The candles guttered. Ripples spread across the mirror's surface like ink disturbed by a dropped pebble. A shadow began to coalesce from the murk, crawling like an insect. Lo fought the urge to step back.

Jaskin's form solidified, his eyes gleaming with a light that wasn't entirely sane. He bore a close resemblance to Nathan despite the centuries that divided them. Both had sharp, angular features, though Jaskin's mouth was bracketed with deep lines as if he habitually scowled. He wore a dark frock coat with a froth of lace at the neck. His fingers were long and monkey-like.

"You're in a pickle, aren't you? A nasty little tickle!" Jaskin let out a gust of mad laughter.

Tijah stepped toward the mirror, and Nathan quickly raised a calming hand. "Uncle, the Grand Menotte has been lost. We must deal with your mortifexes before someone takes control of them. If it falls into the hands of the Duc of Cavet, everything you built could be destroyed."

"The Marcels," Jaskin muttered sourly. "Never liked them. Too big for their hose."

"The new Duc wouldn't hesitate to kill your last living relative and take over this castle," Lo said sweetly.

"She speaks the truth, Uncle," Nathan said. "Tell us where Magnus is before he and the others are summoned to serve a new master."

"At which point, it will be too bloody late to stop them," Tijah muttered.

Jaskin was silent for a long moment. "Very well. But I will show you where he is hiding myself."

"Oh! You mean . . . come along with us?" Lo said.

"*No*," Cas and Tijah said in unison.

"Feh!" Jaskin turned his back. "Then go away and leave me alone."

"We have no time for this shit," Tijah muttered.

"Ah, but I have all the time in the world!" Jaskin flashed her a sly grin over one shoulder. "Those are my terms, you may take them or leave them. Truly, it is a small boon I ask. Do you know how tedious it is to be trapped in a mirror for all eternity? How lonely?"

"That's not fair. I often try to strike up a conversation with you, Uncle," Nathan said. "You refuse to come out."

"Because you are an insufferable bore!" Jaskin exclaimed. "I want to go somewhere! Have an adventure! Here, I will sweeten the offer." His crafty gaze moved to Lo. "I can show you how to make a gate big enough to fly straight to the Cold Sea."

"He's lying," Cas said.

Jaskin Cazal ignored this. "You know it can be done," he whispered silkily. "You must have made a gate before."

"Yes," Lo admitted, "but we're talking about an entire wind ship."

"The size of the gate is immaterial," Jaskin said impatiently. "If you can make a small one, you can make a large one. I have traveled to the Cold Sea many times. I know precisely where to take us. And once we're there, we can join our powers to send Magnus and his followers to the far shore, from which they can never return."

"Is that even possible?" Lo turned to Lady Chaos, who stood in the doorway.

Chaos was only seventeen, yet her dark eyes seemed older. Her twin, Lady Caul, was tall and rather intimidating, but Chaos, for all her diminutive size and softer manner, had powers to speak with the dead and struck Lo as the real leader of the pair.

"It could be," Chaos replied. "There is much about Shadow Souls we don't understand. There are so few. You and

Jaskin. Now this woman from the Western Isles, Morgen Nadezhda, whom I had never heard of before."

"Sweet Morgen of the Isles!" Jaskin sang in a fluting voice. "If she has the box, it will not be long before she opens it."

"She lacks the spell," Nathan said, his mouth grim.

"And how long until she finds it?" Ghoulish mirth glittered in Jaskin's eyes. "Your best hope — your *only* hope — is to take me with you. I will lead you to my vicious little band of mortifexes, and together, we will send their spirits to the far shore."

Tijah rubbed her forehead. "Shut up for a minute," she said. "We need to discuss this in private."

The five of them retreated through the maze of shelves to the bone curtain on the far side of the workshop.

"Bringing that lunatic along was not part of the plan," Cas said heatedly. "There has to be another way."

"Such as?" Nathan said.

Cas glared at him. "This is all *your* fault, you lying, back-stabbing—"

"Every word accurate," Tijah interjected, "and under other circumstances, I'd be happy to hold him down while you beat the tar out of him."

Nathan glared at them both with disdain.

"However," she continued, "Jaskin is the only one who knows where Magnus's lair is. He's an asshole, but he's right about one thing. We are in a nasty little tickle."

"Well, I vote that we take him," Lo said. "There's no choice. Honestly, I don't see what the fuss is."

Tijah and Cas scowled at her.

"What happened to kicking him downstairs to the ninth hell?" Tijah asked.

"I can only do that if I break the mirror and release him first," Lo admitted. "And he might be stronger than me."

"Oh, he's definitely stronger," Nathan muttered.

She decided to ignore that. "My point is that I can't compel Jaskin to do anything and he knows it. But he's trapped in the mirror. What harm can he do?"

"That is true — in theory," Nathan said. "But Jaskin Cazal is quite possibly the most dangerous man who ever walked this continent."

"I hate to say it, but Nathan is talking sense," Cas said. "How can we even consider trusting him?"

"We can't." Tijah turned to Nathan, an evil smile on her lips. "Which is why you're coming, too, necromancer."

Nathan laughed. "Me?"

"Yes, you. You can keep him in line."

"Now I am certain you jest. Do you think he listens to me?" Nathan scoffed. "Besides which, I cannot simply abandon my responsibilities in Vendagni. I have far too much to do here—"

"Like what?" Lo asked. "Be specific."

Nathan started to bluster, and Lady Chaos laid a hand on his arm. "Necromancy is one of the few magical arts that works behind the Veil, and they will need every advantage to defeat Magnus."

Nathan's blanched to the shade of curdled milk. "But—"

"I'll see to things here until you return," she said. "I promise."

Their eyes locked. It seemed to Lo that a great deal was communicated without words. Nathan quite obviously did not want to go, but he also didn't wish to appear cowardly in front of Chaos.

"Then it's settled," Tijah said briskly "Time's a wasting."

"I didn't agree yet," Nathan protested.

"Nor did I," Cas said hotly. "One necromancer is bad enough. Two is hardly an improvement!"

"I resent that." Nathan lifted his chin. "It's not my fault that Delilah lost the Grand Menotte—"

"But it *is* your fault," Cas snapped, "for sending her to Prydwen in the first place. If you hadn't roped us all into your scheming plots, my sister wouldn't be stuck with a band of dead pirates!"

They all stared at him. Cas vented an angry exhale. "Do what you will. I'll get the *Wind-Witch* ready to sail." He pushed through the curtain, sending the bones clacking dramatically, and stomped down the stairs.

Lo caught him at the next landing. "I know you don't trust Nathan," she said. "I don't, either. And I certainly don't trust the man who made the Grand Menotte. But it isn't the worst idea to bring them both along. Think of it as insurance. They can't send us to the wrong place. And Nathan's power could be useful."

"But what if you're wrong? What if Nathan sets Jaskin free? They could have planned this together all along."

"Nathan could have done that long ago if he wanted to," she pointed out. "And Tijah has our backs if it comes down to a fight."

"I still don't like the odds."

"Then I'm open to other ideas. Whatever you got."

He shook his head, frustration writ across his face. "Kaethe's mercy, I cannot think of a single one!"

She took his hand. "Nor can I. But I won't force you to agree, Cas. We're partners in this. Your vote counts."

"I appreciate that," he said, looking calmer. "I thought of summoning Justinian, just to trap him here for a while, to slow him down, but I don't trust Vigo, either. What if he broke the star and let Justinian out? The main thing is that we *have* to get to Magnus first."

Lo wrapped her arms around him. He hugged her back, but she could feel the tension coiled inside.

"I promise we'll find Felippa," she whispered. "Cross my heart and hope to . . . " Lo cleared her throat. "You can stow your things in the captain's cabin. I hear she's promoting you to first mate!"

THIRTY-SEVEN

It was a relief to quit the reflective black walls and windowless chambers of the keep. Cas paused on the front steps, gulping the cool air. When he thought about his sister surrounded by mortifexes, it grew hard to breathe. He reminded himself that Lo's parents had lived among them for eight years. And Felippa was smart. A survivor.

Seeking a task to distract himself, Cas returned to the *Wind-Witch* and began logging the provisions Nathan's dust servants had stowed aboard. Barrels of water and smaller kegs of ale. Oil and vinegar and molasses, dried figs and plums, wheels of cheese and hardtack biscuits.

Every so often Vigo passed through, heaving crate after crate into the hold with the ease of a child stacking blocks. When Cas pried up one of the lids, he recoiled at the sight of pink tentacles floating in brine.

"What the hells is that?"

Vigo bared his teeth in what passed for a smile. "*That* is what dwells at the bottom of the chasm. A bit rubbery, but it tastes better than it looks."

Cas prodded a puckered hole with his knife. "Are those . . . fangs?"

"The creatures have dozens of mouths," Vigo confirmed. "Just remove the teeth before stewing."

"Right." Cas jammed the lid back on, vowing never to open it again. He turned to find the mortifex staring at him, eyes smoldering like banked embers in the dim hold. Cas adjusted his grip on the staff, glad he'd kept it at hand. "Something else to say?"

Vigo glanced at the staff, then sneered and flexed his muscles. "To you, puny little ant? I think not." He hefted a barrel over one massive shoulder and strolled away to the far end of the hold.

"Well, be careful," Cas called after him. "I'd hate for you to strain something."

The mortifex laughed. "Your concern is touching, Reaper. Just know that if my master does not return, I will find you. And next time, you will not live to tell of it."

The boards groaned beneath his boots as Vigo stomped away. Cas let out a taut breath. He was heading for the ladder when a voice whispered, "*Quietus.*"

He turned, the hair stirring on his nape. Vigo had the rumbling baritone of a giant. This voice was as dry and brittle as old parchment. In the darkest, webbiest corner of the hold, Cas spotted an object wrapped in cloth. The covering had slipped down, revealing a dull black surface.

Vigo must have brought the mirror aboard when he wasn't looking. Cas didn't want to go anywhere near it, but he had to make certain it was secure. What if the thing toppled over when the ship took off? Would a single crack be sufficient to liberate the ancient spirit who dwelt within?

Cas cursed under his breath and walked over. He was reaching out to cover it up again when a distorted face filled the mirror from edge to edge, the features bizarrely magnified with bulging eyes the size of dinner plates. Cas jerked back so fast he banged his hip on one of the water barrels. Jaskin erupted in howls of laughter.

"Your expression!" he wheezed. "Like an icy hand grabbed you by the—"

"Do that again," Cas snapped, "and I'll feed you to the squids."

The chortles cut off and the necromancer's face shrank back to normal — which was still sinister. Jaskin regarded him soberly. "I apologize, it has been an age since I had anyone besides Nathan to frighten. It was easy when he was a child, but now he is used to my tricks. Wait!" he cried as Cas reached for the cloth. "Before you silence me, there is something vital you must know."

"What's that?"

Jaskin laid a finger alongside his nose. "How many lives does the young lady have left?"

"That's none of your business."

"Oh, I don't care on my own behalf," Jaskin said carelessly. "I'm merely wondering if she has entered . . . " His voice lowered to a conspiratorial hiss. "The Quickening!"

Let the old man think I've taken his bait. "What's that?" Cas asked with mild alarm.

"A phenomenon that commences once a Shadow Soul reaches the last two or three lives," Jaskin replied. "We are unnatural, you see. Nature abhors us; our very existence is an affront to the rational order of things."

"Get on with it—"

"In short, her luck will sour," Jaskin said, "and so will that of the entire company. Your most meticulously laid plans will go awry. Expect unfortunate coincidences and deadly mishaps. The wind will not be at your back but blowing directly in your face. Fate will do all she can to kill the lot of you."

Against his better judgment, Cas thought of that last day in Prydwen. Finding the Grand Menotte hidden in his own bedchamber, only to lose it to Morgen within minutes. Almost dying to get it a *second time* and losing it to the same bloody person.

"Why are you telling me this?" he demanded. "Why didn't you tell Lo?"

"She would not believe me." Jaskin gave a mordant chuckle. "I've watched her for a while, you know. When she first came to the castle, and later when she talked to Nathan through the mirrors."

"So you spied on them?"

"Oh, please. I was hanging on the wall! Did you expect me to cover my ears? The point is this: our little ray of sunshine will not be the same person behind the Veil." His head suddenly jerked toward something outside the frame of the mirror. Jaskin swatted wildly at the air. "Blasted flies!"

"Know what I think?" Cas said. "You're just trying to plant a wedge between us."

The necromancer put an invisible speck in his mouth and chewed wearily. "By all the gods, you are ignorant. Haven't you noticed something wrong with her already? A certain reckless-ness, perhaps? Poor judgment? Excessive optimism?"

Cas said nothing, though a thread of unease was wriggling its way into his gut.

"The essence of a Shadow Soul is to be divided." Jaskin held his palms up like balance scales. "Half exists in the living world, half in the land of the dead."

"I knew that."

"Yet you do not seem to grasp what it means," he replied testily. "When Delilah passes through the gate, all the traits that were previously suppressed will come to the fore, and those that were dominant will recede. Kaethe made it so, thrice damn that devious woman."

There was something both complicated and stupid about the notion that rang true. "What are you saying?" Cas wondered. "That she'll become evil?"

"No, no." Jaskin waved a hand. "She will desire the same things. Have the same intentions. But how she pursues her goals — well, just don't get in her way, Quietus."

"What does that mean?"

Jaskin paused. "Why do you think I made the Grand Menotte? Would you say forging it was the act of a rational, sane man?"

"Definitely not."

He clapped his hands. "There you are! I was already caught in the Quickening, though I did not realize it at the time. I thought I could use the power of the mortifexes to bring life to the darklands, to restore the great forests, and I did all that — but at a terrible price."

"So you went mad *before* you put it on?"

"A bit, yes." He tilted his head, gaze distant. "I was worse after. Much worse. But I don't care to talk about that now. I'm telling you this so you'll keep a close eye on our captain. And so you will not be shocked by the changes that come over her once we've gone through the portal."

"You keep hinting at what they'll be," Cas said tightly. "Why not come out with it?"

The long, apelike fingers fluttered in the air. "I fear you give me too much credit. I do not know her well enough to say for certain. But . . . well, at my age, one does become adept at reading others." He cleared his throat. "She is quite the liar, for one thing. Scarcely a true word passes her lips. And she seems overly confident in her own abilities. Certain, despite all evidence to the contrary, that everything will turn out well—"

"Enough," Cas snapped, drawing the cloth across the mirror.

"So you may expect the opposite of those things," his muffled voice continued. "I'm certain I'm overlooking a few crucial traits, but it will be interesting to see—"

Cas tuned him out. He wedged the mirror between two water barrels and made sure it was secure. Then he went up the ladder. He found Tijah on deck, staring pensively at the western horizon.

"He's much too far," she said. "He won't make it before we leave."

"Achaemenes?"

She nodded.

Cas eyed the gold cuff she wore around her wrist, engraved with a winged griffin. "You can tell where he is?"

"Roughly." She smiled. "I know for certain that he is well. Achaemenes will find us eventually."

"Where are Lo and Nathan?"

"The necromancer is packing his tools of dark sorcery," she muttered. "Last I saw, Lo was with Lady Chaos."

Cas didn't know Tijah well, but he needed an ally, and Jaskin's claims were too troubling to keep to himself. She listened in silence as he related the conversation.

"You're wondering if any of it is true," she said, "or if he's just messing with us."

"Aye."

"No way to tell," she said slowly. "I guess we'll find out on the other side. But I'm glad you told me." She clapped Cas on the shoulder. "We'll both keep an eye on her."

Lo emerged from Castle Cazal at that moment, sauntering beneath the leering gargoyles with a spring in her step. "Ready to whip some undead arse?" she called, grinning and rolling up her sleeves.

Cas exchanged a quick look with Tijah.

"Don't worry, Jaskin gave me pointers," Lo said, climbing the ladder up to the deck. "I just need to make the gate bigger. I've got a good feeling about this!"

"Sure you know where we're going?" Tijah asked. "There are some dicey neighborhoods in the Dominion I'd rather not visit."

"Jaskin explained it to me. There is a group of islands called Charon's Dice."

"I know of it."

"Magnus's lair is not far off." She waved a piece of paper. "Jaskin directed Nathan to draw the exact configuration of the isles. I will fix it my mind as I make the gate. We'll just pop out right where we want to be! Isn't that marvelous? I wish I'd known about this before."

"That simple, eh?" Tijah muttered.

She turned as Nathan appeared with Lady Chaos. They were arm in arm, Nathan's long stride shortening to match her slower progress with the silver canes. Physically, they were opposites; Nathan tall and lean, Chaos short and plump. He was pale as moonlight, she as dark as the night beyond save for her white hair. Yet even Cas could see the rightness of them together. He felt sure he knew whom the unsent love letters he'd found in Nathan's bedchamber were intended for.

"I will guard the keep until you return, master," Vigo intoned from the steps.

"*Bien sûr*," Nathan replied with a smile that looked forced. "I'm sure you'll do a smashing job."

"Any intruders will be left to wander the blood labyrinth." Vigo couldn't resist a brief glance at Cas. "But next time I will set the Devouring Darkness on their heels."

"Quite right," Nathan said briskly. "Obey Lady Chaos as you would me."

Vigo bowed. "Yes, master."

Four dust servants shambled aboard, carrying brass-bound trunks and elegant luggage branded with the Hand Sinister of Vendagni. Each was as tall as the mortifex, about eight feet or so, with lumpen, featureless heads. Lo directed them to the hatch.

"You're not bringing the ash men, are you?" she shouted down to Nathan.

"Am I permitted to?" he asked hopefully.

"No!" Cas called back.

"Not even a single valet?"

"Sorry, Nathan," Lo said. "If it's any consolation, I doubt they'd survive the gate."

Nathan heaved an audible sigh. "I shall do for myself, I suppose."

He turned and spoke some last quiet words to Lady Chaos, then bent to kiss her hand.

"Be careful," the young Ducissa called, waving one of her silver canes in the direction of the ship. "May you have Kaethe's blessing!"

Thistle greeted Nathan with a hiss when he came aboard, then stalked with a stiff tail to the bow and set about energetically grooming his ears.

"I'll retire to my cabin," Nathan murmured. "It seems your demonic familiar has still not forgiven me."

He vanished down the hatch. Tijah stared after him for a moment, her face impassive.

"You need me on deck?" she asked Lo, who shook her head. "Then I'll go watch him and dear old *Uncle Jaskin*."

"Try not to stab anyone," Lo said absently, her attention

fixed on the fluttering bit of red yarn called a telltale that signaled which way the wind was blowing.

Tijah's bland smile was unnerving. "I was thinking more along the lines of a friendly game of dice."

"See you on the other side then," Cas said.

She held his eye for a moment and headed belowdecks, stepping aside for the ash servants. Cas set about hoisting the sails. *Should I tell Lo?* he wondered. But that might be what Jaskin wanted. To throw her off balance right before she opened a gate to the underworld. If it didn't work, they'd probably be torn apart by unimaginable forces—

"Not getting cold feet, I hope?" Lo asked with a wink.

"Gods, no, I trust you completely," he lied.

Her face grew serious. "I won't let you down, I promise."

Thistle summoned a southerly breeze and Lo cast off the mooring rope. The *Wind-Witch* soared above the misty chasm, leaving the sharp spires of Castle Cazal behind. A single candle burned high up in Nathan's bedchamber, the lone beacon in a sea of darkness.

"No matter what happens, I need you to hold the course," she said. "And buckle in. It's about to get rough."

Cas steadied the wheel with one hand, attaching a harness with the other. Lo studied the map, her face intent. The shadows under her eyes were dark as bruises. A few tense minutes passed, the ship climbing higher and higher, until it broke through the clouds to the starry sky arching above.

Cool, silver Hecate sat low on the horizon, with luminous yellow Selene floating behind the mast. Artemis, the traveling moon whose orbit took a full year to complete, was a small blue dot to the north.

Cas's breath plumed in the bitter air. He heard a dry crackling and realized that the shroud of mist cloaking the ship was turning to ice.

"I have it," Lo said through gritted teeth. "The gate is forming."

The sight of her chilled him even more than the deathly cold. Her skin was pallid and waxen, her ink-black hair drifting about her head as though she were being carried along in a gentle current. In the dappled moon shadows, Lo looked disturbingly like Kaethe.

"Aye," Cas managed, tearing his gaze away. "Ready, captain."

He gripped the wheel, blinking frozen lashes. Icy gusts howled around them and he could feel the ship straining under the relentless assault. The *Wind-Witch* groaned in protest as a fierce crosswind slammed her abeam. Cas spared a glance upwards, dismayed to see the jib shredded and flapping uselessly.

Needles of frost drove into his exposed skin. *Just a little longer...*

Then he saw a starless hole looming ahead, a deeper darkness against the night sky. Blue lightning forked and danced around the rim. It looked like the maw of some cosmic leviathan eager to swallow them whole. The ship hurtled forward, gathering speed as it neared the swirling portal.

"Brace yourself, Sleepy Eyes," Lo shouted, and her familiar voice, strained but determined, gave him courage.

Every muscle tensed as they pierced the veil between realms. The ship bucked and trembled like a terrified horse. His hands, numb with cold, gripped the wheel tighter, holding it steady even as his heart tried to hammer its way out of his chest. Crushing darkness fell; the creaking ropes and luffing sails were the only proof that the vessel remained airborne. Then a faint light appeared and the *Wind-Witch* burst into clear air.

Cas barely had time to whisper a prayer of thanks before

the ship listed hard to port. His boots slid across the icy deck as he fought for balance. A pace from the rail, his harness jerked tight. Both sails were in tatters. Wind whistled through the useless rigging.

"We're going down!" he shouted. "Do something!"

Lo was on her knees, arms curled around the mast. "Brace for it," she muttered.

"Shite!" He looked around wildly. "Thistle—"

The demon cat crawled out from underneath a heap of torn canvas. The yellow lamps of his eyes narrowed, assessing the situation. A gust surged from behind, not the destructive fury of the portal but a gentler, more deliberate conjuring. It filled what remained of the sails, slowing the wounded ship's descent. Cas hurried to Lo across the canting deck. He caught flashes of green water as the sea rushed up to meet them.

"Are you all right?" he asked, crouching at her side.

She blinked, teeth chattering. "I'm c-cold."

"Come here." He pulled her into his arms just as the bow dipped below the waves. A bracing gout of salt spray slapped them both in the face. Then the *Wind-Witch* bobbed up like a cork and righted herself. They stared at other, sodden and dripping.

"You look terrible," she said.

"Not as bad as you," he said. "You look like a feckin' corpse. Not even a fresh one."

She snorted a laugh and tried vainly to untangle her hair. "I suppose you'd know."

"Oh, I'm an expert. I still like you, though."

Their eyes locked and he was about to kiss her, divided soul be damned, when Tijah stuck her head from the hatch.

"By Kavi's nine flails," she called with a wide grin, "I thought we were done for. "

The air was warm, and the ice on the deck was already

melting to patches of water. Cas pulled Lo to her feet. She was looking around with interest, blue eyes bright. Thistle wandered over and twined between her legs.

"I can't believe you actually did it," Tijah said, joining them on deck. "Saved us weeks of travel."

The ship drifted on a calm sea that shifted from azure in the depths to light turquoise in the shallows. Hundreds of forested isles, large and small, dotted the horizon, scattered along atolls like strands of pearls.

"This is the Cold Sea?" Lo's brow furrowed. "I expected it to be gray and dismal."

"No, it is a lovely place," Tijah said. "Outwardly, at least."

Her shrewd gaze took Lo's measure as she said this. Cas understood Tijah's concern, but so far, he'd seen no difference.

"It's nothing like the Dominion," he said in surprise, surveying their new surroundings. "There is a sun. And color!" Streaks of rose-gold, lavender mallow, and fiery orange lit the clouds on both the starboard and port sides. It was a gorgeous spectacle. It also made no sense. "But which way . . .?"

"Disorienting, isn't it?" Tijah said. "One direction appears to be dawn, the other sunset, but the sun itself never rises or sets."

"Now that is *weird*," Lo said, stretching the word out. "Nathan!"

The necromancer, who was halfway out of the hatch, gave a violent start.

"Bring up the black mirror!" she called. "Jaskin can tell us where we are."

The light was soft, but Nathan squinted painfully like an opossum dragged from its den at high noon. He nodded and ducked below again.

"There's weather coming," Tijah said, pointing to the black clouds mounding in the distance.

"It was not I who summoned it," the cat growled. His eyes slitted as he studied the approaching storm. "We must find shelter before the tempest arrives. It will be powerful."

"We need a safe harbor to repair the sails anyhow," Lo added ruefully.

"Careful, boy! Keep me upright, you idiot, I'm not a sack of grain!"

Nathan returned with a long-suffering expression, the mirror listing crookedly in his arms. "I'm trying, Uncle, but you're heavy."

Cas hurried over and helped him prop it against the mainmast. Jaskin pressed closer, and closer still, until a single enormous eye blinked and twitched against the glass. It looked left, then right.

"We are passing Crossjack Bay," he announced. "If the currents favor us, we are four days' sail from Magnus's lair."

"Four days?" Cas's heart sank. "Where is the nearest safe harbor?"

"Dreamhaven," Jaskin replied.

Tijah sighed. "I've been there. It's a pisshole, but we can ride out the storm at least."

"Is Dreamhaven an actual settlement?" Cas asked.

"Of sorts. Mix of demons, lingerers, djinn, a few shady minor deities. If we keep to ourselves, they'll leave us alone. That's the official creed in these parts." Tijah's smile didn't quite touch her eyes. "Mind your own fucking business and never ask about anyone's past."

She joined Lo at the wheel and they set a course for a low, knobby mountain called Summertree Peak. Cas leaned down to the mirror.

"I know you lied," he whispered.

"Did I?" Jaskin sounded amused. "Are you so certain?"

"Aye, look at her." Lo caught him staring and smiled warmly. "Same as ever."

"Captain!" Jaskin called across the deck. "Tell me, what do you think our chances are of succeeding in this endeavor?"

Lo stared up at the clouds for a minute, brows knit together. "One in a thousand?" she hazarded.

Nathan lifted his chin. "Rather more than that, I should imagine," he said haughtily. "Not to toot my own horn, but I am the most feared necromancer in the Moon Courts. When I visit the city, children run screaming and the elderly often perish on the spot."

He glanced at Tijah. "Kaethe's *mercenaire* is disagreeable and bigoted, but I will grant that she is a skilled swordswoman." Tijah rolled her eyes. "And Castelio has a few talents, I am sure. Don't forget the magic staff!"

Lo doubled over laughing. She laughed until tears streamed from her eyes. "Oh, you dear innocent thing," she managed at last.

Nathan's scowl deepened. Cas regarded her with mounting trepidation.

"Tell them the truth!" Jaskin chortled. "Go on! It'll feel good."

Lo inhaled deeply and composed herself, though spasms of mirth still twitched her lips. "Let's start with you, Nathan. By 'the city,' I assume you mean the tiny cluster of thatch houses three leagues from Castle Cazal? We flew over it on the way."

"Well, yes—"

"Which is the farthest you've ever been from home until now."

He opened his mouth, then closed it again.

"You might have turned me into a rat in the familiar safety of your own workshop," she continued, "but you are a man who is so petrified of merely glimpsing the sun that you sent a total stranger to retrieve your priceless heirloom, and we all know how that turned out."

"Oh yes," Jaskin chuckled. "Pathetic but true."

Lo turned to Tijah, who gazed back with narrow eyes. "You are quick with a blade, but without your partner to rein you in, your prickly temper and headstrong nature will almost certainly lead you into trouble."

Tijah muttered something inaudible and ground her teeth.

Cas braced himself, though the look Lo gave him was fond. "Sleepy Eyes. You are brave and kind and reasonably clever."

Reasonably?

"But that staff might as well be a walking stick for all that you're able to use it. Not only are you ignorant of what the runes mean, but you clearly have never fought with a quarter-staff, making it useless on both fronts. Your vials of Kaethe's Tears are gone, leaving a pair of iron knives to battle a hundred mortifexes, when a single one almost did you in."

"I'd say a thousand to one is overly generous," Jaskin put in. "Unless you think she's wrong about any of that."

"As for myself," Lo concluded, "my elemental power is gone. I can't even sense the Nexus."

"You still wield the Shadow power," Cas ventured.

"Which I know nothing about." She glanced at the mirror. "*He* does, but he's mad as a moonlark. He's also just using us to escape his prison, so I expect he will undermine our efforts at every turn."

"She's not wrong!" Jaskin hooted.

"Would you shut up?" Nathan snapped irritably, rounding on the mirror.

"In short, it's hopeless," Lo said, her good humor undimmed. "But we'll give it our best shot anyway." Her cheeks were ruddy, her cloak flapping merrily in the wind. She *did* seem different; it took Cas a moment to realize that the guarded look she always wore was gone. "I love you, Sleepy Eyes. Do you love me?"

She is quite the liar. So you may expect the opposite...

He swallowed, a fist slowly squeezing his heart. "Aye, I do."

"So sweet," Jaskin murmured.

"Tijah, you're like an older sister. Nathan . . . you mean well. And you have good hair." She suddenly looked worried. "I hope I haven't offended anyone?"

There was a brief silence. Then Tijah barked a laugh. She walked over to Lo and slung an arm around her waist. "You're blunter than you used to be, but I don't mind. And you're right about Achaemenes." A shadow crossed her face. "Not that I can't manage, but I do miss him."

Cas drew a breath and approached. "Will you teach me?" He scratched his head with a small grin. "I seem to recall you cutting my legs out with a quarterstaff when we first met."

Lo beamed. "I'd love to."

Nathan raised a tentative hand. "I think I can translate the runes on that staff." For once, he sounded earnest, with no trace of condescension. "They're in tongues," he explained. "The written form."

"By Kaethe, I never even guessed that," Cas said. He still didn't trust the necromancer, but it couldn't hurt to let him try.

Nathan colored slightly. "There are several dialects. Yours are sixth circle — *Sexto Purgatorio*. Luckily, I've studied them all."

"Because you spend all your time buried in dusty, worm-eaten books!" Jaskin eyed them with disgust. "It's still hopeless," he snarled. "A thousand to one!"

"I've beaten worse odds," Tijah remarked. She turned to Lo. "Do you know they have ale in Dreamhaven? It tastes vile, but it'll get you drunk right quick."

The cat — the only one to escape Lo's withering assessment — padded up to the black mirror. Jaskin reared back, peering down his long nose with distaste. Thistle graced the spirit with a menacing growl, then waddled off.

"Never liked cats," Jaskin muttered. "Or demons. Fickle creatures, both of them . . . Wait! What are you doing?"

Nathan dropped the black cloth over his outraged face. Cas grabbed the other side of the mirror. Kaethe, it *was* heavy.

"Time for a nap, Uncle," Nathan panted as they staggered to the hatch.

"But I'm not tired! Put me down at once!"

The sky overhead was darkening to pitch. Thunder boomed on the horizon. Jaskin's spluttering protests turned to peals of deranged laughter.

"The Quickening!" he cried, his voice muffled by the cloth. "It's coming for you all!"

Nathan arched a brow. "What's Uncle Jaskin going on about?"

Cas caught sight of a crescent-shaped bay ringed by twinkling lights. Dreamhaven.

He winked. "I'll tell you over a mug of that ale."

About the Author

Kat Ross worked as a journalist at the United Nations for ten years before happily falling back into what she likes best: making stuff up. She loves myths, monsters, and doomsday scenarios.

Join Kat's list, *The Sorcerous Pen*, and be the first to hear about the next book in the series, *A Wicked Wind*. Her ravens will also deliver a free ebook, along with early access to sales, giveaways, diabolical potions, and arcane lore.

https://katrossbooks.com/newsletter/

 facebook.com/KatRossAuthor

 instagram.com/katross2014

Also by Kat Ross

The Fourth Empire Series

Savage Skies

Rogue & Revenant

The Fourth Element Trilogy

The Midnight Sea

Blood of the Prophet

Queen of Chaos

The Fourth Talisman Series

Nocturne

Solis

Monstrum

Nemesis

Inferno

The Nightmarked Series

City of Storms

City of Wolves

City of Keys

City of Dawn

The Lingua Magika Trilogy

A Feast of Phantoms

All Down But Nine

Devil of the North

Gaslamp Gothic Collection

The Daemoniac

The Thirteenth Gate

A Bad Breed

The Necromancer's Bride

Dead Ringer

Balthazar's Bane

The Scarlet Thread

The Beast of Loch Ness